For my Dad, always in m   Noel
Dempster (25th December   nd to
my Mum Patricia Dempsi   , love
and li   pport.

AUTHOR'S NOTE

"The Thirteenth Pillar of Artemis" is a work of 'faction', a blend of truth, speculation, evidence, supposition and fiction. Some of the characters are, or were real and events relating to those individuals are loosely based on biographical and factual information already well known in the public domain.

References to Diana, Princess of Wales, her family and some of those involved in the Paris car crash are drawn from existing biographical information and presented in fictionalised form.

The characters Fakhar Ul Islam and M. Noel Corbu were real people who met their fate as described, however, the precise circumstances are a matter of speculation. A member of the Diocese of Carcassonne also allegedly survived an incident as described in the prologue, however, the details are vague.

Bérenger Saunière and other characters associated with the mystery of Rennes-le-Château most certainly existed. There are many myths and legends about Saunière's apparent overnight accumulation of wealth and the secrets and treasure he is alleged to have discovered. Whilst many believe that Saunière was the keeper of explosive information which may have been suppressed by the Church and Establishment, there are many who also discredit the countless theories which have flourished around him and Rennes-le-Château . The Church itself has been vocal in casting doubt about the priest's life, preferring a more mundane explanation for his wealth. Whatever the truth may be, Saunière's legend has created a thriving tourist and new age industry in Rennes-le-Château .

All other characters and events are fictional and any similarity to any person living or dead is purely co- incidental. References to the life and death of Diana, Princess of Wales are not intended to cast suspicion, doubt or aspersions upon the character or reputation of any individual living or dead.

FOREWORD

Ever since the death of Diana, Princess of Wales, conspiracy theories have propagated about the circumstances of her demise and the possibility that she may have been murdered. Despite a finding by the jury of an inquest headed by Lord Justice Scott Baker that she was the victim of unlawful killing as a result of gross negligence by the chauffeur Henri Paul and other drivers of nearby vehicles, many suspect that she was the victim of foul play.

Having 'grown up' in Diana's era, and followed her life and death with interest, I have read many books and articles about her. Recently, one theory advanced for the reasons behind her death sparked my imagination and the idea for this book. It will be appreciated upon reading the story that although fictional, it draws from some autobiographical detail already in the public domain about the Princess and her life, and from the fascinating theory advanced by Jon King and John Beveridge in their book "The Hidden Evidence". There is a strong mystical theme in the background of the story with which I have, in the interests of artistic licence taken some liberties in order to explore the possibilities in the context of fiction.

King and Beveridge's theory (although it is impossible to comment on the veracity or otherwise of their findings) certainly proposes a plausible motive for the death of Diana at the hands of a powerful, faceless Establishment. Indeed they describe incidents of pursuit by the intelligence agencies whom they initially believed tried to prevent publication of their book, information for which they assert, was received from a member of the security services in the first place. Subsequently they have suggested that they were elaborately set up to write their book by those same intelligence services on the premise that sometimes the truth is stranger than fiction and that the public would be diverted from accusations of foul play to simply discredit the authors as fantasists and conspiracy theorists.

Either way, we shall probably never know the truth in our lifetime. I would however urge any interested reader of The Thirteenth Pillar of Artemis to read "The Hidden Evidence" and Jon King's follow up book "The Cut Out", (see bibliography). The authors provide some plausible and deeply fascinating insights into the possible reason for Diana's death which they support far more accurately and convincingly with facts and interviews than this work of fiction would hope or attempt to achieve.

I hope that if nothing else, *The Thirteenth Pillar of Artemis* might have amused Diana, who would probably agree that she was neither Goddess nor perfect, but the idea of her possible links to the mystical Merovingian Kings would most certainly have appealed to her and may, if the theory is correct, even have been revealed to her prior to her death.

Jacqui Dempster, August 2015

CONTENTS

Prologue

Southern France

20th February 1967

Fakhar Ul Islam's heart beat faster in time with the rhythm of the tracks beneath him and a smile spread across his face as he savoured the knowledge he'd spent so many years seeking. He was on the Paris-Geneva train having spent some weeks delving into the mysteries of Rennes-le-Château. The strange village nestling high in the mountains of the Languedoc Region had been the focus of his attention for a very long time and soon he would be sought after for the knowledge he'd finally acquired. It held the key for the most elevated members of the Saudi elite to become a major part of the Western political establishment.

Unbeknown to Fakhar though, he was more immediately sought after than he'd first imagined; only not by those with whom he planned to exploit his new found treasure. The train today was quiet as he negotiated the undulating carriages to seek sustenance in the dining carriage. The air was heavy and oppressive with enveloping heat as the train made its way at speed through the rolling countryside.

Unobserved, a smartly dressed man rose from the otherwise empty carriage previously occupied only by Fakhar and himself and followed his unsuspecting quarry. Holding back, he glanced at his watch as Fakhar paused at the door of the train to lower the window for a few moments and breathe in the cooling air generated by the breeze of the moving train. It was perfect timing.

Moments later, Fakhar's eyes widened as his airway was constricted, his throat encircled and gripped with the unyielding strength of a vice. He was vaguely aware in the confusion of the attack and his panicked asphyxiation that the door against which he was pinned was giving way. Seconds later he was propelled onto the tracks with only a transitory understanding of what was happening. He blacked out with the impact of his skull against the steel tracks and did not regain consciousness before the wheels of the steaming iron horse from the opposite direction completed their grisly thundering over his body sending Fakhar into messy oblivion.

Mission accomplished, Fakhar's assailant smiled with cold satisfaction. Gripping the safety rail he leaned out to catch the door as it swung towards him and pulled it shut. He calmly adjusted his monogrammed gold cufflinks and shirt cuffs and straightened his tie before returning to the empty carriage. How pleasing that trains ran so punctually on this line, he thought.

20th May 1968

Just over 15 years had passed since Monsieur Noel Corbu, an hotelier by trade had spent a lonely vigil holding the hand of Marie Dénarnaud at her deathbed. To his great good fortune, he had purchased her former *domaine*, which she had occupied during her lifetime with Bérenger Saunière the erstwhile and now infamous priest of Rennes-le-Château.

Marie, once the priest's live in housekeeper (and many suspected more) had fallen on hard times after a life of accumulating mysterious wealth with the priest and had sold the *domaine* to Corbu. Feeling compassion for the old woman who had spent her life in faithful service and companionship with the priest and who had reputedly kept his secrets after his

11

death, Corbu generously offered her a home at the *domaine*. He had created an extremely profitable business by converting the Villa Bethania into a lucrative tourist attraction and by creating and embellishing a legend of secret treasure to be found at Rennes-le-Château establishing a possible answer to the mysterious wealth of the once impoverished priest. He enjoyed a very comfortable life and a certain notoriety himself with his *Hotel de Tour* as the story attracted those hoping to unearth the secrets and gain prosperity themselves. Although he never found any treasure himself, the *Hotel* brought him unimaginable fortunes for which he was grateful.

In return for Corbu's compassion, Marie promised him the remaining papers belonging to Saunière and, in a moment of indiscretion also promised to tell him a secret before she died which she guaranteed would make him a powerful man.

Marie suffered a cerebral haemorrhage on 29th January 1953 and, true to her word, Corbu reported that she had tried to tell him the secret but stricken by paralysis, she was unable to utter a word of any distinction and thus had never yielded the secret she had kept throughout her lifetime; or so he said.

Either way, M. Corbu's good fortune continued for many years as he dined out on his own version of the secret until his luck finally ran out on the day he climbed into his Renault 16 for the very last time on 20th May 1968. He was never to return to his beloved *Hotel du Tour* after a violent car crash on a quiet road near Carcassonne killed him and, it was said, rendered his lifeless body unrecognisable.

Unbeknown to anyone, only one lonely figure witnessed the incident so cleverly conceived by the powerful institution for which he worked. The incongruously immaculate individual checked the efficacy of his handiwork before walking the few hundred yards along the road in the direction of Castelnaudary to retrieve his own car that had served him well in the execution of his duty – and of M. Corbu.

18th June 1968

The Monseigneur of the Diocese of Carcassonne counted his blessings, thanked God and determined never to meddle with the secrets of Rennes-le-Château again on the day his car veered out of control into a post near Devil's Bridge, Carcassonne.

He regarded his survival less a matter of good fortune than miracle escaping with a crushed chest, broken legs and assorted cuts and bruises. He was well aware that others had not been so lucky. There was no doubt in the Monseigneur's mind that his own near demise was inextricably linked with his investigations into the secrets of Rennes-le-Château. He was equally certain that despite the rumours that his 'accident' was not the result of any curse but rather the concerted plan by powerful entities to suppress the knowledge that he and others had inadvertently uncovered and which in the wrong hands might alter the course of history.

The Monseigneur could not have known at this time that a seven year old girl from the British aristocracy was already destined for similar tragedy some 29 years later as at the time of his own 'accident' she blithely danced and giggled in the gardens of her ancestral home on the sunny afternoon he almost died. He could not have known that the secrets he had uncovered had a direct link to the chubby child who would in time transform into an elegant swan to become one of the most admired and talked about women of the century.

Few would know why her story was inexorably linked with his and that the parallels between them and other less fortunate bearers of the secret knowledge would launch her into the realms of tragic legend, a far cry from the innocent if troubled life she now led. There were those however, who wished it to be known.

Chapter 1 – Hal Bradbury

Late Summer 2014

Hal Bradbury, tie loosened, jacket crumpled and flaccid belly straining his shirt buttons tucked voraciously into a sausage roll. He groaned lazily when Lisa, the London Herald's receptionist delivered her message which she yelled across the office at him.

"Envelope here for you, Hal!"

Taking another bite of the sausage roll which he eyed with appreciative and almost indecent pleasure, Hal retorted without moving his feet from the desk at which he reclined.

"Well it had better be worth it to interrupt my lunch hour," he grunted, spraying flakes of pastry from his overfilled cheeks.

Hal had been a journalist on the 'Herald' for almost fifteen years and far from being the enquiring investigative reporter he had aspired to in his younger days, his stories were now confined to what he regarded as the mundane goings on of 'London Celebrity'. Whilst this might have been a source of great achievement to many of his contemporaries, he had little interest in the vapid, self promoting, egotistical world of so-called celebrity. Fame without merit was now the mainstay of British 'journalism'. He always thought of the word 'journalism' in quotes, no longer believing such a label was worthy of the tosh expounded by the daily rags. He would mourn the day when the last broadsheet disappeared to join the digital age and he would miss the smell and feel of newsprint between his fingers which had been, once upon a time, the substantive embodiment of the award winning writing he had once produced. Like all else, it would join the 'virtual' world where nothing had substance or vitality but was available at the touch of a button.

14

Hal remembered how it had been a source of pride to him when the papers neatly piled off the printers and could be found all over London in newsagents, kiosks and tube trains where commuters devoured the fruits of his labours to alleviate the tedium of their dull, relentless daily journeys. Then, he had things to say with intelligent comment and observation. His analytical powers were now drying up along with his vocabulary since the public had developed a taste for bite sized snatches of prose in dumbed down, easy to read appetisers. Nowadays, he provided merely a superficial glimpse into the world to which many aspired; one which offered reward without effort; his prose designed neither to educate nor edify. He wrote endless diatribes about those famous for plastic surgery addiction; those winning the latest talent show, their endless cover versions replacing the need for originality, musical ability, creativity or talent. Years of this soul destroying crap had ground him into his present apathy. He sighed. *No wonder I eat too much and anaesthetise myself with alcohol every night,* he thought, dolefully.

In no hurry to move, Hal contemplated his burgeoning stomach, his pride and self esteem a thing of the past. Eventually, having demolished the last crumbs of the sausage roll, he reluctantly heaved his heavy frame from his seat. Whenever a story did come in, it was an intrusion to his day. Without enthusiasm he reached the reception desk where Lisa stared at him, her insouciant expression giving way to one of contempt and disgust as his dishevelled, sweaty countenance overshadowed her 'paperless' desk.

"I suppose it would have been too much for you to bring the envelope over to me?" Hal asked without expectation of anything greater than a monosyllabic response.

"Thought you could do with the exercise," Lisa sniped insolently as she inspected him with undisguised revulsion.

Hal picked up the envelope and sneered derisively.

15

"Need your caterpillars re-tattooed love," he said, referring to her eyebrows that gave her a permanently frozen look of surprise. "They're almost becoming expressive." He despised the way that youngsters obsessed about their appearance these days yet worked endlessly to create the 'Stepford Wife' look, devoid of personality, intelligence or charisma. For a moment, he watched despairingly as Lisa compulsively punched letters into her phone, either texting or posting drivel on some social media site. Another mark of the virtual world, he thought. Phones had become like new limbs, permanently attached to their owners, replacing the need for social interaction or friends other than the 790 followers you might have on Twitter where conversations were conveniently limited to 150 characters or less.

Lisa's hair extensions displayed untidy knots at the roots, her false eyelashes transformed her into a drag queen and botox largely froze her expression into vacuity; her skin glowed like a tangerine and her swollen lips metamorphosed her into Daffy Duck. She thought she looked fabulous. Deluded, he thought.

"Watcher lookin' at, Lardy? Dirty old bugger!' she exclaimed in a momentary lapse from her text conversation.

"Not sure," he replied, "but believe me, it doesn't evoke 'dirty'."

"What's 'evoke?'" she quacked from her swollen duck bill.

"Never mind," he sighed helplessly as he glanced now at the envelope he was holding. It was postmarked from Greece. Unusual not to receive e-mail, he thought abstractedly, as he inspected the sealed missive which was to change his life and his fortunes.

Chapter 2- The Paris Match

31 August, 1997

The medical and emergency team worked hastily in the furore and chaos surrounding them at the scene of the accident. Having ascertained her condition and stabilised the surviving female passenger as best they could, she was efficiently and gently removed from the vehicle into the waiting ambulance. It was a slick operation as the injured woman was transferred into the high tech mobile treatment vehicle. She was in pain, barely conscious and yet aware of the severity of the incident, having been momentarily lucid enough to glimpse the apocalyptic scene of her companions in varying degrees of gruesome injury. She had glanced to her left and with horror, regarded the unmoving body of the man she loved, his eyes open, yet unseeing. As she slipped into unconsciousness, she realised that her worst fears, despite all her preparation, had come to pass. She had not intended it to work out this way when she had put her insurance plans into motion; but it was over now. Everything was over.

The team surrounded her and worked deftly to apply monitors and drugs to her body, intent on trying to ensure her survival. In and out of consciousness she drifted, at one moment her soulful eyes penetrating those of the doctor who gazed benignly at her as he gripped her hand reassuringly.

"They did it then," she murmured. "They got what they wanted in the end. I always knew they would." She closed her eyes, certain in the mists of her mind that she was about to enter the next world which she vaguely hoped would offer her the peace, love and comfort so long and cruelly denied her in this one. The ambulance began its slow journey to the hospital which awaited her, the tension palpable amongst

17

those present. Any false move or miscalculation now would thwart everything.

Two men dressed in black formal suits sat at the back of the ambulance, slightly distanced from the medical team. They glanced occasionally out of the tinted glass at the rear of the vehicle. Only the clenching of jaws and the throbbing of neck veins and temples belied their cool professional exteriors, displaying the slightest hint of anxiety as they prepared to carry out the most sensational operation of their careers. The men, together with the medical team, were all hand - picked to be complicit in the orchestration of the most extraordinary event which would stun and perplex the population of the globe for years to come.

The silence in the ambulance was interrupted only by the beeping of the machines displaying the vital signs of the patient and the occasional muttering of the medical team as instructions were relayed and carried out. The ambulance crawled at snail's pace, unusual for the circumstances which would normally have entailed a high speed journey across the city. Away from the chaotic scene of the crash, the streets had been cordoned off and the only other traffic was the motorcycle police who escorted the vehicle on its tentative passage.

Long before the ambulance reached its destination, it slowed to a halt and the woman moaned in pain, her blood pressure reaching dangerous lows. Her eyes fluttered open once more above the oxygen mask which kept her barely breathing. Somehow, she summoned the will to grip the doctor's arm with sudden and unexpected strength; her eyes welled with tears and despair. He in turn, grasped her hand reassuringly.

"Ssh, don't excite yourself," he murmured in heavily accented English. "*Ca va bien maintenant*, it will all be fine. Calm please. We are here to ensure your safe passage."

The heavier of the suited men approached the doctor.

"*Il est temps maintenant.*" The doctor nodded and the suited man gave an instruction to the vehicle's driver. Within moments, the scene was set, the ambulance was opened and the calculated manoeuvre was swiftly commenced. The two men locked eyes and nodded to each other. A barely discernible smile between them displayed a mixture of relief and accomplishment, the plan of action hastily carried out with military precision. They shook hands, the doctor stroked the woman's cheek as she lay helpless and prone below his gaze.

"*Dormez bien ma cherie. Tout sera bien, je vous le promets.*" The doctor smiled and gave the order to his team to exit the ambulance as the new team entered to continue the vital work.

19

Chapter 3 – The Road to Gavdos

Chania, Crete, 2014

Hal couldn't quite believe that just 72 hours after receiving the envelope at his office, he was now descending the steps from the aircraft at Chania in Crete. He'd never been a spontaneous type but that day in the office, he realised that he'd reached his nadir. He needed to do something drastic to set his life back on track. Since Fliss's death, he'd let himself go and become apathetic towards his work, social life and, certainly his appearance. Perhaps, he'd thought, as he read and re-read the letter, this would give him some time out to reappraise things and maybe regain his appetite for producing some decent work again. He needed something to get his self esteem back. If nothing more, it would be time away from the rut he'd ground for himself and the opportunity to think clearly; something he hadn't done in the days since Fliss had died.

The late summer sun was delightfully warm but not excessively hot as Hal made his way to the airport bus which would take him into Chania. It had been many years since his last visit to Crete and he remembered his previous stay with a mixture of fondness and sadness. Perhaps that was why, with barely a moment's thought, he decided there and then that he would go. A sign of a change for the better maybe? The last time he'd been in Crete was during his honeymoon twelve years ago. He and Fliss had enjoyed the setting sun over the Aegean, cocktails in their hands, anticipating the many more holidays and romantic days they would spend together. He laughed inwardly. How quickly the magic of a holiday wears off and the sheer drudgery of daily life erodes the optimism.

Despite his sudden decision to up sticks and hop off to Crete, during the flight Hal found himself wondering what on earth he was doing. What conviction had led him to think this was the right thing to do? But then again, what was the harm? He hadn't taken a holiday for over a year and he'd persuaded Frank, his editor that he needed a bit of a sabbatical. Frank, aware of Hal's visible decline in recent months, was happy to let him take a holiday, plus a few extra weeks unpaid. He knew Hal to be a good journalist when he had his mind on the job and it would do no harm. Frank hadn't seen Hal so buoyed up in a long time and perhaps it would regenerate his work. How could he refuse?

Hal settled back in the coach seat for the short journey into Chania town centre and pulled out the letter once again, just to remind himself that there had been something tangible which had led him here.

Dear Mr Bradbury

I have been entrusted to write to you in the strictest confidence on behalf of my employer, Miss Tasia Artemis. She has followed your work over many years as a journalist and was impressed particularly by many of your earlier investigative stories.

Mr Bradbury, I know that this letter will cause you some consternation, but Miss Artemis has a story to tell; it is one which, I promise will bring you fame and fortune as the relaying of this tale will astound the world. Miss Artemis has asked me to tell you that she will place a villa at your disposal, here in Gavdos for the duration of the project, plus she will pay you a stipend of one thousand Euros per week to allow you to remain here for as long as it takes to write the memoire which she hopes you may one day publish in a book as her final words. The only proviso is that you must wait until the death of Miss Artemis before you publish. Sadly, the wait will not be too long for you as she only has a short time left with us. You see, she is terminally ill and the deterioration in her health has been rapid. You will understand therefore that her need for a

21

quick decision from you is imperative. I have also taken the liberty of enclosing an open air ticket in order for you to make the necessary travel arrangements.

I know that as you read this letter, you will be questioning and sceptical. That, of course, is natural. Why, after all, would you respond to a letter from a complete stranger in another country asking you to drop everything and come here on a whim. Why indeed? All I can give you is my assurance that this is a bona fide request and tell you that I believe you will be unable to resist an interlude in your life that will prove both perplexing and intriguing.

I know that you will come Mr Bradbury and to show my employer's good faith, I also enclose her cheque for £2000 as an advance for your work. Please, feel free to cash this before making your decision. Miss Artemis has also asked me to impart to you that all rights and royalties for the work you publish as a result of your time here will be yours alone. These, I can tell you, will be beyond your wildest imagining.

Finally, I must give you a few words of caution. The project you will be embarking upon is not without its dangers and you must therefore be extremely circumspect about the information you disclose to anyone at this stage. You will find nothing on any media about Miss Artemis, so there is no point at all in researching her. She has, for many years, lived a quiet and spiritual life here on Gavdos with only a very closed circle of friends and acquaintances. Until her death, she wishes it to remain so for reasons which will eventually become clear to you.

I hope then, Mr Bradbury, that we shall have the pleasure of welcoming you to our beautiful island of Gavdos in the very near future. All further correspondence may now be conducted by e-mail, through me on artemigavdos97.gr. If you advise me of your planned arrival on Gavdos, which can be reached by ferry from Chania, I shall be happy to meet you and take you to your villa.

22

I look forward to meeting you soon.
Yours in anticipation
Stergios Tavoularis

Folding the letter back up, Hal shook his head in
wonder at his uncharacteristically impulsive behaviour. Who
knows what he was going into here? It was all so surreal.
And yet, something told him, a little voice in his head, that this
was the right thing to do. He was excited and, as Tavoularis
had suggested, more than a little intrigued. Unable to resist
checking the internet before he left, he had tapped in the
name Tasia Artemis. As promised by Tavoularis, it threw
nothing up which would give him any clues.

Hal arrived in Chania town late in the afternoon. The
next leg of the journey would be a 70 km ride the next day to
Sfakia where he would catch the ferry to Gavdos. This was all
new to him. He and Fliss had stayed in the tourist catchment
area of Chania last time they had been in Crete. They were
both enchanted by the Venetian port with its Moorish
influences and overlooked by an old mosque long dispensed
with as a place of religious worship. Nowadays it housed
various events such as art and craft exhibitions, a long
abandoned artefact of the Turkish influences of yesteryear.

For the remainder of the evening, Hal enjoyed a meal
and a few drinks at one of the tavernas alongside Chania
Harbour. With typical exuberance and the hope of repeat
business, the jovial waiter conversed with him about his visit
and offered him a jug of raki. Pleasantly warmed and his
senses dulled, Hal felt the calming influence of the island
which he had experienced years before. He could be happy
here, he thought. He'd get his life in order, eat healthy Cretan
fare and write to his heart's content. He just needed the
finance to do it – that's where reality bit. Paying the bill, he
bade the waiter '*Yassas*' and ambled along the seafront
basking in the last of the sun's warmth, appreciating the

history and tradition of the bustling harbour before entering his hotel where he gratefully laid his head for the night. He drifted off to sleep with a sense of anticipation and excitement that had long since eluded him.

Chapter 4 – Fairytales and Forests

July 1961

"It's a girl!" the mother beamed at her husband whilst cradling the small bundle protectively in her arms. The father forced a smile at his wife and nodded, barely disguised disappointment the unspoken subtext of their otherwise silent communication. The wife tried to remain upbeat, fighting the tears of hurt for both herself and her new born child.

"We'll try again," she soothed her husband apologetically. "Next time it'll be a boy darling, you'll see." The husband, stiff and formal, nodded wordlessly and exited the room leaving his wife feeling worthless and sad, her joy quashed, her spirit dampened yet again. She had failed; failed her husband, failed the family name and the family line for which the continuation under primogeniture required a son to receive the property of generations.

From that day onwards, the child keenly felt her inadequacy and despite the fact that a brother was born later, she perceived that she was a disappointment. She was supposed to have been the boy and she was less of a person for that. Something deep within her though, told her that in some way she *was* special and she determined that she would show them all one day that her worth was beyond measure. How prophetic her belief would prove to be; but how dramatic the reality was to become even she had no inkling.

Early Years

Growing up the child experienced psychological trauma which, as might be expected, left its mark. Despite all their breeding and aristocracy, there was many a night when she awoke to the raised voices of her parents. All was not well within the household and she knew that within minutes, things would worsen. Tears of powerlessness regularly coursed down her cheeks as she pulled the bed covers over her head to shut out her mother's pleading and to deflect the anger and fear she felt towards her beloved daddy who beat her mother behind the closed doors.

The next day the girl and her brother played together in the acres of garden surrounding their stately home, dashing this way and that as they competed to 'tig' each other, each trying to forget the sounds of the night before; the rows, the pleading, the sobbing of their demoralised and dispirited mother.

"You look happy, Sis," her younger brother commented uncertainly, bemusedly, under the circumstances. She flashed him a steely gaze, her smile stretching her lips, but never quite reaching the eyes which betrayed the sadness which rarely left her. She shrugged.

"I'm like Mummy – always smiling even when she's crying inside. It's a wonderful trick to play on everyone, don't you see, Charles. I can trick everyone because no-one, not even you, will ever know how I am really feeling." And indeed, in the years to come, she used her trick to great effect as she would hide her sorrows and at least some of her secrets from the world.

The mother, eventually broken and unable to endure the abuse, gathered her children and fled the home. Any sense of freedom she may have felt though, soon dissipated as the power of her husband and his position forced her to relinquish her family back to him so that he could spin tales to the impressionable children of her desertion and lack of care for them.

Separated from her mother and under the influence only of her distant father, the girl was convinced by him that Mummy had simply abandoned them and didn't want to know them. Nothing could be further from the truth as the battles

26

over the children raged behind the scenes. The child sought solace in her imagination, taking her mother's old dresses from the dressing up box and, in the way of all little girls she swished and sashayed around her room, pretending to be a princess in high heels and paste jewelled tiara.

Viewing herself in the mirror, she imagined that she was slimmer and more beautiful than she appeared now and dreamt the ultimate fairytale; that a handsome prince would gallop in upon his white steed and upon seeing her beauty, he would stoop down and release her from her misery. In her mind, she was no longer the plump little ugly duckling but transformed into elegant swan casting her spell to enchant the handsome prince. How she loved the fairytale world which released her from the reality and sorrow of her real world.

Little girls however only become aware of the evil nature of fairy tales in much later life. In all the best stories which enthral us, there are dark woods and evil shadows beyond the fairytale palaces. If you stray too far from the pathway the demons lurking behind the knotted arms of the trees in the darkened forest will jump out carrying you off to a world where you are cursed and held by an evil enchantment, perhaps never to see the light of day again.

Indeed, it would come as a shock to the girl, many years later, to discover that there are, even in the modern world dark forces who would deceive us, keeping us wide eyed and in reverend thrall to people, traditions and institutions. As she discovers, they are no more than chimeras; creations of smoke and mirrors which control our mind and movement. These dark forces move silently amongst us, as the child will discover, to perpetuate mystique, symbolism and imagery, their clandestine movements in the shadows protecting the interests of the few and promoting discord amongst the majority. Subconsciously she discovers that there are those with power, entrusted with secrets they say are necessary for our safety and we are programmed in

27

our DNA to believe that these omnipotent forces are beyond reproach. Those, though, who stray from the pathway to discover the truth, or indeed retaliate, will be silenced. For the truth can never be known.

It is fortunate indeed, that few of us can predict our destiny. Destiny, good or bad cannot be avoided. The future opens up ahead of us and we believe in chance encounters and unplanned events. But for some, nothing is accidental, co-incidental or the product of random chance. For this special child, she is nothing but a chess piece and a commodity to be traded. Let her enjoy the fairytale for a while though...

Chapter 5 – A World of Possibility

Hal disembarked the ferry in the port of Karave. He stood on the little island, silently surveying the stunning view before him. The crystal blue sea from the unspoilt beach glittered and twinkled as the sun caught its surface. What struck him most was the silence and the peace. He was the only person to travel that day as he was far outside the normal tourist season. He felt he was standing on a ghost island; a Greek 'Brigadoon' perhaps disappearing, only to magically re-emerge every 100 years. For a moment, he wondered whether he should turn back to the ferry and return to the civilisation of Crete, the loneliness of the island briefly usurping the attraction of its quiet beauty. It was a far cry from the London madness and he wasn't sure as yet whether he was ready to embrace the stark contrast. He was also unsure about what to expect as there was no-one there to greet him.

There had been a couple of emails between Hal and Stergios Tavoularis to organise travel and meeting arrangements. He had expected Stergios to be here at the Port and indeed, there was an array of battered vehicles assembled to meet the ferry which was clearly central to the island's economy but no-one amongst the chattering islanders came forward to introduce themselves as Stergios.

Hal sat down on the beach, arms wrapped around his bent knees as he gazed out to sea where he could just make out the mountains of Crete in the distance. Looking around him, he watched the locals as they loaded and unloaded goods and supplies from the ferry, engaging in good natured banter as they did so. He watched the local priest stride down to the harbour with assurance of his status, his black robes flowing and his chimney pot headwear perched commandingly atop his unkempt bearded head, long grey hair tied firmly back in a ponytail, a throwback to times gone by. As he went, he cordially slapped backs and grasped shoulders reassuringly the locals greeting his presence with respectful fondness.

Although the ferry's arrival, Hal knew, was a daily event, it was clearly something which the islanders anticipated with pleasure, allowing them as it did, to chat and laugh together.

From his own rather scant research about the Island of Gavdos, Hal knew that there were very few permanent inhabitants here. The figures ranged from between 50 and 90 people although it was difficult to gauge exact numbers. He calculated that there were around thirty people here at the harbour representing perhaps over half of the island's population.

He glanced at his watch, a slight unease niggling at him that Stergios had not yet arrived to greet him. What on earth, he wondered, could hold anyone up on an island of such small proportions where the main event appeared to be the daily ferry arrival. Stergios was hardly going to be able to claim traffic jams! Apparently, Gavdos did become busy during the tourist season, attracting thousands of holidaymakers who would set up camp on the beaches, some of which were known to be of the 'naturist' variety. Hal knew however, that the island, although beginning to develop, still didn't provide the kind or number of facilities that would attract package holidaymakers. He supposed that it wouldn't be long before the first gift shop or quad bike suppliers reached this unspoiled idyll of the Mediterranean. He had to confess, the idea of residing on a largely uninhabited island intrigued him but also slightly terrified him.

Hal knew from previous visits to Greece that it was the cultural norm to live in 'Greek Time,' and despite the non-appearance of Stergios, comforted himself with the knowledge that *'siga siga'* (slowly, slowly) was the motto of this very laid back nation. *Probably even more slowly than usual here,* he thought wryly.

He relaxed and enjoyed the view which was indeed breathtakingly beautiful. It was at once, full of lush greenery, rocky terrain, golden beaches and cerulean blue seas. It truly was reminiscent of the island of the 'Bounty Hunters,' he remembered from the chocolate bar adverts he'd watched in his youth. One of the islands off Crete had indeed been allegedly used to film those adverts, although he didn't think it was actually Gavdos. Nevertheless, it was a paradise on earth he thought, as he breathed in the warm, clean but salty sea air.

The rows of battered and spluttering vehicles had begun to dissipate as the islanders completed their business at the portside. Only a few stragglers remained now, huddled in groups as they chatted and laughed together with ease common to those who had grown up and lived together in close proximity. In some ways, Hal thought, that could also be sinister. He noticed the curious and even suspicious glances he had received as he sat here on the beach conspicuously out of season for the normal run of the mill tourist.

As the last of the groups drifted away, one man broke away from the remaining stragglers. He was of sturdy build, and indeterminate age; his chin and upper lips sporting a very black but well trimmed beard. His black, wavy hair was also casual but well cut and he wore a straw trilby on his head. His white, open necked shirt was neatly tucked and belted into casual beige slacks and he struck Hal as looking like 'Our man in Havana,' a rather charismatic and sartorial throwback to foreign office officials of the fifties and sixties, perhaps.

Hal watched as the man bade his companions farewell and moved away from the group with a shared joke as they all laughed amiably, his hand raised in final farewell before casually approaching Hal who now struggled to rise from his seated position, his limbs struggling under his portly frame.

The man strode purposefully to Hal and stretched out his hand to assist him in getting up from the beach. Hal

31

gratefully, but rather embarrassedly accepted the outstretched arm and he felt himself being pulled up with ease by his companion.

"You must be Stergios, I presume?" Hal queried. The man inclined his head and grinned broadly, which, although friendly in manner did not entirely convince Hal; there was something Saturnine in the man's demeanour. He perceived a suspicious, darkly brooding character behind the mask of congeniality.

"Stergios by name and Stergios by nature," the man replied in only slightly accented English. "Come, Mr Bradbury. I bid you welcome to our glorious island and wish you a happy and interesting stay with us. I am certain you will not be disappointed."

Hal brushed down his jeans which were covered in sand as Stergios raised his arm behind him as if to usher him forward. Hal obliged and walked alongside his new acquaintance towards the only remaining vehicle now; one which surprisingly, Hal had not noticed earlier. A gleaming brand new black Mercedes Benz – undoubtedly an unusual sight on an island such as this (although not uncommon in other parts of Greece where the taxi drivers drove their gleaming German cars with pride). The windows were blacked out, perhaps to deflect the rays of the sun, or the gaze of outsiders. The latter seemed unlikely to Hal, given that there were few who would not know his companion on the island anyway.

"So, Mr Bradbury ..."

"Hal, please Stergios," Hal interrupted.

"Yes, quite so; Hal then," Stergios grinned again. "Please get in the car. It is but a short drive to our destination but there are one or two pleasant tavernas on the way. We can stop and enjoy a cold Mythos together, *Nai?*"

32

The thought of a very cold lager in an iced glass was the most wonderful vision that Hal could picture at that moment.

"You know how to welcome a stranger to your land, Stergios," Hal smiled, anticipation of the amber nectar almost too much to bear in the heat of the day.

"Indeed Hal – Greek hospitality starts with a cold beer on Gavdos! You must forgive my rather tardy approach today. I like to observe people for a short while to get the measure of them when they are not aware of my presence. It often tells me more than the things they may say to me."

"That's a little bit mysterious. You seem to know a lot more about me already than I do about you," Hal replied.

"True," he laughed, " but I am a great observer of body language Hal. It has served me well in the past. For instance, you are self conscious, perhaps about your weight which you have gained through a certain discontentment of late. Am I right?"

Hal simply stared at the driver sitting next to him in amazement. He wasn't sure if it was because he was shocked by the very personal nature of the man's assessment of him, or whether he was stunned by its accuracy. Whichever, he was impressed.

"You are spot on, Stergios. Hence the reason I'm here. A change of scene and perhaps something to stimulate an otherwise stultified and stagnant imagination of late. But you might have deduced that simply by the fact that I'm here on a strange island, lured by some weird tale that intrigued me".

Stergios laughed.

"Indeed, I might have made such a deduction. However, the way you curled yourself up on the beach, as though trying to be invisible; the uncertainty in your eyes which display lack of confidence and the agitation in your movements that exhibit a desire to emerge from your chrysalis told me far more."

33

"Well then, I have to agree Stergios, you are a perceptive man indeed."

"Don't worry Hal. I won't be looking too far into your soul. Breathe easy and enjoy your new life here. You will need to open your mind and soul to what you are going to discover here though."

"Very mysterious, if I might say, Stergios."

"There are enormous mysteries in our midst, *o philos mou (my friend)* and you, perhaps, are lucky enough to have come here to find the solution to one of the greatest mysteries of modern times."

A flutter of excitement, or perhaps a frisson of nerves, he wasn't quite sure which, passed through Hal. A tingle of anticipation coursed over the top of his scalp. He felt he was on the verge of something momentous, but equally, it was something terrifying.

After a short journey, the Mercedes came to a halt and Stergios proudly announced that they had arrived in the 'capital' of Gavdos, Kastri. Hal slowly took in the view around him. The title 'capital' in what he saw was something of an anathema. There was no sprawling metropolis, no discernible shops or traffic or nightlife. He saw a cluster of derelict houses which Stergios proudly described as properties for sale which would be desirable residences with 'a few improvements'. Hal didn't voice his opinion that those improvements would include complete demolition and a new-build kit on the otherwise, very desirable remaining sites. Stergios though, was undeterred. Soon, he opined, Gavdos would become a sought after tourist attraction where people would want to come and stay. People would buy holiday homes and create a wonderful new economy on the island paradise.

To be fair, there were signs of building works in the harbour where obvious improvements had been made and Hal didn't doubt that one of these days, the island would not

34

escape the inevitable influx from the moneyed classes, eager to possess their own idyllic retreat.

Stergios had pulled up outside a taverna in Kastri and for Hal it was a most welcoming sight. Tables with chequered tablecloths blowing upwards in the warm breeze, were laid out on wooden decking, shielded from the blazing rays of the sun by a canopy. The two men ordered a beer and Hal, beginning to relax as the alcohol hit his bloodstream looked forward to his new life here. If there was anywhere in the world he would have time and space to write, it was certainly here.

"So, Stergios, when do I get to meet Miss Artemis? I have to say, I'm very puzzled and very intrigued by all the mystery surrounding this project."

"I daresay, Hal, that your intrigue will grow by the day once you get started." Stergios took a deep swig from his glass and ordered another *Mythos* for each of them.

"Miss Artemis is on the main island of Crete for a couple of days. She is undergoing treatment for her illness. She asked me to look after you and make sure that you were fully settled in your new residence here on Gavdos and also to assure you that she will be back just as quickly as she can."

"So what can you tell me about her Stergios? I've been unable to find anything about her on the internet or in any other research I've done. Who is Miss Artemis and why does she merit the writing of a biography?"

"The biography is imperative Hal. The time has come for a great truth to be revealed. You should feel honoured because you are about to rock the world with the story you are about to tell." Stergios met Hal's incredulous gaze with a firm set, serious expression, his steely gaze intent on reading his companion's reaction.

"You said something about it being a dangerous project?"

"Yes, *Kyrie*, you must be careful at all times to whom you speak about this work before its publication. There are,

35

even as we speak, eyes and ears on the island who are trying to elicit the truth about my lady Artemis. They are moving closer; but we too are watchful. If we move carefully and, I have to say as expediently as possible, we should be able to deflect the immediate dangers. Once you get back to Britain, our people will be on hand to help you get the story out but you must learn stealth and maintain utter discretion, even amongst those who live here. There is money to be made and there are those who will exploit the secret we have kept on this island for many years."

Unconsciously, Hal shook his head quizzically. The man was talking in riddles. He'd come all this way, yes, of his own volition, he supposed, but only to discover very little about the purpose. He was becoming slightly irritable now and not just a little uneasy.

"You're going to have to give me something more to go on here," Hal retorted, a barely disguised impatience creeping into his tone.

Stergios smiled broadly, the warmth of the gesture however, never quite reaching his watchful eyes.

"You must trust me Hal; for the moment at least. I promise you, all in good time, everything will become clear. But it is for Miss Artemis to divulge her story to you, not me. I will, where necessary, fill in some of the finer details about certain matters, but only when she has begun her work with you. Now, before I take you to your beautiful new home where you can relax for a couple of days and settle in, we shall have one more beer and I shall give you some important instructions for your comfort and safety, as they say on the best airlines." Stergios signalled to the proprietor with the customary '*parakalo!*' and within moments two further bottles of the chilled lager arrived at the table.

Stergios leaned across the table and indicated for Hal to do likewise as he spoke quietly.

36

"Now Hal, your back story has already been circulated locally. Unfortunately, when a stranger stays on Gavdos for more than a day or two, they become very conspicuous. Gavdos is working its way into the 21st century and for the purposes of the islanders, you are here as a travel writer who will be working and living on the island to produce a series of articles which will promote its growing attractions. The villagers will be happy about this as they are all hoping to make their fortunes as the island becomes known. Miss Artemis is well known and well loved on the island. She does much for the islanders and they believe that she has healing powers. Indeed, we have seen some inexplicable events on the island following her interventions. She is an enigmatic figure Hal and much respected so it will be natural that you would speak to her also about life on Gavdos. As you will discover, Gavdos itself has its own mystique and it is a remarkably fitting place for Miss Artemis to have lived."

Stergios was warming to his story and Hal listened intently, hoping that he would, after a few more beers, drop in some more details about Miss Artemis. However, he was more absorbed with the island itself.

"Archaeologists have been here on the island you know, and their finds have suggested it was inhabited 3000 years before Christ. Gavdos has an impressive pedigree of myths and legends. Many say that it hides the lost city of Atlantis and that it is a source of immortality. This would be a fitting backdrop, as you will discover, to your story about Miss Artemis."

Hal smiled incredulously.

"What on earth are you talking about, Stergios? You're making this whole thing sound not just cloak and dagger but something in the realms of the metaphysical! Let's keep our feet firmly on the ground, shall we?" Hal laughed.

Stergios was apparently less amused.

37

"The metaphysical, you say. Yes, that is a good description of the properties of Gavdos. It is also a very *Greek* word. It derives from *meta* which means *beyond* and *physika*, or physics. It is therefore the study of a certain kind of philosophy, also, you will know, something over which the Greeks famously have a sphere of influence." Warming to his subject, Stergios stretched back in his chair and clasped his hands over his stomach.

"Metaphysical philosophy concerns two basic questions, Hal; 1) What is actually *there?* And 2) What is it *like?* It is a method by which we have tried to define our existence, the means by which we understand the world; things like our very existence, the existence of objects, the meaning of space and time, the relevance of cause and effect and the notion of *possibility*. I think, Hal, these are matters which you will have to contemplate in the days and weeks to come and above all, keep an open mind as to *possibility*. If you close your mind to this, then you are not the man for us. Of course, metaphysics is regarded less as a philosophy today than a science, by which empirical study seeks to prove the metaphysical realm. Before the 18th century though, it was a natural philosophy and you are going to encounter in your work with us much of the metaphysical".

"Stergios, you're losing me I'm afraid. What are you saying? Miss Artemis has some sort of metaphysical properties? Is she a ghost? Something from the supernatural? You said she's regarded as having some sort of healing abilities? Come on, you've got to explain yourself!"

Stergios chuckled.

"I've already said more than I should have done. All in good time, Hal, all in good time. Enjoy the experience of unravelling a mystery and of drawing your own conclusions. You are about to embark on a fascinating journey on Gavdos. Whether you believe or disbelieve the things you will uncover, you are, shall we say, in for the 'ride of your life.'

38

"Stergios, you're talking in riddles! I wish you'd just give me a straight answer to a straight question. I'm a journo, not a philosopher or a scientist. I deal with facts, things that are discernible. I'd lose all credibility if I started writing New Age claptrap."

"And you haven't already lost the credibility of your previous years' cutting edge journalism with some of your more recent celebrity stories about botox, big boobs and Big Brother?"

Hal, in one moment coiled himself to offer a sharp retort to the stinging criticism but in the next found himself open mouthed, unable to justify any argument against Stergios' assertions. It was true, his readers wouldn't have a clue what words such as *metaphysics* or *philosophy* meant. Even he felt 'dumbed down' by his recent efforts. He wondered if he could even find it within himself to use an extended vocabulary these days. He drew a deep breath and conceded.

"You're right Stergios. In the old days, I covered important stories with depth and meaning and consequence. Now, I'm consigned to the superficial stuff; no investigative journalism, no expression, no room for objective or reasoned discussion. Just who's shagging whom and who's got the biggest boobs. And yeah. OK. Maybe you are spinning me some wild stuff; maybe you honestly believe you're involved in something weird and wonderful. You're paying me, I'm in a beautiful place and, if nothing else, it sounds intriguing." Hal lifted his glass in toast and Stergios lifted his clinking them together.

"To the metaphysical then!" Hal laughed.

"To the metaphysical and beyond!" Stergios replied amiably.

Hal and Stergios, the ice having been broken and Stergios happy that he had at least broached some of the difficult areas he knew Hal would struggle with, continued to get acquainted over a good home cooked Greek meal of souvlaki, tzatziki, aubergine salad and fresh green salad topped with salty feta cheese. The food reminded Hal of happier times when he had honeymooned with Fliss, enjoying the sunset over Crete as they held hands and anticipated a bright future together.

Stergios meanwhile wanted to tell Hal all about Gavdos. He was genuinely excited and entranced by the myths and legends which it apparently spawned. He explained how the island once had a population of 8000 during the Byzantine times; a sharp contrast with the 50 or so inhabitants of today. He also revealed that Gavdos was once known as 'Ogygya' and was the subject of Homer's Odyssey. Legend had it that the Goddess Calypso had made a shipwrecked Odysseus her immortal husband on the island. Whilst Odysseus wished to return to his wife Penelope, he was detained by Calypso in the hope that he would settle with her. Eventually though, the God Zeus sent Hermes to tell her that it is not the destiny of Odysseus to remain with her and she must set him free, which reluctantly, she does.

"So you see, Hal, mystery abounds on Gavdos. Calypso herself is both a positive and a negative goddess; a rescuer but also the mistress of concealment". Stergios raised his eyes and with a knowing glance, continued, "You will find that the story of Miss Artemis contains similar intrigue, I am sure. She has, in some respects, become synonymous with Gavdos and Calypso. And of course, she is named after another of our Greek Goddesses."

Hal, feeling mellow and not just a little worse for the wear by now having supplemented the beers with local wine and the customary raki, leaned over the table, slurring his words slightly as he spoke.

"Stergios, now, you're not going to tell me that I'm here to interview a *metaphysical Greek Goddess* are you?" He giggled slightly as he slumped back in his seat, the heat and the rigours of the day having caught up with him somewhat suddenly and unexpectedly.

"I'm not suggesting anything to you Hal. Just remember what I told you about metaphysics and be open to the realms of all *possibility.*"

"Hrrmph! Riddles again Stergios. My brain hurts now."

"Hal, my friend, I'm forgetting myself. Of course, you have had a very long, hard couple of days travelling here. Drink up and we'll head off to your villa. It's very close to Miss Artermis' house so you won't have far to go when you're working with her."

After a very short drive along a twisting, dusty, and under developed road, through pine trees, cedar trees and shrubs, they came to a clearing and stopped outside a very new and very beautiful modern villa.

"So, here we are," Stergios announced on their arrival. "This is your new home for now, 'Villa Gaia'. I hope you will be comfortable."

Having unloaded the cases from the Merc, Stergios led Hal into the coolness of the air conditioned villa. Hal was impressed. Marble floors, tasteful decor and the best of household equipment was placed at his disposal. There was even a small area of garden which had been cultivated to give the property a homely feel. If nothing else, he could anticipate a luxury stay on Gavdos. Stergios briskly showed him around, explaining the water, electrical and air conditioning systems.

"So Hal, I suggest you get some sleep and settle in over the next couple of days. The real work will begin shortly. Now, just before I bid you goodnight, one or two other matters of housekeeping".

Stergios led Hal to the upstairs balcony in the villa's bedroom and flung open the doors. The view was breathtaking, the flora and fauna growing in wild abandon around him. Stergios pointed ahead.

41

"You can't quite see it all because of the trees, but if you follow the track up the hill you will come to Villa Artemis. There is a car at your disposal in the garage as you will need to either go to Sarakinikos or Karave for basic supplies. You will probably want to take the ferry to the mainland once in a while to stock up or place orders for the incoming ferry. I will provide you with a list of suppliers who are happy to despatch to the island. You can either walk to Villa Artemis; it will take you 10-15 minutes, although the hill can be difficult on the hottest days; or, of course, you may take the car and drive up. I have left the key in the bowl on the table in the kitchen."

The two men made their way back downstairs and Hal thanked Stergios for his hospitality. Just as he was leaving, Stergios turned back to Hal, a grim, serious expression on his face.

"Be vigilant, Hal. Keep your cover story straight. There is a time of great upheaval and consequent danger coming. We believe the secret may already, at least partly, be suspected by those who would seek to manipulate the world to their own advantage. If you see or hear anything suspect, play dumb but let me know immediately. You have my mobile number – call me anytime; day or night and help will be on hand. We have surveillance around both Villas Gaia and Artemis and we are watchful at all times, but sometimes," he shrugged, "things get missed or wily characters avoid the technology."

Hal listened to the warning, wide eyed, and felt an involuntary shudder. He was excited, but now, very wary. What on earth had he let himself in for this time?

"I have to say, Stergios, you're terrifying me."

Stergios gripped Hal's shoulder.

"All will be fine. Just be cautious is all I am saying. I am not far away so just call if you need me."

He placed his trilby back on his head and waved farewell to Hal who quickly shut the door and made a tour of the Villa to make sure everything was locked up for the night. He was shattered and needed some sleep. Gratefully, but uneasily, he threw himself on the large double bed and soon he was oblivious to the rest of the day.

43

Chapter 6 – Chariots and Swords

London, June 1997

The young woman, blonde, statuesque and beautiful displayed a serenity she didn't feel as she alighted elegantly from her car. She had a driver today. Parking in central London was a nightmare and she was in no mood for it. She wore large sunglasses, her beautiful face masked and anonymous, her eyes tired and swollen from the tears she had shed. She had lost the man she believed was her true love. After days of crying, hurling things at the walls and even screaming in displays of frustration and despair, she was spent; as far down as she could possibly go whilst still living. She needed hope today, and that's what she had come to find. She needed something to cling onto; someone to tell her that all would be well; things would come right in the end. And so, she had picked up the telephone and dialled the number of one of her advisers who would give her the guidance she needed.

Sitting now, in the psychic's Knightsbridge rooms, the woman gazed hopefully at the clairvoyant she had visited so many times before, desperate for words to calm her greatest fears and give her the lifeline she needed to go on.

"So, come on then Mary, let's do it," her quiet, clipped tones were softened as always by her slightly whispered and breathless cadence.

The psychic, by contrast was large, brash, blousy and spoke in a jovial cockney accent, a laugh or quizzical exclamation never far from her lips.

"C'mon then my darlin'," she breezed, "you know the score. Take the cards, shuffle them up a bit, hold 'em in your left hand and cut the deck. Then pick me ten. And cheer up darlin' we'll sort it, whatever the problem."

It was just what the younger woman needed to hear. Instantly, she felt calmer. Once this was done, she'd know what to do. Even if it meant camping outside his bloody door all night until he'd changed his mind! If that's what Mary told her to do, she'd do it, no matter what!

Mary took the cards selected and began to lay them out.

"Ooohh! This looks exciting," she exclaimed.

"What? What are they telling you?" her client looked up and gazed at the psychic coyly from under her heavily kohled eyelids and lengthy eye lashes.

"Well, my love, looks to me that you're going on a lovely sunshine holiday where you'll be cared for by a very special someone."

"Really? Is it, um, you know .... him?"

The psychic wanted to say yes, but with clients of this calibre, she didn't want to raise false hope. This was a client who raised Mary's own profile to the higher echelons and was bringing her a great deal of prestige business. She sighed, giving a visible impression that she was deflating.

In her most placatory tone, Mary replied, "No, luvvy. It's someone new! I know that's not what you wanna hear, darlin' but believe me, this is good. Really. Go with it and trust me on this. You don't think so right now, but you're going to be crazy about this guy very soon."

Mary's client didn't look convinced. In fact, she looked as though she was about to burst into tears. This wasn't what she had come for. How could she possibly fall in love again when she felt this way about him? It just couldn't happen. Mary reached for the woman's hand as huge, fat tears spilled from her doe eyes, falling in great puddles upon the wooden table at which they were seated.

"Shh now, luvvy. Have I been wrong before?"

Taking a handkerchief from her Chanel handbag, the young woman wiped her tears and reluctantly conceded by a shake of her head that no, the clairvoyant had never let her down before.

"So, no need for tears are there? C'mon now. I'm tellin' you this is great! You're going to feel so much better in just a few weeks. Yes, it's always hard after a break up but this is all looking great! I think you're going on water, yes, that's it, a boat, I think. Wherever you are, it's gonna be really hot and ... ohhh look! I think the kids are going too!"

Momentarily, the young woman cheered a little. That would indeed be a great idea. She needed some 'us time', away from the madding crowds with the boys.

"Right, good," Mary continued. "So, there's a new man on the horizon and this is gonna be something special. He represents a complete turning point in your life. Hmmm...," the clairvoyant's brow furrowed a little.

"What's wrong? What have you seen?" Mary's client looked slightly nervous at the hesitation.

"Nothing bad, darling. I was just gonna say .... I don't think he's British. But he's very well connected in Britain, darlin'. Can't tell much more than that from the cards just now. Anyway, let's go on".

The clairvoyant turned each card which she was confident brought the young woman more hope and peace with each progression. Finally, there were three cards left to turn. Mary was glad that she had practised composure and a constant cheery demeanour whatever the turn of the cards showed. On this occasion, her mask very nearly slipped as, swallowing a gasp she let out a panicked exclamation followed by a coughing fit as the last three cards were revealed. Although she maintained an outwardly calm facade, inside, Mary was shaking. Behind the smile, she was stricken. This combination of cards rarely came out but in her experience, when they did, the result was always the same. Keeping her hands steady, she placed, face up, the Death card, the ten of swords and the chariot.

Her client's eyes gazed in fear as the death card was revealed.

"Mary! What does this one mean? The Death card? Does it mean I'm going to die?"

Mary, practised in her cool 'bedside' manner shook her head.

"No darlin'!" she exclaimed, perhaps a little too cheerily. "The death card," she continued truthfully, "just means the death of an era, radical change. Sometimes it can be hard darlin', but overall it means renewal. Taken with what's gone before, that all makes sense now doesn't it? The end of one thing but the beginning of something better."

Slightly appeased, her client sighed in relief and a reluctant smile lightened her face a little.

"And the other two cards? The ten of swords and the Chariot?"

"Just more of the same, darlin'. Means an irrevocable ending, but the start of something new. Together with the chariot, it suggests travelling, possibly even a new car for you darlin'."

Shortly afterwards, the young woman, though not ecstatic with her reading, left the clairvoyant with a warm hug. Mary gripped her a little harder and with affection usually reserved for those whom you may never see again, or at least, not for a long time. She closed the door behind her client and leaned back upon it for support. Her legs felt like jelly. She had seen this combination of cards on so many occasions. She knew what it meant. Soon, it would be over for this young woman. Truthfully, the Death card without accompanying ones usually didn't mean death, but renewal. Together with the Ten of Swords, 'irrevocable end, pain, disaster' and the Chariot 'travel, often in a vehicle, a car'. Put them all together, death, irrevocable end, pain, a car, medical intervention and destruction. This young woman was about to face her end and there was nothing Mary could say to her. Don't travel in a car? That would be absurd. Don't step out of your front door, ever? No. Even a warning was against professional ethics. What would be, would be. There was nothing Mary could do about it and there was no point in telling this poor sad creature, whose life she had followed and advised upon for so many years that she was about to find everlasting peace. One thing troubled Mary though. One part of it that didn't quite make sense. She would have to meditate on that one. The spirits were trying to guide her; she could hear their voices but indistinctly at the moment. There was something else...

Chapter 7 – Tasia Artemis

In the gleaming new hospital in Chania, the creation for which she had actively campaigned and to which she had anonymously donated money, the woman, though tired and weak remained luminously beautiful and serene. Her dark, Cleopatra bob shone in the sunshine as she reclined in the hospital grounds, exhausted but satisfied that she had offered comfort to others in the hospital's care.

Although sick and weakened herself after the latest round of aggressive treatment, her greatest source of energy was that which she gained from the happiness she brought to others, many of whom were children. When she had the strength, she would spend endless hours playing with them, telling them stories and creating a place of enchantment for them. She remembered the joy that her own children had brought her before she was wrenched from them so cruelly but so necessarily.

Although it wasn't something she could control, there were times when she would grasp a hand in support, or brush against an arm and a force, like the crackle of electricity would pass between her and the other person. It was a *connection* which she had learned might be channelled to help the other. On a number of such occasions, after moments of intense concentration whilst gripping a needy hand, she would 'see' pictures of the other's life and she was able to pinpoint what ailed them. She would see the ugly virus or the invading tumour in her mind's eye and target a mental blast of love, warmth and healing against them. She was deeply moved the first time one of her terminally ill companions was miraculously found to have been cured. It didn't happen immediately but began with the noticeable reduction of fever or pain followed by discovery that the sickness or tumour was in remission.

49

It had been a source of wonderment and delight to her whenever this happened but she also knew that it was no co-incidence. It was the destiny of those who survived that they should live because, like her, they had a particular purpose, a role to fulfil. Although she possessed the strange power she could never tell when it would work its arbitrary magic.

These occasions were discreet affairs and no connection was ever made between her quiet intervention and the sudden recovery of patients in the hospital. The closest she had come to being discovered was when young Georgios had blurted out to his mother,

"It was all because of *Kyria* Tasia Mamma. She made the electricity kill my sickness. I felt it!"

Fortunately for Tasia, she was an expert in modesty and downplaying her role. She simply smiled her characteristically serene, shy smile and in her gentle, clipped English accent which belied her Greek origin, simply responded,

"No darling. It was all down to you. You stayed positive and willed yourself to get better. Now hush. Don't go saying things like that or you'll get me into all sorts of bother."

Both of them though knew differently and when Georgios ran to bid her farewell on the day he was discharged, he whispered, "*I know it was you, Kyria Tasia, who made my sickness go away. I saw it in a dream.*"

"Well, let's just keep it as a secret between us, shall we? Promise me Georgiou. Never speak of it again."

The child hugged her as she bent to pick him up, his little arms firmly wrapped around her neck.

"Our secret," he promised her. And to date, she had never come close to being discovered again.

Tasia was of course well used to harbouring secrets. Indeed her whole existence was a secret. Nothing about Tasia Artemis was as it appeared. She was a mirage, nothing more.

50

The downside of her healing powers however, was the slow absorption into her own body of the ills she had cured. For each person who recovered, a little of her own health deteriorated and no-one in the medical profession really knew what ailed her. Tasia knew it was beyond medical diagnosis. Her ill health was put down to an auto-immunity meaning her body's defences attacked themselves emanating in a variety of deeply unpleasant and debilitating symptoms. No diagnosis or prognosis had ever been reached beyond this very general and very wide ranging illness. Although she was a medical mystery Tasia knew that this was the way it must be and that her days were limited, especially if she used her energies for many more healings.

This was just the latest secret in 17 years of secrets and lies that she had kept. The ministering angels and gods who had brought her here ensuring her safety and sanctuary now gently decreed that it was time to make the revelation she had been dreading. In her heart, she knew that the truth must out and thus she had decided to lay it in the hands of a person whom she knew she could trust. He would disseminate the astounding information she and her colleagues had to impart and he would defend it with integrity and impunity; providing of course, there was still time before those who would bury the secret, and her with it, caught up with her again.

Stergios had phoned her yesterday. She smiled upon hearing his familiar and trusted voice as he relayed the coded one line, 'Odysseus'.

"Odysseus has landed." She knew that the latest SIM card he had used would be immediately discarded following the call, to be replaced by yet another.

Today though, Tasia was tired and all of her energy was taken up in meditation as she tried in vain to heal her own illness. She sighed. Although she was aware that her current life cycle was nearing its end, death never became easier. Despite the knowledge that others rarely possessed, even she grew to love life and clung on to it with determination. With a stick to steady her, she slowly and painfully made her way to the private room she occupied and hauled herself wearily into bed. She needed some regenerating sleep before she could contemplate the difficulties of the coming weeks. Drifting off into a fitful somnolence, she dreamt now of earlier times and the vocation she'd be destined to follow .

As a young woman, she'd been educated in England by the private and finishing school systems. She lived as a member of the aristocracy and had been groomed to expect a good marriage. As strange as it would seem to most folk, arranged marriages amongst the upper classes were still the thing. They were tacit affairs of course, designed to perpetuate a system that fuelled political and financial ambition and furthered status in the higher echelons of British society. In effect, she, just as many of her aristocratic forbears, had been sold as a brood mare, duped into the belief that she had attained a fairytale ending.

After an unsettled and somewhat fragmented and unhappy childhood, as a young woman, she'd developed a certain resilience and determination. In her early twenties, she had her sights firmly fixed on one man for her husband and he was within her grasp. In retrospect, she knew that she had fabricated a vision of her future existence with this man, projecting onto him the perfection she felt she had missed in her childhood. He would be her Prince, her knight in shining armour who would stand by and protect her, no matter what. She had looked forward to the dazzling life she was promised this time around.

Sadly, no matter how elevated, Tasia would discover that all humans are flawed. The mixture of her flaws and his were to prove a toxic combination leading them both to years of sadness and bitterness.

In her slumber, Tasia smiled as she recalled the day when finally, the opportunity had arisen to 'bag her man.' It was at a shooting party, which, of itself, was of no interest to her, but she pretended otherwise, of course. She confided to her friends that this man was to be her destiny; *"I have an intuition about it,"* she laughed. *"Don't you know I'm psychic*?" If that was true, her predictions, if accurate in one sense, served her badly in the long run.

Contrary to the popular myths that satisfied popular convention and aristocratic tradition, the young woman was not inexperienced with members of the opposite sex at the time of her marriage. As with all good fairytales, turpitude was concealed beneath the surface.

In pursuit of her quarry, she employed every one of her womanly wiles to engage and ensnare him; flattery, sympathy, empathy with his interests, flirtatiousness at every opportunity so that he was smitten and convinced of her attentions. Behind every good match in these circumstances, there were families engineering the process for their own benefit. They wheedled, negotiated and calculated to produce the desired result often ignoring the glaring faults that would blemish the dream.

The press had been a tiresome burden but there was no doubt that their interest had been crucial to fruition of the plan. She was not above courting the marauding hacks to ensure that she was seen leaving her lover's home at various times or in his company at public events. Indeed, she became the darling of the press, creating so much speculation and excitement that the poor man was almost forced into the marriage by public demand. In fact, his family agreed that not to have married her would have been seen as a most terrible slight; humiliation on the grandest scale from which she might never recover.

Having spent months laughing a little too hard at his every joke, pretending not to be bored as he enjoyed his country pursuits, batting her eyelashes and sympathising as he mourned the death of his favourite uncle, eventually she won her prize and in the midst of great excitement, the fairytale wedding for which she had longed finally took place.

The wedding should have been the most exciting day of her life but already, cracks were beginning to show. She was uncertain of her husband's love or fidelity and several events had transpired to suggest that perhaps the joyful facade of their wedding day was flawed and in danger of collapse. Still, it was too late to back out now, and truly, did she really want to? Surely it would all come right once the fuss was all over?

The facade was maintained in public at least. However, she soon found in her older husband a stuffy, often selfish, insular and self absorbed man who could no more understand her desire for youthful pursuit and romance than she could comprehend his love of old buildings, gardening and country pursuits. His arrogance and indifference to her became daily more pronounced and soon they found they had nothing in common. She enjoyed shopping, pop music and fun with her girlfriends; he preferred reading philosophy, politics, learning about environmental issues and architecture. In short, she was as bored with him as he was apathetic to her and whilst they endeavoured to find common interest, within a few short years, rows and tantrums drove a wedge between them and their relationship crumbled. He was not in tune with the social mores of her youth; she was out of kilter with the staid, regimented lifestyle to which he was accustomed. But the young woman understood that she had a role to fulfil as part of the bargain of her marriage. Like her forbears, she was a commodity, a vehicle for primogeniture, just as her mother had been before her. Once she had fulfilled that role she was cast aside, no longer required except to fulfil her public duties with a fixed smile that reminded her of her childhood when she could 'trick everyone', never allowing them to know what she was really thinking or feeling; hugging the secret of her pain.

54

Her demons came to the fore as she became convinced yet again that she was a disappointment; despite and often because of the public adoration, she was never quite good enough for her husband or his family. Her doubts and increasingly tortured mind replaced the once carefree and jolly girl she had epitomised for her husband. That girl was usurped by a vengeful, manipulative harridan who was unrecognisable either to herself or to her husband. Her unhappiness and insecurities manifested themselves physically. Convinced that she was unattractive and hence the reason her husband preferred the attentions of an older, plainer woman, she first comforted herself with food binges followed by regular purging of all she had consumed. It gave her control in her otherwise uncontrolled existence. She had always been a girl with a voracious appetite which she indulged with abandon. She ate as much of the food she loved and as her weight reduced and her cheeks became chiselled the demons urged her on to destruction.

In the midst of tantrums and accusations and half hearted suicide attempts, at first, the mask rarely fell in public. Few, other than insiders knew that the marriage was over in all but name with the couple living separate lives; he with the woman he really loved; she, sidelined, desperate and lonely. She consoled herself with one doomed relationship after another, each coming to an end because of her self-destructive and obsessive nature.

She continued to court the press for her own manipulative ends throughout this time and became the media darling. She had grown from slightly plain duckling of the early days into a gliding swan, an icon of the modern age rivalling Jackie Onassis and Princess Grace of Monaco. Her allure eclipsed even the legend that was Marilyn Munroe. She was not to know that tragedy of similar proportions would strike her or that her apparent demise would result in speculation involving conspiracy and lies.

55

But that is the story for Hal to tell, she thought dreamily as she slowly awoke from her restless slumber. She looked forward to the moment when the final story would be told and a shocked world would wake up to the astounding truth.

Chapter 8 – Balalaikas and Ballerinas

Hal spent his first days on Gavdos settling in to his new home and getting to know the immediate area. Not that there was much to explore, the island itself only being about 10 square miles. It was an island of contradictions. Despite the harsh climate (it had been around 40 degrees the last couple of days), it was nevertheless remarkably green, covered as it was by lush pine trees and scrub land.

As he explored further, abandoned and derelict houses and terraces could just be detected under the carpet of greenery indicating that at some time there had been a thriving community on the island.

During his forays, Hal rarely met another soul. It was nearing the end of September and those who were drawn to the island to use its beaches for free camping and experience the hedonism of its naturist beaches had dwindled considerably.

Curious, Hal made his way up the hill, along the dirt track to see where Miss Artemis lived and was surprised by the opulence of the building which was his closest neighbour. It was a modern building, but built in neo classical style with a traditional Greek Colonnade forming a portico across the entrance to the property. It was also a large building reminiscent more of official premises than a house. It was stunning and dominated the horizon as Hal came over the brow of the hill. As he neared the building the panoramic view which the property overlooked was breathtaking. Miss Artemis was clearly a lady of money and good taste, he thought.

He wandered around the perimeter of the building hoping to look in a window or two. He was disappointed however, as all were located considerably above the ground and without actually climbing up, he was unable to simply look inside. He felt it would be too much of an intrusion to consider this. In any event, most of the huge windows had curtains and blinds drawn across them. Hal thought that there was a surprising amount of privacy for one who lived on such a sparsely occupied island. She was hardly going to have a stream of passers by invading the property.

Stergios had called earlier to let him know that Miss Artemis would be back on Gavdos within the next 24 hours or so. Hal contented himself in the knowledge that he would see inside the palatial residence soon enough.

He made his way back down the track towards his own villa which was extremely comfortable when suddenly the roar of a vehicle tore through the peaceful silence and his thoughts. He stopped, wondering from which direction it was coming when suddenly, at great speed and with aggressive acceleration as it came around the bend, a motorcycle hurtled straight towards him. He barely had time to throw himself off the track, out of the way of the motorbike before it roared past him never veering from the route upon which only seconds before he had been walking. The motorcycle disappeared up the hill leaving a thick cloud of dust in its wake, covering Hal who was now sprawled in the scrubland adjacent to the track. Deeply shocked and unnerved, he inspected the cuts and bruises he'd sustained in avoiding the motorcycle.

"Bloody idiot," Hal muttered out loud, drawing himself up from the ground and rubbing dust from his clothes and face. *If I didn't know better, I'd almost believe that was deliberate*, he thought. But then, whoever was on the motorcycle probably had no expectation of there being anyone else on the track. It was hardly a public thoroughfare, after all. It had all been so fast and he hadn't had time to get a decent look at the rider. All he knew was that he was dressed in very smooth leathers with a somewhat sinister black helmet, with a Perspex visor which was also tinted black. It seemed to be something of a habit on Gavdos to drive vehicles concealed behind shadowy and anonymous shields.

Hal consoled himself that it had just been an accidental near miss. Even so, the cyclist must have seen him throwing himself from the road. You'd think he would have stopped to check if he was OK and at least offer some sort of apology. Uneasily, Hal continued on his way, this time, keeping a vigilant ear and eye both ahead and behind him. The motorcycle hadn't stopped at Villa Artemis as Hal heard it continue in the distance, presumably in the direction of Kefali.

On returning to Villa Gaia, Hal changed out of the dusty clothes, had a shower and patched up the cuts he had sustained from the somewhat rough terrain he had fallen on earlier. He needed a few basic supplies and so he picked up the car key from the bowl and opened up the garage. Inside, he found a brand new 'A' Class hatchback Mercedes Benz. '*Surprise, surprise*, who'd have thought it, he smiled to himself. This time, however, the windows were clear glass.

For the remainder of that afternoon, Hal busied himself in finding his way across the island (courtesy of a map left by Stergios) and he headed over to Sarakiniko where he had been told there was a supermarket. Nothing on the scale of Tesco, he thought ruefully as he scanned the shelves of the small shop, but, he was able to buy some bread, eggs, fruit, cereal and a few frozen items to keep him going until he could put an order out to suppliers in Crete. After that, he took a walk around Sarakiniko where there was some new building work going on and later, he walked down towards the beach where he found a taverna. Following a hearty late lunch, Hal set off again, this time driving through the port of Karave where his island adventure had begun. There was a great deal of activity once again at the harbour where the ferry was due in shortly. He wondered if Tasia Artemis would be aboard and thought he would wait around for a while to see if he could catch a first glimpse of his new employer. Stergios had

59

assured him she would be back on the island today and his natural journalist's curiosity was plaguing him.

Hal was to be disappointed though. The ferry arrived without any passengers and stopped simply to unload the supplies. He watched, puzzled, as it sailed off into the distance, back towards Crete. It didn't look like Miss Artemis would be back on Gavdos after all. Not today anyway.

Driving back to Villa Gaia, Hal's gaze was drawn to the sky by the distinctive roaring of helicopter blades. He stopped the car and got out to get a better view. It was close and appeared to be descending. He watched for a few moments more as the sound of the rotating blades grew louder and nearer by the moment. Yes, it was definitely coming down and appeared to be travelling towards the North side of the island. After a short while, the aircraft disappeared from his view until only the faint whirring of the blades could be now be heard in the distance to announce its presence.

After a quiet evening in the villa with a bottle or two of Crete's local wine (which took some getting used to, but, after the first bottle, it got easier), Hal decided to turn in. He was becoming restless now, eager to get on with the job he had come to do and slightly irritated with Stergios who hadn't contacted him again with an update on the arrival of Miss Artemis. With only 50 people on the island, he didn't have much contact with other members of the human race and he felt the tranquillity and isolation was actually becoming oppressive, which surprised him.

Hal awoke from a restless sleep and glanced at the clock on the bedside table. It was just after 2.30 a.m. and the moonlight shone brightly into his room, casting a ghostly illumination, which although nearly as bright as sunshine, cast different, colder shadows in every corner. He had forgotten to pull down the black-out blinds in his slightly hazy, wine dulled state, succeeding only in throwing himself fully clothed on top of the bed after staggering somewhat uncertainly into his room. It wasn't just the moonlight that had woken him though. Somewhere in the distance, he could hear music. Not the type of music which might be heard on most of the other Greek Islands at 2.30 a.m. It was a strange, haunting sound. Some sort of pipes and possibly the balalaika. It was distant, but clearly audible. It unnerved him as he couldn't conceive of where it might be coming from in the middle of this near deserted island. Against his better judgement, he decided that he would go outside and investigate.

Hal's head still felt a bit woozy but looking forward to cooling sea breeze, he managed to navigate his way out onto the balcony. The music was more distinct from the outside but still, he couldn't tell from which direction it was coming. Maybe a couple of out of season tourists camping nearby, he thought.

Fully awake now and his curiosity aroused, Hal decided to take a walk and see if he could find the source of the haunting melody. He remembered stories of Sirens calling ships and sailors to their doom by their beautiful, hypnotic singing and shuddered slightly. It was a little bit spooky with the moonlight casting its ghostly glow across the island and the hairs on the back of his arms stood up a little as he made his way up the hill from Villa Gaia. He followed the music which seemed to be getting louder as he ascended the dirt track. He was going in the direction of Villa Artemis. As this was his nearest neighbouring property, Hal deduced that the sounds must be emanating from there.

Villa Artemis loomed above him, its imposing architecture slightly sinister against the cold silver illumination of the moon. From behind an area of shrub, concealing him from view of the Villa itself, Hal gazed across the wide expanse of landscaped courtyard and garden area and was astonished to see the figure of a tall, elegant woman, seemingly draped in the ancient Grecian style floor length dress. A loose scarf or cowl snood covered her hair obscuring

61

her face. More astonishing, because he had never seen another on the island, a deer stood behind her, one moment grazing, the next looking up as though watching over her. The music was definitely more discernible now. A lilting, slightly mournful melody, reminiscent of, but perhaps more classically composed than some of the traditional music he had heard on Greek radio as he travelled in the car.

Hal was riveted as he watched the woman first swaying gently in time to the music. Transfixed he gazed at her as she then began to dance with the grace of a fully trained ballerina, dipping and pirouetting in one moment, her body forming an arabesque with great agility the next, her arms held aloft, leg poised and stretched out behind her. In and out of the trees, she moved, a sylph, the diaphanous robe rippling with each easy movement, timed beautifully to the melody she followed.

Hal remained rooted to the spot, unable to take his eyes from woman who performed her slightly melancholic choreography, lonely and unaware of his presence. He didn't want to make any movement in case he startled her. Finally, the music came to an end with a flourish of swaying and twirling until she threw herself to the ground in a stylish and controlled finale, her limbs impossibly but beautifully posed, one long leg behind her, the other to the front, her torso and head bent over her knee, arms outstretched and her hands and fingers, gracefully poised in front of her, looking for all the world like a Degas masterpiece. She remained in position for a few long moments, her upper torso moving rhythmically as she breathed deeply in and out. The deer moved gently towards the woman, bowing its head and nuzzling her own bowed head. He heard her giggle as the deer appeared to push her head upward and push closer into her face. As it did so, she threw her arms around its neck and cradled it as though it were a pet dog. Still, Hal was unable to see the woman's face, though he craned his neck over the shrubbery in an effort to do so. He was entranced and despite the weirdness of all he had just witnessed, he couldn't help but smile, taking pleasure from having seen such a gentle and beautiful display of art and empathy with nature.

He hardly had time to digest the scene however, when, without warning, a cloud sailed by, obscuring the moon plunging everything into darkness. It took a moment for his eyes to adjust and he inadvertently moved backward, tripping on the exposed root of a tree, causing him to fall backwards with a startled cry. Seconds later he felt himself being grabbed from behind, roughly and without ceremony as an arm was wrapped around his chest impeding his arms and what felt like the cold steel barrel of a gun under his chin. Terrified now and sweating in fear, Hal yelled out.

"Don't shoot! I'm sorry ... I didn't mean to intrude! What the hell's going on? Who are you?"

His captor, never relinquishing his grip on Hal whispered aggressively in his ear in a cool, smooth American accent.

"Well, I might just ask the same question of you, Sir. What are you doing trespassing here in the middle of the night?"

"I just heard the music that was all," Hall blurted out, gasping slightly as the tightness of the other man's grasp hindered his breathing. "I was sleeping, down the track at Villa Gaia and then I heard the music and I followed it. I saw the woman, dancing and ... I was transfixed."

"Think you're hallucinating, Sir! No music, no lady dancing. Maybe you've had a little too much to drink huh? I can smell it on you. From down the track, you say? Are you the dude from the UK?"

"Yeah, that's me, Hal gasped."

The man released his grip and the cloud shifted away from the moon allowing Hal to see his captor. Turning around, he could see the unsmiling man was dressed in a black suit, white shirt and tie. More disturbingly, he clicked the gun he was holding and replaced it ostentatiously in the holster strapped to his chest.

"Well now Sir, I suggest you make your way back down to Villa Gaia before the moon disappears again. It can be mighty dangerous for strangers in these parts. If I may suggest, Sir, there are more, shall we say, conventional ways of paying a visit to the neighbours at more appropriate hours of the day. It leads to fewer misunderstandings."

"Yes, yes of course. I am expected. I'll be on my way now, thanks. And, er, sorry again".

The heavy set man remained impassive, though at least polite now.

"Yup, we're aware of you. You'll be contacted to make the necessary arrangements. In the meantime, I'd take more water with it in future." The man shook his head and laughed, a little derisively, Hal thought, and said "Music and dancing women. I need some of what you had man! Be on your way now. G'night Sir."

Shaken, Hal stumbled off in the direction of Villa Gaia but turned fleetingly to see the American striding off towards the big house, looking around him warily as he went. Neither the woman or the deer were anywhere to be seen.

Hal was awoken the following morning by the vibrating of his mobile on the side table next to him. He stretched his arm out lazily to grab the phone and the name 'Stergios' flashed up on the screen.

"Hi, Hal speaking," he muttered sleepily.

"*Kalimera,* Hal," the voice on the other end chirped brightly. "Just thought I'd let you know you're to report for duty with Miss Artemis this afternoon," he announced.

Hal sat up, his senses slowly coming together having been roused from a deep sleep.

"OK, what time should I arrive? I met her henchman last night and I don't want to get on his wrong side again."

"Her henchman? Stergios queried. "Aah, you must mean Kyle Masters. He's her bodyguard. Actually, he's a pussycat once you get to know him and he trusts you."

"A pussycat?" Hal exclaimed. He seemed more like a feral wildcat last night."

"You must have made him nervous, Hal! What on earth were you doing?"

Hal related his story about how he'd been awoken by the music and seen Miss Artemis dancing in the moonlight when Kyle had emerged from the bushes.

Stergios listened intently, but chuckled as Hal finished his tale.

"Well, I think you were either hallucinating or very drunk, Hal. Miss Artemis struggles to move easily these days without the help of a stick. I don't think it was her you saw dancing last night. And, as for Kyle, he was doing his job. If some stranger is poking about in the shrubs in the middle of the night, any security officer would react that way, don't you think?"

Hal reluctantly agreed that he couldn't really blame Kyle, but as to the dancing woman? He knew what he'd seen but right now he wasn't in the mood for arguing. It was a mystery he'd solve all in good time. There must be some rational explanation, but he didn't think it was either hallucination or drunkenness on his part.

Stergios rang off after confirming that Miss Artemis had returned by helicopter the previous day. Apparently, there was a largely disused heliport in the North of the island and although in disrepair, it still boasted a useable landing pad which the islanders used mainly for hospital transportation. Hal was to report to the big house at 2p.m. that afternoon.

At the appointed time, Hal, somewhat apprehensively, rang the bell of Villa Artemis. He was surprised to note it had a very old fashioned, 'ding dong' style ring. He was equally surprised when a tall, elegant woman, whom he assumed to

65

be Miss Artemis herself, arrived at the door and welcomed him warmly. He felt self conscious as the perspiration from the walk uphill in the heat of the day darkened his shirt and ran down his face. He struggled to catch his breath.

"How lovely to meet you at last Mr Bradbury. Actually, is it OK, if I call you Hal? It's such a frightful bore being so formal and I just know we're going to be great pals." The woman grasped his hand with a firm, business like, but warm handshake and her beaming smile would light up a room, thought Hal, as he took in her strikingly beautiful and friendly countenance, framed by luscious dark bobbed hair. A real Helen of Troy, he thought. Her face would indeed launch a thousand ships. He felt slightly awestruck.

"Of course, call me Hal," he smiled.

"Wonderful. And you shall call me," she hesitated for just a moment and finally added, "... Miss Artemis!"

Hal, unsure how to respond to her own suggestion at formality, simply stared in surprise when she giggled, pleased with her little joke at his expense.

"I'm kidding, of course, Hal," she laughed. "Never could resist a little fun! Call me Tasia (she pronounced it *T-ay-zhia*, as in Anastasia).

Hal warmed to her immediately. She was clearly from upper crust British stock, but her charm and humour was intoxicating.

"Well, it's an honour to meet you at last Tasia. I'm intrigued as to what all this is about, but I'm looking forward to starting work."

Just then, a voice from behind them interrupted their introductions. It was solicitous, perhaps even slightly agitated.

"Now then, Miss Artemis, what do you think you're doing; running about answering doors yourself? You know you're supposed to be taking it easy. Come along, let's get you back to the study."

66

The voice belonged to an older woman who came scurrying up to Tasia. She spoke with a Greek accent but her English was very fluent. She eyed Hal with slight annoyance, as though it was his fault that her mistress had been disturbed in this way. He thought she was slightly scary, a little reminiscent of the housekeeper in 'Rebecca'.

Tasia, unperturbed, touched the woman's hand which was now gently grasping her under her arm.

"Now, now, Sophia. Don't fuss, so. I'm fine. In fact, much better today. Look, I didn't even have to use my stick to get here."

Indeed, Hal thought, Tasia looked the picture of radiant health. Nothing like the sad picture he had in his mind. She was dressed casually, but expensively in designer jeans and t-shirt. He couldn't quite pinpoint her age, but he guessed her to be in her early 50s although very well preserved. Something niggled him about her though. Something he couldn't quite put his finger on. She was sort of familiar, but he didn't think they'd met before.

They reached the study, and though Tasia walked slowly, she was poised and self assured, despite whatever it was that ailed her. Sophia tried to fuss around her, but Tasia was having none of it.

"Sophia, be a darling; would you go and make us some afternoon tea? Perhaps with some of the lovely cakes I brought back from Chania? I'd do it myself, but it would be terribly rude of me to leave my guest alone. Anyway, knowing me," she laughed, "I'd stuff all the best cakes down before they reached you, Hal."

Hal couldn't quite picture this slim, lithe woman emptying the contents of the fridge and devouring all the cakes. That was more his *modus operandi*. Judging by her height and stature, he felt more and more certain that this was the woman he'd seen in the grounds last night although he'd been unable to see her face as the cowl hood had obscured her features from his vision. Hal decided that discretion being the better part of valour that he wouldn't raise it at this point as it might have embarrassed her to think she'd been seen dancing in the darkness while he looked on like some peeping Tom. It sounded a bit creepy when you thought about it.

They sat down and Sophia bustled off, muttering in Greek but obviously solicitous of her ailing mistress. Tasia reclined and stretched out on a chaise longue, resting her head against plump cushions.

"Do forgive me lying down on the job, so to speak," she chuckled. "I find it more comfortable to stretch out. I have a little arthritis; legacy of a bit of an accident some years ago. Just one of my rather annoying medical problems. It really is all such a bore."

"What happened to you?" Hal enquired.

"Car accident. Well, when I say 'accident', that's something of a euphemism, but we'll get to that later, Hal. First things first. Sorry about the cloak and dagger approach, but, there are reasons why we must be very careful about how we do things here."

"Well, you have a careful, and, if I may say, very attentive bodyguard." Tasia laughed.

"Ahh, Yah, I heard you'd met under rather *unusual* circumstances last night. He was a bit worried you were some delusional madman. Said you'd seen a woman dancing in the grounds or something?"

Hal flushed, slightly embarrassed at having been caught out in his omission to mention the previous night. He confessed that he had been awoken by the music and that he had indeed seen a woman in the grounds, whom he had thought must be her.

Tasia appeared to be considering her response before she spoke. Her head was bowed in thought, but eventually raised her eyes, which he saw were sapphire under thick, long, lashes. A smile played around her lips and she at once

68

looked both shy and knowing. She could seduce a man with just a flash of those eyes, Hal thought. He also thought she was very aware of the power she wielded in that respect and guessed that she used it to her advantage whenever possible.

"Greece is full of myths, legends and mystery, Hal. You don't strike me as being given to wild fantasy, so perhaps you did see something. And perhaps not all is quite you think it to be," she finished cryptically.

Hal recalled his conversation of a few days ago with Stergios when they had discussed metaphysics and openness to possibilities. *They all talk in riddles, here, he thought.* He didn't say anything more but it felt it was very odd that his vision had coincided with Tasia's earlier arrival that day. And there was no getting away from it, he would swear it had been she who danced so beautifully that night even though he could see that her movement was now restricted, causing her to wince painfully at times.

The slight awkwardness which had now descended upon them was broken by Sophia opening the door, wheeling in a tea trolley that rattled with the sound of delicate china. It was laden with a selection of savoury dishes; *Spanokopita, Tiropita* (delicate Greek spinach and cheese pies); dips, *Tsatsiki*, fresh bread, feta cheese, ham and olives. In addition to the traditional *baklava*, oozing with honey, there were a selection of the finest, most mouth watering cakes and sweetmeats he had ever seen.

"Wow!, This looks something else," he gasped appreciatively.

Tasia slid into a sitting position, a look of delight on her face.

"Tuck in! I'm going to," Tasia replied, stretching as she did so to grab a plate which she filled mainly with a selection of cakes. "Don't you think the *zachariplasteios* are just fab Hal? I just love to go in to all the different ones when I'm over in Crete and stock up on all the fancy treats. Can't resist all

69

that chocolate and creamy loveliness," she smiled, biting into a very large hunk of chocolate fondant and cream filled gateau.

Hal was surprised to see how voraciously Tasia attacked the goodies on the trolley and he joined in with gusto. So much for his resolution for healthy eating, he thought. He remembered fondly his holidays with Fliss when, on their way home after an evening out in Chania, they would stop off at the patisseries, which were open decadently late and stock up with sweet goodies to eat later on the balcony of their apartment.

Tasia and Hal chatted amiably for a while about Crete, London and various innocuous topics which revealed nothing to Hal about why he was here. Eventually though, the conversation turned to the reasons why he had been asked to come. It was clear to him that Tasia found it difficult to know where to begin, but finally, she took a deep breath, readying herself for the moment of revelation.

"So, Hal, you're the journalist and I don't know where to start. Ask me something first. It might lead me into a logical starting point."

"OK," Hal obliged. "Who are you and why do you want me to write a book about you?" He wasn't prepared for her cryptic response which took him no further.

"In truth, Hal, I am no-one." She laughed. "Nemo! Very topical for our location. Once upon a time though, I *was* someone and I made a difference in the world. The story I am going to tell you about my life, my demise, and the reasons for it will stretch credulity but it is imperative my story is told. I am going to reveal to you the truth about the secret world which exists just beyond our understanding and how it affects everyone. When you publish the book, you will be met with derision and disbelief. They may even try to say that you are mad, just as they did with me. There are many myths surrounding me, Hal. If you asked most people, they will say that I was at the centre of a conspiracy. In actual fact, they would be correct; only now, they will find out just how complex a conspiracy it was and even the theorists will be astounded at what you will reveal to them."

Hal shook his head as though trying to clear his way through a fog in his mind.

"What exactly do you mean, when you say that you don't exist? You look pretty real and solid to me?"

Tasia laughed. "Well, I'm not exactly going to have a conversation with you about existentialism, although it might be interesting! Yes, I am real, I'm here, I'm flesh and blood, just like you. However, the *real* me no longer exists, Hal. I ceased to exist a number of years ago when I was, let's just say, 'killed' in a car accident."

Hal felt they were travelling in ever widening circles and it was starting to irritate him a little. Tasia continued.

"To all intents and purposes, to my family, my friends and the wider world, I am dead. I am now living a lie, but that is how it must remain. Just for the record, though, I should add that I did clinically die several times over after the incident but thanks to the miracles of medical science and metaphysical mysteries I am able to sit here and still enjoy tea with you. The experience changed me beyond recognition, Hal, as you shall discover.

There are those, if they knew of my current existence, who would ensure that it ended because I still represent a danger and what I am about to tell you represents possibly the end of powerful forces who control our society in the western world." Tasia leaned forward and grasped Hal's hand in both of hers, a look of concern darkening her face.

"Hal, you will also be in danger if they get to you before publishing this story. Once it's out, you'll be safe, it'll either be supported or ridiculed. But mark my words well; if the wrong people discover what we're doing, neither of us will survive long enough to complete our work."

71

Hal paled at her words. He wasn't sure what to make of anything he was hearing. He wasn't sure he wanted to. Yes, he had craved a good story to work on, but what if what she was telling him was true? Was he prepared to risk possibly his life for a story? And what story could possibly be so toxic that anyone would be prepared to kill in order to keep it quiet? He wasn't even sure that he could trust this woman or anything she was telling him.

She retained her grasp on his hand and he noticed a strange sensation coursing through his arm. It was a frisson, like static electricity.

"So, Hal, what's your answer? Are you ready for an adventure? I can feel your hesitation."

"I'm not sure, Tasia. I thought I was. I thought I was ready to take on something new and different but now I don't know."

"You'd given up of late hadn't you?" It was more of a statement than a question. Her eyes were closed as though she were reading him from within. The static seemed to intensify through his arm. "If you succeed in this, your life will change in every sense. Some of it, you will welcome, but, as with everything, there is a dark side and you must be prepared for that." She opened her eyes and in them, he perceived a deep sadness; a sense of loss. "Be strong for both of us," she implored him.

Her grip on him loosened and, apparently drained, Tasia flopped back on the chaise longue, her shapely, endless legs stretched out languidly in front of her.

"Forgive me Hal. I tire easily these days. Give me a moment and if you wish to continue, we'll begin. Time is running out for me in more ways than one."

Hal took a moment and excused himself. He needed to think. Letting himself out into the grounds, the heat of the afternoon sun washed over him, energising and healing. It didn't take him long to make up his mind. He was here now and if he didn't find out what all this was about, it would haunt him forever. Stepping back into the cool hallway of Villa Artemis he made his way back to Tasia who was waiting for him. She looked up.

"You've made your mind up then?" she asked, a smile creasing her lips. Hal nodded.

"And...?" she raised a quizzical eyebrow.

"And ... Let's do this!" he responded with a laugh.

He wasn't prepared for Tasia's jaw dropping first revelation.

"I'm going to tell you the story of a Princess Hal; a Princess who was murdered in cold blood by the Establishment all because she was the legitimate heir to the British Throne!"

Chapter 9 – Tantrums and Tiaras

"Sir! Something has to be done! She's locked herself in the study and in floods of tears; she is quite beside herself again even bordering on the hysterical, I'd say." Tom Dunsmore, in all his years as a private secretary had never encountered anything like this. *I mean, really,* he thought, *I'm just not equipped to deal with this sort of thing.* He'd thought the woman had **breeding** for God's sake. She was **trained** from an early age to do her duty, wasn't she? Really! He'd come across race horses with more backbone!

The other man looked up from his desk. His heart sank and he visibly shrank upon hearing Tom's words. His long suffering expression displayed distress and anxiety, worry etched on his brow. He sighed.

"What's wrong with her this time, Tom?' he asked wearily, a slight tinge of exasperation in his voice.

"She's been asked to do a couple of engagements with the Business Federations. I'd prepared all the background information for her and I was trying to fill her in and encourage her to read it and discuss it so that she could converse with some degree of knowledge, Sir. But she's having none of it. Just keeps saying how it's all such a complete bore and she doesn't want to read the information I've put together for her." Tom wrung his hands in consternation. "I'm afraid she took all the papers and threw them out of the window Sir."

The other man covered his face with his hands and shook his head.

"I can only apologise for my wife once again, Tom. I'll go and see her now." In truth, he avoided his wife as much as possible these days and he didn't relish having to intervene now. Their home was large enough to maintain two separate households and his own busy work schedule thankfully kept them apart for lengthy periods.

He stopped at the door of her study and listened before knocking. Sure enough, the storm seemed to have abated. Tom had told him that she'd started throwing things around the room again. He really couldn't cope with that sort of tirade. Never, in all his years had he encountered such lack of control in a woman's temperament. She didn't respond, so he opened the door tentatively, just enough to allow him to see inside but insufficient for him to be hit by flying missiles. He saw her bent over on the couch. She was sobbing deeply, but quietly now.

"Darling, are you alright? May I come in?" he enquired apprehensively, unsure of the welcome he would receive.

"Go away! Leave me alone, why don't you? You only come to see me when you want something from me anyway!" The woman was sobbing heavily and sniffling noisily. He couldn't help but feel utter distaste for such a display of self pity. Didn't the bloody woman understand British fortitude and a stiff upper lip for God's sake? And in front of the servants too! He knew better than to go wading in to voice his displeasure though. It would become a battlefield for who knew how long if he reacted with anger to her. He had become quite accustomed to her tactics for goading him into a reaction and it never ended well.

"No,no my dear. We're all just worried about you. Can I help at all?" He kept his tone, against his better judgement and all his instincts, calculatingly soothing, placatory. She gave another sniffle and signalled to him to sit with her.

Damn, he thought. In many ways, he preferred it when she refused point blank to engage with him. Warily, he stepped closer to her surveying the room as he moved. He noticed its ornate and tasteful decor was punctuated by her own attempts at, he thought, trashy modernity. Everything he hated.

He looked at her with a feeling of revulsion. She was dishevelled; mascara ran in dirty tracks down her face and cheeks and her nose was unbecomingly reddened by crying. She certainly wasn't the so called 'icon' she was hailed as in the popular press. If only they could see her as she really is, he thought ruefully. They'd at least understand him better if they knew how he suffered. As it was, she could do no wrong, and yes, he was bitter about it. They didn't see the depth of unhappiness she was capable of bringing, both to herself and to him. He took a deep breath but wished he had a brandy for a little Dutch courage. Approaching her warily, he placed a rather stiff arm around her shoulder, infuriating her with a placatory pat on her back as though she were a recalcitrant child. *He has all the emotion of a fish,* she thought angrily. He thought he was doing rather well until she venomously shrugged off his fatuous embrace causing him to recoil.

"If you can't do fucking better than that pathetic excuse for comfort, just don't bother to come fucking near me!" she blazed furiously. He winced inwardly at her fishwife's vocabulary. The next moment, standing up, she emitted a guttural moan, rising to a scream as she picked up a rather valuable statuette and flung at the wall. It whistled past his ear, narrowly missing him by a whisker. He made a mental note to get the most valuable stuff removed from the room and have it replaced with disposable items. This was becoming something of a regularity.

"Bloody hell," he fired angrily at her. "I was only trying to comfort you and see if I could do anything to help. I can see there's going to be no reasoning with you though, so I'll bid you good day and we'll speak when you've recovered a little dignity about you." He turned away from her stiffly and marched brusquely off towards the door. He just managed to close it behind him before narrowly missing another antique missile hurtling towards him from her stock of armaments. Collapsing backwards onto the closed door, he felt despair wash over him as the heart rending crying began again. He just couldn't understand it. Where had it all gone so terribly wrong? Why was she so deeply unhappy? He *did* care, he really did. But the poor man had never come across anything like this. He'd never treated her cruelly or even unkindly. It was all such a mess and he didn't know what to do.

In the study, her shuddering breaths and racking sobs finally abated. No-one would ever understand that these 'crying jags', as they were commonly referred to released the terrible grip of pain she held in the middle of her stomach. At first, she'd thought the pain was physical. It was only when she'd experienced the utter relief after a particularly soulful bout of crying that she realised that somehow, miraculously, it temporarily released the evil demon that gnawed at her insides and that it was a necessary and regular means of pain control. She knew now that the pain was the accumulation of anger, frustration, sadness, insecurity and loneliness that fused inside her, growing like a poisonous tumour until, it was lanced in a fit of rage and desperation. Unfortunately for those around her, its poison splattered over those who often least deserved it.

Today, she just couldn't cope with the demands of her position. Her focus and concentration were shot to pieces. The engagements they wanted her to attend didn't interest her at all; what did she know about business federations, for God's sake? Moreover, she just didn't have the confidence to face all those strangers, making conversation with people with whom she had nothing at all in common. She just didn't even have the energy to make herself look presentable or to shine as she always somehow managed to do in front of the cameras. She was too tired; too tired to deal with this life any more. Every particle of control over her own life had been eroded. Her days were mapped out for her; her behaviour was scrutinised and criticised on a daily basis by the family and their minions. Why didn't they see what the world could see? She was doing a marvellous job. She had brought them into the 20th century and given them more popularity and profile than they had ever enjoyed. They should be *fucking grateful* to her, not criticising her! Every day, her face was splashed over the newspapers, her radiance belying the truth of her crucifying unhappiness that she wanted to scream to the world. She wanted the world to know how, like Rapunzel, she was locked inside an archaic world of protocol and tradition that was slowly suffocating her. She imagined throwing down her hair and a handsome hero coming to rescue her. One day, she thought, one day, she would let them see the pressures she endured and however much adulation she received, they were slowly killing her, as surely as if they piled rocks onto her chest. That was how it felt to her. A slow, crushing death. Of course, most would say that she had a wonderful, privileged life. The truth was disguised very professionally. Now, the young woman was trapped in the four walls of her own mind and she mentally clawed to escape them. Rationally, she was aware of her privileges. Materially, she could want for nothing. She was probably the most loved and admired woman on the planet outside the confines of her private life but all she saw was a gaping black pit of hopelessness and nullity. A vacuum of misery opened up as the promise of her future.

The woman had discovered in her youth that she had one means of control and it provided her with huge relief at times like this. She could indulge herself with guilt free pleasure which in itself gave her a little lift. Calm now, she opened the study door and surreptitiously checked the hallway. Satisfied that all was quiet, she headed for the stairs. Her husband, she knew, would be too terrified to approach her again until he received word that stability had been restored. Reaching the bottom of the stairs, she headed off to the kitchen. *Good!* The staff were on their break just now. She'd timed it well. Quietly, she moved around the kitchen with the skill of a seasoned thief, pulling out vast quantities of food from the fridges and cupboards. Everything from cooked chicken and cold potatoes to huge quantities of trifle, crisps, chocolate, cans of coke were piled on to her tray. She was grateful to the frugality of her mother in law who never liked to throw away leftovers, despite their wealth. It was the one positive trait that had rubbed off on her husband. Admiring her handiwork she inwardly salivated at the thought of tucking in to the goodies she'd amassed to cheer herself up. Just as she picked up the tray to sneak back up to her study, one of the chefs walked in and stared in astonishment at the mountain of food piled on her tray.

"Can I help you with that?" he enquired dutifully.

"No, no, Antonio. As you can see, I'm perfectly capable of seeing to myself." Most people would have been embarrassed by the contents of the tray, but not she. Her mind was quite elsewhere and she was more intent on getting back to the study with her booty. She flashed a smile at Antonio as he held the door open for her to exit.

To an outsider it might have looked more a case of being spoilt for choice rather than simply greed that made the troubled young woman pile on the variety and huge quantity of food on her tray. Nothing though, could have been further from the truth.

Back in her study, she waded into the morass of food like a wild animal which had been abandoned and starved. She tore into it with the voraciousness of a lioness with its meaty prey. Her eyes were glazed as she stuffed mouthful after mouthful into her face; all pretence of manners dispensed with at her lonely banquet. Only once she was sated and the stripped carcass of chicken and remnants of trifle graced the tray, packets strewn around the room, did she appreciate what a disgusting sight she must have presented. Moments later though, the familiar rising of the food from stomach to throat caused her to gag, the desired lurching and contracting signalling the necessary endgame. She bolted from the study into the lavatory opposite and purged herself of everything she'd just consumed. Long ago, as far back as her teens, she'd been thrilled to find that she could combine her need for massive quantities of food and yet control her weight to perfection maintaining the facade of a model known for picking at her food and eating like a bird. It was the one thing she could control, but just lately, even that hadn't felt so good. Unfortunately, she had no idea that her small grip on autonomy was actually having devastating psychological effects because of the chemical imbalance her dietary habits caused.

Slightly ashamed now, the rage abated, the hunger sated, but sadness still very much her companion, she returned to the study to clear up the evidence of her binge. She knew the below stairs staff would be gossiping amongst themselves about her appetite but they would keep quiet.

Exhausted, after another traumatic day, she retired to her lonely bed and gratefully drifted into sleep where she could escape her own tortured soul.

As was often the way, the young woman 's contradictory behaviour stunned those around her and it was no different when, on the following day, she called Tom to her study at 7 a.m. sharp and to his astonishment, she was cheery, calm and full of the charisma for which she was loved. She apologised for her behaviour and worked attentively, studying for the engagements with the business federation. To Tom's delight, she acquitted herself perfectly, undertaking her work with aplomb, both charming and impressive in her knowledge. This then, was her life. Alternately battling with demons but bringing to bear her strength so that her sense of duty presided. She was again, the toast of the city and she drew strength from it, even as her life and marriage disintegrated.

Inevitably, the consequences of her moods and tantrums drove away the one whose love and attention she had craved the most. She never once realised that it had been her own tortured mind that had sent him into the arms of his former (and in her opinion, inferior) lover. She blamed him for her deep unhappiness and she failed to connect that his initially clandestine infidelities were precipitated by his own sorrow and powerlessness to make her happy. He had needed comfort, reassurance and refuge from the battlefield of his marriage and so he had turned to familiar arms and the one who really understood him. He would have wished for it to be otherwise, but the years of turmoil had taken its toll and no matter how hard he tried, he could no longer love the beautiful woman that everyone else adored. He recognised that of course, there may have been fault on both sides. Perhaps they were both victims of a system which created and upheld tradition and order so vehemently that individual personality was stifled. Certainly, she was too young when they married and he, experienced in the controlled world of his upbringing was too old for her, both in years and intellectual maturity. They had been doomed from the start, had they both only known it.

Eventually, the couple reached some tranquillity in their lives, co-existing for the world and presenting the display of unity the public craved. Beneath the surface, the demons continued to visit her and she sought the love and attention of a string of lovers. Just as she was suffocated though, she suffocated most of those who were not strong enough to withstand the demands of her love. She and her husband lived separate lives and she experienced at least some freedom, as did he. As long as they both adhered to the requirements of absolute discretion it was a workable arrangement. They conducted their *Affaires de Coeur* whilst continuing the masquerade of happy families in public. In truth, she genuinely hoped that one day, she and her husband would reunite, that the true love she felt for him would somehow conquer all. Indeed she worshipped him, *as a God*, she would sometimes tell friends. But such all encompassing and demanding love was not for him and never again would he return to her, the woman the rest of the world regarded as a beauty icon and living saint. How cruel the reality had turned out to be. She had dutifully served her purpose, fulfilling her obligations under primogeniture to provide her husband and her country with an 'heir and a spare'.

If there was one aspect of her life which made her truly happy and whole, it was motherhood. Even her parenting style though was frowned upon and criticised by the rigidly aloof family. Her tactile and hands-on approach was disapproved of loudly but she determined that she would never relinquish her role as a loving mother or bow to the dysfunctional and distant parenting her husband had endured, which, had left him in her eyes, an emotional cripple. For the sake of her children, if no other reason, she determined to maintain the status quo and provide them with the stability and security that she, of all people knew was essential to a child's well being.

But eyes were already upon her. Suspicion grew that she confided too much to her young and that she was manipulating and exerting pressures upon them that children should not encounter. More dangerously, the eyes that watched her believed her motives may be darker for there was a world of shadows just behind her that she was only just about to encounter. Those shadows were more fearful than her demons and they fed upon her for their own purposes. They operated just out of peripheral vision but her understanding of them was to become more terrifying than anything which she could conjure herself.

As her marriage disintegrated, her freedom grew but the demons were too deeply rooted to be exorcised by the benefits she gained. The correlation between freedom and the diminishing attention of her husband cancelled out any feeling of happiness she would temporarily experience with each new romantic diversion she found. Consequently the demons continued to feed from her dissatisfaction that she still couldn't control major aspects of her life.

It was during this period that she became aware of 'The Watchers,' as she called them. It began when she overheard Tom, her private secretary, speaking on the telephone, unaware of her presence just outside the study door which stood slightly ajar.

"Yes Sir, I'm keeping an eye on her. The mood swings are still frequent and I'm concerned her irascibility is going to come out at a public engagement one of these days. She's also raising a few eyebrows with her latest dalliance. Yes, she barely bothers to disguise it from anyone below or above stairs. Tongues are wagging. Something needs to be done about her in my opinion."

She took a deep breath, a frisson of fear causing a shiver to ripple through her. *'Something needs to be done?'* *What did that mean,* she wondered. There wasn't much they could really do was there? There'd be public mayhem, she was certain, if they did anything that might harm her standing. In truth, they'd find it difficult to force her to do anything without fear of a backlash and adverse publicity, she comforted herself.

She did however decide to tone down her latest affair and conceded to herself that she had become a bit feckless in the conduct of the liaison. In truth, she'd quite enjoyed throwing it in the frosty faces of the establishment, sticking two fingers up at them metaphorically as she emulated the hypocrisy which they blindly espoused as her husband pursued his own indiscretions.

The choice of her latest lover of course raised eyebrows because of his class. It just wasn't the done thing to be cavorting with the staff, even if it was her personal bodyguard. It was hushed up for members of the blood family if they chose to pursue an unsuitable consort, but as usual, she was treated very differently when she tried to find a little happiness.

Jerry, her latest protection officer was everything a woman could want. As was common, these men were chosen for their build, fitness and social aptitude as their positions demanded that they be able to mingle with all social classes and backgrounds. She'd been thrilled when she was put on his watch.

It had all started innocently enough as she flirted, laughed and joked with him. As the weeks went on, he saw her at her best and experienced her at her very worst. She was the mistress of seduction though and he soon fell under her spell, becoming her most trusted friend, confidante, comforter and lover. Eventually, throwing caution to the winds, they would disappear together, not returning for hours until the household was frantic. Sometimes they were left wondering whether she would make it back in time for an engagement, or worse, perhaps she was kidnapped and the family would be horribly ransomed and blackmailed for her safe return. Usually though, just in the nick of time, she and Jerry would turn up, sharing secret jokes and laughing in the stony faces of secretaries and organisers who were beside themselves with anger at her increasingly unpredictable and irresponsible behaviour. She cared not a whit or a jot. They were getting all that was coming to their haughty, self satisfied hypocritical selves.

One day, after just such a foray, she was confiding in her best friend on the telephone.

"So, we just drove and drove Anna. I said to Jerry, 'just keep going – let's never go back. We'll just disappear and get ourselves a little cottage somewhere. I can cook shepherd's pie and we can drink wine and it'll be just heavenly.'"

"But," Anna began warily, "isn't he married darling? You really need to be careful. You don't want your heart broken again and think of the scandal when it comes out you've broken up a family!"

Her expression darkened. She didn't like to hear the bad things. Why couldn't people just be happy for her and let her live in her bubble for a while? It simply was so unfair, she thought. Just as she was about to make a sharp retort that would probably have resulted in her cutting Anna off as a friend, at least for a while, she heard a strange clicking sound on the line. Instead of replying to Anna's concerns, she said, "Anna, did you hear that? I think there's something wrong with the line. You still there? Can you hear me?"

Anna confirmed that she could indeed still hear her friend, but nothing else unusual. But, thought the other woman, you could definitely hear a *click, click, click* noise, something like you used to hear on party lines, or when the old telephone wires got crossed when she was a child. She recalled how, when chatting to her friends in those days you would sometimes hear a complete stranger's conversation or they'd be listening to you and suddenly pipe up with a comment on your private conversation. You could even sometimes hear them turning the old ring dial over your call and there'd be a sort of clicking then.

She suddenly felt cold. Those old telecom systems were obsolete now and technology was now much more sophisticated. Come to think of it, she'd heard that noise when she used one of her mobiles as well.

A dawning understanding washed over her. The phones were tapped! She was being spied on! Without wishing to draw attention to what she'd stumbled on, she made her excuses and promised to call Anna back later. She felt violated and afraid. Why would they want to spy on her? What did it mean? More to the point, who was it? Suddenly, she felt more alone than ever as it dawned on her that she could trust no-one. She was a twentieth century girl, not one from the mediaeval times who could be removed at a whim.

She also knew though, that there were those whom she might, in another era, have regarded as dangerous enemies. How, she thought would they translate to today? She shuddered. Who could she confide in? Jerry? Or was he a 'plant' himself, ready to betray her? Perhaps he was even doing so now. No, she decided. She could trust him. She would speak to him as soon as he came on duty and avoid the phones until then.

Later that night, when Jerry came back on duty, she presented him with a note explaining her suspicions which had already grown to include the possibility that not only her phone was tapped, but perhaps the whole apartment was bugged. They spoke only in code and about general matters of interest to avoid suspicion as Jerry scoured the apartment, sweeping his fingers behind mirrors, pictures and under tables. He checked the phones, but found no tangible evidence of any bugging.

Eventually, he signalled to her that they should take a walk in the grounds where they could speak more freely.

"So, d'you think it's clear up there?" she now asked Jerry as she slipped her arm companionably through his.

"Well there's nothing tangible in there, but it doesn't mean you're not under surveillance. We've moved past the little devices pinned under tables and screwed into telephone handsets nowadays. There are much more covert means of watching someone". Involuntarily, he took a look over his shoulder, checking to see if there was anyone following them or lurking in the bushes. He went on to explain in a whisper, "They can use remote systems now using really high tech exterior vans. I'm not really up on the science of it, but they use the mirrors in people's homes or offices to transmit signals."

She gasped, incredulously.

"Oh my God, really? But that's just ghastly! I mean terrifying." She shook her head and turned to face him.

"Jerry, I know they're watching. They want to catch me out doing something that can be presented as bad to discredit me. Maybe even to push me out altogether. If they'd go to those sort of lengths, well, who knows what they could do? We must be more careful darling."

"I agree. I don't want my wife getting wind of any of this either; not like this. It just wouldn't be fair." He looked pensive, the risks of his actions perhaps taking on a new reality for him.

"When you say, 'they', who do you think 'they' are?" he asked.

She shrugged.

"I'm not entirely certain. I think the family feel I'd be better off sidelined somewhere, but I don't think they'd go that far. There are others though. 'Establishment' figures and organisations I suppose who don't approve of me. 'Friends' of the family who really run the whole bloody show." She crossed her arms protectively in front of her.

"You know there are those who are the puppet masters behind an awful lot that goes in our system of Government and politics," Jerry warned. You wouldn't believe for example, how much influence the secret services control."

She laughed, without mirth, just disbelief at what he was suggesting.

"You mean MI5 and MI6 and all that sort of stuff? Spies? Why would they be interested in me? I'm hardly Mata bloody Hari, am I?"

Jerry wrapped a protective arm around her shoulder. Perhaps he'd said too much. He was spooking her. He pardoned his own pun.

"I dunno, hon," he replied evasively. But you need to tread warily is all I'm saying. Be careful who you speak to; what you do. Don't get into things that might antagonise political or business organisations. Keep your profile low and keep smiling sweetly is my advice."

She snorted derisively.

"Just play the dumb blonde, as I've always done and do what I'm told you mean?" He looked at her earnestly, trying to convey with his expression just how imperative it was that she listened to him.

"That's exactly what I mean, my love." His look and his tone said it all.

Within days of this, her world was to be shattered. She had just finished getting ready to go and open a new hospital wing when she called for security to escort her to the car. She was looking and feeling great today and she couldn't wait to see Jerry's admiring glances as he accompanied her to the engagement. She loved the solicitous way he looked after her, his manly presence deflecting any approach that may signal danger. All the while, the delicious secret of their burgeoning relationship simmered until the precious moments arrived when they could be alone together. She had felt happier in the last few months than ever before, safe in the knowledge that Jerry was always close by and ready to give her all the attention she craved. She felt strong for perhaps the first time in her life.

She flung open the doors of the study where it was customary for Jerry to wait for her. She felt radiant and her face glowed with anticipation. But her smile fell away and a dark cloud hovered over her as soon as the doors opened to reveal a shorter, stockier, ruddier man dressed in similar fashion as all the protection officers adopted. Her heart and mood plummeted instantly.

"Hi," she greeted the man civilly, looking around and behind him as though Jerry might be hiding somewhere in his coat tails, ready to jump and shout, '*Surprise!*'

"Good afternoon, Ma'am," the man replied formally. "My name is Matt."

She tried to keep her voice under control as she replied.

88

"Sorry Matt, don't mean to be rude, but where's Jerry?"

Matt looked apologetic. "I'm not sure of his exact location today, Ma'am, but I understand he's been assigned to new duties."

"New duties?!" she shrieked. "How long for? When is he due back? I want Jerry here now!"

Matt looked sheepish, helplessly clasping his hands and parting his feet as if to ground himself before an inevitable attack. His charge's tantrums were legendary. He mentally noted the location of any inanimate objects that may become flying missiles.

"As far as I understand it Ma'am, he won't be assigned back here. I'm afraid you'll have to make do with me."

She was enraged but utterly desolate in equal measure. How dare they, she thought. Who had authorised this? It must be sorted immediately. She simply wouldn't accept this level of interference in her household. Tom, who had been lurking in the shadows in the hall, now entered the study uncertainly.

Looking at his watch, he began to usher her out of the door.

"Ma'am we really have to go now. Your car is waiting."

"Well it can bloody well wait forever as far as I'm concerned. I'm going nowhere until I have answers and Jerry is brought back."

Tom recognised the danger signals. It was essential he got her out of the door.

"Yes, yes, Ma'am. We'll discuss it later. I'm sure we can sort it out then. Perhaps a misunderstanding. Yes, that'll be it. A misunderstanding. I'll get on to it straight after the opening."

A knowing glance passed between Tom and Matt. Uncertainly it was Matt who replied, "I may have got it wrong, Ma'am. I only get told what I'm doing really, not what the others are up to. Shall we go now and we'll make enquiries for you when we get back?"

Her eyes flashed angrily. She knew what they were up to. She wasn't stupid. But equally, she knew she had to play the game to have any hope of answers. She took a deep breath, her heart pounding and consoled herself with the knowledge that oh yes, this **would** be sorted. And quickly.

The papers were full of her after the hospital opening. They described every detail of her perfect performance, her perfect fashion choices and her stunning beauty. No-one was aware of the turmoil she was in. She smiled and seduced the cameras and tricked the world again in hiding behind the smile that belied the desperation she felt.

Her diary had been deliberately left clear for the next ten days. Tom knew exactly the kind of storm that was brewing. She pleaded, cajoled, screamed and cried until finally, she needed sedation as it became clear that nothing was going to bring Jerry back from the mundane duties he'd apparently been assigned. She tried his personal mobile, over and over again, but to no avail. She left dozens of voicemails which went unanswered, until the last time she rang, the robotic impersonal voice on the other end advised her that his line had been discontinued. It was the final straw and she collapsed helpless on the floor, a low guttural noise emanating from her that built to a screaming crescendo. She remained shuddering, kicking, screaming and punching the floor until the hysteria was spent and finally her doctor persuaded her to take something to calm her and help her to sleep. When she finally came to, her spirit was broken. For the next few weeks, she was like an automaton. A hopeless marionette dancing to the music of time.

Hal had remained motionless as he listened intently to the story Tasia was telling him. He had begun to feel uncomfortable as the story sounded very familiar to him. He recognised it from accounts he had read in the past, although now, it seemed to be coming from a new perspective; straight from the horse's mouth, as though she had seen it; lived it even. However, the woman before him was straining credibility. She wasn't unlike the Princess, he thought; about the right build and height. And yes, her mannerisms and voice were similar. He wondered momentarily if he was actually looking at the supposedly dead woman. Tasia hadn't made any such claims about her identity though. He wasn't sure if he was dealing with a raving lunatic but he felt it was a distinct possibility. If that was so, he'd need to be careful how he dealt with it. He decided to keep quiet for now, not to scare her. He was intrigued as to why this woman would be spinning him such a tale, but equally intrigued as to where it might go. The book she wanted may yet be written, but perhaps not from the perspective she might be anticipating. Hal decided to go along with her for now and see where it took them.

Throughout her tale so far, he'd given no sign of recognition or suspicion. He wanted to dig deeper. There was after all, something here; something that struck a chord with him.

He was weary now though. It had been a long day. He decided just to ask a few more questions before he took his leave.

"So, did you ever see Jerry again?" He asked the question, but he knew, in his heart, what the answer would be.

Tasia shook her head, her eyes filling with tears.

"No Hal. You see, they wiped him out shortly after that. Afraid he'd talk, d'you see? There had been some rumours about him being about to sell his story. Tosh, of course. Jerry would never have betrayed anyone like that."

Hal had phrased his question in the second person – '*did **you** ever see Jerry again*?' Significantly, she hadn't flinched or corrected him.

"What do you mean, 'wiped him out?'

91

"Killed him of course. It was the first inkling I had of the lengths to which they'd go. I still didn't really know why at that point. That would come later. But I knew from the terrible moment I heard the news of his death that I had to keep my eyes and ears open. I – we were all - in mortal danger."

"How did Jerry die Tasia?" Hal probed gently.

She sighed. "Ostensibly a car crash. The way they always do it. Make it look perfectly ordinary. He was on a motorcycle with another rider. Teenage girl just passed her test mowed into them. She and the other rider survived. Just him dead."

Hal pondered a moment. He'd heard the basic story before, but hadn't been aware of the details. He'd need to check them out later.

"Just a few more questions and we'll give it a rest for today Tasia." She nodded, her expression solemn now in remembrance of Jerry.

"First, just to clarify... who are **they**?

"MI5, Hal. Just all in a day's work for them."

Wow. She'd read the conspiracy theorists then.

"OK so how do you explain MI5 setting up a 17 year old girl and another cyclist so that they survived and he didn't?"

"The girl would have been under surveillance. Her usual movements, her driving weaknesses. The other cyclist was in on it. Like a stunt driver, they're trained to orchestrate these things. They set it up; the other cyclist makes a sudden move – bingo! Looks like there was simply a collision with a newly qualified driver. They wouldn't actually care if the others died or not. Once they were down, either the complicit cyclist, or someone who 'arrives at the scene', pumps Jerry full of drugs, sufficient to kill a horse probably. They make sure that their own doctors deal with it and pronounce him dead. Inquest is primed to find some injury consistent with a fatal accident. It's all so very simple you see when you have that kind of power."

Hal's mind was reeling. She seemed to have it all worked out. Every intricate detail. She was also a damned good actress or delusional, he thought. Time to call it a day. He needed a drink and time to reflect on what was going on here and how he should deal with it.

Chapter 10 – Meddlesome Messages

"*Nai?*" Stergios answered the phone with the customary '*Yes?*' greeting which Hal always found to be strangely brusque and unfriendly.

"Stergios," Hal responded. "We need to talk."

"Ah, Hal! I hear you've had a productive day with Miss Artemis. She tells me you worked through a lot of material today."

"Well, yes. I heard some of her story, but, as I say, we really need to talk. I'm uncomfortable with all that's going on here. You're all either playing games or Tasia is delusional and you've all fallen under her spell."

Stergios listened intently, but laughed upon hearing Hal's conclusion. When he replied however, his voice was steady, stern almost as though wishing to make himself absolutely clear.

"No games Hal; no delusions and no deception. I understand your concerns though. Perhaps you are already beginning to see parallels with history. The story Miss Artemis has to tell is astounding and your belief will be tested. Do not though, be tempted to pre-judge. Stick with it. You wish to meet with me you say?"

"Yeah. I think that would be a good idea, Stergios." They arranged to meet for dinner in the taverna at Sarakiniko later that evening and Hal bade Stergios farewell. After a short nap and a refreshing shower, Hal drove the couple of kilometres to Sarakiniko. When he arrived at the taverna, Stergios was already there enjoying his first Mythos of the evening. He stood as Hal ascended the wooden steps to the canopied restaurant and clasped his hand in a friendly handshake, slapping Hal's left shoulder genially as he did so as if to provide further reassurance of his friendship.

"Hal, good to see you. Let's have a drink. What would you like?" Hal returned the greeting cordially, but warily. He

94

wanted to remain slightly aloof, unwilling to display any signs of gullibility. Hal joined him in a Mythos and without further attempts at small talk, he launched in.

"Ok, Stergios, what is going on here? The story Tasia is telling me – well, I guess you know what I'm thinking?"

"What did I tell you when you first arrived Hal?"

"You mean about staying open to possibilities?" Stergios nodded. "Yes, but what you're asking of me is to accept *impossibility*. The woman whose story she's recounting to me is dead Stergios. She's been dead for 17 years for God's sake."

Stergios looked ponderous, holding Hal's gaze as he considered how to proceed.

"Are you receiving any new insights on the story as you know it?"

"Well, yes. It has a personal dynamic I guess. If it were true, that is."

"Keep listening, my friend. You haven't even begun to scratch the surface of this story yet. When the time is right, the proof you want will be provided to you. Kyle Masters and I will corroborate much of the information and we have documents which we will reveal to you in good time. For the moment, just do one thing for me?"

"And that would be...? Hal's consternation and indeed irritation with the man was growing. Why the hell couldn't Stergios just be clear instead of stringing things out and talking in riddles?"

"Take Tasia's story at face value; as though you have never heard any of it before. Suspend all preconceptions about what you know, or think you know and come to it all as if it were new. That way, you will hear and write the truth, uncoloured by your own judgement. You have the unique chance to unravel and share a remarkable story and one which must be told." Stergios paused. "What, after all, do you have to lose?"

Hal was silent for a moment, then, reluctantly, he conceded.

"Nothing, I guess. Except my credibility. Who is ever going to believe any of this?"

"As I said Hal, you have much to learn yet. You are hearing only the background so far. You are only aware of the story to a certain point. What you will find out after that, will, I grant you, challenge all that you once thought to be the world as we know it. But, you will discover an exciting and intriguing new perspective. Please remember to believe in **possibility.**"

Hal looked down into his glass of Mythos as though the answer may, like a crystal ball, lie in the froth that swam atop the golden liquid. He was conflicted. He couldn't understand why he had been brought here and why he was being paid so handsomely. What was the agenda? He wasn't big enough that anyone would find him worthy enough to ruin his career in revenge for some past story by making a fool of him. On the other hand he couldn't fathom why anyone would stage a highly elaborate hoax at his expense. It was clear though that Stergios wasn't going to enlighten him further tonight. He had to admit, his curiosity was aroused. And at least Stergios was now aware that he wasn't going to be fooled too easily. They both knew that his suspicions were aroused. Hal threw himself back in his chair and raised his arms as though in defeat.

"OK. I give up," Hal replied. I'm prepared to suspend disbelief just for a while. But, things had better start to become clear soon." He gave a wry smile before taking a deep gulp from his beer. "Just tell me one thing."

"If I can..." Stergios replied.

"Who is she really; Tasia Artemis?"

Stergios laughed. I could say that is for you to discover. I think though, that you already have your suspicions. But let us not confirm anything either way. I could also ask, who is anyone?

"Riddles, Stergios. Always bloody riddles," Hal responded with barely concealed annoyance. Stergios merely laughed again before continuing with his line of thought.

"Take me. I am Stergios Tavoularis by name and Stergios Tavoularis by nature. The origin of names is fascinating, don't you think Hal? I often think they actually shape what we are; who we become."

What is he going on about now? Hal wondered. Undeterred by the raising of Hal's eyebrows, Stergios went on.

"Take my name – Stergios. It comes from the word 'stergo.' It means to take care of; to show love, affection, commitment and to strengthen. My life's work is the commitment to take care of Miss Artemis and I do believe that she derives strength from me."

"And do you love her Stergios?" Hal enquired, wondering if this might throw up any more clues.

"Not in the way you infer, Hal. I love her as though she were my own daughter," he smiled. "And yes, I do wrap my arms around her to give her the affection she deserves. We have come through a lot together Hal. I also act as her secretary, which is quite co-incidental given my surname," he laughed.

"Tavoularis. And that means what...? Hal asked. Stergios chuckled.

"Secretary, literary assistant of course! Very apt, don't you think?"

Hal had to concede the point. *Must remember to look mine up, he thought.*

Hal returned to Villa Gaia, parking the Merc outside just before midnight. The evening with Stergios had continued with very little discussion about his mission here. Instead, they discussed Crete and Gavdos in general terms, Stergios never giving way to any real personal details about himself.

As Hal turned the key in the lock, he felt uneasy entering the Villa. Something didn't feel right. It was instinctive at that moment. Nothing Hal could put his finger on. His feeling was vindicated however when he switched on the lights revealing the remains of what appeared to have been a tornado swirling around the house. Everything was thrown around; drawers were pulled out, lamps overturned. In the bedroom, his clothes were strewn around the room; his passport, various credit cards and the keys to his London home had been tossed on the floor beside the drawer where he kept them. Hal felt himself blanch. What the hell...? He looked around, afraid to move. What if the intruder was still here, hiding in the bathroom or in a cupboard? He was hardly fit enough to tackle a burglar intent on escaping without being recognised or caught. He was breathing heavily now and he tried to control it, calming himself as he crept quietly out of the bedroom, sideways, trying to keep his eyes moving around himself in case something moved. He edged back out of the front door and into the Merc, his hands shaking now as he unlocked the driver's door. He drove without stopping back to the relative comfort of 'civilisation' in Sarakiniko before he lifted his phone once again and pressed out Stergios' number.

"*Nai?*" Stergios' voice uttered the familiar greeting but this time, it was sleepy.

"Stergios!" Hal responded urgently. His voice was unconsciously kept to a whisper as though afraid there may be unseen ears listening to him in the car.

"Hal? Whatever is the matter? I thought we'd heard the last of each other for the night," Stergios answered amiably enough.

"I've been burgled. Someone had been in Villa Gaia by the time I got back. Everything was thrown about as though they were looking for something. I just rushed straight back out in case they were still there. I want to call the police. Can you do that for me?"

Stergios was now alert, throwing the sheet of his bed aside.

"Was anything taken?"

"Not that I could tell. My passport and credit cards had been pulled from the drawer but ... yeah ... that's odd. If they didn't want money or anything from the villa, what were they looking for?"

"Have you written anything down yet?" Stergios demanded of Hal.

Puzzled, Hal answered, "No, not yet. Everthing is on my Dictaphone and I was carrying that in my pocket. I didn't take it from my jacket before I came to see you."

"Good. Then perhaps it is not too late. Have you noticed anyone around the villa? Anyone hanging around? Strangers coming to the door, anything like that?"

"No...Oh, wait! Damn it, yes! Something odd happened to me the other day when I went up to Villa Artemis the first time when I was finding my bearings. A motorcycle came flying up behind me at full speed. It damn near could have killed me if I hadn't thrown myself into the bushes. He didn't stop to see if I was OK or anything."

Stergios was clearly rattled. "Why didn't you tell me any of this Hal? It could be important!"

"I didn't think much of it really. Just thought it was some irresponsible young gun showing off his macho abilities to the fat guy."

"Did you see his face?"

"No, he was covered head to foot in black leathers and helmet. Even the visor was tinted black so I couldn't see anything."

"OK Hal. Stay calm and stay there. I'll call you back in a moment."

Hal's hands were still shaking as he pressed the 'end call' button on his phone. He wasn't sure he ever wanted to stay at the villa again. He was terrified out of his wits and he couldn't shake the feeling of violation that came from the thought of someone ploughing through his personal effects. It was a mystery though that nothing had been taken. Nothing of value that he could tell at the moment. He wondered why Stergios had asked whether he had written anything. Why should that be of interest to anyone? He nearly jumped out of his skin when his mobile rang, disturbing him from his thoughts.

"Hi Hal, it's me. OK, you can head back to Villa Gaia now. I've alerted Kyle Masters and he'll meet you there. He'll be there by the time you arrive and says he'll wait outside for you."

"You didn't call the Police?"

"No," Stergios replied. "Best not to involve them. Not much they can do anyway. Kyle's security training is far superior. We'll deal with this. Don't be afraid. You'll have all the protection you need. Tell Kyle everything that's happened and he'll check Villa Gaia with you to see if anything is missing."

Hal, feeling a little better drove slowly back to the villa. He didn't want to take any chances that Kyle might not be there by the time he arrived.

Kyle was standing outside Villa Gaia, peering into the window as he stood just to the side of it so that his body was hidden by the wall. He was dressed, as Hal had first seen him in formal black suit, white shirt and tie, his hair slicked back. He looked every inch the protection officer. He clearly wasn't trying to be incognito in his security role, thought Hal.

"Hey Man!" Kyle greeted Hal.

"Hello Kyle. I'm glad to see you on this occasion," Hal made a half hearted attempt at humour to lighten his mood.

"OK, shall we go in?" Kyle asked without any further niceties. Hal drew a deep breath and replied, "Let's do it." Kyle slipped his right hand inside his jacket where from previous experience, Hal knew his gun to be. Hal had left the villa without stopping to lock it. Stupid, he thought. Giving them easy access next time. The light was still on in the living

100

room. It looked the same as when he had left it – untidy, violated.

Kyle went through the villa with a fine tooth comb, gingerly opening doors, whilst standing to the side of them lest an intruder was lurking within waiting to pounce. All the time he was poised to draw his gun. Hal was careful not to make any sudden movement in case he spooked the protection officer into shooting in his direction. In fact, Hal tried not to make any discernible movement at all as Kyle inspected every room, cupboard, nook and cranny for evidence of the intruder. Finally, satisfied that there was no-one in the villa apart from himself and Hal, he went into the living room where Hal was waiting.

"All clear," he announced before sitting on the sofa. Hal sat on the armchair opposite and breathed a sigh of relief. "So, do you think there's anything missing?" asked Kyle.

"Not that I'm immediately aware of. Shall I take a look around, just to be sure?"

"Yeah, I think you ought to. I'll just call Stergios and tell him all is quiet at the moment." Hal made his way around the villa, trying to recall all that he had brought with him and their location. Nope, nothing of any value seemed to have gone. Weird, he thought. Suddenly though, something did catch his eye. He approached the table in the kitchen where his laptop lay. He knew that he had left it closed. It was always his habit to shut down and close the top. Now though, it was open. Not only that but the on button was lit up. Someone had switched it on! They weren't interested in taking it, but finding out what was on it. But they'd need a password to get in.

Hal pressed the return button and the screen lit up from its stand by slumber. Instantly he could see that whoever had been there had managed to hack in as it was his user documents and screensaver that flashed up. He hoped fervently there wasn't anything on there that would lead them to personal or financial passwords. He stared at the screen.

101

There was a tab open at the bottom; a word document. He moved the arrow downwards and clicked on it. The document came up and to his horror, there was a message on there, written in red 'chiller' font.

"GO HOME – DON'T MEDDLE IN THINGS YOU DO NOT UNDERSTAND.

His heart beating heavily against his chest, Hal read the message open mouthed. "Kyle!", he shouted, panic evident in his voice. Kyle came rushing through to the kitchen and followed Hal's gaze to the computer. Calmly, he closed down the computer, unplugged it and signalled to Hal to follow him.

"OK, so I've spoken to Stergios and Tasia. You're going to stay with us up at Villa Artemis tonight until we work out what's going on here. Don't worry, we have it crawling with security so you'll be safe up there. They can't infiltrate us so easily. I guess it was kind of a risk leaving you alone down here. Stergios tells me there was an incident on the track the other day as well?"

Hal nodded. "Yeah, thought I was a goner for a minute or two. Just thought it was some reckless kid showing off his motorcycle at the time."

"Doubt it from the description Stergios said you'd given. Sounds like they're onto us. It was only a matter of time I guess."

"Excuse me...?" Hal queried. "Look, far be it from me to pry, but is anyone going to give me the slightest clue as to what's going on here and what all this is about? I get subterfuge, dangerous missions and being open to possibilities and coded messages about meddling, but no-one actually gives me a joined up sentence connecting all these things. I am able to understand things you know. I'm not a complete idiot."

102

Kyle nodded. "Yeah. Sorry. I guess you do deserve some explanation but in some ways, the less you know until the time is right, the better it is for you and for us. Once everything is recorded there's no way of taking it back and protecting the information is much harder. So, we just figured, once we get to that point, the bit where you have the full story, is where our job in keeping it and you safe really starts. It looks as though we'll have to step up security on you immediately though. They're onto us faster than we thought. Not sure how though."

"So you're not going to tell me? My life is in danger and you're still not going to tell me how or why?"

Kyle shook his head. "All I can say is that the job you've been assigned is of a highly sensitive nature and one which concerns matters of national security for Britain specifically, but also impacts on the rest of Europe and indeed, my very own US of A, Hal. It's big; real big and there are those who will want to destroy the evidence, just as they did before. Only this time, they'd prefer it to be a little less *public*, shall we say? So, Hal, please, take it from me, we have to be careful about the knowledge you have and when you receive it as we have to protect it appropriately. We'll step up your security right now. I can assure you, we'll also be investigating who is on the island to discover who the motorcyclist was. We'll have a team of security officers scouring Villa Gaia in the morning for any clues, fingerprints etc that we can check against databases. No stone will be left unturned and all precautions for your safety will be in place. Now, it's getting late what d'you say we head up to Villa Artemis and get you settled so we can all get some sleep."

Hal, deeply relieved that he wouldn't be alone at Villa Gaia tonight gratefully accepted Kyle's suggestion and they headed for his car, a Merc of course. Before getting in, Kyle pulled out a device from his jacket and checked around the

103

vehicle. He seemed happy and unlocked it. Hal asked what he had been doing.

"Checking for any explosive or electrical interference. Just a precaution. In case your visitor might have decided to attack us again tonight. We'll check yours tomorrow for any interference before bringing it up to Villa Artemis. Can't be too careful you know."

Horrified, Hal listened to Kyle speak of sabotage as though it was a day to day event. He never even considered someone might have interfered with his car. God! They might have cut his brake cables, or put an explosive device under the vehicle. Of course, his earlier putting two and two together about Tasia's story was starting to make some kind of sense if the conspiracy theorists were to be believed in the aftermath of what was in the public knowledge. I guess if you asked 90% of the public, most of them would say that foul play had been involved in the disposal of the woman whose story Tasia appeared to be adopting. It had always been denied of course and, from the purely logical perspective, it hardly appeared to be foul play. It was only the circumstantial evidence which might have suggested it. But, here he was, immersed now, in something which he'd only read about in spy novels, never imagining that he would be the epicentre of something potentially momentous and deadly. Fatigued, Hal lay his head back on the headrest. His mind was swimming. It was too late to pull out now though. If he could be guaranteed of his safety, he intended to get to the bottom of it if it was the last thing he did. And, he thought wryly, it just might be the last thing he ever did if tonight was anything to go by.

Back at Villa Artemis, he was shown to a sumptuous suite, complete with bedroom, sitting room/study area, dining area and bathroom. Kyle bade him goodnight and assured him that security would be in close proximity all night and he shouldn't concern himself. He hadn't taken much to Kyle's curt and gruff style at their first meeting but now, he was grateful for his clear focus on the job and glad to have him on his side. Nevertheless, Hal did not spend a comfortable first night in his luxury suite and 'slept' with one eye open most of the time. He didn't feel particularly refreshed to commence the day's work with Tasia when she called him down to her office next day.

Chapter 11 - Spiritual Pursuits

To the world, they were still a happy couple, but the reality was by now quite different. No longer did they share the home that she had lovingly restyled to her own tastes of modernity. In a way, she was pleased when finally, she no longer had to keep up the daily pretence of civility that living in close proximity dictates, even if just for one's own peaceful state of mind. It was agreed that she would have her own apartment in Central London staying at one of the magnificent grace and favour stately homes owned by the family who were also reconciled to the irreconcilable nature of the relationship which lay in tatters at their feet. Her husband too was happier with the new arrangements. Almost immediately after she had taken her leave, he called in the interior designers to restore the building to its former antiquarian magnificence thus washing his hands of the youthful mores to which he had been exposed by his wife. Everyone breathed a sigh of relief as some normality was restored to their lives.

The young woman, now cast adrift found her life a confusion filled with contradictions. She lived for love. She wanted to eat, sleep and breathe it. She received it in spades from the entire world who admired and envied her but was cruelly deprived it from all those whose affection she craved. She would gladly surrender the public adoration for the true and enduring love of one good man who would sincerely admire her for her beauty, strengths and deep down goodness. Sadly though, that was the hardest kind of love for her to find. Her neediness and suffocating, all consuming displays of ardour always had the same ending – shattered hopes and shattered dreams. Of course, other matters played their part. Anyone she became in the least bit close to had to be wary of offering her true love because she was trapped, and always would be in the facade of a highly public marriage

106

which could never be revealed to show cracks; much less the fissures that now undermined the stability of an entire dynasty. Consequently, there was no future in any relationship she might forge, no matter how heartfelt and sincere. She could promise nothing to any of the lovers who passed through her doors. They would live with the fear of exposure and now, possible death if Jerry had been anything to go by. She knew she had to find a permanent way out. She had to divest herself of the shackles that bound her if she was ever to find true contentment.

Each day, she would rise early and demand that the morning's newspapers be brought to her so that she could scour them for any stories about her. Her addictive personality soaked up the fame and adoration, giving her the validation she so badly needed. She had never been academic and, in the presence of her husband, self esteem had slowly eroded as she persuaded herself that she could never match the highbrow knowledge of his education and interests. Consequently, she hated the responsibility that went along with her fame, resisting at every turn the requirement to learn and understand the world in which she lived. She knew that she had to turn herself around now and take control of her life if she was ever to genuinely believe in herself.

It wasn't until one of her closest friends gave her an ultimatum that the swirling fog around her began to disperse. Of course, at the time, she was furious. How dare she issue ultimate to someone of her standing? Who the fucking hell did she think she was, threatening to go to the press if she didn't get some help for the bulimia which her friend believed was slowly but surely killing her. Part of the illness of course, was denial and it was only when threatened with public exposure that she agreed she would do something. First, she consulted the professionals in the area. It helped her to some extent, but she needed more. She turned her attentions to alternative therapies and to her joy, she found that they struck a chord with something deep within her. She found something she could believe in and she immersed herself in every type of holistic therapy she could find. Her days were filled with people who would indulge her sense of self and she grew to understand the nature of a more spiritual existence replacing so much of the negative with the positive. She experimented with new diets devised by her newly found holistic experts and discovered that she could indulge her ever present greed for food but still stay slim by combining different types of food. She grew healthier by the day and with that she found a new way of living. It didn't stop with alternative medicine. Now, she turned more and more to advisers who could give her spiritual advice so that her emotional, intellectual and spiritual sides could work together in a greater understanding of the universe. She laughed with her friends about the revelations she encountered along the way.

"God, I'd have been burned at the stake for witchcraft in years gone by," she joked one night as she enjoyed a night with girls, telling them about her latest set of advisors. They included astrologers; different ones for different purposes. She consulted one for self discovery, another for telling her the future on every day matters of life and latest love affairs. She became obsessed, barely able to make a move without telephoning them several times a day to check whether she was doing the right thing. Sometimes, she heard things that didn't please her. She would never, she was told by one trusted astrologer, inherit the title she most craved and expected in later life. The astrologer however, did not expand on exactly why this was the case. It was against their ethics to say that death was most certainly on the cards for this poor, searching creature. Nevertheless, she learned to take the negative with the positive and each day, there was an endless procession of psychics trooping into her apartment; mediums, tarot readers, palmists, crystal therapists all tended to her spiritual needs and her daily plans. Meanwhile, her perceptions were altered to change her approach on the world with the help of hypnotherapists and psychotherapists who allowed her to pour out the angst which she harboured deep within, exorcising the terrors which had invaded her psyche since childhood. Her physical health was improved and tended by aromatherapists, acupuncture needles, osteopathy, colonic irrigation and reflexology, all indulging her tactile needs, revitalising her and bringing strength to the body which had begun to waste and seize up under the influence of her bulimia.

Eventually, she felt strong as her armoury of therapies and spiritual support network grew. She had found something to believe in.

"So, she really believed that the answers to her problems lay in the occult arts?" asked Hal as Tasia paused for a moment.

Tasia laughed. "Of course! She did and I do too! It's been my saviour, the reason I'm still here at all! I take it you've never tried it, Hal? Too 'mumbo jumbo' for you?"

Hal conceded that she was right. It wasn't something he'd ever tested, but he believed that it was simply a bunch of frauds feeding off the vulnerable. He pondered her answer – 'she did and I did too...' So what was she now, he wondered. Schizophrenic?

"I think maybe at the end of this project, you may have a different view, Hal," Tasia smiled knowingly.

He grinned. "Doubt it, Tasia. A cynic through and through I'm afraid. Tell me though, why do you set such store by it all?"

Hal's question was one she'd had cause, over the years to consider carefully. In truth, she hadn't known the answer in the early days; not until she'd grown sufficiently to understand who she was. In some ways, Hal could have been right. She'd been at the most vulnerable stage in life and she

109

needed a higher power to believe in; something that would perhaps set her free from her gilded cage. Certainly, there was nothing with any earthly power that was likely to help her and so it had given her hope. She thought carefully before answering Hal. It was complicated, as she had later discovered.

"I believe these things are in us, Hal. I was somehow – just as she – was - *drawn* to all things spiritual. It was as though something had awakened inside me, perhaps because of everything I'd been through. Somehow, I just *knew* that there was truth and light in the spiritual pursuit. Later, much later, the clues were there. I'll come to it later in the story Hal, but I am, shall we say, genetically predisposed to the occult arts. It's been in my family for centuries as my genealogy will show. The sensitivity and the ability to use the spiritual arts is my inheritance and for those, like me, who have it in their blood, we will always find it, or it will find us. In fact, as you shall see, it is a central factor to what happened to me and why I come to be where I am now."

"Tell me, Tasia, does *anyone* on Gavdos speak plain English and offer a straightforward explanation to anything?"

Tasia laughed. "Well, if you ask me what the weather's like outside or whether I like chocolate cake and chips, I can give you a straight answer. It wouldn't make great reading for your book though, would it?"

"I guess not," Hal agreed. They were interrupted by a knock on the door.

"Come in," Tasia called and a moment later, they were joined by Kyle, his face serious as usual.

"Kyle! Where have you been? I missed you this morning. I was getting really worried."

Kyle's features visibly softened as he saw Tasia, stretched out in her usual position on the sofa. When he answered her, his tone was surprisingly gentle, tender almost.

110

"Hey! Howz my girl? he asked in untypically informal fashion which surprised Hal, considering he was her protection officer. "You know you don't have to worry about me. Just been over to Villa Gaia checking out the damage from last night." He turned to Hal, his usual abrupt tone returning. "Nothing to report over there really. Whoever entered the property was careful. No fingerprints; wore gloves probably. We've scoured everything but no sign of anything dangerous. I think they were just trying to give you a warning but we're onto it. The island is being checked for strangers as we speak but it's difficult to monitor. We still get a few tourists coming over daily. We're following up the motorbike though. Checking ferry records to see if such a vehicle was brought over from Crete in the last few days. I'm guessing the two events were linked. Anyway, Hal, I think we're decided that you should stay here for the time being, right Tasia?"

"Of course! Gosh, I'm sure you'd prefer to be here anyway Hal? The suite's private enough for you, is it?" Tasia looked up and smiled at Kyle and his eyes softened as he met her gaze. Hal detected more than a professional relationship between them. Kyle's hand rested on the back of the couch and he noticed Tasia's hand brush, intimately against it as she spoke to him.

Hal was genuinely relieved that they didn't expect him to go back to Villa Gaia. He didn't think he'd ever sleep again if he found himself isolated in the dark of night down the track. He shivered slightly at the thought.

"I'd feel much happier staying here if it's OK with you guys. As you can see, I'm not quite the Action Man that Kyle is!"

Tasia laughed and a slow grin spread across Kyle's face. He clearly liked being referred to in front of Tasia as 'Action Man.'

111

"OK then. I'll get back to work. Tasia, Ben and Samuel are keeping an eye on things here. I'll be late back, so don't be worried. I'll phone you later."

"Great, make sure you do! You know how I hate it when you're not here." For a moment, Hal thought Kyle was going to kiss her upturned lips as he hesitated before taking his leave. The air was palpable with things unsaid as he exited. Tasia watched him until he had left the room. Her face was glowing. It was clear that history was repeating itself. He guessed she didn't really meet too many other people she could get this close to.

"So, where were we? Oh yes, I was explaining the genetics of the occult arts wasn't I? Well, we'll come back to that. It's all part of the jigsaw, you see. Now, tell me Hal, why are you so sad? Why have you given up? No, let me tell you. Your wife died, right?"

Hal was flustered now. He detested the word 'died.' Perhaps in his heart, he did need to believe she was somewhere else; not simply gone, snuffed out as though she'd never been here. Tasia's words stabbed his heart. Quietly, he acknowledged it was true.

"How did you know that? You carried out some research on me I guess? Before hiring me?"

Tasia didn't respond to his question. "She's still around you Hal. Don't you see her out of the corner of your eye sometimes? Don't you smell her favourite perfume in the room occasionally?"

Oddly, Hal had noticed the gentle waft of her Prada perfume sometimes. It always made him look around, expecting to see her. It was odd how a familiar smell was so strongly evocative of a person and the memories they shared. He put it down to someone else wearing the perfume, even when there was no-one else around. Brushed against someone in the Tube perhaps or in the flat, smells lingered in the walls or the floorboards. He'd never thought of it in terms of her having come back to visit him though. And as for catching things out of the corner of his eye, well, didn't that happen to everyone? A flicker of the light, a fly passing, an optical trick perhaps? Strangely though, all of these things when they happened always made him think of Fliss. He missed her with agonising sorrow. He'd never really let himself grieve properly. He felt that if he opened up the chasm and allowed it to happen, he may never be able to stop it and carry on. Sometimes, he really didn't want to carry on without her but he'd promised her he would. And a promise is a promise. For her, he'd do anything. He pushed back the overwhelming emotion threatening to wash over him as he thought about it now.

"It's OK. I'm sorry Hal, we won't talk about it just now. I know you're not ready. Take comfort though. She *is* still with you and she will prove it to you when you're both ready." She hesitated a moment, nodded her head and smiled. "Prada *'Infusion d'Iris,'* – that's the perfume she wore isn't it?"

Hal simply gaped at Tasia. She may have been able to research him to know his wife was dead, but how the hell could she have known that? He nodded, words failing him. Tasia simply smiled.

"Like I said, Hal, have faith. You have a lot to learn."

That night Hal slept fitfully but this time, he was disturbed not by fears of the intruder but dreams of Fliss. He relived the night that she had finally given up the long fight with cancer she had endured. He saw, once again, her wasted, pain wracked body as she lay on the hospital bed, tubes everywhere; dehumanised and exposed to every indignity imaginable. She hadn't properly regained consciousness at all on the last day and as he sat there, gripping her tiny hand as though trying to prevent her from leaving him, now in his dream, he relived the moment of her death. It hadn't just been a physical sign that she was gone, although that had been obvious enough. He'd heard of the

113

death rattle before; the moment that fluids build up in the respiratory system of the dying person signalling the end. He'd heard it sure enough, but just moments before, her eyes had fluttered open fleetingly and Fliss spoke. It had become unnaturally cold in the room and almost simultaneously with the change in the temperature, she said, clearly and articulately, "They're here! They're all here! They've come for me. Grandad, Mum, and look! Oh look! Buster...! She sighed heavily, taking a last breath as her chest rattled and then, nothing. He looked at her, tears in his eyes and saw that she was smiling. He felt a tingle and thought he saw a feint shining aura around her. As it dissipated, he knew that she'd gone. The machines sounded her departure and the nurses ran in. For a short while, there was a bustle around him as vital signs were checked until finally, her MacMillan Nurse, Katriona knelt beside him. Taking his hand in hers, she confirmed what he already knew. Fliss was gone. His best friend, the one who'd truly known him; the only one who understood his humour and all the different sides of his personality. The one who'd loved him and whom he had loved more than life itself. Of course, he knew this day would come and he thought he'd prepared himself. But he hadn't. He was lost and alone and he didn't know how to live without her. It was an odd feeling. Once he'd been an independent adult living life perfectly contentedly. But then he'd met Fliss and they'd become a unit. Now it was unimaginable to contemplate life without this necessary part of him. He was numb, barely aware of the nurse beside him. Absently, he said,

"She spoke. She said her mum and grandfather were there and her old dog, Buster. It was so cold as she left me and then, I saw a light around her. It was like a halo. A halo for my angel." The nurse smiled sympathetically.

"It often happens," she said gently. "Lots of patients, when they pass, they see family and friends. I've seen the light myself many times. I think it's a good thing to believe, don't you?" she asked gently. "That people you've known and loved come to meet you and take care of you? She's at peace now. Look."

His eyes were swimming with as yet unshed tears as he looked back at Fliss. Strangely, she did look at peace. Her face had lost the greyness and the strain. She looked more as she had done before the vile disease had arrived to torture her. The tears now flowed from him like a waterfall and he sat with her, sobbing until he could sob no more. The nurse left him for a while to say his farewells and returned later to gently persuade him to end his vigil and get some rest. In a daze, somehow, he made the journey but couldn't remember any of it. He'd simply found himself back in the flat they had shared and it was the emptiest building he'd ever set foot in.

All of this, he relived in the dream, but part of it changed. In the dream, after Fliss had died, he saw her standing in the corner, looking radiant and healthy. Two people stood hazily behind her and in her arms, her beloved Buster, the Jack Russell Terrier who'd been her only other true love. He wagged his tail with joy and licked her face as she smiled broadly. Fliss spoke to him.

"Don't grieve for me Hal. I'm well and I'm happy. I'll always be with you. Don't think that this is the end. We will be together again when the time is right. Make the most of your life and always remember, when you're sad or afraid, I'll be there. Just look for me and you'll see."

Hal woke with a start, beads of perspiration on his face. He sat up, his heart beating rapidly in the darkness. The air seemed thicker than usual and he took a breath. There was no mistaking it. *Infusion D'Iris.* She was there with him now. He called out, *"Fliss? Is that you?"* There was no answer and seconds later, the air was clear and normal. She'd been there though. He knew it and he beamed, the smile spreading across his face, easing the knot of grief which usually accompanied his waking hours. For the first time since Fliss's death almost two years earlier, he felt relief and contentment and the possibility of a new beginning, safe in the knowledge that he would see her again. He thanked God for meeting Tasia Artemis and Stergios Tavoularis, who'd awakened him to, yes, *possibility.*

Hal was on top of the world the next morning and he walked almost jauntily into the breakfast room where he'd been invited to join Tasia. A breakfast fit for a king was laid out on a long table where he could help himself. Moments later, Tasia breezed in, a huge, warm smile on her face as though she was greeting an old friend of many years.

"Good Morning!" she beamed. "Did you sleep well, Hal? I certainly did and I'm looking forward to tucking into a good old Full English breakfast. God, I'm absolutely starving." She eyed up the table, lifting covers to reveal bacon, eggs, sausages, kippers and just about everything you could hope for at breakfast.

"I slept like a baby, thanks Tasia. Must be the soft bed you've given me!"

She laughed. "Yeah, I had them imported. The Greek beds are a little bit on the hard side for me. Concrete bases as well! You'd think they'd use something a bit more lightweight but I suppose the Greeks don't tend to move house as much as we Brits! She caught a glimpse of Hal's face as he turned to her and gave him a knowing wink.

"I think the Greek air must be agreeing with you Hal! You look so much more relaxed than I've ever seen you before. It's like a big black cloud has lifted from you." She chuckled. "Or maybe the spiritual world is teaching you what you need to know?"

Hal gave a wry smile. "Who knows, Tasia, but whatever. Yes, thank you for our talk yesterday. Perhaps it's given me something to think about."

116

"My pleasure. Now, shall we get on with breakfast before it gets cold and then we'll continue with our work."

"Sounds good to me," Hal replied as they both set about the table filling their plates. Hal stared in astonishment at the mound of food on Tasia's plate.

"You're wondering how I can eat all this and stay so slim aren't you?" Tasia was voraciously attacking her plateful of food. "It's really simple actually. It's called the Hay Diet. I've used it for years and it's certainly done the trick for me."

"No, don't tell me, you substitute some meals for a bunch of Hay? Well, that'd certainly curb the appetite," he joked.

She poked him playfully in the ribs.

"No, it means you can eat all you like as long as you don't mix carbohydrates and proteins. Maybe you could give it a go Hal?" He was a little taken aback at her forwardness but he wasn't offended. He knew he needed to shed some weight.

Teasingly, he feigned offence.

"Well Miss Artemis, I've never been so insulted in my life. Are you saying I is fat or something?"

Tasia giggled. She was enjoying herself. It had been a while since she'd had a new person to tease.

"Not *fat* exactly. Maybe just a little bit *under thin?*"

"You'll give me a complex. I might get an eating disorder you know!"

Tasia looked serious then. "Yes, you're right. I shouldn't tease. It's how these things get out of hand. I'm sorry. I of all people should know better."

Hal could have kicked himself.

"Hey, I was just kidding. There's no way I'm going to develop an eating disorder, don't worry! However, I might just take your very welcome advice on the Hay Diet. It sounds great. Now, if you could just point me in the direction of the nearest barn...?" She giggled again.

117

"Well, I think you'll have to join me at every meal then Hal because it's always a Hay diet in this house. *Except,* of course when we have guests. Good toast and hash browns with your bacon and eggs then Hal?"

Hal was chewing happily on his third piece of toast when he realised that if he was going to manage this diet, the bread and potatoes would not be a part of future breakfasts.

"Better make the most of it today then hadn't I?" he joked, helping himself to another couple of hash browns in memory of his old ways.

Chapter 12 – Tape for Tape and Tit for Tat

Though many scoffed at the young woman's new found reliance on her alternative therapies, there was no doubting for those who knew her that it was instrumental in helping her to turn her life around. She had found a coping mechanism which gave her the strength to move forward and the ability to discover new skills and depths which she now wanted to put to good use. Her spiritual quest had resulted in her finding a sense of worth. She wanted to share her new found contentment and greater happiness with those less fortunate than herself. She needed to find a niche for herself which allowed her to use her position, the responsibilities of which she had hitherto found generally boring and tedious, to benefit others. She threw herself into charity work and discovered that she genuinely cared for those whose lives were blighted by one difficulty or another. In many ways she identified with them. She researched various charities, became patrons for many and worked with other philanthropists to raise profiles and bring support to the homeless, sick children, AIDS sufferers to name but a few. In her youth, she had trained as a ballerina and the desire to dance, or at least be involved in it in some way never left her. She worked closely with the arts, allowing her not just to help promote and fund them, but also to be involved in them, often turning up at rehearsals, dressed casually and immersing herself as she watched performers being put through their paces from stage right or left. When no-one was watching, she would practice the moves, swirling happily to the music, her grace and ability unquestionable. She appreciated that the publicity she brought to her work helped her charities enormously but there were many times when she worked secretly; away from the eyes of the press. These moments brought her and those whom she helped much greater fulfilment. She wanted to bring comfort to the

sick and the dying. She felt their pain and their sorrow.
Somehow, when she went out on her secret missions, she
knew that she was truly helping. The joy and surprise that she
brought with her did so much more than drugs in bringing a
lightness of being to those she visited. She was happy and it
made her appreciate that her life really wasn't so awful. She
was privileged in a way that most were not and she was now
so much healthier in mind and body. She did of course enjoy
the recognition for the public work she did, but she had a
deeper joy in the work that went unrecognised. She could
now combine enjoyment of her work with a deep personal
fulfilment.

     The more charity work she did, the more she realised
she was capable of taking on and she spoke to her advisors
about becoming even more involved, perhaps on the political
level with humanitarian work. The powers that be were not
too keen on her becoming involved in matters which they
considered she did not fully understand and so her desires
were kept at bay, at least for a while. She was a determined
individual though. She had always been wilful and when
someone told her she couldn't do something or tried to put her
'back in her box', it was a red rag to a bull. She *would*
become a serious humanitarian she decided but she needed a
few more tools in her box to help her along the way.

     One thing she really detested was having to speak in
public. Her speeches were prepared for her and whenever
she watched them on the telly (after Eastenders usually), she
cringed at the stilted, halting cadences of her own voice and
the body language which screamed her lack of confidence; the
refusal, or more accurately the inability to meet the eye of the
public and convey the sincerity she truly felt. This was her
next venture on self improvement. She found herself a good
coach in public speaking skills and her work paid dividends.
Although she never quite got over her confidence issues
completely, she was able to confront the crowds to deliver a

confident and persuasive speech which demonstrated conviction and sincerity. She was now the mouse that roared and for good or bad, people began to take more notice of her.

The one area of her life which still lacked any control of course, was her disembowelled marriage. She swung between indifference and longing for the fairytale romance to magically rekindle, although in truth, she had to admit, 'romance' had been sadly lacking.

Some weekends, she stayed with the children at her husband's residence but they rarely socialised. Depending on her mood, she was sometimes cordial with him and willing to make conversation, occasionally even, joining him and the boys for meals. Usually though, she preferred to make a statement by remaining in her own rooms to eat and to freeze out the man who had betrayed her so deeply. It was a punishment, for he genuinely wanted to maintain a friendly relationship with the mother of his children but her vengeful and resentful streak festered and scorched the pathway to geniality. She was still lonely and in that respect at least, she was still trapped in the gilded cage, never able to truly spread her wings or have the freedom to live the 'normal' life which she craved. It was now that she made another, possibly deadly mistake.

She had spent a sleepless night, tossing and turning, resentment again burning in her veins. She knew somehow that she had to divest herself of this marriage if she was to have any opportunity of finding some happiness. How could she ever forge a life or make new lasting relationships if every man who came along knew that she would forever be tied to another man? And a powerful man at that. Of course, she was attracting the wrong sort just now. Opportunists, all of them; fascinated by the prospect of a no strings fling with the most admired and sought after woman in the world. What could be better? Anyone who was straightforward and reliable would give her a wide berth. And try as she might, she could not foresee living her life essentially alone, without 'a rock' to support her? It was unthinkable to her. She had to come up with a way. Unfortunately, she came up with her first idea after a bout of insomnia when the exhausted and delusional mind can come up with wonderful schemes which clarity of mind would discount from the outset. When she awoke next morning, she called one of her old school friends whom she knew to be an expert in the security services.

She donned her simplest outfit and a pair of dark glasses and made her way through the affluent streets of London whilst it was still relatively quiet. A full brimmed hat hid her face as she approached the telephone box to make her call. She had learned her lesson with telephones. Now, she always had a full phone card to make those private calls when she might reveal information of interest to the 'Watchers.' She also had three mobile phones and she changed the sim cards with regularity but somehow, she always felt more secure in the anonymity of a red telephone box. She always used different ones in rotation so no-one would be able to second guess her calls.

"Tim?" she said as a sleepy, gravelly voice answered. "Sorry, did I wake you? I know it's awfully early but I couldn't sleep. Listen, I really need your help. Can you meet me in Kensington Gardens? Half an hour?" Tim knew it was pointless to argue. Once she had a bee in her bonnet, she wouldn't take no for answer. He agreed to see her at the appointed place.

She had just come to the end of another love affair. It had been an important and lengthy one. He though, had accepted a military posting overseas and she had seen this as the ultimate betrayal, even though rationally, she knew if he refused he would be court martialled. To soften the blow, she had taken up with an old flame she'd known since her youth. It suited them both and she was gratified that this time, it was he who was keen. Quite the contrast from years previously when he had spurned her and she'd been moved to throw eggs all over his shiny new car in delicious revenge!

Contrarily, she was also living in a wistful phase of wanting to try again with her husband. It would of course need to be on her terms however. At times like this she fantasised. She thought she might actually still love him and she harboured romantic dreams that perhaps second time around they could really make it wonderful. Wouldn't it all be so much easier if they could just be in love again, she thought. Even as she considered it however, she bitterly recalled his words at the announcement of their engagement, *'whatever in love means.'* She winced. Those words still jarred on her.

No, she thought sadly. Her terms would never be met. For him it would mean giving up everything that absorbed him; all his interests. She wanted him to devote himself completely to her to the exclusion of everything and everyone but their children. Only that would prove his love for her. Of course for her part, it would be necessary to eliminate the main barrier to her happiness. No progress could be made whilst he was besotted and making a complete fool of himself with the other woman who had her claws firmly in him.

She sighed. No it was highly unlikely she would overcome all the obstacles that stood in the way of happy reconciliation. If that was so, then she would have to remain trapped in this hiatus of a sham marriage, forever in limbo; a life of suspended animation that would prevent her from ever finding happiness. The alternative was to create the circumstances in which she would be released. Neither option would be easy but she found the second option more realistic and at least offered a glimmer of hope of a new life and the autonomy she craved. She spent many sleepless nights pondering the options and finally, she had come up with a plan. She was popular; far more popular than her husband. Many a resentful scene had played out when he petulantly derided her after a public engagement when he'd been sidelined in favour of her presence and beauty. The fact of her popularity meant that there would be sympathy for her in spades if somehow he could be publicly exposed for his behaviour whilst showing her to be the innocent but rejected victim of the piece. There would be an outcry if the public became aware of his infidelity and the obvious comparisons were drawn between her and his consort of choice. She smiled, relishing the deliciousness of the prospect of seeing him and his flighty piece squirm in horror. The moral high ground would be hers. Genius, she thought. There would be enormous pressure on him to either give up his sordid little affair and genuinely make an effort with their marriage or he would be forced to allow her the separation she otherwise craved to pursue her own life. She had it all worked out and Tim could be very useful to her.

They met in the gardens as arranged and strolled along, never stopping long enough for anyone to grasp anything of their conversation.

"So, you see, Tim, he's always on the telephone to her when he's not with her. I've heard him talking to her and my God, he doesn't hold back! X-rated doesn't even begin to describe the disgusting things he says to her. Now, what I need, is proof of it. D'you see where I'm coming from? I know it's possible to tap the phones and all I want you to do is catch him *in flagrante delicto* so to speak. Pick up one of his juicy conversations and then somehow, get it out to the public. Then everyone will know what an unfaithful sod he is and something will have to change."

Tim groaned inwardly. This was the last thing he would ever want to be involved in. If he was caught, it would be the end of his career. There was a lengthy silence before he replied. How could he help her without being directly involved? He knew there were those who would gladly be party to bringing the family into disrepute, but he had to make sure it was someone he could trust. Finally, reluctantly, he promised he would make enquiries. She was delighted. To her, it was as good as done. She didn't, however, consider the fact that her own infidelities may tarnish her 'rejected wife' persona or bring greater troubles to her own door.

Tim was as good as his word and, through his contacts, the incriminating recording was made. The next thing though, was how she would become the inadvertent recipient of the damning information contained on it. It needed to be broadcast or picked up by the press but she couldn't simply approach the tabloids. They of course would be overjoyed at receiving the story but not without very difficult questions being asked as to how it had been obtained. It couldn't, under any circumstances lead back to her. It was Tim who came up with the plan. It would be broadcast on radio frequencies calculated to reach the Ham radio buffs who would hopefully believe that they were picking up on a live telephone conversation.

To an extent, the plan worked wonderfully but it would be some time before the true ramifications would be apparent and it would not be without pain for her in the long run.

Far from being overjoyed at the prospect of reporting such a scandal the press, to her horror and anguish, having heard the incriminating tapes, spoke with her husband and his Family. Of course feathers flew but the media were persuaded to suppress the story in the interests of maintaining good relations. The scandal revealed by the recordings was unprecedented for these modern times and no-one could predict how publication of something so volatile would affect the media relationships. It was duly negotiated away. The tapes were locked away for the foreseeable future.

Behind closed doors there was outrage, horror and embarrassment. Crestfallen, she had to shelve the anticipation that his lover would be positively lambasted by the public with the photographs depicting the wronged wife, grief stricken and tearful; headlines screaming, 'How could this *'cad' of a husband reject his beautiful wife for such an inferior model?'* Everything had backfired.

She revelled in the discomfiture and outrage the tape had caused for her husband and his Family. They were mortified at his indiscretion and carelessness and now they were living on a knife edge. The matter was never discussed with his wife personally. She now found herself shunned even more as the family suspected that she was the source of the tapes but she resolved that it was even more imperative now to make her move. With no-one willing to engage with her she found herself in the humiliating position of having to make her demands to senior staff.

'Damn him,' she thought, he didn't even have the courage to face her. And so, she laid out the options as she saw them to a private secretary; either he returns and works at the marriage on terms she could accept, or, he grants her a full public separation so that she could have some semblance of independent life without vilification from the public. The secretary simply sneered at her his thin lips creased with obsequious derision.

"Don't be ridiculous. Your marriage is for life. You'd do well to remember that, Ma'am," he responded scornfully. And as for a reconciliation, I don't think that is likely under the circumstances, do you?" She was unnerved. She sensed that there was some hidden meaning behind the man's words. What did he know, she wondered?

She was as naive as she was vengeful. Her vengefulness however was borne from powerlessness. She was a pawn in a centuries old game of chess where women were traded by their families for their own selfish ends. Her family knew what they had encouraged her into. In years to come, she thought, she would be the subject of a popular historical romance, the plotting and manipulation of the families laid bare for the world to read, just as it had in the lives of other unfortunates who had come within the control of this establishment. She thanked God they didn't behead people these days or lock them up in the Tower of London. She felt sure that would have been her fate in years gone by. However, she shivered. They have other ways these days, she thought ruefully. Nevertheless, she had to tread warily. Something was afoot, she knew.

Sure enough, her pleas went unheard and she continued to live in a hiatus, waiting for the move in the chess game of her life. It was like living in suspended animation, she thought. Living out her days like some marionette, dancing to the tune of her position but never having the right of autonomy; stymied at every turn.

Meanwhile, the shadows worked behind her and stepped up their amorphous activities. She could never be one step ahead of them. They were the 'Watchers'. They knew everything. They infiltrated, they listened, they watched her, they plotted, much more effectively than anything she could come up with. They knew it wasn't a chance broadcast on a random radio frequency that had outed her husband's nefarious activities. The young woman and her supporters hadn't been quite as clever as they thought. It was clear to the 'Watchers' that it was a set up job, from the inside; and the wife was the prime suspect. She was painfully aware of the precariousness of her position and she knew without shadow of a doubt that storm clouds were gathering around her when another tape, this time detailing her own compromising conversations came to light. She had sought solace in various doomed romances and all the while she knew that 'they' were plotting her downfall. Eventually she was hoisted by her own petard when it became known to her that she too had been caught not only indulging in her own indiscretions but openly disparaging the Family, demonstrating her unbridled loathing for them. It was gold.

Something had to be done about her. She had to be silenced and prevented from her resolve to destroy the reputation of the Family. The Watchers had played her at her own game but they too were thwarted in their revenge strategy. For now. The incriminating call was broadcast on the ham radio frequencies mirroring her own plot and of course, it came to the attention of the newspapers. She was alerted by sympathetic media insiders and whilst she had no control within the Family, she begged and pleaded with her media friends not to release it in the public domain. She was the media darling. She sold their newspapers and they needed her co-operation. The Watchers weren't overly concerned. Newspapers were fickle. It would come out sooner or later and perhaps it would have reflected badly on the Family just now anyway, heightening the danger that her husband's tape would also be released. Would have looked like tit for tat. Anyway, the *hoi polloi* would simply have said *'Good on 'er Guv! Wot's sauce for the goose is sauce for the gander!' 'Well, who could blame 'er, the poor love! Look wot she's 'ad to put up wiv!'* They could anticipate it all. No, their revenge would come later. Revenge was always the dish best served cold. So the Watchers continued to watch. And wait.

"So, Hal, it was another two years before they published the story of the taped conversation; followed closely by publication of his conversation. Of course, everyone on the outside simply speculated that the conversations had been live. Most people never realised it was a tape and they certainly never put two and two together and came up with me as the mastermind behind it." She looked thoughtful now. "I'm not proud of my actions though. I hated every minute of it. I just had to do *something* to try and loosen the chains. But, they had us at every turn. Once you're in the Family, you're in and there's no release for good behaviour. Anyway, it all backfired later." She laughed, mirthlessly. "They released the recording of her first and she never got to play her wronged wife bit. Taught her a lesson, didn't it?" she murmured, a tinge of – what – bitterness in her words, Hal wondered.

"What happened after the newspapers agreed not to release the tape?" Hal wanted to know.

She shrugged and spoke, her eyes glazed and far away, as though in a trance. "She just got on with it I suppose. Her discontentment grew. Her fears grew. Obviously, it was a UXB having that tape sitting in the media safe. She knew they'd use it one day when news was slow and perhaps she'd pissed them off. She was living on the edge. She broke it off with the guy she was seeing when the tape was recorded. If anything had come out about him, I don't think her image would have been enhanced, shall we say. God! Look, sorry Hal, I'm feeling a bit unwell now. Speaking about this part of my life – it's sort of like reliving it. She shivered and laughed uncertainly. "Silly me! Well, there's a lot worse to come, so I'd better get used to it now!"

The session was over for the day and Hal excused himself. He really didn't know how to approach this situation. Tasia was a wonderful woman, but clearly delusional. She was reliving by proxy the life of another woman. It was fascinating because she was so utterly believable. Her demeanour, her voice, her mannerisms all screamed that it was her. She looked nothing like the woman whose life she was describing though. At some point, he would have to ask the question; why are you impersonating a woman long dead? What do you think you have to gain from this? And yet, recent events persuaded him to stay quiet for the moment. Let her tell her life as 'Tasia Artemis.' If he challenged her, she might just call the whole thing off and he was enjoying it. It was fascinating. Perhaps there was a story there. He just wasn't quite sure who it was about or where it was going. He sat at his computer now. Time to start writing, he decided.

Hal tossed and turned that night, unable to sleep. He was perplexed by the biggest question for him. Why was Tasia telling him this story? When was she going to drop the bombshell and admit who she was purporting to be? Should he broach the question himself, he wondered. If her state of mind was fragile, as he suspected, a blast of reality may not be welcomed by her. It might be the end of his tenure here in Greece. And what about Stergios and Kyle Masters? What was their role? He was deeply suspicious of them, despite the cordial relationship with Stergios and the rather more glacial association with Kyle. They obviously had something to gain and they were following some sort of agenda. Either they were simply humouring Tasia, or it was in their interests to be fuelling the lie she was clearly living. Now *this,* he thought, is the real story.

It was hot and stuffy in his suite tonight and he arose to switch on the air conditioning, grateful for the icy blast of cooling air. As sleep was going to be elusive, he approached the balcony and threw aside the shutters. What he saw below him in the grounds confirmed one of his suspicions.

Tasia and Kyle were strolling around the gardens, deep in conversation. He was dressed casually tonight, light trousers, the usual white shirt with sleeves rolled up and the neck unbuttoned with no tie. She was wearing a flowing maxi dress. They walked, each with an arm around the other's back, whispering together. Occasionally, she would laugh and turn her face upwards towards Kyle's. They kissed with passion, but also with the familiarity of people who had known each other intimately for a long time. He remembered how he and Fliss had been after a few years of marriage. There was no longer the need for open, hopeful flirtatiousness between them but the easy conversation and laughter between a couple who knew and accepted each other's flaws, enjoying them as much as their finer points. Tasia and Kyle looked extremely comfortable with each other as they huddled up together, contentment issuing from every one of Tasia's pores. Hal had to admit, he felt slightly disappointed for a moment. Irrespective of the strange circumstances he found himself in with Tasia, he was developing a great affection, possibly even attraction for her. He brushed off the feeling though, knowing it was ridiculous. Someone like Tasia Artemis wouldn't give him a sidelong glance in that respect and, in truth, it was probably for the best. He may have to alienate her by forcing her to expose the truth soon. There was no way he could keep up this pretence. How, after all, could he write yet another book about the most iconic woman of the modern age only this time claiming that she was alive and well and living in Gavdos? Isn't that where this story was leading, he pondered. Canary Wharf would never look at him again. He'd be derided as being as mad as a box of frogs. No, this was going to have to take a completely different perspective and somehow, he would need to use all his guile and investigative abilities to peel away the layers. He looked out into the courtyard again. The couple had taken a seat at the table on the far side and were enjoying a glass of wine together. They were quiet now, seemingly lost in their own thoughts. Kyle reached over and grasped Tasia's hand, whispering something to her, their heads now close. She looked worried but then smiled as Kyle drew her close, his arm firmly around her shoulders and kissed her gently on the top of her head. Hal carefully closed the shutters. He had seen all he wanted to. It was time to give them their privacy.

The next day, Hal received a message that Tasia was feeling unwell and that she wouldn't be able to continue with their work until she had rested. Hal decided to make the most of it. He checked with Kyle first that it was safe to use the car as he planned to go out and explore the island.

Kyle was cordial that day. "Sure Hal. I've had it swept for any bugs or sabotage. It's OK and in the garage. Make sure you have the cellphone with you and call me if you're worried about anything. Keep your wits about you."

Hal felt slightly less bold about going out when it came to the moment of driving away from the safety of Villa Artemis, but he needed to clear his head. Kyle had told him that the motorcyclist situation had been 'resolved' and he needn't worry about that again. He refrained however from explaining exactly what 'resolved' had meant but Hal had a feeling that the cyclist perhaps hadn't come off well from it.

He started off with a visit to Sarakiniko. This was probably, apart from the Port, the only other area of the island under visible construction. There was a taverna which also had rooms to let and the proprietors now knew him from his visits with Stergios. They welcomed him enthusiastically.

Kyrie Bradbury! *Kalimera, Ti Kanete?* How are you? Spiros and Helena only spoke a little English, the requirement for fluency being much less than in other areas of Greece. Most of the visitors to Gavdos went self catering in their tents on the beach so conversational skills weren't much needed for now. Serving up a Greek Coffee, thick and bitter, Spiros told him in very broken English, "We are trying to learn to speak *Anglika Kyrie.*" He produced a CD which was a BBC English Language course. Spiros tried out a few stock phrases which he spoke hesitantly and emphatically. "My name is Spiros and I come from Gavdos." He enunciated proudly. Hal joined in. "I am pleased to meet you, Spiros."

"How are you today? It is very hot." Spiros, warming to his theme continued.

"I am very well thank you Spiros. It is very hot. How are you?"

"I am also very well thank you Mr Bradbury." He smiled, nodding his head, waiting for another response with which he might continue the conversation. Hal was a bit stumped as to what else he might ask, when Spiros came in with another volley.

"Are you here for work or holidays?" he asked.

"I am here for work, Spiros. I am writing for a newspaper about your beautiful island." Spiros frowned slightly. He had understood the work, but not the description of it. He nodded, trying to work out what he had been told. Helena, who had been standing behind him as the conversation developed stepped in.

"Are you enjoying the island, Mr Bradbury? Perhaps your story will bring us more people who will stay in our rooms?" Hal was impressed. Helena had obviously progressed a little more than her husband.

He laughed. "Well, I will do my best, Helena. I can certainly tell them what a wonderful taverna you have here and what lovely people run it." Helena smiled graciously. She was pleased with herself. Hal continued. "And you must call me Hal. *Me lene Hal,* he attempted in his very limited Greek.

"Ah, yes, Hal," Helena acknowledged, as did Spiros, glad of the return to Greek.

"Milate Hellenika? Do you speak Greek?" Spiros enquired hopefully.

Hal shook his head and shrugged apologetically. *"Ochi,"* No, he said. Spiros and Helena, stood there for a few moments giving a little uncertain laugh, not quite knowing where else they could take their conversation. Helena slipped back into her kitchen and Spiros started to set another table, busying himself so that he could avoid any other complicated exchanges. It was hard work for everyone exchanging pleasantries. Hal had hoped perhaps to find out a bit of the gossip in town about Villa Artemis and its occupant but clearly that wasn't going to be an easy ask. Instead, he drank the gloopy coffee down and pulled a face as he swallowed.

Well, he thought, it would wake him up if nothing else. Afterwards he wandered into the supermarket and picked up some chocolate and a packet of crisps before remembering he was going on a diet. He put them back and picked up a bottle of water and some fruit instead. He had to admit, it wasn't as appealing as his first choice but he remained resolute.

Back in the car, he drove around the island. It was only 9km long and about 5km wide so his circumnavigation didn't

133

take him long. It was a glorious day and although the sun was shining, there was a slight breeze offering cooling respite. In Kastri, he discovered there was a medical centre and a post office. He stopped at a couple of the beaches, getting out of the car to admire Aghios Ioannis. The tiny village boasted 10 inhabitants and the beach next to it was apparently the usual location of choice for the naturists where there were trees for shade. He was relieved to find that there was no-one lying there in full glory that day. He was astonished that the travelling hordes had not yet claimed the island as their holiday destination of choice, but glad all the same. It was refreshing to come to an island as yet unspoiled by seedy nightclubs and drunken Brits cascading down a manufactured strip of pubs and noisy clubs. No doubt, it wouldn't last, he mused. He sat down in the sand to eat his low calorie lunch and take a drink of the bottled water. A moment later, his mobile beeped and a text came through from Tasia. She was feeling much better now and wondered if he felt like doing some work later that afternoon. Refreshed, he replied that he'd be with her in about half an hour and drove off back to the Villa wondering what the day would reveal.

He didn't have long to wait. Tasia was anxious to get started. She looked tired and drawn today, her usual good natured exuberance tempered by seemingly painful movement. She greeted Hal, as usual, with her warmth and generous smile and apologised for having been unavailable that morning.

"I have good days and sometimes, very bad days, as you can see, Hal. My injuries are playing up and it's difficult to sleep when it's like this."

Hal resisted the temptation to suggest that if she didn't sit drinking wine in the early hours of the morning, she might feel more rested. However, he realised that there was more to it than that and felt a little ungracious in his thoughts.

134

"I think it was reliving the memories yesterday. I tense up a bit and that plays havoc with me in the night. Anyway, let's get on, shall we?" she smiled. Hal helped her to the sofa and plumped up the cushions behind her.

"Are you OK?" he asked. "Comfortable enough?"

"Just perfect, thanks, Hal," she replied, gratefully.

Chapter 13 – Revelation and Resurrection

The way Tasia described it, the woman's life did sound like a living hell. Despite the trappings of privilege, what could be worse for a young woman than the prospect of a loveless marriage with no possibility of escape? Any hope of fulfilment of dreams, whether they be romantic or the simple pleasure of making one's own life choices were dashed. She had played her cards well, but for the time being, the effect on her life was nil. Her husband refused to consider any form of legal separation. She was trapped, but now with the added burden of her husband and family's utter contempt which they barely managed to contain. Consequently life was extremely uncomfortable and she felt there was no-one in the world she could turn to. The natural result of this is that the mind of the long term prisoner begins to work overtime to produce more and more crazy ideas which the rational among us would discount in view of the longer term effects.

Some days, she was so far down in the depths of her own underworld that she failed to see the light at all. She felt 'utterly desperate' and despaired of ever finding the freedom for which she was prepared to risk everything.

Unbeknown to her, the Watchers were muttering amongst themselves. A momentous mistake had been made in choosing her for the role, but how could they have known it would take this dreadful turn? There were few amongst the families of either her or her husband who knew that the significance of their coupling was far greater than anyone could begin to imagine. The underworld meddling of certain individuals had a distinctly sinister purpose which only those in the highest orders of secret echelons were aware of. Few in the modern world would have believed, let alone understood the reasons for the machinations of those individuals who operate as shadows, deep beneath the consciousness of the populace, manipulating and plotting to disguise the true source of world power and ensure it is never fully discovered. This was the background to their marriage. She was a complete innocent; embroiled in what was sold to her as the fairytale but which now crushed her very soul and subsumed all vestiges of her true self. She was determined never to give up the fight to release herself from the life sentence she had willingly entered, never understanding the danger or deadly agendas in which she unwittingly interfered.

Hal stopped his Dictaphone.

"Whoa, whoa!" he exclaimed as he struggled to take in some of what she was saying. Something though, had grabbed his attention.

" *'Higher powers of secret echelons...'?"* he queried. "Tasia, where are we going with this? Who are you referring to?

Tasia considered for a moment before replying.

"I'll come to it later, with the help of Stergios and Kyle who can fill you in with more of the detail. Suffice to say that what few people knew at the time was that this particular young woman was chosen to marry her husband, not just because she was a suitable brood mare from the right background but for the most astonishing reasons relating to her genealogy. Essentially, those in the know wanted to mix her blood with the blood of her husband's to secure their position and at the same time eliminate any challenge to their standing. It wasn't until some years later that the shocking truth of this was brought to her attention and when it was, oh yeah, she was ready to stand up and be counted. Suddenly everything began to add up. She began to understand why she did certain things; why she believed as she did; she began to understand who the person inside her really was and why her life was so difficult. The greatest things come from adversity they say, don't they? Well, she resolved that her adversity would yield results for everyone."

137

"OK, so you're not going to elaborate on this just now, I take it?" Tasia smiled, her face lowered but her eyes looking up wistfully at Hal. "You're so impassioned, I could almost believe you were talking about your own life. It sounds as though it was you who experienced all these things."

"I know, I'm a terrible tease, aren't I Hal? But it's important that you understand the story as it unfolded to me. Otherwise, I'll be all over the place trying to explain all the very complex threads. Also, much of it is Stergios and Kyle's story to tell." She leaned across to Hal and patted his arm, which could have felt patronising, but for the fact he knew it was just part of her tactility, her constant need to reassure the other person and herself; her need for human contact.

Hal nodded. He knew better than to try and derail her from the track she was on. He'd find out in due course. He was slightly irritated though. This was something entirely new to his knowledge of the story she told and it was by far the most intriguing.

"So, the young woman's efforts to force her husband into either a separation or reconciliation had failed and now, there were two very explosive tapes hidden away somewhere. Tell me what happened next," Hal recapped to get his and her mind back to the story.

"Well, as if her meddling with tapes wasn't enough, she hatched another, crazy plan which she felt would be bound to force their hand. God! How could she have been so utterly stupid? Why didn't I see what the inevitable result would be? Why didn't I warn her?" Tasia shook her head in disbelief.

"You see, she really was consumed with madness at that time. She gave them every ammunition to label her with mental illness. She must have seemed completely barking to everyone around her. It's what it does to you though, eventually. Hopelessness..." she added sadly. "You feel like nothing you'll ever do will work; nothing good will come out of anything you try; so you'll do anything, no matter how

138

outrageous it might look to everyone else because how much worse can it get? It seems perfectly reasonable to you when you're doing it but you look completely bonkers to everyone else." She paused for a moment as though formulating her next thoughts. She continued.

"A number of things happened at this point which I guess, was the beginning of the end for her. First, an acquaintance, an author, offered to write her biography which at first, was agreed would be sold in aid of her charities. There was massive charity fatigue at that time, you see. All of them were suffering and loads of them were going to the wall. Well, she agreed. But, as usual," Tasia sighed, "she insisted on it being on her terms. Unfortunately, it didn't go quite to plan." She laughed. "Nothing new there then!"

Tasia explained to Hal that the woman had stipulated to the biographer that if a book were to be written about her life and with her involvement, it must reveal the truth, warts and all (at least to reveal the warts she wanted to expose). She had naively believed that if the outside world understood fully her struggles with bulimia and its causes there would be such sympathy evinced by it and such criticism of the family that they would want to be seen doing the right thing by releasing her. In advance of the book, she took the precaution of leaking her illness to the press and her somewhat airbrushed view of herself as a sexual innocent, free from tarnish.

"She thought, you see Hal, that by leaking the details of her health before 'the men in grey' could use it for their own ends, she'd stolen a significant march on them. When the book came out, the public wouldn't be so hard on her because she'd admitted her battle and overcome it. If the 'Greys' wanted to use it against her by leaking to the press themselves, it would reduce the negative effects."

"The Greys?" Hal queried? Tasia laughed.

"I make them sound like extra terrestrials don't I? Well, maybe there were similarities," she added bitterly. They were

139

the stuffed shirts who surrounded us, organising our lives, always ready with a disparaging remark or a forbidding tone when we stepped out of line. Some of them were Watchers, feeding back to the head honchos. She'd become very suspicious and paranoid about them. They waited and took every opportunity to trash her. They preyed on her greatest fear; that her children would be taken from her as they portrayed her as an unfit and unstable mother. In holding that over her, they knew they had control. By addressing her own mental health problems, she trounced them a bit; outfoxed the old foxes."

In reality, Tasia explained to Hal, the book, as it unfolded wasn't quite what the biographer had in mind to publish. The young woman, enthusiastic about the new platform it would give her, poured her heart out to the author. There were no holds barred as she described her husband as a 'perfect beast', how he and his family had callously used her to provide the heir and spare, and finally, the cruellest blow; how she had been cast aside for another, far less beautiful woman as soon as she'd fulfilled her purpose. She described bouts of self harming and suicide attempts as she desperately tried to regain the affection of her husband and demonstrate the pain she was in.

The biographer however moved in the same circles and was shrewd enough to create a more balanced account. In the resulting book, the bulimia was played down and her 'suicide' attempts dismissed as insincere cries for attention. It also, to her dismay, included accounts of her less than white past with other men. In short, the plan backfired on her. It was impossible to promote it for sale in aid of the charitable purposes as originally intended as the charities would have distanced themselves fearing they would alienate the family as patrons and supporters.

"Of course, her life became hell after that. Friends and family openly criticised her for washing her dirty linen in public.

It simply wasn't the right thing to do, revealing one's innermost hopes and fears. If she wasn't desperate before, she certainly was by now. She honestly felt she would die if she couldn't escape from this living nightmare. She was a tortured soul. But, her latest hope was thwarted – or so she thought. But then, another glimmer of hope presented itself and without hesitation, she seized it, never thinking of the horrors which might yet result. All this time, she never really appreciate the mortal danger she was in."

Whilst Hal found it all very interesting to hear Tasia's explanation of the motives of a woman whose mantle she appeared to be openly usurping, he was frustrated by the continued pretence. What could Tasia Artemis hope to gain from it? And yet, as she spoke, he felt the pain in her, as though she was truly recounting to him from personal experience. It brought him a greater appreciation of the tortured workings of a desperate mind. Clearly, there would never have been any actual intent to cause harm to the poor, long dead creature but it would have taken someone very strong, single minded and yes, *ruthless* to survive. If a person had any individuality, he could appreciate how they would become crushed and broken very quickly. Of course, from his earlier years as a journalist, he knew what had gone on. There was little here that was new thus far. Most of it was in the public domain and had been rehashed *ad nauseam* by various biographers both at the time and posthumously.

Hal was growing weary now – there was nothing he could successfully publish in any of this, he sighed. How much longer would **they** keep up the masquerade? It was then that Tasia gave him his first surprise; a new twist that caused his wilting journalist's antenna to perk up.

Chapter 14 – Crowns and Coronets

The young woman was reeling after the publication of the biography and scanned the papers after it was first serialised. Furiously, she read comment after comment, some critical of her behaviour, some simply highlighting her fragile mental state and others sympathetic. She was on very friendly terms with some of the editors who relied on her to boost their sales and she spent the next few mornings on damage limitation exercises, leaking more personal information to counter the stories which were less to her taste. Fury and anguish fuelled her pursuit. She was going to have to do something really drastic. Her life had become impossible and she was determined that one way or another, she would get what she wanted –legal separation from her husband and a way out of the turgid routine of duties which neither interested her or gave her an outlet for her own creativity and caring nature. The 'Greys' were trying to stifle her activities though to keep her out of the public eye as much as possible. Her diary was sparse and she was bored and discontented; never a good combination in this young woman which was likely to lead to extremes of behaviour.

Just as she had put one of her three mobile phones down, another one rang. It was her old school friend, Tim who had helped her with making the incriminating tape.

"Hi! It's Tim!"

"Hi Tim, how are you?"

"Great thanks. Listen," he said urgently, "I need to see you. Don't say anything but can we meet up somewhere?"

"Of course, but you sound a bit edgy Tim, what's up?" She was alarmed. Tim wasn't one of her usual social companions these days and they hadn't got together since the tape was made. They both felt it was safer to distance themselves so as not to arouse suspicions as to his identity.

"Nothing. Nothing's up, don't worry. I just need to talk to you about something."

They agreed to meet later that day at an open air restaurant near the river where prying and eyes and ears would find it more difficult to eavesdrop their conversation. She drove herself, dismissing her chauffeur and telling her security officer he wouldn't be needed. It was another reckless habit she was getting into. She was tired of having to be accompanied everywhere and she always felt she had to be looking over her shoulder, never quite certain who was on her side and who was reporting back on her movements. Her protection officer argued with her, fearing that it would be his neck on the line if anything happened to her on his watch but she was having none of it. She wanted to be a normal woman on a normal afternoon out. She did take the precaution of wearing dark glasses and a wide brimmed hat as some measure of disguise. It usually worked for short periods as long as the press didn't get wind of her being out and about. She knew the staff in the restaurant would find them a quiet table somewhere away from unwanted attention.

She was the first to arrive and she was discreetly welcomed by the Maitre d' of the restaurant and shown to her table. It was quiet there at this time. She had taken the precaution of booking outside the usual lunchtime rush.

She glanced up from the menu she had been reading just in time to see Tim, his tall frame striding over to the table. He had been in the military after Oxford and before he joined what was mysteriously termed, the 'Security Services.' He was smart and confident, looking every inch a former Officer. She admired his good looks and poised self possessed bearing. He was, she knew, a suave operator with the ladies and she didn't intend to encourage anything more than already existed in occasional friendship between them.

"Hello Darling," he inclined his head in casual greeting to her and kissed her on both cheeks as she rose from her

143

chair. He kept it informal though. Nothing overly formal that could lead to speculation as to her identity from other diners or that might invite curiosity. Instead of sitting opposite her, he took the chair immediately to her right so that they might speak quietly.

"Tim, great to see you. At least the furore over you know what has died but as you probably know I'm in hot water again." She laughed uncertainly.

"Hmm, yes, I've seen the papers. Whatever possessed you?"

She pondered the question for a moment, her expression serious.

"You know, Tim, sometimes I think 'possession' is the right word. I just get an idea and I have to run with it. I'm so desperately sad and unhappy you see. I can't bear it for much longer. Everyone hates me. They're all being perfectly beastly to me. If they'd just listen and see reason, we could all be shot of one another and there'd be no more of this unpleasantness. They're just so bloody dyed in the wool difficult."

Tim laughed. Same old, same old then. Ever since their schooldays she had blown hot and cold with her friendships and relationships. It was all fine when things were going her way but her over sensitivity and sheer bloody mindedness whenever there was a perceived slight led to the shedding of many of her friendships. Sometimes, they would be resurrected but often the offending parties were cast aside and frozen out, never to be invited in again.

"Tell me, what is it that you *really* want? Do you just want to be a simple commoner again, free to do as you will? Because it's hardly likely now, is it? The fact you are the mother of the two most important children in the country would hardly permit you the opportunity to buy a two up, two down in Camden and buy your vegetables in the market to make the tea for your 9-5 hard working hubby now would it? Can't see the kids being able to stay with you in those circumstances."

"Ohhh God, don't!" she buried her head in her hands in despair. He had brought the reality far too close to home. In some strange, other world that existed in her own mind, that was exactly what she wanted. Just *ordinariness*. The chance to do things that interested her without the interference of the family and to spend her time with loved ones as a normal mum and yes, perhaps wife again one day. But he was right of course. She would never, ever, achieve the mundane existence she thought she wanted. But, if the truth be known, fame was her lifeblood. It validated her as a person. She *needed* the world to be talking about her but only about the things she wanted them to talk about. The good stuff. Not prying into her every private moment. In her heart of hearts, she knew she could never have the roses round the door cottage where she would meet the kids at the picket fence after school with the smell of freshly baked apple pie coming from the window. She would probably die of anonymity if that was where she was consigned. No. There would have to be much more of a negotiated compromise between herself and the family. One that would give her the status and role that she wanted whilst acknowledging her maternal position and the role she would have to play in her children's lives.

Tasia paused in her story for a few moments and pulled her legs off the sofa to turn into a sitting position opposite Hal. She looked sombre and closed her eyes for a moment, breathing deeply.

"Are you OK Tasia?" Hal asked, his expression creasing into concern as he threw down his notepad and Dictaphone. He knelt down in front of her and looked up. She opened her eyes and nodded, smiling.

"I'm fine, Hal. I guess I was just bracing myself. We're now coming to the bit I think you've been waiting for. I can't tell you the rest of the story now without coming clean. I'm

145

sure you've already guessed my secret haven't you? And probably discounted me as a complete imposter or a fruitcake."

Hal's heart was beating. Was this really going to be the moment? He hoped so. He was going to burst if he had to listen to much more of the story without them acknowledging who she was really talking about.

"So, Hal, tell me, who do you think I really am?" Hal felt uncomfortable in revealing his thoughts. This could go very badly.

"I think," he hesitated, "that you truly believe that you are...," he was trying to put into words carefully his thoughts as he didn't want to cause offence. "...Princess Diana..." There. It was out. "Deceased..." he added, just to show that he was buying none of that fiction. Of course, he wasn't even sure that she truly believed it, but she was certainly trying to make him believe it.

Tasia smiled enigmatically. "Good! She laughed. Just what I thought you'd say. "There, now that wasn't so bad was it?" Hal gazed at her, waiting for her to say something which might explain her actions.

"So, you think that I merely *believe* I am Princess Diana then? Not that I *am* her?"

Hal had to admit that yes, that was what he was going with for now. He was treading warily.

"And there is absolutely no reason you should think anything different. I totally understand that Hal. After all, the world was told that Diana died in 1997. To all intents and purposes, she did. She went out in a blaze of glory. But, the story is somewhat different from that which the world was told Hal and there are only a handful of people who know it. You are now one of the privileged few. To quote, or rather misquote Mark Twain Hal, 'reports of [her] death were greatly exaggerated." She smiled, waiting for his reaction. Hal meanwhile didn't know what to do. How could he respond?

He had been unconsciously holding his breath as she made the confession he had expected, yet still evinced incredulity from him. He stood up and walked over to the window, turning his back to the woman who was wringing her hands on the sofa. She was utterly mad. There could be no denying it now, he thought. He wheeled round, ready to say that it was impossible, he couldn't be an accomplice to this lie but, he was stopped in his tracks, almost winded with the shock of what he saw. Tasia was pulling at her Cleopatra bob and as she did so, it came off, revealing a shorter, blond bob much more reminiscent of the real Diana. She shook out her real hair, combing her fingers through to reveal a woman who, though still not *exactly* the way Diana looked, certainly was a very good, if older, look alike.

Hal approached the woman; Tasia; Diana; whoever the hell she was. He was close up to her now and yes, the eyes had the soulful depth of the real woman. The face, though a little older and perhaps a little greyer due to ill health looked for all the world very like Diana. The mouth when smiling could have a cheeky, mischievous twinkle whenever she joked or take on the defiant steeliness as the lips drew taut whenever she felt annoyed; sometimes the familiar biting of the lower lip when she was anxious or unsure. Her eyes crinkled with pleasure when she was happy, were beautifully doleful when sad and on occasion, could narrow with spite when she 'recalled' her mistreatment of previous years. Her nose appeared to be different though and this did give her face a slightly different look. It was smaller, more pert and straighter than he recalled Diana's. Hal couldn't be sure. Yes, the woman was a very good substitute for the way Diana might look today but there were differences. He'd seen some fantastic doubles from specialist lookalike agencies and, after careful scrutiny, he could put her at no higher than a possible 7 out of 10 for similarity of face. As he gazed at her in wonder, Tasia couldn't help but giggle. As she did, her face lit up and she was for a moment, the spitting image of the woman he believed to have been dead all these years.

"I feel like a waxwork in Madame Tussaud's with a tourist scanning me to see if I'm real," she laughed. "I'm trying to stay really still for you." Hal suddenly became aware that his behaviour probably wasn't particularly appropriate. He was indeed examining her like a laboratory specimen.

"Sorry, Tas..., Diana... What do you want me to call you?"

She bent down and picked up the wig again, placing it carefully back on her head as she stood in front of the mirror.

Just stick with Tasia Hal. I don't want anyone overhearing or you making any slip ups outside. Remember, to the whole island, aside from a few within my own household here, I am simply Tasia Artemis; philanthropist and rather eccentric hermit with random healing powers. As for any other identity I may, or may not have, I shall let you make up your own mind."

Hal shook his head as though trying to clear a fog. It was just so unbelievable.

"Tasia, I admit you are an amazing likeness for Princess Diana, but not an *exact* match, I have to say. I can't with all certainty just sit here and believe that you are who you suggest and let's face it, you're ... she's (he corrected himself) dead for God's sake! There was absolutely no doubt of that. How could Diana just suddenly emerge on the remote island of Gavdos and expect the world to believe she's somehow miraculously alive. We had investigations, speculations, conspiracies, a coroner's inquest, bodies, autopsies...!" He reeled on her grasping his aching head in frustration and disbelief.

"Sorry Tasia. I'm outta here. I have to think a bit, but I don't think I can go on until I get some answers." Hal stormed out, angry that anyone could take the piss to such an extent

148

and think that he'd been born yesterday. Why would she do it anyway?

Tasia slumped down into her seat. Of course, she had feared this would be Hal's reaction. What else could she have anticipated. It was hardly your run of the mill royal story was it? *"Princess Diana Returns from the Dead!"* A bit like '*Aliens turned my kid into fish fingers*' or '*Elvis seen in Lancashire Chippy.* Yes, she could see why Hal was having a bit of difficulty. She couldn't help but giggle – maybe the photo accompanying her headline would be of some ghastly zombie, grotesquely vacant with flesh hanging off it. No, no, she thought. You're getting hysterical now. There would be no headlines of that sort. No, when this story was complete, the world would take it seriously and with any luck, the secrets she would tell would make it a better place. She knew though, that she wouldn't be around to see it – or Hal's reaction when the final truth was revealed.

Chapter 15 – Lies, Damned Lies

Hal took the Merc from the garage and drove off at speed from Villa Artemis. He was angry at being made a fool of. Kyle Masters watched impassively as the car sped down the track. She'd obviously told him then. Kyle had been involved, no, instrumental in orchestrating the operation that had been designed to fool the world and he knew every detail of Tasia's life since their first meeting when she had exploded into his life. It had been a gradual process, the burgeoning of their relationship. Boy! She'd been a difficult dame to deal with in the early days and he'd had to give her some tough love. It was hardly surprising though.   Nothing of her old life could be resumed. All that was familiar to her and loved by her was torn away and all he could promise was the possibility of the truth revealed in years to come when the world was ready and when it was finally time. Time was running out and they would be lucky at this rate if they'd ever reach the point of being able to reveal the truth. He was becoming frustrated. All the work and sacrifices they'd made to preserve the secret and protect her so that she could finally have her moment would be for nothing if Hal didn't get a move on. Her health was failing rapidly, although she hid it well.

Kyle remembered how it had been like breaking in a wild mare dealing with her in the immediate aftermath of the tragedy. As she grew stronger, she wanted to go back, full of fury and indignation at how the Establishment had tried to wipe out a life and caused the death of innocent people in the process; how they were prepared to kill off the mother of the future monarch. She railed against him as he tried to reason with her that she had to accept, in the eyes of the world, that she was dead to them. She must now live a new life, one that she'd longed for in anonymity and that he, Kyle, would always be there to protect her. There had been arguments of course, screaming, hair pulling, hot-headed tantrums but he'd been as good as his word and his cool, laid back American personality had eventually intrigued her as she understood that his loyalty and later, his love were assured. It had taken him by as much surprise as it had her that they had grown closer as each day went by and that he had come to worship his 'Goddess' as much as she worshipped him for the love, passion and loyalty that he offered her and that she'd craved all her life. Finally, her knight in shining armour had come to save her, quite literally and they'd never been separated from that day to this.

Now though, he had another battle on his hands. He and Stergios would have to rein Hal in to get the job done. He hoped that diplomacy would suffice. He quite liked the Li'l Guy as he thought of Hal. He gave Hal a head start and got in his own car to follow him. He didn't want any unpredictable behaviour that might blow the whole thing now.

Kyle caught up with Hal but kept a distance behind him. Hal was either ignoring the vehicle behind him or just wasn't being as vigilant as he ought to be given the dangers he'd been warned of. Hal stopped back in Sarakiniko and, striding over to the taverna he ordered a large Jack Daniels and a beer. As he was giving his order to Helena, the American voice behind him said "Make that order twice, please Ma'am." Helena smiled at Kyle in greeting before heading off to the bar to fetch the drinks. He took a seat next to Hal.

"Tough day buddy?" Kyle enquired casually. "You sure took off like shit off a shovel a while back. I was kinda worried you might get yourself into trouble." The Jack Daniels arrived and Kyle threw his back in one gulp. "Good choice. Bring me another, Helena? Thanks."

Hal merely regarded the man, suspicion and anger darkening his expression.

"Hardly surprising is it? Just what kind of a fool do you all take me for?" he spat. Kyle casually looked around, checking to make sure no-one was in earshot. Coolly he

151

replied, "No bigger fool than you're making of yourself right now," his mouth drew into a tight scowl. Kyle drew himself menacingly up to his full sitting height, his powerful frame dwarfing Hal's slumped figure. He spoke slowly, meaningfully enunciating every word.

"Look, I ain't gonna sit here and spend hours trying to persuade you to do the right thing and hear her out. You're employed to do a job and you're being paid real well to do it. If you don't wanna do it buddy, say the word now, but mark my words, if you breathe a word of anything you've heard so far, without my say so, you'll live to regret it. You got me? There's more at stake than you realise and you haven't got the first idea of what we're all up against. Now, the time isn't right for me to fill you in on the rest of it but I will give you what you need when Tasia's come to the end of her part. It would only confuse things more for you." He leaned back, waiting for Hal to make a response.

"You called her Tasia, not Diana. I know you're close to her. I saw you both in the grounds the other night. If she's who she says she is, why don't you call her by the right name?"

"Buddy, we've taken every precaution to keep her away from the wider world all these years to protect her anonymity. What d'ya want me to say? *'Hey Princess Di? Howya doin' this fine day?'* Might be a little bit **obvious** don't you think? Might sound a little odd maybe? And OK, I could call her Diana, but that's how mistakes happen, Hal. A little slip of the tongue here, a few loose words there. We've all known her as Tasia since we first met and that's how it stays. Anyway, you've still got a lot to learn Hal and don't yet make assumptions about Tasia or her identity." Helena had returned with the beers and Kyle's second Jack Daniels which he now downed. "So Hal, what d'ya say? We go back and finish the job or we sort out the alternative?"

152

Hal didn't quite like the way that Kyle mentioned 'the alternative' and wasn't sure if it was meant as a threat. Thinking, Hal spun through the day's events in his head. He'd always known where this was going hadn't he? And, he'd resolved to stick with it whatever. There was a story here without a doubt, but he was damned if he was going to let them think he'd swallowed their lies. Eventually, his lips pursed, he met Kyle's intense stare. He's psyching me out, he thought. Trying to decide if he can trust me. Hal actually didn't like the idea that Kyle might not trust him. He felt it might not be in his own best interests. Finally, his mind made up, he answered, steadily and resolutely.

"I'm going to co-operate Kyle. I don't believe any of it but I'm going to hear you all out. You're right. You guys asked me to a job and I don't walk away from a deal, however far-fetched it might seem. I'll write the story as it's told to me, but just don't ask me to put any spin on it that might suggest that I think it's true. It'll reflect the 'facts' as they are given to me, but it will be through the eyes of other parties, not as I may or may not see it. I must be allowed to keep my integrity in this. Are we agreed."

Kyle nodded.

"Yup! That'll do for me Hal. I think though," he smiled enigmatically, you may yet change your mind. Just stay open to poss..."

"*Possibility*" Hal interjected. "That bloody word again. Yes Kyle, I'll do just that." Hal signalled to Helena and held his JD glass up. "*Theo - Two, parakalo?*"

An uneasy understanding had been reached. Kyle got up to leave. "Be seeing ya later bud," he said as he threw down Euros in payment. Hal decided to stay at the taverna and eat that night, unable to face dinner with *'Princess Di'* for this evening anyway.

Chapter 16 – Misfits and Mystics

All was quiet and still when Hal returned to Villa Artemis that night. Aside from the outside lights illuminating the courtyard and the surrounding parts of the house, it was in darkness. Everyone must have retired early, he thought. He entered the house and quietly ascended the stairs to his suite. Something was on his mind and he wanted to check it out.

"*Stergios Tavoularis by name, Stergios Tavoularis by nature,*' the phrase uttered by Stergios was repeating in his mind. Stergios had been trying to make the point that one's name revealed more about a person than might otherwise be obvious. He fired up his laptop and poured himself a nightcap as he waited for it to load.

Sitting at the desk, he Googled the name 'Tasoula.'

'Tasia: derivative of Tasoula - *The meaning of Tasoula is 'resurrection,'* he read on the first website. Then, as he read on, he noticed, *'Tasoula and its derivative, Tasia, is the Greek form of* **Anastasia'.** Quickly, Hal did a further search to find out if there were any deeper meanings for the name. Another website told him that a person by the name of Tasia was 'emotional but also secretive and introverted but would open up when comfortable in her environment'. '*She is a mysterious misfit and just beyond human understanding. She is fascinated by all that is odd or unorthodox'*, he read. 'There may be a tendency to oscillate between periods of high energy; sociability, enthusiasm, intense communication and optimism and lows; misanthropy, scepticism, reticence, pessimism and *even depression.*' He continued to scan the page, '*The supernatural appeals to her inquisitive nature, and sooner or later she could be drawn to investigation of spiritualism, mysticism or parapsychology. Her emotional life is rarely simple because she never exposes her deepest feelings, even when she is at her most loquacious!*'

Wow, Hal thought. The description could apply as easily to Tasia as it could to Diana. Whoever this woman was, she'd chosen well. Next, he keyed in the name, 'Artemis'. 'Of course,' he slapped his forehead as it dawned on him. *'Artemis was the Greek goddess of the moon and hunting, the twin of Apollo and daughter of Zeus and Leto. She was known as* **Diana** *to the Romans.* The clues were all there had he picked up on Stergios' hints the other night. He was trying to tell Hal to look at the significance of names to discover who Tasia really was (or at least was purporting to be). *"Damn!"* he cursed himself for being so slow on the uptake. At least this was beginning to make some sense.

He was exhausted now but there was something, something he couldn't quite put his finger on. There were more clues here. He'd have to sleep on it though. Hopefully it would come to him when his mind was clearer.

When Hal woke up, it was around 6 a.m. He was still tired and a bit fuzzy so he turned round and tried to get back to sleep. The revelations of the previous day were weighing heavy on his mind and his mind was determined to triumph over his weary body as disjointed pieces of the puzzle flashed through his thoughts.

OK, he thought. So, it seems she claims to be Diana, Princess of Wales. So, where do we go from here? There were a thousand interpretations he could place on this. Is she claiming that she never died in the accident which left the world aghast and stunned in 1997? Or, as her chosen name is now Tasia, meaning 'resurrection', is she claiming she is dead, but miraculously returned to life like a modern day Lazarus? Does she and her posse really think that he would believe that he is talking to a spirit? Or is she just a complete crank with an agenda of her own to gain fame and fortune – perhaps some sort of medium who is possessed with the spirit of Diana? She certainly looked and felt like flesh and blood so he discounted the idea that she would claim to be a ghost.

155

"Wait a minute though...!" Something else had occurred to him. Tasia was a derivative of the name 'Anastasia'. He flung the sheets aside and swung himself out of bed to switch on his computer again. He searched for 'Anastasia' and recalled, as he read, the details of one of the biggest mysteries of the 20th century; the emergence of the woman who claimed to be the Grand Duchess Anastasia, daughter of the deposed Czar Nicholas II who, together with his family, had been murdered by firing squad. Two years after the shootings, a woman, rescued from a suicide attempt in Berlin had eventually claimed that she was Anastasia and that she had escaped by using jewels sewn into her clothes allowing her to buy her way to freedom with the help of some of her captors. For years, Anna Anderson caused controversy. There were similarities between the two women and, like Tasia, Anna had what appeared to be some intimate knowledge of the family history. Even relatives were torn as to whether this woman was indeed Anastasia. It wasn't until after Anderson's death in 1991 when all of the bodies were exhumed and two remaining bodies were found that DNA evidence proved that Anderson could not be Anastasia. The public though, taken with the mystery wanted to believe that Anderson was Anastasia and even today, there were those who claimed the Russians doctored the DNA to discount the story.

Hal sat back. Was Tasia simply emulating the woman who had gained, if not fame, notoriety and, for a time, adulation and assistance through her insistence she was Anastasia? Perhaps she was simply some crazy, fame hungry individual who thought she could weave a terrific story around the similarity of her appearance to Princess Diana?

Hal rubbed his eyes and yawned. He threw himself back on the bed and despite himself, he fell asleep again. He slept peacefully until he was awoken by the house coming alive with the rattle of china and silver platters containing the wonderfully aromatic cooked breakfast. He overcame all resistance as he was lured to the dining room by the waft of bacon and eggs which had drifted upwards. Clever ploy by 'Princess Di', he thought.

When he reached the dining room, Tasia was already seated. She gave him a sheepish 'Good morning' which he returned a little curtly. Neither really knew what to say to the other under the circumstances. She was conscious that he now distrusted her, he was deeply uncertain of everything in his world.

They ate in silence for a while, the uncomfortable chinking of cutlery against china the only sound cutting the ominous atmosphere between them. Eventually, Tasia could take it no more.

"Look, I'm sorry Hal. What I told you must have come as a huge shock. Of course, I understand your disbelief. I'm asking you to consider what must sound like the most impossible situation in the world. All I can ask of you is that you hear it all. Please, don't dismiss me as a lunatic just yet. You *will* understand as we continue, I promise."

Hal considered how to respond. He was torn between packing his things and returning to London and curiosity. What if there was something in what she said? What if there might just be some grain of truth in all of this? He would have the story of a lifetime if there was. If not, he would be the laughing stock of the publishing world if he continued. In the event, curiosity won the day.

"I'll stay," he stated definitively. "Don't get me wrong. I'm not saying that I believe anything of this but, I'll hear you out." He sighed. Tasia smiled gratefully.

"Thank you Hal," she said.

"Well, the breakfast is good here," he replied, looking up into her oh so doleful gaze.

They laughed, the ice broken between them.

157

"So," Hal began, clicking the switch on his dictaphone. Shall we go back to where we left off before you dropped your bombshell? You - or shall we say, 'The Princess' and Tim were at the restaurant."

The 'catch-up' chat between the woman and Tim had concluded and she wanted to know why he had been so anxious to meet her that day.

"You know who I work for, don't you?" he asked her now. She nodded, although in truth, it was all a bit evasive.

"Something in the security services isn't it?" she asked uncertainly.

"Yes, but a little bit more specifically, MI5." She looked at him aghast.

"Wow! You're a real life James Bond then?" she asked incredulously. "I hadn't quite thought of you in that role," she laughed. Tim on the other hand did not break a smile.

"Look darling, you need to listen to me. You have no idea how much MI5, MI6, the CIA and other groups work together and how much they watch and listen to what is going on with the lives of those in power. I've come to tell you that you are in danger. There is whispering about your mental health and the damage you're bringing to the Monarchy. They will leave no stone unturned to bring you down if you don't toe the line." The young woman gazed at him wide eyed with fear.

"What do you mean – 'bring me down?'"

"It could mean any number of things but they will stop at nothing if it becomes necessary."

"You mean they might kill me?" she asked, her voice rising in pitch, eyes widening.

"Sshhh," Tim cautioned her. "Keep your voice down. But yes, it's possible. It won't be the first time someone in high position has been silenced so you have to tread more warily. Now, what you must also understand are that within these organisations, there are different factions. There are

158

opposing views; secret groups within secret groups. There are those, for example, who believe that you should have greater influence in the Monarchy and those who will fight to the death to prevent you from taking your rightful place. The latter, believe me, are in much greater number than the former."

The Princess felt that her heart would beat out of her chest at any moment. She bent closer to Tim.

"My '*rightful*' place?" She asked him.

"Yes. Now, this is going to come as a bit of a surprise to you I'd imagine but some would say that you personally have a greater right to claim the British Monarchy than the 'usurper' Family who enjoy the privilege of royalty today. I can't explain it all to you here, right now darling, but your bloodline leads to the Stuart kings who were deposed of their rightful inheritance." He hesitated a moment. "And their bloodline, well, this is where it all gets very complicated, can be traced back in time to even more powerful sources. The truth about these sources has been used and manipulated throughout history to grasp political and financial power by all of the most formidable institutions of the Establishment including the Church of England, the Church of Rome, various European monarchies and now, the most powerful oligarchies of business and finance. They have all successfully used the bloodline to create myths, deceit and manipulation of the common people into believing that monarchy is somehow untouchable; worthy of such reverence that their subjects believe they are extraordinary in an almost mystical way. Have you ever wondered why a family of, let's face it, quite ordinary, but highly privileged human beings are able to enjoy the hero worship of the majority of society? Why do we kneel, bow and curtsey to a handful of people who haven't got a clue about real life?"

She had to admit that if she thought about it, she couldn't really give any reason why the family, or others in

159

various countries took on such special significance. It was just the way it was and, she supposed, because they were descended from those who had held such elite power throughout history. It really was, when she thought about it, quite ridiculous that such deference was given to a particular family when they didn't really do very much. Society, without question, just accepted their superiority through tradition. It wasn't as though they held any real power in the country.

"Exactly!" said Tim. "No-one knows why; *except* those who put them there and those whose agenda intend to keep them there. But, just suppose, the family didn't have a true right to be there and there was *someone* – someone here today, who could genuinely make a difference to the monarchy and *who did* have a clear right to claim the throne?"

"Well that should be made clear and the rightful monarch should be restored of course!" she responded. They fell silent for a moment and Tim waited for the penny to drop. The young woman laughed. "Oh no. C'mon Tim! You're surely not saying that because of my genealogy, I have the right to go to my mother in law and the family and say '*Move aside you lot, I'm the real Queen around here!* I'd be laughed out of the UK and beyond. They'd really think I'd gone barmy!"

"That's the point. They really wouldn't. They *know* of your bloodline. You were positively *chosen* to be Princess of Wales because of that. The Royal family have some of the true bloodline in them but it's been diluted and mixed with other strains. The mixing of your blood with theirs through marriage and the birth of your sons strengthens their claim to the throne and it keeps those whose powers derive from that very happy."

She was dumbstruck. She couldn't take in what Tim was saying. *She* was the **true** monarch? It was just ridiculous.

160

"Look, I can't tell you much more now. It's a highly complex situation. There are others who will help you to understand though. As I said, there are two factions here; one which actively supports you and what you represent and another which will fight to the death to ensure that you are either suppressed in your current role or removed from the picture altogether. That's why I've come here; to warn you, but also to ask you to be ready as your support grows in the murky underworld that exists beneath our so called *democracy*. They would like to see you take greater control of the monarchy and lead it to greatness through your sons. I have been asked to bring this to your attention. Now, I have to go. Promise me you will think about all of that I've said?"

She nodded her assent, although in truth, she was sceptical and very confused.

"If you want to do a little bit of research, check out the Merovingian dynasty of Kings. They're highly relevant to your story. We'll be in touch further in due course but in the meantime, keep your nose clean and stay wary. There are rumblings of discontent in the corridors of power."

Tasia told Hal how the young woman had been completely shaken up by Tim's words. She had somehow sensed all her life that she was different and that she was following a destiny but there was nothing tangible to say why or how that might be. In recent times, she had felt frustrated by the whole idea of monarchy and she had, in her own small way, been fighting to try and change the way it was operated. She wanted it truly to be a force for good. They were in a wonderful position to use their power and privilege to change the world but aside from the stuffy facade of fulfilling charitable engagements they didn't really become involved or make any real inroads to changing things. But then of course, the family didn't have any real power in themselves. They were criticised for making public any political opinion or for being outwardly supportive of change in any meaningful way. Her

161

husband had suffered for being vocal in his views and opinions many times. The Monarch was only the constitutional head of the country without any real power. As titular head, no political involvement was permitted because ostensibly the power came from democracy; the government elected by the people. The lessons had been learned long ago that power vested in one supreme monarch was open to abuse. Why, then, did Tim reckon that she had a role to play here? And how would that be possible given the democratic system?

Something in Tim's words had struck a chord with her and, headstrong as ever, it gave her confidence and conviction that she was on the right path. Somehow, she still had to free herself of the current situation, just sufficiently for her to regroup and start to make inroads in reform of the monarchy. Now Tim had planted the seeds and her ideas began to germinate. However, she became careless and never was the old adage more true that 'a little knowledge is a dangerous thing'. The knowledge that she'd gained gave her confidence. She knew that there was support for her in the corridors of power but she discounted, for now at least, the dangers that Tim had warned of. She had renewed optimism which she would put to good use.

Hal was stunned by Tasia's latest revelation but he had to admit, he was intrigued. He knew of course that the lines of power in Great Britain were not as perceived by ordinary people; that there was a complex network of dealing and counter dealing; secrets that most people would never be privy to. Could there be any truth in what she was telling him? He intended to find out. The strings of her story did however seem to have elements that when tied together, made some sort of sense.

He asked her to go on and tell him what happened in the aftermath of Tim's revelations.

Tasia sighed deeply.

"She played it all wrong of course. It was as you know, imperative for her to free herself from the immediate clutches of her husband and his family. It's true that her fragile mental state made her utterly reckless. She was determined though and by the time she met Tim that day, she'd already started a process that was to go completely out of control. She arranged for another book to be written about her. This time however, it was going to be completely within her control. She had to be careful though. She couldn't be seen to have direct involvement so it was agreed between the Princess and the author that she would supply tapes to him from a distance and a number of her friends would be cited as the contributors. They would be held out as the sources for all of the information in the book. Well Hal, as you no doubt remember, the book was published and all hell really broke loose. Her life and reputation was just about destroyed. It rebutted much of the content of the previous book and, in her eagerness to tell her own story she embellished it presenting it from, shall we say, a rather subjective perspective. She really did think she was telling the truth, but of course, the mind does have a rather clever way of distorting things, especially when it is as disturbed and unhappy as hers was at the time. It was so essential to her that this time she was presented in a favourable light and I guess, she distorted the truth in some respects." Tasia hesitated a moment. She looked unhappy. "She wasn't proud of what she did but what else could she do?"

Hal remembered the book she was talking about. It was written by a Fleet Street journalist who was eager to make his name. Princess Diana's 'True Story' caused a storm when it was published and the controversy it created was unprecedented for the royals.

"Anyway, her bulimia was fully revealed and she spoke about her husband's infidelity which in her mind had been the cause of it. Truth is, she had suffered from the illness before

163

her marriage. She was pretty cruel and vitriolic about her husband and the family whom she felt hadn't prepared her properly for the royal life. I'm afraid she chose to present herself as whiter than white and completely contradicted everything that had appeared in the previous biography. When she looked back she really wished she'd handled everything so very differently but she couldn't see it at the time. She was in a very self destructive period you see. After Tim had spoken to her about the possibility that she had some sort of claim to the throne, she thought that she could command more of a role in the family. She thought she was invincible and that her popularity would win through.

Of course, there was hell to pay once the book was published; a terrible furore. In terms of royal scandals, this was probably one of the worst in living memory; a complete betrayal of the family and of course her husband. She lied her way through it of course. She simply denied everything and placed it squarely on the shoulders of the friends who'd agreed to take the rap. However, she did want the world to know that she approved of the book and its contents so she openly and publicly supported her friends, arranging for journalists to be there when she 'happened' to visit them. It was a terrifying time for her. She was living on a knife edge, not knowing what was going to happen. It was then that she was called to a family meeting."

When she'd entered her mother in law's office that morning she'd received an icy reception. As well as her mother in law, who could be a formidable character when pushed, she was dismayed that her husband and father in law were also present. Her husband gave her a stony greeting, her father in law could barely look at her, such was his contempt and disgust. A hasty meeting between her husband and his mother earlier had forced them to recognise that she was ill and they resolved that they should be sympathetic. The last thing they wanted was any more scandal with the possibility that she might take even more drastic steps to seek attention. If they didn't handle the situation with kid gloves, they knew that she had the power to destroy the whole royal institution.

"My dear," began her mother in law, without preamble. "You must be aware that the publication of this book has caused irreparable damage to us all as a family, as an institution and also to yourself." The Princess nodded miserably, her head held low, her gaze averted from the steely countenance of her mother in law.

Her father in law, who had been pacing the room impatiently and didn't feel particularly sympathetic to the bloody woman who was intent on creating so much devastation around her interjected impatiently. He couldn't be doing with all this softly softly approach. She needed to understand the seriousness of her actions.

"Look," he barked. "Just tell us what the bloody hell it is you want woman, hmm? A divorce is it? I'm sure it can be arranged but good God you stupid little airhead surely you can see how disastrous that would be for everyone? Including you hmm?" He shook his head angrily and paced, or rather strode around the room menacingly, his hands clasped behind his back. He had been fond of the girl in the early days. She felt sad now that the betrayal she'd felt to be so necessary was hurting everyone. They were clearly saddened and disappointed in her. It was almost more than she could bear but she had to remain strong. This was her moment to negotiate the best deal she could for herself. She steadied herself, drawing herself up to present a more confident front. Taking a deep breath, which came out as a sob as fear and sadness mingled she said, "I'm so sorry for the hurt that's been caused by the book. I wouldn't have wished for it to happen."

"Did you, or did you not give the information to that seedy bloody journalist?" her father in law spat at her?

165

"No, Sir, I did not," the young woman lied with ease. "I'm afraid that I was perhaps over candid in confiding in my friends about my unhappiness and the effects it was having on my health. They really just wanted to help by telling my story. They felt that it would be cathartic for me if it were out in the open and that perhaps it might help things to change in some way. I truly didn't know what they were doing. I'm so sorry. I do understand however that now it has happened you will want us to work together to rectify things."

Her mother in law nodded, her husband remained tight lipped and unwilling to speak. Her father in law snarled in derision. The woman must take them all for bloody fools, he thought angrily.

"So?" he growled. "What is it you want then? Out with it."

Tasia explained to Hal that the Princess had felt hugely intimidated by the situation. She was truly alone. It didn't help either that she was lying through her teeth and despite her selfish motives, it wasn't something she was enjoying or felt comfortable about. But, this was her chance and eventually she summoned up the courage to announce her wishes.

"I want a full legal separation from my husband but I want to help maintain the status quo as well," she began uncertainly. *Here goes*, the young woman had thought. "Although we will be legally apart, I absolutely want to remain a member of the family and set up my own court. I can do so much work for you and I really want to be able to do good in the world and help to restore and enhance the royal family as a respected institution. Please, let me have my own responsibilities. My husband and I can still present a united front but concentrate individually on the things we do best." She smiled in the most appeasing way that she could, hoping to persuade the family whose faces now registered utter disbelief at the suggestion she had made. She hoped they would see sense but their reaction belied any such

166

expectations on her part. Adrenalin was coursing through her veins as she waited for a response. It was a tense few moments that felt like hours before anyone managed to respond. Her father in law's eyes blazed with anger and shock.

'Preposterous!' was all he said as he again began to pace the room, anger and perplexity evident in equal measure.

It was clear to all that there could be no firm solution reached at this time but eventually, after further discussion, a compromise was reached. She and her husband would remain together in a show of unity for a further six months and the matter would be reviewed then. It wasn't the ideal solution for anyone but the family knew that she was still regarded highly by the populace and that it was necessary to tread warily in order not to alienate the masses against them.

She bit the bullet. At least it gave her breathing space she supposed and perhaps, just perhaps, they would come round to her way of thinking. Why ever couldn't she and her husband remain family but simply do their own thing? In a strange way, the desperate young woman was emboldened by the information she had received from those who supported a new era for the family. Since Tim's initial revelation, she had been put in touch with another contact who simply called himself by a code name, *Hermes.* She felt that there were allies out there who also felt that she could be the catalyst for change in age old traditions which, to her mind, were outdated and needed modernising. She would soon meet up with 'Hermes' who promised to explain fully the reasons why she should be a contender as a senior figure in the family and the idea thrilled and excited her. There was a small part of her that wanted to wipe the complacent smiles from their faces when she confronted them with her rightful heritage but she knew she must tread warily for the time being so, although impatient, she agreed to the cooling off period of six months when she would be better armed with information to support her arguments. Mistakenly, she felt invincible and smiled inwardly with excitement as she contemplated the possibilities which would open up to her. She pushed the fear and paranoia to the back of her mind, safe in the belief that there were those supporting her cause.

Tasia sighed.

"But of course Hal, her peace of mind didn't last long as you will no doubt remember."

First of all her popularity had to be addressed if the Establishment were to have any chance of ridding themselves of the former rose who had now become an almighty thorn in their side. This was achieved by the re-emergence of her taped conversation which became front page news as her own blemished character was exposed with details of her love life and familial disloyalty splashed across the media. The Princess's 'true story' was exposed for the fabrication that much of it undoubtedly was. Her mental health took a turn for the worse as she came under increasing pressure resulting from the enormity of her actions. She was frozen out from the family whose betrayal and anger were understandable but for whom the revelations boosted their public position as she was revealed to be more sinner than saint.

"To his credit though Hal, her husband didn't retaliate even though she had thrown him to dogs," Tasia reflected. "In fact, several in the family recognised that she was suffering from illness and treated her with incredible kindness, although at that time she didn't appreciate it. She stayed indebted to those who treated her well during that awful time and she was sorry for many of the things she did. It's only as a grownup that she understood how beastly she really was." Tasia wiped away tears as she recounted her story. She seemed genuinely remorseful, as though it was her own story she was telling - or a very good actress, Hal thought. She blew her nose before continuing.

168

"God, she really miscalculated the whole thing. The way she went about it all was so reckless and stupid when I look back. It was no wonder the Establishment wanted rid of her. She felt a complete fool. If she'd kept her powder dry until she knew the full facts, perhaps things would have been different but she was in such a hurry to change everything. It was the only light on her horizon you see. She wasn't able to rationalise. Now, everywhere she turned, she saw only enemies. She'd created a situation that she couldn't get out of and she had to play it through. Can you imagine the terrors that filled her at night as the consequences of her actions unrolled? She didn't know where to turn so she turned to everyone she knew for advice. Of course, they all had a different view. She listened to their advice, but, and she'd admit this herself, she was so pig headed she just ignored everything that she didn't want to hear and went her own way anyway. The columnists in the newspapers analysed every aspect of her character which was now being slowly destroyed. Her integrity was questioned and there was anger that she had undermined everything that the British people held dear. She was being branded a bitter and twisted demon and a complete crackpot. Far from the icon she had once been, she was becoming infamous and a laughing stock."

The young woman complained bitterly about her friends after the publication of '**that** bloody book!' She forgot completely that she had orchestrated the whole tenor of the biography and now began to blame the author and her friends for the disastrous effect it was having on her life. The Princess cut off the friends who had gone out on such a limb for her in order to deflect her own involvement with the content. All the while her mental state deteriorated further under the increasing stress. Everywhere she looked she saw barely disguised fury and disgust written on the faces of those who served her. Mutterings of *'Little upstart! She should be grateful for the privileges she enjoys',* could be heard in

169

whispers behind the hands of those who would smile to her face. They would fawn around her, their obsequious platitudes designed to keep her onside in case her maverick behaviour should lead to some other disaster which would shake the foundations of the British Establishment.

Since Tim's last contact with her and *Hermes'* initial contact, she heard no more from those who would elevate her to blood royalty and her initial ebullience began to fade. Instead, she imagined that everyone was complicit in plots to be rid of her and as her paranoia grew, her behaviour became more erratic and unpredictable.

She was convinced that her former sister in law, also under scrutiny for her conduct, had been set up with compromising photographs of her own indiscretions as a warning of what would happen to her should she step out of line again. Somehow, security wasn't properly set up during one of her sister in law's trips abroad; something that would never have happened in the past. She knew that should she decide to leave the safety of the family, just as her sister in law had done, they would stop at nothing to expose every move she made to try and destroy her reputation. Even now, whilst still in the fold, she trusted no-one. She obdurately refused to show weakness though, and even played fast and loose with her husband's right of access to the children, thwarting him whenever she could to prevent him from spending time with them; changing her plans at short notice and manipulating the truth to show herself as the perfect mother; he as the cold, distant father. At every photocall she attended with her husband she played the victim to perfection, pain and sadness carefully etched into her expressions. When photographed alone she ensured that she looked carefree and happy.

"Oh yes," Tasia nodded to Hal. "She was a complete pro when it came to making her husband look like the most awful creature that ever lived. She actually couldn't believe how hideous she could be towards him. I know now of course that he did really love her and had the best intentions when they married but she was too pig-headed to see that it was she who was destroying much of what they could have had."

"Well, Diana was very young at the time," Hal mused. "Unfortunately it is usually only with the benefit of hindsight as we get older that we realise the truth and become willing to admit the mistakes of youth."

Tasia nodded.

"Yes," she sighed. "But she felt ashamed, Hal. She caused so much unnecessary pain for him. "And for herself. It was like an unstoppable train though. She couldn't, or wouldn't put the brakes on. Eventually, her husband's patience was exhausted and after the most traumatic and turbulent six months came to an end, he snapped and the lawyers were brought in."

It had happened after one of her now frequent changes of plan when her husband was due to see the children. During a heated exchange over the matter, her final outpouring of vitriol led to the result she had worked for. He had pleaded and reasoned with her until he was exhausted and defeated.

"Well, if you want me to be reasonable," she had announced imperiously, "*you* had better start to meet me halfway." She smiled, ready to deliver her final blow. "If you are so determined to stay married to me then remember I can play as difficult as I like with your access to the children." She lowered her eyes, uncoiling to release the venomous strike. "However, if you were to grant me legal separation of course, we would have to make a legal agreement about access to the children. I wouldn't be able to spoil your plans then, would I?" She lifted her eyes to meet his gaze now, knowing that she had thrown the winning volley.

"So be it," her husband uttered quietly, his energy and will depleted. "Have it your way. I'll speak to my lawyer immediately." There was momentary relief between the two of

171

them as the twilight of their relationship was finally acknowledged. Of course, she knew that the future was desperately uncertain now without the absolute protection of her position but she would fight tooth and nail to ensure that she protected herself. There would be no agreements without every 'i' dotted and every 't' crossed, she resolved.

"Co-incidentally," she explained to Hal, "Or rather not so co-incidentally, Tim contacted her again at around that time. Those who were in the know about everything had got wind of what was about to happen and the factions now began to regroup and prepare for action. Tim told her that this would be the most dangerous time and that she had to know everything in order to exert her proper influence. It was to be the most incredible roller coaster of her life. It was when "Ares" and "Hermes" came into our lives."

Hal looked confused. *Ares and Hermes? What the hell was she talking about?* Tasia laughed at his obvious consternation.

"Yes Hal, they're Greek Gods. But what you need to understand, these were code names for my two guardians. Otherwise known as Kyle and Stergios. They couldn't let their true identities be known at that time. Remember they were rebel agents in the secret services. They operated in the underworld of establishment power and they were, although part of a growing number, still very much in the minority. They had discovered the most explosive information that could rock the entire foundations of both British and European royal history, impacting on the most powerful institutions worldwide. If they were discovered imparting the secrets which have been held for centuries in secret archives they would have been killed instantly. The consequences of this information being released into the public domain would shatter everything that the modern world has believed in and trusted in. It is this knowledge which convinced me of my own destiny. The information you are about to learn will change your understanding of the events leading up to the Princess's 'death' and you'll begin to understand how it will change the face of modern democracy and all of the institutions which work tacitly to control every aspect of our lives."

Hal was silent as he digested all that she had said. The familiar feeling of unease ran in his veins. So Kyle and Stergios weren't just bodyguards to a wealthy eccentric. If Tasia was to be believed in any way (and he was still largely unconvinced), he was dealing with highly trained killing machines from the secret services. He would have to tread more warily.

Tasia rose from the couch. The session was over for the day. She had such a habit of leaving him just at the point that things were getting interesting. He had to admit though, he was tired and needed some space to get his head around all that he had heard.

Chapter 17 – Democracy of Deception

It was yet another sleepless night for Hal. The day had reached forty degrees despite the time of year and Tasia's incredible tale was troubling him. After tossing and turning for what felt like hours he decided to clear his head with a stroll on the beach. He stepped onto the balcony to find a full moon illuminating the night, casting its ghostly glow over the grounds and he was reminded of his first visit to Villa Artemis. He recalled now the lilting, yet haunting music which had roused him from sleep and drawn him here. He also remembered the nocturnal performance by the dancer who now made him question his very sanity.

Hal quickly pulled on a pair of shorts and a tee shirt, both of which, he was gratified to see, were beginning to hang a little looser on him. For the first time since he arrived here, he inspected himself in the full length mirror that was hanging on the inside of the closet door. He was shocked to see the extent of his transformation. His generous face and double chin, gained through endless days and nights of comfort eating now displayed contours that he hadn't seen for years. His features were slowly restoring to the chiselled look of his youth. His stomach had shrunk, no longer billowing like marshmallow over his waistband. It was amazing what a few weeks of healthy eating and a measure of stress could do for you he thought. Hal had stopped looking in mirrors as self disgust grew with his expanding waistline. Food had become his only pleasure, his safe haven after Fliss's death. He could empathise with Tasia ... *Diana* ... anyone who found comfort in food. It offered a distraction, just for a short while, from the pain which defined him, filling the hungry void which in truth, could never be sated. Once the endorphins wore off, depression and emptiness soon returned. In Gavdos, Tasia had taught him a way to regain control and with it, self esteem.

She had become the distraction he needed and his unwitting mentor.

Hal crept quietly down the stairs to the hallway and let himself out. He crossed the grounds and passed through the gate onto the path leading down to the beach. There, he sat for a while, lost in the simple and calming pleasure of the rippling sea washing up to the shore where the moonlight provided a backdrop to the silhouetted pine and monkey puzzle trees. He closed his eyes and wished with all his heart that Fliss was here to share the beautiful serenity of the island with him. An explosion of suppressed memories came to the fore and hot tears stung his eyes. From somewhere there was a howl of such sorrowful intensity, piercing the night. It was seconds later before he realised that the wailing had come from him, giving him a sense of relief. Hal gave into the sadness allowing it for the first time to completely engulf him, releasing the long held grief, permitting it finally to wash over him. As it did so, he became aware of the familiar scent evoking another place and time, transporting him back through the years to a happier place.

He was startled from his reverie by a voice calling his name. It almost twinkled through the air; real, but slightly other worldly; muted, as though carried on the wind or through radio waves. Hal stumbled up from his sitting position and scanned the beach around him. In the distance, he saw a figure. A woman. She was facing the sea, watching the rippling waves as they lapped the sand. Her long dark hair blew in the slight breeze that had suddenly picked up causing her gown to cling around the contours of her body. There was no mistaking it. Hal fell to his knees.

"Fliss?" His voice was weak and uncertain; disbelieving.

The woman turned around as he called and, to his utter joy, he knew it was her. She was smiling and he could feel her warmth and love radiating towards him, as comforting as a hug. She was illuminated by the moon, her beautiful form and

175

features etched in relief against the silvery backdrop. Hal ran towards her, but, as he did so, she seemed to shimmer and become less tangible, translucent even. She continued to smile, holding her arms out towards him. With each step Hal took towards her, she appeared to recede more into the distance, always just out of reach. With each moment, she seemed to be a little less *there*. In his head, he heard her voice again.

"I have to go Hal. Let me go for now. I'm never far away from you. Remember that. We'll meet again I promise, but it isn't time yet. Be happy, live life and do what you must do." Fliss raised her fingers to her lips and blew him a kiss which he felt as warm and real upon his lips. Fliss faded into the darkness but as she did so, Hal saw another figure move where her ethereal figure had lingered. It gambolled along the beach, long, gangling legs prancing like Disney's Bambi in the sand. He watched as the baby deer now turned and ran towards two figures in the distance. One, he recognised instantly as Tasia. She was wearing the same diaphanous floor length ancient Greek style dress he had seen that first night as she danced in the Villa grounds. This time, her head was uncovered and the Cleopatra wig was removed to reveal herself looking for all the world like Princess Diana. Next to her stood Fliss who waved to him and smiled her farewell before they both appeared to glide into the distance and fade away. The moon was suddenly erased by a cloud and Hal was plunged into darkness, alone again. He was overcome by fatigue, his emotions raw and spent. He lay on the sand and allowed his eyes to close. Soon he drifted into a deep and more peaceful sleep that he'd experienced for a long time.

Hal was rudely awoken the next morning by the urgent calling of his name. He stirred, unsure whether he was dreaming or not before he became aware of the heat beating down on his face. He groaned as he realised he'd spent the night asleep on the beach. A shadow blocked out the searingly bright sunlight.

"Hal! What the hell are ya doin' lying here dude? Any longer and you'd have been fried!" Hal shielded his eyes against the sun and as his sight adjusted, he saw Kyle Masters towering above him. Kyle knelt down, inspecting him for signs of illness or sunstroke.

"You OK? You had us all going for a while there. It's not a good idea to go off on your own – you know the dangers." Hal pulled himself up stiffly.

"Yeah, I'm fine thanks Kyle. I just couldn't sleep so I took a stroll last night. I guess I must have just dosed off."

Kyle was unusually agitated, his generally composed feathers slightly ruffled. He looked tired and somewhat dishevelled this morning and he was wearing scruffy jeans and a crumpled t-shirt. Not his usual sartorial and perfectly turned out style. His usually passive expression was creased with strain and fatigue.

"I went to look for you in your room to tell you that Tasia had been airlifted off the island last night. She's real sick." There was a slight tremor in his voice.

"What happened? When?" Hal asked. He'd only seen her a few hours earlier on the beach. How could that be, he wondered.

"Happened just after she'd wrapped it up for the day with you. She felt faint before dinner so she went to lie down. She called me shortly after because she had chest pains. We got the helicopter over to Crete about 9 p.m. last night. You didn't hear the commotion?"

"No, I was in my room working. I had my headphones on listening back to the recordings. I wasn't aware of anything. How is she now?"

Kyle rose to his full height, and stood, shoulders slumped, hands in his pockets. He gazed out towards Crete as if by staring hard enough, he might just catch a glimpse of the woman he loved.

"Not so good," he said quietly.

"Why aren't you with her?" Hal asked. Kyle sighed before answering.

"She wanted me to come back and keep the work going with you. To fill in the, shall we say, technical details so that she can finish the story. She's asked me and Stergios to tell you our part in all of this and when we're done, you'll go over to Crete and finish it.

"She isn't coming back soon?"

Kyle's eyes were shining, tears held back, determined not to crack the tough exterior he adeptly displayed to the world.

"She doesn't seem to think so," he replied cursorily. "And she usually knows," he finished enigmatically.

Now, back at the Villa, Hal stood motionless, supported by his hands splayed against the glass shower booth allowing the warm water to cascade over him comfortingly enveloping his body. The last few hours had given him a lot to think about. He felt kind of hung-over, a feeling of unreality permeating his senses, saturating him almost as much as the water now surging over him. Last night, the visions of Fliss and Tasia had seemed real but now, in the cold light of day, how could it have been? Fliss was dead and Tasia had been airlifted from Gavdos hours earlier. Hal was afraid that he'd become delusional or there was trickery going on for which there was no obvious rhyme or reason.

Refreshed and dressed, Hal made his way to the study where he'd arranged to meet with Kyle. This morning, there was no breakfast laid out, just the aroma of strong coffee filling the room as he entered. He was met with a curt nod of the head from Kyle whose usual cool ebullience was absent, his face drawn and pale.

"Coffee?" he offered Hal, who gratefully accepted. Kyle's hand shook slightly, rattling the cup and saucer as he poured the coffee.

"God damned helluva thing when you get close to someone, Hal." He laughed without humour. "Always said in my profession you should never mix business with pleasure. It never works out good. First and only time I ever did it. Never really cared for anyone until I met Tasia. She just bowled me over and I never looked back."

Hal could sympathise completely with Kyle.

"It's hard, I know. When Fliss got sick and then died, I was lost without her. Never really found myself again if I'm honest. One minute she's there, all full of life and laughter, next minute she's gone and life is like an interminable winter, devoid of warmth or comfort and everywhere I go I find hollow emptiness." He shuddered as though trying to throw off the bleak abyss he'd faced for so many years.

"Man, I'm sorry. I'd forgotten you had your own sorrows to bear. I've known it would come to this for a long time. Thought I was prepared for the worst. Guess I've just been fooling myself. It's just hittin' me for real now."

Hal felt powerless. There was nothing he could say that would make Kyle feel better. The worst, he knew, was still to come for him. It was the first time he'd really been able to relate to the usually brash and surly American and it was refreshing to see that he had the quality of finer feelings.

"Nearly twenty years I've known her Hal. Haven't been separated for any length of time for seventeen of those years. Long time," he reflected. "God she's been trouble though. First dame to make me really laugh. First real friend I ever had since I was a kid. It was always safer to stay detached. The only one I've ever loved. When she's gone, my whole reason for living dies with her. Gonna miss her."

Hal listened in dismay.

"How sick is Tasia? I mean she seemed OK yesterday."

"It's bad," Kyle confirmed, exhaling a deep sigh. Each time she gets a little bit worse. I guess the strain is taking its toll on her poor heart. She's had a lot to bear over the years I've known her. I guess I was able to take the edge off some of it, but she has deeper sorrows that broke her heart."

Kyle sat in the armchair as he spoke. His head was bowed, his hands so tightly clasped in front of him his knuckles blanched at the strength of his grip. Kyle was holding on bravely. He managed to gather himself from the engulfing emotions and, squaring his shoulders as though to defend himself from the onslaught of pain, he stood and strode purposefully to the window. His voice steadier, he cleared his throat and adopted a 'ready for business' approach.

"Well, best thing we can do is to get on with her story. You must be wondering what kind of crazies you're dealing with I guess?

Hal nodded.

"It's been a surreal kind of time," he acknowledged. He decided not to mention anything about seeing Tasia on the beach, or indeed his own visitation from Fliss. It could only have been his imagination playing tricks on him.

"OK, so here's the plan. She wants you to go over to Crete in a few days, so we'll get started." Kyle poured himself another strong coffee before settling down.

"After I left the military, I joined what we loosely call the 'Secret Services. In other words, the CIA. I wanted the excitement of working in intelligence and I wanted to make a real difference in the world, you know? My illusions were shattered within a short time though Hal. I had these high ideals of protecting my country, my people, guarding the principles of democracy and all that the US and we in the Western World hold dear. It wasn't long before I discovered

180

the truth though and it was a bitter pill to swallow, believe me. The cyanide capsule for idealists you might say.

What I actually discovered was that far from protecting our utopian understanding of how the world works, the intelligence services are really committed to covering up the truth and protecting the interests of a very select and elite few."

"So let me get this straight. You were a spy, that's what you're telling me?"

"Not *was,* Hal. I still *am* a spy. But I'm one that's caught in a dangerous world because I use the information I have to disrupt the causes of the organisations I work with. I believe what I do is for the greater good. I'm not so deeply entrenched these days, but you never truly leave the service. I have contacts I'm still working with but from a distance nowadays."

"And Tasia? What has she got to do with all this?"

"She's the reason I am where I am. She was the final straw to break this camel's back Hal. We'll come to that though. Bear with me. First you need to understand more about how the secret services work and what we're dealing with.

Now, the CIA, MI6 and MI5 all work closely together as you'll appreciate Hal. Very shortly after I joined the service, I was sent to Britain to work with MI6 on various assignments in counter terrorism and dealing with subversives who weren't playing ball and threatening to derail various plans of our respective governments. Let me ask you a question Hal. Who do you think runs your country?"

Hal knew that the obvious answer wasn't the one Kyle was looking for.

"Well, I guess most people would say our democratically elected governments ultimately."

"Yeah, you'd think, huh?" Kyle's question was rhetorical. "But of course, it isn't the case. Our governments are puppets; the official facade for much more powerful agencies whose interests must be served. Your so-called 'democracy' is exercised by a very powerful elite and underwritten by oligarchs; industrialists, financiers, politicians. They are an evil cabal who don't give a shit about what happens to individuals. They engage the covert operations of the Secret Services to serve their own interests."

Kyle had been a successful member of the Marines and had that typical 'jock' physique, athletic and powerful. He was atypical of that type though in that he had an alert, intelligent and enquiring mind which enjoyed philosophy and politics. He had witnessed atrocity and despair in many warzones throughout the world and he departed the marines hoping to make a difference. He was just thirty when he entered the shadowy world of the CIA. When he was posted to the UK, at first he revelled in the British eccentricity and tradition and he settled comfortably into his new life. At first, he enjoyed the work, undertaking surveillance exercises on those deemed to be a threat to the West. As his knowledge grew though, he found himself questioning the reasons for some of the assignments he was undertaking.

As an undercover agent, it was often necessary for him to ally himself closely with those who were deemed enemies of the state, or at least labelled as potential threats. All too often though, he was discovering that many of these individuals simply questioned the motives and protested about issues which they felt were wrong. Kyle found himself agreeing with the views of those he was detailed to either derail and sometimes, destroy. He began to question why those who were clearly working on the humanitarian front and exhibited more empathy for the world than he perceived from his organisation were accused of threatening the status quo. Increasingly he was discomfited by the work that was required of him but never dared to speak out for fear that he too would be targeted as a threat. He knew that the day would come when he would no longer be able to live with the duality of his beliefs against the actions that were required of him.

One evening, whilst off duty, Kyle was having a drink with one of his colleagues, a dapper, highly eccentric individual by the name of Stergios Tavoularis. Although born in Greece, he had been educated within the bastions of the British public school system which was finished by studies in Politics and Law at Oxford University. His distinctly Oxbridge presence overshadowed his Greek nationality and for all the world he was a member of the British upper classes. He, like many of his forbears and peers had been recruited into MI6 from University when he'd been approached by the 'talent scouts' of the intelligence services.

To Kyle's amazement, on that particular evening, Stergios, in an unguarded and angry moment, voiced his outrage over the fate of one of the so called enemies of the state he had been investigating. Stergios was convinced of his quarry's innocence and honourable intentions and horrified when he discovered his demise after committing 'suicide'. Of course, the suicide had been carefully orchestrated on the man's behalf for daring to speak out vociferously against the nuclear policies of the west.

Stergios whispered furiously.

"We are nothing but official mercenaries, Kyle. I feel that I am destined for hell if I don't do something about the injustices I see every day." He stared into his pint of real ale, contemplating the horrible end for a man for whom he had developed respect and friendship whilst simultaneously betraying his every thought and movement to his employers.

Kyle looked around him, making sure that they were out of earshot.

"Stergios, you need to be careful what you say. As it happens, I agree with you but we're trapped. What can we do about it except keep quiet and try to exit the organisation without suspicion?"

183

"No Kyle. We cannot exit. That would just allow these monsters to continue their atrocities, silencing and murdering innocent people. We have to *do* something about it and we can only be active whilst staying with our ears to the ground."

Unbeknown to Kyle, Stergios knew exactly what he was doing when he staged the conversation. They had known each other a while and through casual conversations Stergios had elicited enough about Kyle's character to understand that he too was discontented with his lot. There was already a dissident group, substantial in number within the intelligence services who were avowed to work together in secrecy to thwart those activities which they deemed not to be wholly conducive to protection of the state but which promoted the corruption increasingly evident to them. They were effectively spreading counter intelligence, not in support of any other state or individual power but in the name of altruism and righteousness. It came as a relief to Kyle to find that there were others who were willing to take action against the wrongs which they perceived were being perpetrated in the name of Western security. Of course, it crossed his mind that perhaps Stergios had been primed to elicit Kyle's dissident views but he took a chance having developed ostensibly at least, a close working relationship with the man. They had been in some hairy moments together and their shared mutual trust had been instrumental in helping them to extricate themselves from danger. Kyle decided to be open in his own views with Stergios.

"Of course Kyle, if you join us in our undoubtedly mutinous circle, your life will be in greater danger than it is now. The Secret Services will seek to eradicate anyone who defies their interests and those of their puppet masters." It was a risk that Kyle was prepared to take. He couldn't continue working against all that he believed in.

Kyle was introduced to others within the circle and indeed, they placed themselves in situations of unprecedented

184

danger when they 'failed' to carry out a mission or information was 'accidentally' leaked to the public about covert operations. They worked with stealth and care, opposing and undermining much of the organisation's work for what they believed was the greater good. If they were to succeed as a dissident group, they had to remain expertly duplicitous. As a result Kyle, Stergios and other noble rebels lived on a knife edge, never quite sure whom they could trust and aware that if their acts of ostensible treachery and counter intelligence were discovered, sudden disappearance and almost certain death awaited them.

"So, Hal, to let you understand, the world at large lives under the total misconception the intelligence services, the CIA, MI5, MI6, Mossad, whoever you wish to include, all work for the benefit of citizens, protecting democracy and eradicating threats to our own countries and on a global basis." Kyle shook his head sadly. "But not so, Hal. *Nothing* could be further from the truth."

"As our 'dissident' group expanded, I learned more fully the context in which the CIA operated. The world believes that political decisions are made at government level and that our secret services are the guardians of freedom. The truth is though that the CIA and MI6 are financed by the Corporate world who 'sponsor' our governments."

Hal wasn't uninformed and knew well enough that few things are as presented in politics and government. He wanted to be sure though, just exactly what Kyle was suggesting.

"So what you are saying is that the secret services are in the pay of businesses to orchestrate democracy?"

"That's exactly what I'm saying. The situation developed during the 2ⁿᵈWorld War when large corporations funded the US, Britain and even Hitler. After the war ended, these corporations wanted their debts repaid. Governments wanted to co-operate with them and directed huge funds into corporate development of the tools of war in all sorts of areas, nuclear, pharmaceutical and aerospace. The corporations began to monopolise, operating cartels organised by the US and Britain who were underwriting research and which recruited scientists, engineers and others. Many of those who control the intelligence services, the CIA, MI5 & MI6 are on the boards of these companies, orchestrating everything from arms sales, oil production and every aspect of the media and communications industries. You can see then how our view of the world is completely influenced by these powers. It's terrifying. The whole point of the secret services is to protect the financial and political interests of the oligarchs who in turn finance the various intelligence agencies to do their bidding and influence the entire system of democracy. Not only that but the 'godfathers' who mastermind all of this use the intelligence agencies as a facade to protect all kinds of operations behind a veil of respectability and altruism. In fact, the corporate oligarchs are undertaking all sorts of scientific research and experimentation, covert programmes and secret military procedures for their own financial and political gain. It isn't for the common good, let me assure you. In Britain, the Official Secrets Act allows these operations to be carried out under the guise of national security."

Hal took a sharp intake of breath. What Kyle was telling him was explosive. He didn't think he could write about this. If it was all true, he could see why there were individuals who would be anxious to stop the information going into the public domain. If he was going to be the one to make any kind of exposé on the intelligence services it was no wonder that nefarious characters were stalking his movements and trying to run him off roads.

"What about accountability though Kyle? That's the saving grace of all of our institutions surely?"

Kyle laughed derisively.

186

"Really, Hal? You really think that we have the Utopian world where questions will be asked in the House and everything will be sorted? No my friend. It doesn't work that way largely because anyone to whom these organisations are 'accountable' all have a finger in the very profitable and rotten pie.

Within MI6 itself is the most powerful and unaccountable of all the covert operations, the Special Operations Executive or SOE as we call it in the trade. You won't find it listed in any official publications Hal and you won't be able to put in a call because officially, it doesn't exist despite having hundreds of millions of pounds budget in addition to the subsidies it takes from the corporate sources."

"You're right," Hal agreed. "I've never heard of it." He was becoming more uncertain by the minute whether he really wanted to hear any more. The deeper entrenched he became in Kyle's purging of secrets, the harder it was going to become to plead ignorance and go back to the relatively safe world of celebrity reporting and a pork pie behind his desk. Sure, he'd done investigative reporting before, but nothing on this scale and nothing that might have placed him in any real danger. He was scared and beads of sweat were breaking out on his top lip as he considered the potential consequences of his acquaintance with Kyle Masters. He couldn't deny he was intrigued though and given he was something of a captive audience now, he allowed the conversation to continue.

"So, the *'SOE'*, this must be something of a new organisation, right?"

Kyle burst out laughing and shook his head.

"Not unless you call the reign of Elizabeth I a recent event Hal. Because it was during her reign that the basis for the organisation is said to have been founded by her paymaster, Sir Francis Walsingham."

Hal's mind whirred and now he started to put parts of the jigsaw together.

187

"You're saying that the monarchy has some historical connection with the SOE?" he asked.

"Exactly right," Kyle confirmed. "Ever since the reign of Good Queen Bess, monarchs including those of Hanover-Windsor descent have been reliant upon secret agents. I guess we all know from history that particularly during these and subsequent centuries, espionage and treachery were part and parcel of the monarch's life and that enemies had to be flushed out."

"And now? Surely you're not suggesting that the current monarchy is in bed, so to speak with the SOE?"

"It's more subtle these days, Hal. No, you're right the connection isn't quite as it once was. Remember in the days of Elizabeth I and subsequent monarchs, up until I guess when Cromwell came along, there was a great deal of power vested in the monarchy. They were more like tyrants and dictators in those days and held political power whereas today..."

"...the monarchy is only the constitutional head and without power." Hal finished Kyle's explanation. "But the Monarch is still the titular head of the Government in Britain and therefore must still influence and be influenced by the intelligence services, surely?"

Kyle stretched and rubbing his neck, stood with his back to Hal facing the picture window overlooking the grounds of the Villa. He was weary and worry was etched on his face. He was trying to keep it business as usual, just as Tasia had wanted but it was difficult knowing that she was fighting with her illness, sad, lonely and in pain and separated from him by the cobalt expanse of sea between them.

"Yeah, of course, the monarch is still top dog but democracy requires that her country is run by the government who in turn work hand in hand with the various agencies. In that sense I guess the monarch still dominates the organisations but won't be intimately acquainted with, shall we say, the more despicable acts except in the broadest sense. The monarch can't be linked to any form of moral turpitude. There is no doubt that current monarchs will be aware that things go on outside their specific knowledge but they would be protected from knowing the specific details and are unlikely to be asked to sanction any proposals from these agencies. MI6 is ostensibly accountable first to the monarch followed by the Foreign Secretary and lastly to the House of Commons Intelligence and Security Committee. Within MI6 there is a hierarchy of ever more secretive compartments and divisions who work with the oligarchy of the Establishment to uphold and protect the British Monarchy. Whilst the royals may hear whispers and briefings about these covert departments, other than the official body MI6, it seems unlikely that there is any plotting or discussion of their activities. In 1909 the Military Intelligence Department 6 became a formal body, ostensibly formed to infiltrate the military powers, industrial organisations of foreign powers and to gather intelligence. Later, in the 1920s it became divided and the SOE as it then became known was formed to look after corporate and international affairs rather than democratic matters. It's these guys who dominate the worldwide corporations backed by European and American powers."

Hal's mind was spinning. In his head, it all made sense. Money buys power; power breeds the desire for more money and more power and ultimately absolute corruption. His heart, as a patriotic Englishman didn't like to believe that all he held good about the exercise of democracy in Britain was no better than a very highly organised and secretive dictatorship which benefited only those who were part of the gentleman's club.

"So, Hal, we're nearly at the end of what I can tell you about the CIA, MI6 and the organisations which are at the root of the British Establishment and its American counterparts. They do however have a bigger role to play in the story that we're telling you about Tasia and for that there is just a little bit more you should know before Stergios fills you in on some of the more colourful detail. The European Union also has its roots in the machinations of the secret services. It's also central to the story. The SOE, with its corporate, financial and publishing interests had the aim of creating a United States of Europe and after the Second World War, it was instrumental in the creation of European Lobby Groups to underwrite and bankroll the mission. During the war itself, it worked in tandem with the American intelligence agencies which now form what we know as the CIA to undertake covert operations with resistance movements and infiltration of enemy groups to sabotage them and obtain intelligence to co-ordinate raids and thwart plans. Although the SOE was officially dispensed with after that, the truth is that it still exists and continues to act in secret pursuit of a United States of Europe."

Kyle paused and Hal exhaled in astonishment.

"It all sounds very Masonic. Secret aims and covert activities to cover backs and promote self interest of the chosen few," Hal ruminated.

"A good analogy and actually, very apposite as Stergios will explain to you."

"So, if you're working against all of this Kyle, how have you managed to survive? I mean the duality of your life must drive you demented not to mention the danger you must surely face."

Kyle pursed his lips reflectively as he nodded.

"It sure isn't an easy life to choose," he acknowledged. "Truth is Hal, I've had to do many a thing I'm not proud of and wouldn't have done except it was the only way to keep my cover and save my own skin. The only consolation I have is that I did it for the greater good so that suspicion was kept from my door while I tried to subvert even worse strategies of the organisations I work for. I've killed, maimed and threatened people whose beliefs ran contrary to that of the

Establishment and the underpinning agencies whilst at the same time covertly trying to protect others of their number and credo to allow their voices to be heard and the truth to be known. Duality is a good description. Sometimes it does make you a little schizophrenic and every day you wonder who you're going to be."

The two men sat in silence for a moment, then Hal asked,

"And Tasia? What has she to do with your world?"

"Everything." Kyle answered simply and earnestly. "She *is* my world."

Hal caught up with Stergios later that day and they sat at their usual table in the taverna. Kyle had left for Chania to be with Tasia but Hal was eager to continue with the work, his appetite having been whetted by Kyle's revelations.

"So Hal, Kyle's been telling you something of the nature of our business I understand." Hal drank deeply from the tankard of Mythos he'd been caressing appreciatively moments before.

"Yes, and from what he tells me you and Kyle have a somewhat, *colourful* association, shall we say?"

Stergios nodded thoughtfully. "Indeed we have. Never a dull moment in truth. However, it is a part of our lives we shall return to shortly. First though, a digression. I'm going to take you back to a time well before ours which may help you to understand where we are going with Tasia's story. It is an essential detail which I believe may set what we're telling you in context. So, this takes us to late 19th century Southern France and to the world of a parish priest by the name of Bérenger Saunière. He is central to the understanding of just how a 'commoner' princess was discovered to hold the *de facto* and most authentic entitlement to the British throne and the key to the mystery of her death."

191

Hal retrieved the Dictaphone from his pocket and switching it on, he sat back in the sunshine allowing Stergios free reign to resume the story.

Chapter 18 – Penury, Parchments and a Pecunious Priest

Rennes-le-Château 1891

It had been an unremarkable week so far for Bérenger Saunière. He had officiated over a wedding, three funerals and a number of masses as well as performing pastoral duties in the parish over which he had presided since 1st June1885.

Now, on a gloriously sunny afternoon, he strolled through the village greeting those of his flock he encountered along the way, his black cassock absorbing the heat causing him to wipe away beads of perspiration from his forehead.

It was market day in the village of Rennes-le-Château nestled high amongst the mountains in Southern France. Although only populated with around 200 souls, local merchants gathered together each week to sell their wares and bring the scant population together with a real sense of community. Saunière stopped to peruse the merchants' goods in the busy square.

"Father, you must take some peaches to quench your thirst on this hot day," the fruiterer insisted, refusing payment from the priest who accepted gratefully; for Bérenger lived in abject poverty amongst his flock. He was despatched by the Church in exile for daring to give controversial sermons that were not to the taste of the state and which had ended his stipend and branded him a militant reactionary. When he arrived in the remote village, he'd found his Church, St Mary Magdalene in a state of complete disintegration and the Presbytery in which he was expected to live squalid and derelict. For a while, he'd had sufficient money to pay a disagreeable and avaricious old woman, Madame Marro for the use of a room for which she charged him an unashamedly high rent. More recently though, he'd made do with a decaying shack in which to rest his weary bones at night.

Wandering slowly amongst the trestle tables laden with local produce, each of the stallholders would smile warmly and offer him the pick of what they had, each hoping that their generosity to one of God's own would ultimately incite The Lord to smile upon them with good fortune, protection in this life and everlasting peace in the next. At such times, they forgot their daily transgressions and hoped that their token altruism towards God's representative in Rennes would suffice to atone for their sins if provided in tandem with a good confession later.

Saunière always took his constitutional on market day. God knew, his life of parish priest in the village of Rennes-le-Château was austere and miserable and the charity of his parishioners was all that kept hunger at bay. Sometimes he questioned his life and longed for a few luxuries to brighten his Spartan existence. By taking to the square each week he knew that the goodwill of the kind folk of Rennes-le-Château would provide him with the sustenance he needed until the next week and afforded his flock spiritual comfort from their offerings. It was indeed, a win win situation, he thought happily as the hessian bag which he always carried on such occasions strained with savouries, cured meats, fruit, baking and sweetmeats which kept his surprisingly generous frame nourished. Today he was particularly delighted with the latest batch of red wine provided to him in a stone jar by the local vintner. Saunière looked forward to the evening when he would put his feet up to enjoy the heady brew as he prepared his sermon for the weekend. A good glass of wine always aided his creative and spiritual abilities, he found.

Sometimes, Saunière questioned his vocation and wondered what it would have been like had he studied law or accountancy rather than theology which provided him with few material pleasures and fewer philosophical answers. Still, he

194

didn't do so badly he supposed. Some priests were not so respected or well cared for by their parishioners and he was grateful for that which God had provided for him.

Saunière sometimes (and he hesitated to use the word) *envied* friends and family whose lives had taken a very different and more comfortable direction than his own. Were they happier than he though? Perhaps, in some respects, he inwardly confessed. True, their wealth and status often caused them great consternation but there were times when Saunière would have liked to experience the love and sensuous touch of a woman and the sound of children playing happily in his home. At times such as those, when he wistfully longed for a secular existence, he would throw his energies into tending the gardens around the church. There were many attractive young women in the market that day, all of whom threw him admiring glances. He was aware that his tall, broad shouldered frame and lively engaging eyes set in a heavy jowled yet handsome face enhanced with dimpled chin and a bush of thick dark hair attracted women who dreamed of seducing him. His independent spirit and strong personality radiated like the feathers of a peacock as he strode purposefully through the village. Although he wasn't beyond the occasional tryst, he planned to distract himself from sinful thought by throwing his energies into a little hunting and fishing later that evening.

Saunière waved a friendly farewell to the occupants of the square never realising the momentous nature of God's plans for him when he returned to his cheerless existence that night. His thoughts were preoccupied with sadness and frustration about the state of his Church which he regarded as an ignominious location for the worship of God. He fervently wished that he had some way of restoring it to the Glory worthy of its purpose. He entered the shack which had been cleaned for him by a loyal 18 year old local girl Marie Dénarnaud who, taken by Saunière's sturdy good looks had begun to work for him as an unofficial housekeeper much to the consternation and wagging tongues of the villagers who believed there to be more sin than saintliness attached to the growing friendship. Saunière set his bag down on the unsteady table and had barely started to empty the contents when there was a light knocking on his door. He found Marie outside, flushed and yes, radiant even, breathless in her excitement to see him. She held out her hand in which she was clutching a sealed envelope.

"For you Monsieur Le Curé!" she smiled engagingly. "I was working in Couiza today and I collected the mail for the village. This one arrived for you." Marie for now combined her housekeeping duties for Saunière with her job as a bonnet maker in the town.

Saunière visibly appreciated the healthy and vital countenance of the young woman before him and realising that perhaps he stared at her a moment too long, gathered himself and beckoned her inside, a frisson of excitement passing between them when his hand brushed hers as he grasped the letter from her. He motioned her to sit for a moment to gather herself from the uphill walk she had just completed on his behalf and offered her a glass of the precious wine he had procured earlier that day. She accepted gratefully and silently watched him as he first scrutinised the envelope then carefully opened it. The frown of concentration on his face turned swiftly to a broad grin when he had finished reading.

Saunière's hands shook as he poured himself a generous glass of wine and sat down next to Marie who was looking at him expectantly. He laughed; a joyous, glorious sound and not one that Marie had heard in his company before. He leaned over the table and grasped her two hands that were perched demurely upon it.

196

"Marie, you have brought me the greatest of good news today and for that I cannot thank you enough. Now, do you like your work making bonnets?" he asked.

Confused and non plussed, Marie looked at the priest as though he had taken leave of his senses.

"Why, it pays me a wage Monsieur Le Curé although it is intricate and tiring. The travel to Couiza is often difficult too. Especially in the winter."

"Then your days of bonnet making are over my dear," he replied enigmatically. "If you wish it to be so. Marie, will you be my housekeeper on a more permanent basis?"

Marie's chin dropped in shock at the Curé's question.

"Well I should like it to be so; more than anything else," she assured him. "But, with the greatest of respect I need the money that my job brings."

Saunière chuckled. "Don't worry your pretty little head about that Marie. I shall match whatever you earn now." Marie flushed even more at the compliment but didn't know what to say. How could he possibly pay her when he could barely afford to eat and lived in this ramshackle hut? Saunière supplied her with the answer.

"You see this letter, Marie?" She nodded; of course. Hadn't she been the one to bring it to him?

"A very generous benefactor, my predecessor no less, Abbé Le Pons, now sadly deceased, has left 600 Francs to the Church God bless his soul! I can begin to repair the Church and the Presbytery. In good time, you can even become my live in housekeeper!"

Marie was shocked and delighted. She longed to be close to this man with his profound good looks and imposing spiritual aloofness. There was indeed something other worldly and compelling about him. She could not refuse and decided to trust in God that her decision would be the right one.

Shortly afterwards, Saunière engaged local tradesmen and the most urgent repairs were completed. Masses were no

197

longer carried out with the rain falling on the worshippers and at last, the Presbytery was made into something of a residence, albeit still decrepit for the Curé and his housekeeper.

Once begun, Saunière developed an obsession for improving the Church and although the funds were soon exhausted, he was determined to continue with the transformation. Somehow, he managed to persuade the Municipality to lend him a further 1400 francs and work started in earnest in 1891.

Saunière decided that the High Altar should be the starting point for the works and engaged two masons to undertake the work. Saunière himself supervised and joined the men, hitching his cassock higher in his belt to facilitate movement. He was a great scholar having taught himself Latin, Greek and a little Hebrew during the leaner years and the Curé was fascinated with history of his Parish and concerned to preserve the ancient artefacts embedded in the Church itself. The High Altar lay upon two ancient pillars created by the Visigoths, a Germanic tribe that had flourished and migrated under the Roman Empire and settled in these parts. Carvings and hieroglyphs adorned the pillars which Saunière couldn't help but study with interest, slowing the work to accommodate his fascination. Before they could evaluate the restoration work, the stone altar table had to be removed. Carefully, the three men strained and stretched to grasp the heavy slab. Eventually, it was lifted and carefully placed on the floor. Saunière was busily inspecting it when he heard a gasp from the workmen still perched above and now scrutinising the pillars.

"What is it? What have you seen? Saunière enquired, clambering up to see what had caught the attention of the two masons.

"Seems to be something inside one of the pillars, Monsieur Le Curé," Babou the mason replied scratching his

198

head. Reaching down inside the pillar, Babou produced a handful of dried fern.

"Is that it?" asked Saunière. "Just dried fern?"

"No, no. There's something else, I just can't quite reach."

"Let me look," Saunière gently ushered Babou aside afraid that he might damage something of historical significance. He could just see the outline of something cylindrical within the pillar. Thinking quickly, Saunière despatched the two masons off for lunch; he wanted to explore the contents of the pillar himself and savour whatever knowledge may be hidden inside. Bending over the pillar, he stretched his arm down inside and pulled up the cylinder. He looked down again and saw that there were two more similar containers which he quickly retrieved from their resting place. He sat down and inspected the cylinders closely. They were wooden and sealed over with wax. Working quickly, he released the seal of the first container and peered inside. There he saw a rolled up parchment. Concerned that exposure to the air might damage them, he decided to take the three cylinders inside to the newly repaired Presbytery where he could more carefully remove the parchments and lay them out on the table. He barely acknowledged Marie as he rushed past her in the passage leading to the kitchen. She prepared some lunch for him but was surprised to find that the study door was locked. His voice came from inside.

"Leave me a while Marie. I have some important work to do. I will call for you when I am done here." It was unlike her Bérenger to refuse her admission. The pair had become close and she his most trusted confidante in recent months. To say that they were now just friends would have been to deny the moments when their relationship had deepened beyond what would be acceptable between a priest and a woman. They were content though and if discreet, their

199

relationship could flourish with no more than speculation from the outside world; something that bothered neither of them.

Saunière's thoughts were occupied with something other than his burgeoning though illicit relationship with Marie. Something seemed to grip him; an inner voice, urging him to discover the contents of the box for they would change his life. The voice was insistent and unrelenting in its promise that he was on the verge of something life changing and momentous.

Saunière took the cylinders into his still Spartan study and laid it reverently on the wooden table which he had covered in paper. He carefully took a knife around the lid, loosening the aged wax seals on each cylinder. Inside each was a similar parchment to the first. Fearing they would simply disintegrate on exposure to the air, he gingerly pulled them between thumb and forefinger one by one from their containers. The smell of earth and damp was overpowering, reminding him of a burial ceremony next to the newly excavated grave on a dank and miserable day. He shivered slightly fearing the curse of age old artefacts. He unfurled and smoothed out the first parchment. It was covered in writing but difficult to decipher on a first reading. Absorbed now however, Saunière's classical education encompassing Latin and old French served him well as he studied the scrolls, one by one, his breath held, his eyes widening as he realised the magnitude of the secrets they imparted. He immediately recognised their importance although it would take him nearly two years to fully decipher them but more significantly, his hands shaking as he read them, he recognised the potentially disastrous impact they would have on his own Church and the many organisations affiliated to it.

Rennes-le-Château was the site of horrific massacres in the 14th century when the Cathars who had occupied the area were murdered at the hands of the Church of Rome and the monarchy. The Knights Templar, a secretive order of Christ's soldiers and crusaders were also tortured and massacred in the area by Pope Clement V and King Philippe IV who mistrusted their secretive organisation and desired their infinite wealth. In fact both the Cathars and Knights Templar were said to have held untold wealth and as Saunière read through the parchments he began to understand why they had died so violently.

The Cathars, he knew, were said to be the guardians of a secret so sacred that it would change the political, monarchical and religious beliefs of the world. He had read of their Judaic origins and descent from the Merovingian Kings whom it was said, had issued direct from the Royal Dynasty of Kings David and Solomon and had ruled France in AD350-750. Of course tales of the secret were all myth and conjecture, never taken very seriously by him or other scholars. But now, as Saunière avidly studied and translated the parchments, they contained what appeared to be compelling evidence of the Merovingian bloodline from David and Solomon having continued in France. As he read on, he discovered that the parchments had apparently arrived in France after Jewish militants were executed in Rome during the 7th century. They referred to the Church of Rome plundering the Ark of the Covenant when the treasures within were removed to Rome including ancient parchments, gold, silver and jewels and texts. Later stolen by the Visigoths, they eventually found their way into the care of the Cathars and later the Knights Templar, who it was said, held the secret of the Judaic bloodline and, most importantly, of Jesus Christ himself.

Taking stock for a moment, Saunière put all he had read together. So, the Merovingians, it appeared were the direct descendants of David and Solomon and ultimately, of Jesus Christ. This meant that the true French Royal bloodline were the direct descendants of Christ. He continued reading the third parchment which, to his astonishment announced that this very potent bloodline continued and provided

201

evidence that any descendants of the Merovingians would have a claim to both the thrones of France and Britain, should they be traceable. His translation of the third parchment suggested that the Merovingian bloodline, the relations of Christ, should be restored once the secret was revealed. Saunière drew a deep breath, his hands trembling. What was he to do with these texts which seemed to provide evidence that perhaps the European monarchs, most of whom were interrelated, may not be the true heirs to the thrones they occupied. Moreover, what did this mean for his Church which had effectively promoted the idea of Christ's death on the cross without family or children as a supernatural and omnipotent being, the Son of God? These parchments suggested that he was a mere man although a true King of Israel descending from the Houses of David and Solomon whose bloodline and right to the thrones continued through the Merovingian Kings. The reason for their massacre had become both explicable and chilling. The Church, Monarch and others who benefited from the mythical version of Christ stood to lose everything if this secret was exposed.

Over the coming days, Saunière pondered his find and was surprised to receive a visit from the Mayor who'd got wind of rumours emanating from the masons that something had been found. He considered it his duty to point out to Monsieur Le Curé that if there was something of importance discovered it should be handed over to him for the village archive.

Saunière however was a wily fox and appeased the Mayor with the suggestion he should sell the parchments to antiques collectors in the City where they would undoubtedly fetch enough to repay the loan for the Church refurbishments.

"Very well," agreed the Mayor, "but I want faithful copies of these made before they leave the parish.

"I undertake to make the copies myself Monsieur Le Maire," Saunière agreed.

In fact, it took Saunière a full two years poring over the manuscripts to fully decipher them and the many secrets they held. When he felt the time was right, he paid a visit to the Bishop of Carcassonne who sat wide eyed as Saunière explained the historical significance of the parchments but was careful not to reveal everything he had discovered. That was a secret he shared only with one person. His faithful housekeeper, Marie. They were now inextricably entwined, not just with the secret of their relationship which she guarded jealously, but also with that of the parchments that would change their lives forever. Both he and she knew that if nothing else kept them fixed together, the contents of the parchments surely would. He could never risk her leaving him, nor she of upsetting him if they were to benefit from the secrets.

The Bishop of Carcassonne considered his words carefully so that the meaning could not be lost on the wily Saunière.

"Bérenger ," he began slowly, "if what you say is true, we cannot sell these parchments. They could destroy the Church and the Monarchy if you are correct. Now, for the good of all, will you be happy to release them into my care and allow some experts in Paris study them?"

"Monseigneur, I would of course wish to accede to your request but I have already promised the *Maire* in Rennes-le-Château that I will sell them in order to repay the loans made to me for the refurbishment of the Church."

The Bishop's eyes narrowed, momentary fear evident in his gaze.

"How much have you told the *Maire?*"

Saunière smiled. "Not much. He knows they have great historical significance and probably great value but I have been careful not to reveal anything which might damage the Church."

Relief spread across the Bishop's face.

"In that case my boy, you will tell him that you have simply kept your side of the bargain and sold them to an antique collector. I shall ensure that you have enough money to repay the debt and more to continue with your work on the refurbishments. Now, is it a deal?"

Saunière considered his position for a moment before giving his answer.

"I feel troubled that I must tell a lie before God in such a covert fashion but I have no choice than to accede to your wishes."

The Bishop visibly relaxed. "Fear not my son. You are absolved for the lie. After all, it is to protect God and therefore I take it upon my shoulders to give you absolution in this matter."

And so it was that Saunière, somewhat richer for his meeting with the Bishop was hastily despatched to Paris to meet with the Director of St Sulpice, where the parchments were deposited into his safe keeping for scrutiny by experts. In Paris, Saunière had the time of his life when he was royally entertained by the Abbé's nephew, an expert in language, palaeography and cryptography. His own star would rise later in life when he would study the occult and secret societies at the Vatican itself.

In the meantime, Saunière made the most of his excursion to Paris where he indulged himself in the purchase of paintings for his Church and began a liaison with a beautiful and talented opera singer Emma Calve. He enjoyed the high life to which he'd been introduced and safe in the knowledge that this was a life he could maintain thanks to the parchments, he eventually returned without them to his little parish in Rennes-le-Château .The *Maire* was delighted to receive repayment of the loan with interest.

The villagers noted that Saunière became ever more mysterious as work continued in bringing the Church to a glory it has never before seen. The workmen were suspicious when

204

one day the priest ordered them to dig a hole in the Church floor to a depth of one metre.

"Monsieur Le Curé!" one exclaimed as he struck a pot full of shining tokens. Saunière appeared unsurprised at the find and, delving into the hole, he pulled them out for inspection.

"They are nothing," he assured the workmen. "Just worthless artefacts of a long past time. Now, why don't you leave it for today. I think we have done enough here gentlemen." The workmen were dismissed and Saunière ushered them from the Church, watching as they retreated towards their village homes. Once satisfied they were gone, he excitedly returned to the excavation inside the Church and worked like a man obsessed uncovering yet more treasures below, just as he knew he would.

Fascination and suspicion surrounded the priest and his housekeeper as the villagers noted strange goings on. For a while they would leave the Church on a daily basis, ostensibly to gather stones along the plateau which was, he told observers, for the purpose of building a grotto and 'prettifying the garden.'

Like some ghoul, Saunière upset the village by clandestinely shutting himself in the cemetery. When he emerged it was discovered that he'd moved and defaced the inscriptions on two of the tombstones.

Saunière was summoned to the Bishop of Carcassonne who, puce with rage demanded to know the reason behind the Curé's distinctly odd behaviour.

"What in Heaven's name d'you think you're doing? We've had multiple complaints that you've been disturbing sacred graves in the cemetery. What am I to tell your parishioners?"

Saunière was calm and assured.

"Monseigneur, the answer is quite simple. The cemetery is full at Rennes-le-Château and I have no room to bury the dead. I was simply removing the bones contained in the most ancient of graves to create an ossuary where they may be respectfully contained thus leaving room for the newly dead. I am sorry if this has caused some consternation."

"Consternation?" the Monseigneur spluttered. "They think you are committing necromancy or some such practice up there. Now, I demand that you leave the dead to rest in peace. Your domain stops at the gates of the cemetery and you have no right to remove the bones."

Saunière nodded his acquiescence and took his leave. The Monseigneur shook his head in disbelief. Whatever was his Curé up to? He must have taken leave of his senses.

Quite mysteriously, the work continued on the Church amidst lengthy disappearances of the Priest who covered his tracks with the aid of the faithful Marie by leaving pre-signed letters of response to be sent to anyone contacting him during his absence thus giving the impression he was still in his parish. Unbelievably, the ploy worked leaving the priest to travel far and wide. The extravagance of the works and the apparent ascent in Saunière's wealth and lifestyle caused bewilderment to all who observed it. Meanwhile, the Church was transformed as he brought in artisans from Toulouse and Bordeaux to create art, sculptures and stained glass windows.

The Bishop was intrigued to receive an invitation to inaugurate the newly completed works at the Church of Rennes-le-Château .

"Monseigneur, welcome!" Saunière greeted him warmly. "Now, after we have a glass of wine, I shall escort you to my proudest achievement." The men sat cordially chatting for a while before heading into the Church. The Bishop took in the sumptuous surroundings of the Presbytery, now a far cry from its previous condition. He could not fathom how Saunière had managed it on the loan and the few extra francs he had been paid for the parchments. He must have a wondrous way with money, the Bishop thought wryly. Like the loaves and the fishes, he thought.

The two men reached the entrance to the Church but instead of filling him with joy, the Monseigneur recoiled in horror as he saw the words above the door, *"Terribilis est locus iste,"* which he instantly recognised as Jacob's cry at Bethel, *'Yes this place is indeed terrible."* His revulsion and unease exacerbated as he surveyed the vulgar and hideous imagery presented to him as adornments of this place of worship, the worst of which was a life sized Devil poised in the entrance which as some kind of Christian oxymoron held the Holy Water Stoup. Saunière was oblivious to the distaste and discomfort of his colleague and continued happily with the tour. The Monseigneur was more than happy to leave the Church and wondered whether the younger man had been possessed by evil. It would certainly explain his sudden and unexplained riches.

Over the years, Saunière's extravagance and spending remained unabated. He bought more land and built an impressive villa, *'Bethania'*. Later he constructed an orangerie complete with park and water features. A library was created and his house was filled with antiques; the gardens populated with exotic birds, fish, dogs and even monkeys. He mixed with the nobility and artists of all descriptions who stayed at *Bethania* in luxury.

Tongues in the village speculated that Saunière had either been smiled upon by God or was in league with the Devil. No-one could be sure which, for even as the priest spent on everything from finery to the completely bizarre for his own comfort, he also donated huge sums of money annually to the village coffers and provided generous gifts of thousands of Francs to the poor families of the parish. His renovations, more folly than beautiful edifice, created the impression of a disturbed if brilliant mind. And, after all, if the Church itself accepted Saunière's ostentatious lifestyle and

207

questionable relationship with a mere servant girl, who were the parishioners to comment? He didn't actually cause them any harm. In fact, he was seen as very much 'one of them' in most circles. A man's man whose generosity was clear if the source of his funds was less so.

It was 1902 when the Church finally tried to curtail Saunière and draw him back into the fold. A new Bishop, Monseigneur Beausejour was suspicious of the wayward priest and over the years not only sent him on retreat in a monastery to remind him of his holy vows but some years later offered him a new parish.

"You won't go, will you Bérenger ?" Marie worriedly asked him as yet another letter demanding Saunière's attendance with the Bishop arrived.

"Of course not *Ma Cherie,* I could never leave Rennes-le-Château; as you of all people well know." Marie smiled. She was nonetheless worried that her beloved companion would be unable to resist the demands of the Church.

"Speak to the Doctor and ask him to provide me with another medical certificate. We can delay his demands a while longer yet."

Eventually however, Saunière, despite best efforts, could not delay the inevitable summons to the Bishop in Carcassonne. He arrived to a frosty welcome and without any preamble an enraged Monseigneur Beausejour launched into his tirade.

"Saunière, we meet at last," he observed humourlessly. "Don't think I am fooled by your constant excuses to avoid this discussion. Now, I must ask you to fully account for your unprecedented wealth. If no-one else in this Church will ask the questions, I certainly will."

Saunière bowed his head respectfully and with great composure responded to his Bishop.

"Why Monseigneur, I am afraid that I cannot divulge the information you request. You see the money comes from

208

donations from those I have absolved from sin. It was given to me personally in gratitude for the solace I have brought these people. As such, I am not accountable to you either from whom it comes or for what purpose the money was given. It is, as you will understand of a highly confidential nature between the sinner and his priest."

The Monseigneur reddened as anger overtook him. He would not be made a fool of by this philandering, profligate upstart! But the wind was taken from his sails as Saunière continued.

"If I may also respectfully remind your Honour, I am saddened by the nature of your insinuations especially given that I have lovingly restored the Church and extended its property at my personal expense. I have not made it publicly known but I intend for it eventually to become a retirement home for priests."

"In the name of the Lord God," the Monseigneur erupted. "Enough of this! You will provide me with a full and complete set of accounts showing your income and expenditure over the period of concern. Make sure it is with me within the week. Now I bid you good day." Saunière was summarily dismissed. He was angry at the intrusion but largely untroubled by the Bishop's demands. In the following days, he and Marie created a set of accounts, but one which displayed only 20% of the true figures pertaining to his financial affairs.

One morning Saunière received notification in his mail that he was to be prosecuted for simony, trafficking in the masses.

"Can you believe it Marie? That man will stop at nothing to persecute me. Look at this!"

Marie was visibly upset by the summons for prosecution.

"But what does it mean exactly?" she asked.

"It means they believe that I am charging the faithful for masses that I have not said. It isn't strictly illegal and to be honest, most priests do supplement their income by it but as you and I know Marie, it is not something I have ever committed. They are determined to find something on me though and it is troublesome if nothing more. They won't find any evidence or advertisement from me to do masses."

"Will you attend the Court?"

Saunière shook his head. No. He would not dignify them with his presence and he was thus tried in absentia. He was declared guilty and *suspens a divinis;* forbidden to say mass or administer the sacraments. But Saunière was made of stern stuff and successfully appealed against the decision. His victory was short lived however when the Bishop of Carcassone further appealed and an interdict was issued ordering Saunière to hand over his Church to a new Abbé .

The Bishop was near apoplexy to find that he was once again outwitted by Saunière however. He had, unbeknown to the Bishop, taken advantage of the separation of the Church from the State in 1905 meaning that the Church and its buildings had become the property of the local community. At that time, Saunière had staked his claim to the property having secured it in Marie's name from the community. The new Curé of the parish now had nowhere to live and such was the erstwhile priest's popularity that the parishioners refused to attend mass with their new priest preferring instead to attend Saunière's chapel adjacent to the Villa Bethania. Had he not been a religious man, Saunière might have relished the last laugh.

He and Marie continued to live with their mysterious wealth for a few more years until World War 1 curtailed Saunière's ability to travel which appeared to all to have been a significant detail in his accumulation of money. The legal battles had cost him dear and although the priest suffered some inconvenience, he was confident that the source of his wealth would soon yield for him again and he committed himself to several new projects including a new Chapel, library and the provision of running water for the village.

Before Saunière could complete his plans he collapsed from a stroke on 17th January 1917.

"Ah Marie," Abbé Rivière greeted his friend's housekeeper and confidante warmly. She was pale and distraught. "How is he?"

Her grief rendered her barely capable of forming a sentence.

"Not good Monsieur Le Curé." She wiped away her tears with a handkerchief and sobbed uncontrollably.

"He is in here?" the Curé asked.

Marie nodded and gestured for him to enter. Abbé Rivière was shocked as he saw the once strong and vital man helpless and incapable of movement. Nevertheless, Saunière seemed to recognise him and managed to say a few words. What was said remained a secret between them but the man left wordlessly and in such a rush he even forgot to say farewell to the sorrowful Marie. It was later said that the man never smiled again, so shaken was he by the final words of his friend Saunière and left without administering the last rites. Saunière's soul departed his body on 22nd January without the preparation of his Church, a matter unprecedented in the Catholic faith.

Upon his death, those with an interest were perturbed to find that Saunière had died penniless, owning nothing. Everything had been transferred into the name of Marie Dénarnaud long ago.

211

Chapter 19 – Of Demons and Devils

Hal listened attentively, barely managing to keep up with the twists and turns of the tale unfolding before him and trying in vain to work out what any of this had to do with Tasia and the late Princess Diana.

Hal frowned quizzically as he pondered the latest revelations from Stergios. Stergios, his elbows resting comfortably on the checked tablecloth gripped the jug of Mythos in both hands, thumbs slipped through the handle. He explained that he had studied history at University specialising in French mediaeval studies. Later though, as he became involved in the British intelligence services his involvement with the Merovingian parchments had become far more than simply academic interest.

Finally breaking the contemplative silence, Hal said, "So let me get this straight. This priest, Saunière, finds these parchments and, correct me if I've misunderstood, they hold a genealogical secret which says that the descendants, the children of Jesus Christ were exiled in France and became the Merovingian Kings?"

"That's correct Hal. Very good. In other words, the true heirs to the thrones of France, and thereafter through family blood ties also the throne of Great Britain, would be those who descend from the Merovingians and carry the Judaic bloodline of Christ."

Hal exhaled as he tried to follow the story.

"And we're saying that because Jesus descended from original royalty, the Houses of David and Solomon, only the Merovingian blood line is therefore true royalty now in Europe."

Stergios smiled, nodding.

"Again, correct. True royalty is absolute power. And now perhaps you understand why royalty achieves the reverence it still holds today. Since time immemorial, the monarchy has been held in awe as thought they have some sort of God given power which makes us hold them in great esteem. Of course today, most people just accept that they are in some way powerful families without really knowing the foundation of that belief. The truth is that the few who have been privy to the secrets through the centuries have ensured the Monarchy's continued demi-god status for precisely the reason that there is a blood link to the 'Son of God'. What the common people do not understand is that although there may be a diluted link back to Jesus Christ in the European Monarchs, it has been deliberately modified and blended by heredity and that there are true descendants with an even stronger link to the Merovingians who escaped the massacre and continued the bloodline.

To have that blood link is a symbol of power in the highest proportions and those who surround and protect that power derive great influence themselves."

"What exactly do you mean when you say the bloodline is 'diluted' and 'deliberately modified'?" Hal asked, perplexed.

"We'll come to that but let's just say that when the secret bloodline was discovered by powerful organisations who had their own brand of royalty, they felt it was in their interests to intermingle the bloodline with those who were not of the Judaic origin and therefore diluted the connection between the dynasties of David and Solomon and thus Jesus Christ. It allowed these outsiders to maintain the influence they enjoyed with their selected royals whilst introducing the mystique of the Judaic royal bloodline. The 'Establishment' and the existing 'monarchs' were thus able to retain their powers and influence whilst still able to claim that in some sense they were descended from the true royalty of Christ. Now, what do you think would happen if the truth came out that there were truer pretenders to the European monarchies than those who enjoy those privileges today?"

Hal, still grappling with all that he was learning could only surmise the possible effects of that secret.

"I guess that those pretenders could usurp the existing monarchy and thus upset the existing Establishment and the benefits they achieve from their selected royals."

Stergios nodded in agreement.

"Quite so Hal. Not only that but the supplanted true monarchs may not agree with the system of government or constitution as it works today. They might want to change things, perhaps. As the Merovingians preferred, they may wish to work for the greater good of the people they rule rather than protect the self interest which pervades monarchy and establishment today."

Hal was beginning to understand. The Establishment of Europe would be keen to suppress the contents of the parchments and would probably do so at any cost to protect their own manufactured royals. To do otherwise would cause nothing less than possible revolution and destruction of their comfortable world.

"So Stergios, I'm guessing that Saunière benefited from his new friends in high places in return for his silence and the handing over of those parchments?"

"Exactly. Now you are seeing the bigger picture. His rise to fortune and popularity was rapid and unprecedented. He was fortunate really. It could just as easily have led to his demise in today's world. Of course, there were also rumours that his wealth was increased by the discovery of treasures hidden in the area which were also documented in the parchments."

Hal still wasn't sure exactly how Jesus Christ fitted into all of this. He wasn't a particularly religious man and all his knowledge had come from Sunday school. Jesus, he had understood was a supernatural being, the Son of God who died for us on the cross. The Bible, to his knowledge, hadn't

214

included a wife or children had they? Stergios looked surprised.

"You haven't read the book or seen the movie of the 'Da Vinci Code' then Hal?"

Hal admitted that he had of course read the book but had taken it as pure fiction. Stergios conceded that the book had indeed been fiction but that it had been based on various hypotheses contained in several other works. He explained to Hal that many researchers had investigated the history and agreed that there was overwhelming evidence to suggest that Christ had indeed taken a wife, most probably Mary Magdalene (who incidentally had not been a prostitute as advocated by biblical stories but a member of the Royal House of Benjamin) and that they had produced children. Following Christ's death the historians agreed that the family had fled to Europe where they settled. The children had married into the families of other exiled Jews who became the Judaic Teutons and the Merovingian Dynasty was formed with the royal bloodline of David and Solomon secured. He explained that it was the bloodline itself which was the Holy Grail referred to and sought after by so many in mediaeval history. The searches were to find the true bloodline.

"It's the secret that the Knights Templar and the massacred Cathars knew. As guardians of the secret and the riches from the Ark of the Covenant they accumulated great wealth to which their enemies aspired."

Wow, thought Hal. He'd never considered the biblical stories to have much real relevance; just a belief system based on a book which he'd never considered would be a reliable historical source. But to now consider the possibility that Jesus Christ had continuing political and economic relevance was profound stuff. Hal voiced his thoughts to Stergios.

"Yes, it's true Hal, I think many people do have an understanding that Jesus was a real person but he is

215

generally thought of as a supernatural being with omniscient powers. But here is the truth – cover your ears now if it will destroy your illusions or faith. Research has established that yes, Jesus Christ was very real and he was undoubtedly a *de jure* king of Israel. In truth he was a freedom fighter who together with the Zealots tried to oust out the Romans to reclaim the throne which they had passed to the Herods. Jesus was fighting for his right to rule Israel as a bloodline monarch; he was fighting to remove the usurper Herod Kings and for that he was crucified. Now, consider the Bible stories. What the historians have found is that much of the New Testament is simply written in code which creates a new persona for Jesus as a prophet, a mystic and spiritual leader. The Roman Catholic Church, seized on this to lend itself, as the instrument and representatives of God and Jesus Christ the idea that it assumed higher powers. Thus it created a belief system designed to maintain public order and to keep citizens subservient and willing to carry out its bidding. Think of the power that the Church has over its members Hal. Think of the money the Church can generate simply by perpetuating the myth that we are all governed and watched over by an all powerful and sometimes vengeful God. It's much more powerful than worshipping a mere mortal freedom fighter who wanted to be restored to the throne. Think also of the power the church has had over monarchs throughout the centuries; remember, the British Monarch is the Head of the Church of England and defender of the faith. This is a very powerful alliance between monarchy and church."

"So are we saying that Christ wasn't the Son of God and that he didn't have all the powers that we attribute to him as a prophet, a healer, miracle worker?"

"Ah, now that is more difficult to say for sure. We know that the Merovingian Dynasty, descended from Christ's children were said to have healing powers and knowledge of the esoteric arts. Jesus may well have been an extremely

216

wise man and philanthropist and who knows, there are many people who claim to have supernatural powers. Who is to say that he did not and that those powers continued through the Merovingian Dynasty? I should say that anything is possible Hal. The Church of Rome took those powers very seriously and for that reason they sought the destruction of the Merovingians and the secret of their powers for themselves. It all added to their own strength you see and to the omnipotence of God and His Son."

Hal, though perplexed and having difficulty absorbing all that Stergios was telling him was nevertheless fascinated by all that he was hearing. He was grappling however with the relevance of all this and how it was significant to Tasia's story, or for that matter, Princess Diana. His head spinning, he ordered another beer and the two men paused for some food and refuge in their own thoughts.

"Have you heard how Tasia is?" Hal enquired, changing the subject for a moment as they tucked into a traditional Greek Plate of Dolmades, Tzatziki, Aubergine Salad and various other appetisers. Stergios nodded sadly.

"Yes, Kyle called. She's very weak but determined to survive until her mission is complete. That is why we must proceed as quickly as possible Hal. She is waiting until we finish our work but deep down she wants an end so that she may find peace. She's had enough and it is her time. We all know this."

Hal shook his head sadly. Although he hadn't known her for long or particularly well, he liked this strange woman despite the mysteries surrounding her. She was very human; she loved a joke and her warmth and caring shone through regardless of the rather selfish and self absorbed past she had confessed in their meetings. She and Hal had become firm friends and no matter what his beliefs were, he wanted to help her and wished that she was in good health. It saddened him

217

to think that another wonderful woman in his life was going to leave a void in his heart.

"Kyle must be devastated," Hal commented sadly. Stergios nodded in agreement and empathy.

"Yes, but he knows how it is and he is prepared. He also knows that it is not the end. It is never the end. He draws comfort from that."

"You mean in a Christian, 'life everlasting' sort of way? The way you seem to be actually debunking? Hal queried.

"In, let us say, a *spiritual* way. Perhaps the *Merovingian* way."

Hal's head was pounding. The heat, the alcohol, the sheer depth of conversation was too much for his brain to process.

"OK so let's go on," he said finally, if a little reluctantly. "To sum up now, we have original royalty, the David and Solomon bloodline from Israel. The Herods have been put in power by the Romans and Jesus, who may or may not have supernatural powers, but definitely royal connections, is dead. He was married and the royal line was continued through Europe through the Merovingians until again, they were seen off by the Holy Roman Church because they held the secret and the true claim to the thrones of Europe."

"Yes, just about right in a nutshell Hal. Well done. You're following it well." Stergios explained that the importance of this information was in the maintenance of power and many organisations were attracted to the source of that power, the Church. During his time as an undergraduate and postgraduate student at Oxford he had begun to consider the political and economic consequences of such power. When he was finally recruited to the intelligence services, he saw at first hand the consequences and benefits of the power which, alongside many others, had sickened him to the core. It all flew in the face of democracy and benefit for the common man.

218

"I'm not quite clear on how the bloodline was kept pure when Jesus' family married other Europeans. You said that the monarchs of Europe carry a diluted form of the bloodline now. What did you mean?" asked Hal. As usual, he kept his digital recorder running but also kept his trusty shorthand notebook next to him."

"Thousands of Jews were exiled during this period. Many married the Teutons, a Germanic tribe of the period. They settled in France and Germany. When the ancient Royal bloodline arrived, they were welcomed by the Judaic Teutons. Their intermarriage preserved and strengthened the Judaic Royal line. The present line of monarchs were cultivated by mingling part of the Judaic royal blood with blood of no Judaic origin whatsoever. Thus the line became diluted in the current European monarchs."

Stergios waited whilst Hal, frowning, made some notes on his pad. Eventually, pencil between his teeth, he nodded and Stergios continued.

"The Merovingians were, unlike other Royal dynasties known for their liberal views and their distaste for warmongering Hal. They were an enlightened people who embraced tolerance in all things including politics and religion. They espoused knowledge, education and understanding as the antidote to war. Their enlightenment however was regarded with awe and suspicion, not least because they were also known as the Sorcerer Kings; adepts of the occult, practitioners of magic. In effect, they were pagans, polytheistic in the worship of many deities, believing that divinity is found in nature and in the mind. Quite the contrary to the traditional views of Christianity or Judaism in fact. Remember, despite their being descended from Christ, it was not the Merovingians who created Christianity. That was the Church itself. It was thought that Merovingian blood had healing powers and they often practised the laying on of hands; it was widely believed that their robes held the power

219

to cure the ailing and create miracles for the hopeless. You can see where the ideas for the Christian religion and Christ's attributes came from."

"They must have been revered for their purported mystical powers," Hal added.

"Indeed, but sadly, as with anyone who has a tendency towards altruism, kindness and rationalism, it is seen as weakness. Because of a reluctance to fight back, they often fall prey to less worthy influences; influences who seek to use them for their own political and financial advantage. It was just so with the Merovingians who were largely destroyed by the Holy Roman Empire who took their occult powers very seriously and wanted to use the bloodline for their own purposes. The Holy Grail is what we now know to be the bloodline itself; the thing that was so highly sought and prized by the Knights Templar and many other secret organisations including the Freemasons."

Stergios explained that the Holy Grail, just as many modern researchers had agreed was not a tangible 'thing' as was widely believed. It wasn't a cup or a dish or indeed any vessel which many thought had contained the blood of Christ. It wasn't a relic at all but a purely figurative vessel of Christ's blood; a metaphor for those who perpetuated and physically carried Christ's bloodline. The Merovingians in other words.

"The Grail is derived from old French, *San graal* or *Sang Real.* The former means Holy Grail, the latter, Holy or Royal Blood which, as we have seen carried on from the Diaspora, the Jewish Exodus and continuing through the descendants of Christ in Europe."

"Wow, it's almost too much to take in," Hal shook his head in disbelief. "How sure are you of all this?"

"I have seen the parchments Hal. I have been privy to their scientific and academic scrutiny and I have been part of the conspiracy to protect the information contained in them."

"You've actually *seen* them? How? What happened to them after Saunière discovered them?

"Let us say that Saunière's rise to fame and fortune was stellar Hal. Those documents were sought after by just about every secret service in the World because they would, if ever released into the public domain, destroy the power base created through networks of Masonic, religious and corporate organisations who have worked in tandem with the Church and monarchy to perpetuate the Christian ideology and suppress the true bloodline. All public order is based on our religion in the west and much wealth and power is derived from it. Imagine what would happen if the truth was exposed and the dismay of the followers who have been duped for so long. Our society would potentially implode and the established order may be annihilated. Perhaps now you see why the intelligence services have such an interest in protection of those secrets?"

For Hal, it was all indeed beginning to make some terrible sense. He was wearying now as the sun disappeared over the horizon and a cool breeze drifted over the tavern like a portent. Stergios drained the last of his drink and regarded Hal, the intensity of his gaze boring into him.

"People have died throughout history keeping these secrets Hal," he continued. "The mystery of Rennes-le-Château didn't end with Saunière. If anything it was only just beginning. Many people have since tried to discover what it was that he and Marie Dénarnaud knew. Many were seekers of truth, others simply seekers of the wealth believed to be hidden in the village and its surrounds. We know of at least three others who died undoubtedly for stumbling upon the truth of Saunière's 'treasure', or as some would have it, 'curse'. Take for instance Fakhar Ul Islam; mysteriously died in 1967 having 'fallen' from a moving train onto the tracks. He'd been delving into the secretes of Rennes-le-Château. In 1968, Noel Corbu, the then owner of Saunière's domaine died in a horrific road accident on a quiet country road near Carcassonne. He'd bought the *domaine* from Marie Dénarnaud and made a fortune from tourists seeking the treasure in the village and nearby parts of the Languedoc region. It is believed that Marie may have imparted the secret to him on her deathbed although he always claimed she was unable to speak following a stroke and that she never revealed anything to him. Another man survived a car crash in June 1968. Monsieur Boyer, Vicar General of the Diocese of Carcassone escaped with injuries from the accident at the rather appropriately named 'Devil's Bridge'. He too had been engaged in researching the secrets and no doubt discovered more than he should have done. He resolved from that day on to discontinue his work so convinced was he that his life would always be at risk should he carry on."

Hal's eyes widened.

"There seems to be a theme here right enough," he acknowledged. "Car crashes ... Oh my God! Of course! Diana! The most famous car crash in living memory! But Stergios, are you saying this is why she died? Because she too discovered something about the secret?"

"Rewind a moment Hal. Remember, she was told she had a greater claim to the throne than the present Royal Family. Now, from what I've told you, why do you think that might have been so?"

Hal's jaw dropped as the pieces began to click together.

"You're saying that she carries the true undiluted bloodline of the Merovingians aren't you? And that's why it was so important for her to be removed and silenced?"

Stergios smiled with satisfaction.

"As you say Hal. The connections are becoming clear, *Nai?*"

"And that is the treasure of Rennes-le-Château?"

222

Stergios nodded. "Yes, although it's possible there was also tangible treasure to be had that might also have added to Saunière's everlasting riches. He was undoubtedly in the pay of influential people to remain quiet but there is also evidence that he may have come into money by other means too. It would explain the reasons for his regular journeys to various European destinations perhaps to sell the precious artefacts he came upon in his searches.

It's a fascinating village, Rennes-le-Château. Very beautiful even today but pervaded by a very strange atmosphere."

"How do you mean?" Hal asked.

"Oh it's full of New Age residents, philosophies and shops mixed with ancient superstition. Although people live there, it never quite seems inhabited or if they do, you imagine that they're a world apart. Living in another dimension even. On the one hand, it's a tourist destination with people running businesses but on the other, you never quite feel that anything is quite ordinary while you're there. Hard to explain really."

"You were saying about the treasure," Hal backtracked. Stergios considered a moment before responding.

"Mmmm, yes. Remember, Saunière had been a penniless priest, yet between the years of 1891 and 1917 he had actually spent between 15 and 24 million francs. The exact figures aren't known but certainly a calculation of the works he carried out and the activities he engaged in give us these parameters. It's quite inexplicable except that the area has been known to yield treasure in the past. Visigoth, Merovingian, perhaps even, as has been suggested, the contents of the Ark of the Covenant rumoured to have been hidden there. What we do know is that Saunière is documented as having given various gifts to poor parishioners; priceless coins, jewellery, even a chalice on one occasion. Remember, his wanderings with Marie? Ostensibly they were to find stones for the orangery."

223

Hal frowned in deep concentration. Stergios reached into the inside pocket of his jacket and pulled out a handful of photographs, some old, some more recent. He handed them to Hal who studied the broad handsome face of the man who'd been at the centre of Stergios' story. Bérenger Saunière. He looked friendly and strong willed but not particularly mysterious. Hal continued through the pictures. Some showed the steep approach of a mountain road culminating in a neatly kept shrubbery on the side of the road adorned with brightly coloured flowers and a welcoming sign with the name of the village printed on it. Others showed the village itself with shops, cafes, houses with charms and horseshoes decorating the windowsills as though warding off evil spirits. The priest's former property was depicted including the Magdalene Tower, the *domaine*, the Church, the cemetery and the garden cafe. It all looked very quaint and chocolate box beautiful to Hal. Despite the peaceful beauty of the village however, Hal had to agree that there was the suggestion of eerie menace lurking in the corners. He flicked through the photographs one by one until finally, he recoiled in horror as he came to the picture of an ugly life sized demon or devil that apparently sat inside the door of Saunière's church.

Stergios watched Hal's reaction as he scrutinised the vile statue that appeared to have no place in a church of God.

"What's with the devil?" Hal frowned. "Why would Saunière want this in his Church?"

"Some would say it was just representative of the artwork of the time. It was known to be somewhat crass, gaudy and garish. Others suggest it has much more significance."

"In what way significant?" Hal asked.

"As a map, indicative of the places at which Saunière may have found actual treasure. The priest commissioned the statue for his church; take a closer look."

224

Hal placed the picture on the table between them and Stergios pointed out various details as they pored over it.

"See here, the Devil or demon is in a seated position but he doesn't actually have a chair. Instead he is simply bent as though sitting. His right leg, here, is twisted and he rests five fingers of the left hand on his knee."

Hal looked closely and saw that the Devil's right hand held its thumb and forefinger in a circle and that the chest seemed to be misshapen or deformed. It was flat on one side, the nipple incorrectly placed.

"But what does it all mean?" Hal asked puzzled. There were no obvious clues. "How is it a map?"

"Taken together with coded journals left by Saunière, we can speculate on the symbolism. It is said that Solomon entrusted a demon, Asmodeus to guard the cave where he'd hidden his treasure. Solomon wanted to retrieve his seal but Asmodeus refused to allow him entry. The story goes that Solomon managed to drive Asmodeus out into the desert. Thus we have the first connection with Saunière alluding to the wealth of Solomon. There are myths that this treasure was now to be found in Blanchefort, an area also said to be guarded by the Devil. Other clues point to a place call 'Devil's Armchair' which is actually a nearby plateau or rock shaped like a chair."

"The seated devil then?" Hal concluded.

"Yes. Then there is a location in the region known as *Pla del la Costel,* the flat chest; another known as the 'Devil's Breast'."

"Signified by the misaligned nipple presumably?" Hal added.

"Very good. Now, between the rivers Blanque and Sals, we have a place called 'The Holy Water Stoup'."

"Which the statue supports here in the picture!" Hal was warming to the clues.

225

"Now Hal, look at the five fingers. Another nearby rock, 'Bread Rock' contains five hollows said to be the imprint of the Devil's Hand."

Hal shook his head in awe and wonderment. Where could all this possibly be going he wondered? Strange priests, spooky hilltop villages, treasure, The Devil and finally, the Death of a modern princess somehow connecting all these disparate clues together.

Stergios continued to explain.

"The placement of all these clues have been shown to correspond with the orientation of the locations I've just mentioned on the ground. Now, either Saunière genuinely knew something and was encoding the information for posterity or he was creating a diversion from the truth of how he came by his riches."

"Ah, back to the sacred bloodline of Christ and eagerness of the Church and other organisations to keep him quiet with handsome payments..." Hal mused. "But then, why didn't they just kill him?"

"Who knows? Fear that he'd already created safeguards upon his untimely demise perhaps? Maybe he was in a position to blackmail the authorities. Perhaps in that sense he was safer alive than dead to the Church and Monarchy. One odd thing though..."

"What? Asked Hal, now completely enthralled by the Saunière mystery.

"Five fingers on the devil's knee. Referred to as *Cinq Genou*. Take it a little further and we have *Saint Genou*." Stergios looked up and met Hal's questioning and intense gaze.

"Saint Genou's day is celebrated on the 17th January Hal."

It took Hall a moment, but soon it dawned on him. Of course! The day that Saunière suffered the stroke; five days before his actual death.

226

"So," Stergios continued, "foul play or natural causes? One might conclude that someone played him at his own game and arranged a symbolic death from his own cipher."

Hal had found the whole tale intriguing and resolved to visit Rennes-le-Château for himself one day soon when all this was over. He was fascinated, attracted and repelled all at the same time by the picturesque little village presided over by demons who now pervaded his thoughts. He wondered if he would survive the end of this tale.

Chapter 20 – Huntress with the Lazarus Touch

Eventually Stergios and Hal decided to call it a night and bade each other farewell after arranging to meet at Villa Artemis the following day. Hal's mind was restless and he doubted that sleep would come easily as the latest revelations spun around his mind. The information to which he'd become a party, if true, was capable of bringing death and destruction by those determined to protect the secrets. Was there any truth in what he'd been told? It certainly sounded plausible and hadn't he already felt the repercussions, the warning of things to come if he didn't leave well alone?

It was hardly surprising that Hal couldn't shake off the feeling of ominous dread as he stepped into the entrance hall of the Villa. All was quiet and still as he made his way swiftly up the stairs keeping his steps light, fearing that any creaking might awaken the bogeyman he felt lurking in every corner. Hal tried to reassure himself that it was nothing more than an overwrought imagination that was making him feel jumpy. Nevertheless, he was uneasy; the air felt heavy and his senses were screaming out to him to be wary. It wasn't just the nature of the information he now held that unnerved him; ever since he'd been here there had been a sense of unreality. Fliss felt near, Tasia was a complete enigma and the combination made him feel as though he was living in a fantasy world and just beyond was a door or portal dragging him as though towards a vortex of discovery.

He hesitated before entering the room and he felt the hairs standing up on his arms. He shivered and told himself it was probably just a reduction in temperature from the air conditioning in the Villa. Still, however, the nagging fear wouldn't leave him. He admonished himself for having an over active imagination and turned the handle cautiously, not quite understanding his reluctance to enter. Stepping gingerly

228

inside, the moon was the only source of light bathing everything in an eerie glow. As his eyes adjusted, he immediately became aware that his instincts were correct. The desk at which he worked had been disturbed and he could see in the dim light that the drawers had been opened and his belongings were strewn around the floor. His stomach sank in horror with the realisation that not only had his room been raided but his laptop which he had uncharacteristically left open on the desk was gone. Hal stood for a moment, gaping open mouthed and unsure whether to reach for the light to survey the damage or simply flee from the room and find the villa staff. He had no time to contemplate what actions to take as the door slammed violently behind him. He turned in shock to see the cause of the sudden noise and as he did so he saw the form of a tall but stocky man standing there. The figure was clothed from head to foot in black his face covered with a balaclava, only the eyes visible. In horror, he saw that the man had his arms raised above his head and in his hands was a long implement like a metal bar or a piece of wood. Before Hal was able to move aside to avoid him, a heavy blow crashed down on his head causing him to sink to his knees, stars forming before his eyes. Seconds later more blows rained down upon him which he tried to deflect by raising his arms protectively over his head. Barely conscious, he became aware of the door opening and the man running down the stairs towards the front door. Hal was dimly aware of a wet trickle running down the side of his face. Summoning strength from somewhere, he managed to pull himself up, gripping the sideboard as he did so. He felt dizzy and barely able to think but survival instinct prevailed. Staggering towards the window he was astonished by the scene playing out in the courtyard below. The black garbed figure whom he recognised as his assailant was running towards the main gates gripping his computer when suddenly, emerging from the shadows ran a young deer speeding gracefully towards

229

the retreating figure. It ran directly in front of the man causing him to trip and drop the computer. The figure, visibly shaken, tried to scramble back on his feet but as he did so, another figure, female this time, shimmering and wraith-like in the moonlight slowly and purposefully approached from the shadows. She was carrying a bow and arrow which she raised steadily before her, bringing the man into her sights. Unhurriedly, she loaded the bow and calmly took aim, drawing the string back smoothly with the determination of an assassin. Meanwhile, the black clad figure seemingly in the woman's thrall remained rooted to the spot as though in a hypnotic trance. There was a smooth whooshing sound as the arrow expertly met its destination and with horror, Hal watched as it sailed through the man's skull. As though in slow motion, the man sank to his knees emitting a howl of pain, shock and fear before falling to the ground where he remained shuddering and jerking until moments later, the death throes over, he was still. The woman lowered the bow and gazed up at Hal's window, a slow smile spreading across her lips. It was Tasia, looking for all the world as serene and beautiful as a goddess; a goddess once known as Diana. She lowered her eyes momentarily as the deer now circled her. It nuzzled its head into her and she hugged and stroked it. She turned her head back to Hal who was beginning to feel sick as a wave of cold clammy dizziness swept over him. He saw her smile and wave to him before he also fell into a deep unconscious slumber.

Hal came to with several of the household buzzing around him with warm flannels and the acrid smell of antiseptic assaulting his nostrils. At first, he was barely aware of who he was or what was happening to him. There were no memories or thoughts at all, just indistinct noise and the awareness of people around him. It was like being no-one, *Nemo*, he thought. I am nowhere. He felt as though he was just a collection of senses; of noise, of colours flashing and worse, of thudding agonising pain. Moments later, he found that he could open his eyes briefly but the brightness of the room exacerbated the pain and he quickly closed them. He didn't know where he was or what had happened. He became aware of a familiar voice. American.

"Hal? Can you hear me Dude? Speak to me if you can. Open your eyes."

His eyelids fluttered as he recognised the voice and after a few moments he was able to open them again, this time long enough to see the hazy features of Kyle bending over him.

"You're gonna be OK Hal," Kyle said reassuringly. Then, in whispered tones, "Jesus Christ Doc, he sure looks a mess." Hal heard the pragmatic reply, "He will be fine *Kyrie* Masters. It looks worse than it is. I think whoever did this was in a hurry and didn't take accurate aim, fortunately for *Kyrie* Bradbury. Once the swelling goes down, he will look a lot better. He will probably be concussed and feel rather sick and sore for a few days but I don't think there is any lasting damage. He should have an x-ray at the hospital. Perhaps we can book the helicopter for him?"

"Yeah, sure, good idea. I'll get on it now," Kyle agreed. Before he went to make the arrangements, he spoke again to Hal.

"Don't worry. We'll get you the best treatment and you'll be on your feet again in no time. We'll take you over to Chania by helicopter."

"Whaa th'fckppend?" Hal tried to speak but it came out as a thick and barely recognisable string of sounds rather than words.

"Don't try to speak. Save your strength. We'll talk once you feel stronger. Get some sleep now." Hal tried to nod but his head would barely move, weakness and pain inhibiting everything. It felt as though his head had doubled in size and was too heavy for his neck. Tired now, he fell into another

231

deep sleep where he saw the ghostly archer smiling benignly at him. From behind her, Fliss emerged and stroked his head. Her hand felt cool, comforting and familiar on his head and he nestled into her now, contented in her embrace. A happy, if tight smile formed upon his swollen and disfigured face as the pain was washed away giving him temporary respite. Kyle patted Hal's arm reassuringly and set off to make the necessary arrangements for the airlift to Chania.

Hal awoke properly the following day and found himself in a private room in the hospital. His head was pounding and he still felt like the Elephant Man as he tried to sit up. He was unaware of the person sitting next to him, unable to turn his head sufficiently to see anything except straight ahead. Even then everything was blurred and hazy. It was only when he felt a soft hand grip his own that he realised that he was not alone. Hearing the familiar soft tones, the warm smile evident in her voice, he recognised them at once.

"Well that's another fine mess you've got yourself into," Tasia said, a humorous lilt in her voice.

"Tasia?" Hal spluttered weakly. "Is that you?"

"Yes Hal, it seems we're both in rather a decrepit condition," Tasia replied.

"What happened? "

"I'm afraid we were a little lax on security back at the villa. There were security officers on the premises but without Kyle there to supervise, they weren't quite as vigilant as we'd hoped. Someone who doesn't have my best interests at heart got in and tried to steal your computer for the information stored in there. Don't worry though, he had a bit of an accident on the way out and we got it back."

As Tasia spoke flashes of the night's events came back to him; the abiding memory reawakening. Struggling to speak, his mouth and jaw groaning with stiffness and pain, he managed to form a few words.

"Accident? Tasia, you shot him with a bow and arrow. You were dressed up like the Goddess Diana; Artemis, if you prefer, and I saw you. You'd give Pocahontas a run for her money," he struggled to give a little laugh.

Tasia giggled. "Hal, I think the injuries to your head might be fuelling your imagination. "I've only tried archery a couple of times and that was with a target. I was completely useless at it. Missed every time and it was so painful afterwards with all the straining I never tried it again. Not my sort of thing I'm afraid. If it had been I might have caused a lot more damage long before this, she laughed." Her voice was soothing like smooth butter on a burn.

Hal strained his neck to see Tasia sitting to his right.

"Nope. It was you. No doubt about it. I've seen you dressed like that in the grounds before."

"Stuff and nonsense!" Tasia laughed. Your mind is making connections that aren't there," she brushed aside his protestations.

"Now Hal, we have to get you better. There isn't much time left. Now, I want you to close your eyes. I'm going to take your hand and when I do, I want you to think about your injuries healing and all the pain disappearing. You must concentrate though."

Hal wondered what on earth she was talking about this time. He laughed.

"What witchery are you practising on me now?" He managed to turn just enough to see her eyes crinkle into a warm smile. She really did look for all the world like the late Princess Diana; a bit older but just as statuesque and beautiful as he remembered her. There were subtle differences however. Her nose was smaller and the chiselled features a little fuller. Tasia looked tired and drawn as she gazed at him intently with her cobalt eyes. She was paler than when she'd been at the Villa. Her skin looked like parchment and she'd

233

lost weight. Dark circles framed her eyes. She was clearly still unwell."

"No 'witchery', Hal. Just a few holistic techniques I've learned through the years. Now, come on take my hand and hold on tight. Close your eyes."

He did as she told him. Her hand in his felt comforting. He felt her love and friendship through her touch. He concentrated on all the parts of him that hurt and he felt her hand tighten in his. Moments later he became aware of a tingling sensation, like pins and needles but not as unpleasant. Heat seemed to radiate through his body. He concentrated on his aching head and his tight swollen face. Miraculously, as the tingling continued to radiate, little electric shocks passed through him, the pain and tightness began to recede. He regained some clarity of thought as he remembered the brutal attack that had brought him here. They sat, hand in hand for several minutes, silently willing his injuries to improve. Eventually, Tasia's grip loosened. Almost immediately his movement felt easier and amazingly he was able to sit up further in the bed and turn his head so that he could see her properly. He was shocked at what he saw. Although she had looked worn out and strained a few moments before, she now appeared barely able to hold herself up. She was slumped slightly in the chair, her breathing laboured and fast.

"Tasia? Are you OK?" Hal was alarmed at her sudden deterioration. Tasia, without looking up simply nodded. "I'll be fine," she gasped. "It's just – just something that happens with healing. Energy flows from me into the other person and I have to wait until it returns," she gasped.

"Do you want me to call a nurse? Where's the call button?"

"No no," Tasia replied. "It'll all be fine. Just give me a few moments."

234

He slumped back into the pillow, acutely aware of how much better he was feeling and how much easier it was to move. Hal closed his eyes, intending to rest for just a few moments but actually fell into a deep sleep. When he awoke, he saw from the clock that it was two hours later. The pain had diminished and was all but gone. Astonished, he turned to see if Tasia was still there but the chair where she had sat was empty. He felt a little sad. Moments later a nurse bustled in with a trolley. Her eyes widened when she saw him alarming Hal.

"What is it? Is there something wrong?" he asked her in panic. She didn't respond and went running from the room calling out in Greek. His heart was thumping. Did he look that bad, he wondered?

The nurse re-entered with a man who appeared to be a Doctor. He looked equally astonished as he examined him.

"What – what's up? Why is everyone looking at me like this?" Hal ventured.

The doctor continued his examination and shook his head in disbelief. When he spoke, it was with good English.

"Well, you seem to be quite the miracle patient Mr Bradbury. How do you feel?"

"Actually, I feel fine. All the pain seems to have gone."

"And all the swelling and bruising seems to have gone as well. I've never seen anyone heal this quickly before. We were looking at around three weeks before you would begin to look normal. We took a scan of your head and there was bruising and swelling in the brain. I'm going to have you taken down for another scan so that we can see what's happening there."

Within two hours, Hal had been taken in for another CT Scan and returned to his room. The Doctor came in with the results.

"You are indeed a baffling case Mr Bradbury," he said. The haemorrhaging has stopped and the swelling is no longer

235

visible in your brain. We thought we were going to have to relieve the pressure surgically. You have been a very fortunate man. It was quite a serious condition you were in. In all my years I have never seen anything like it. You should be written about in the medical journals. There is no way you should be in this condition at this stage of your treatment. Not that I am unhappy for you Mr Bradbury, but I am as you say in English, quite baffled."

Hal's mind was reeling. Inadvertently, he voiced his thoughts.

"Tasia Artemis came in to see me earlier. She held my hand and there was this warm tingling. She said she was healing me. She really is a woman of mystery."

The Doctor looked perturbed as he listened.

"No no. You are quite wrong Mr Bradbury. That is impossible. Miss Artemis has been unconscious. She is an extremely sick lady I'm afraid. There is no possibility that she came here to see you. Sadly, there has been even more deterioration in her condition today. We really don't know at this moment how much longer she will be with us," he said sadly. "I think you were hallucinating but it appears to have done you a great deal of good. Faith can be a tremendously powerful healer in itself. Perhaps you have managed to take advantage of it."

Hal opened his mouth to protest that the Doctor was wrong and that Tasia had been sitting here as real as he. Thinking better of it though, he decided to say no more. The Doctor wrote up some notes and placed the board at the end of his bed.

"If things continue like this, it seems you will be able to leave the hospital within a day or two Mr Bradbury. Now, I suggest that you stay resting for the time being and we'll check on you again tomorrow."

Next morning Hal was finishing breakfast when Kyle and Stergios stopped by.

236

"Morning Dude! I heard you'd made a miraculous recovery. Wow! You look almost normal! That's amazing!" Kyle scrutinised Hal all over searching for the signs of his injury and finding none.

"Hey Kyle. Good to see you. Yeah, I really don't know what the hell's going on here but apparently I'm a medical mystery." He decided to confide in the two men hoping that they wouldn't look at him as though he was crazy as the Doctor had done.

"Kyle, Stergios," he began. "You have to tell me. Tasia; is she unconscious?" The two men looked sombrely and earnestly at Hal before they each pulled up a chairs on either side of him. Hal looked from one to the other.

"It's just that, well, yesterday morning, when I regained consciousness myself, she was here. Sitting in that chair where you are now Kyle."

Hal saw Stergios steal a glance at Kyle who nodded as though giving him consent to speak candidly.

"It is true Hal. She hasn't moved in almost a week. She hasn't even regained a short period of consciousness. We're not expecting her to last much longer. A lot of damage was done to her in the accident many years ago and she also did lasting damage to her organs with her eating disorder in her youth. Her body is fighting itself now."

"So how did I see her, Stergios? She was here, I swear, holding my hand and in some way – I don't know – in some way she was healing me. That's why I'm looking and feeling as I am."

Stergios nodded. "I can only ask you to have faith and understanding Hal that there are more powerful things in heaven and on earth than you can possibly contemplate. I am certain that what you say is true and that Tasia came to you in your hour of need. We weren't sure that you would make it after they found the bleeding and pressure on your brain. We

237

could have lost you in surgery. You have been blessed indeed."

"So what you're saying is that she came to me in a kind of out of body way?"

"Perhaps so. Perhaps that is the best way of describing it. She certainly couldn't have moved physically. Not only is she unconscious but she is tied up in wires and drips which are keeping her alive. She may never come round."

Hal was crestfallen to hear the news but shocked. He'd been certain that he'd felt her hand as real flesh and blood.

"What is it about Tasia?" he asked. "There are things you are not telling me."

Stergios paused a moment before answering. He sat in the chair, head bent forward, his hands clasped before looking up to meet Hal's gaze.

"She is a Merovingian," he answered simply.

Thoughts rushed through Hal's mind; conversations with Stergios which had taken place only days before but in some ways seemed like months ago. He had to process the information which only slowly clicked into place.

"So what you're saying is that she has the Merovingian powers of healing then? That's how she came to me and that's why I've recovered so miraculously?"

Stergios nodded. The strange thing was that Hal fully believed it. So this is where Tasia joins the story then, he thought.

"And as such you're telling me that's precisely why she is also the true heir to the throne of Britain?" Hal ventured somewhat tentatively, barely willing to believe that those words were leaving his mouth.

Again, Stergios nodded.

"And that's why she is under constant security over here and why I'm the target for nutters trying to kill me I take it."

238

"Quite so Hal. That is exactly it. Your computer contains for the first time the full unexpurgated story of Tasia Artemis. It is information which our counterparts in MI5 and MI6 would seek to destroy. You will have a very high price upon your head but there are only one or two in the intelligence services who are aware of Tasia just now. Most of those who know of her existence at all believe that we are working on their side; that we are here to suppress the story. We are aware however that there is a small faction within our organisation who believe quite the opposite; who suspect the truth – that we are here to protect her and spill the beans so to speak."

"Which you are – right?"

"Yes, of course Hal. I know it must be difficult working with people who have been double agents, working on all sides but it is important that you trust us. Kyle and I are both members of the faction within the organisation who are unhappy with the style of monarchical and establishment power that exists today. We believe, just as Tasia does in a better world and we are here to help her fight for it. Her fight is nearly over but we have to get the story finished and released to the public. It will be a long struggle but at least we will start the world questioning and perhaps one day it will lead to the reform we want to see. A reform which will lead to more equality and fairness in an uncertain world; a reform which will see the monarchy taking a greater and more selfless role in healing the ills which are all around us. That is why you are here."

"So do you think that we're going to get Tasia – or is it – *Diana* - pronounced as the true Queen in Britain and somehow usurp our current monarchy?" Hal asked incredulously.

"No Hal. That is not the way things will happen. We are here to sow the seeds; to get the world questioning; to give them the information they require to begin seeking

239

reform. Through Tasia's bloodline though, through her own children, she hopes to see the changes we are all working for." Hal puffed out his cheeks and slowly exhaled the air he held in them.

"The guy who broke in and stole my computer. He's dead, right?"

"He was taken care of buddy," Kyle now spoke.

"Tasia killed him didn't she? She shot him with a bow and arrow."

"Remember Hal, Tasia was still in Chania on the night of the attack," Stergios replied. "The man was apprehended and presents no danger to us. We've stepped up all security around you and the Villa so don't worry. Your computer survived and we have taken backups of your files."

"You haven't answered my question, Stergios."

Stergios nodded sagely. "I think I have. Remember there are more things..."

"...in heaven and earth than we can possibly know," Hal finished the sentence for him. He knew that he wasn't going to get any more enlightenment at the moment. He turned to Kyle.

"So how are you bearing up Kyle?" he asked. Kyle looked tired and sadness shone from his eyes.

"It's not easy buddy. She's been my lover and best friend for nearly eighteen years. I know, just as you do, that she is a very special individual. Her strength and love has sustained me through difficult times. All I can say is that I'm bracing myself for the end but I too know that even when she's gone, she'll never be far away from me. It's the only comfort I have to hold on to. Right now, I have to be her eyes, ears and mouthpiece so I have to stay focused and make sure her incredible story is published for all the world to know what a truly amazing person she is and the difference she has been making even in exile. You're not the first person to have been healed by her in such a miraculous way Hal."

240

"So," Hal said finally, "I guess we'd better get back to work as soon as possible then." Despite his reservations, he knew deep within himself that this was indeed a remarkable woman and that her story, however the ending turned out, was one that would enthral and enchant generations to come. He had a feeling also, that the most remarkable part was yet to come.

Hal was discharged from hospital the following day but before he left, he went with Kyle to visit Tasia. Just as he had been warned, she lay as still as a corpse, all life drained from her, the only indication that she was still alive came from the breathing apparatus and beeping computers showing that her vital signs continued. He bent down and took her hand in his. He felt the frisson of electricity pass between them again but weaker this time. He closed his eyes and willed with all his might that she would get better and that he could hear her laughter and see her bright personality ringing through the villa again. He wished with all his heart that she could be healthy and happy with Kyle, a man whom he now came to regard as one of strength, loyalty and deep integrity. He regarded them both as friends, though God knows what they'd got him into. Still, Tasia had brought him life where there had been none and hope where there had been a void. He vowed that he would do all he could to return the favour.

Chapter 21 – Kings and Oligarchs

Hal wasn't entirely comfortable about returning to Gavdos and Villa Artemis after the vicious attack but, he surmised, if he wasn't safe there he was at decidedly greater risk alone. It was agreed that he would travel back with Kyle on the helicopter.

On the return journey, Kyle was distant. In the last few days he'd appeared to age. Lines which hadn't been apparent to Hal previously were now etched upon his face displaying clear signs of strain and worry. He didn't want to intrude on Kyle's thoughts or his evident grief with idle chatter but he was concerned for the man with whose misery he could fully empathise.

"I know how it feels Kyle. To lose someone precious I mean. I can't tell you how very sorry I am that you are having to suffer this."

"Yeah. It's kinda tough." Kyle had never been the master of overstatement so Hal knew that 'kinda tough' meant unbearable in most people's estimation. Kyle was staring out of the helicopter's window as he spoke but Hal could just see the glisten of unshed tears in his eyes. He recalled the searing pain of impending loss as Fliss had deteriorated during the final weeks of her illness. He remembered how he'd been unable to truly believe that within a short time the person he'd loved most would not be there. Looking at Kyle, he felt again the gnawing pain in his stomach, like a growth; the intermingling of pain, grief and helplessness. In some ways it was the worst pain he'd ever experienced because nothing but the outpouring of tears could relieve it – and that was just temporary. What made it worse of course was that one couldn't go about daily life constantly bursting into tears. For one thing, other people didn't understand and for another, it was important to stay strong in front of Fliss and other loved ones. And so the grief tumour simply grew and became more painful. Eventually of course it would have to burst. In Hal's case it was after Fliss died that he was finally able to release his sorrow. To have done so before would have meant giving in to the inevitable and he hadn't been prepared to acknowledge that she was going to die. Had he cried then it would somehow have been affirming the prognosis he refused to accept. When death had finally arrived to claim her he still couldn't quite believe that his beautiful, vital wife was no longer there. The loss was of such momentous proportion that he could barely conceive it was possible. Even now he couldn't quite take in that life was snuffed out and a once vibrant person was replaced with nothingness. What he'd experienced over the last few weeks suggested however that perhaps Fliss hadn't really gone. Perhaps it was true that only the body dies but that the spirit lives on in another dimension or world as yet unseen by most of the living. He'd never been a great believer in such things but he'd seen Fliss hadn't he? He felt her close, smelled her perfume and been comforted by those things.

Hal was drawn from his reverie by Kyle whose captive pain, for the initiated at least, was clear to see.

"I was supposed to kill Tasia you know." The revelation came as a bolt to Hal who stiffened and became alert to what he was hearing. Kyle looked him in the eye. "Yeah. Kill her. A beautiful soul was meant to have been disposed of quickly, quietly and without fuss. That was my job. Like I said before, I killed many innocent people to keep up the subterfuge that allowed me to know the terrible secrets which I knew had to be subverted. Others, like Tasia, I worked to save. Stergios too. We're both murderers. We've both taken out people's loved ones to keep our own skins safe and to try to protect the greater good. Only now I know the pain I must have caused others. It's almost too much to bear."

243

"How were you meant to kill her?" Hal asked nonplussed.

"We'll get to that. But it was all very well stage managed. Stergios and I were the broken cogs in the wheel for them. I'm not sure we really did her any favours though. She hasn't really had much happiness from it. Perhaps I should have left well alone."

"She's been happy Kyle. I've seen the way she looks at you. You're her very reason for living. It's obvious."

"Yeah, maybe. But she had to give up a lot to live in secrecy and fear. There hasn't been a day gone by when she hasn't wept for her children who know nothing of her existence. We've constantly had to reassure her that it's for them that we're doing all this."

Before Hal could question him further, the helicopter began its descent onto the helipad in Gavdos. Wordlessly, the two men stepped out, the blades creating a noisy whirlwind around them. A Mercedes awaited their arrival. Kyle got in the passenger seat and Hal took his place in the back. He still felt tired and disoriented so he rested his head on the back of the seat and enjoyed the scenery of Gavdos once more as they travelled in silence back to Villa Artemis. Sadness filled the very air around them all.

Later that evening, Stergios and Kyle waited for Hal in the gardens. They sat around the table, a bottle of wine and three glasses set for them. Hal went down to join them after a short rest. He knew the men wanted to expedite their business with him as quickly as possible so he took his place at the table prepared with recorder and trusty pen and pad.

"Where would you like us to resume the story for you Hal?" Stergios was relaxed and ready to continue as he flashed a welcoming smile to the reporter.

"I guess I really need to understand who you both work for and where you fit into this story. I'm not sure I'm really clear on it all."

244

Stergios agreed that this was an essential part of the jigsaw. Kyle, still distracted concurred.

"You understand that we work for the British Secret Services? At least ostensibly we work for them. Indeed we have done a great deal of the good work for which they are generally known. However, we would probably be called traitors for the other activities we have undertaken. We like to think of ourselves more as *conscientious objectors* than traitors. We try to work for what is right, not for what others would have us believe is right if you get my drift."

Hal listened intently. "When you say you work for the Secret Services, who exactly do you mean?"

Stergios continued. "I work for MI6 now but we have also worked for MI5. Kyle works for the CIA but he has been seconded to Britain and the sister organisations for many years. What you must understand is that the majority of the British Establishment and much of the American Establishment are completely unaware of the real activities of the Secret Services, most of which are covert and known only to those in the higher echelons of the organisations. When you hear therefore of the Home Office working with our organisations, most of the personnel do so in complete innocence of the more sinister operations in which we are frequently engaged. We keep secret dossiers on people who are regarded as, shall we say, *troublesome* and the organisation operates under its own laws and practices, unbeknown to those whom it is supposed to serve."

"It sounds chilling Stergios. Almost like a secret police."

"Quite so Hal. Indeed there are those who have compared it with just such organisations. MI5 is split into many different divisions, surveillance, personnel, vetting Government personnel, spying on suspected terrorists both national and international, monitoring the Royals, counter intelligence, working with the SAS when drastic action is needed. Some of this work is contracted out to private

245

security firms, largely when MI5 wants to dissociate itself from certain unsavoury activities. When we carry out surveillance on various persons, it can literally be anyone regarded as potentially dangerous to Establishment aims. At least those aims known only to the few who truly orchestrate power in our country. Some might say, as both Kyle and I do, that these 'subversives' are actually simply people with strong beliefs; people with high morals who want to expose the terrible nature of things that happen. They can be anyone from journalists, rock stars, political activists, nuclear protesters, people who campaign for animal and human rights. Anyone in fact who may be regarded as overstepping the mark and coming too close to the truth. Remember this Hal – it can even include those in Royalty if their populist support begins to destabilise society from the norms which our organisations work to maintain."

Stergios paused for a moment to refill their wine glasses.

"The secret services have a long, illustrious and bloody history. MI5 is tasked with domestic security and MI6 with international security. Within the secret services, there are more secret organisations, notably the Special Operations Executive or SOE which as you know looks after the interests of the monarchy. The continued existence of the SOE is not publicly acknowledged, though it is a well known 'secret' in the highest echelons of British oligarchy whose primary aim is to protect and uphold the British Monarchy. The SOE had a very clear policy to create a powerful United States of Europe after the Second World War and continues to covertly pursue this aim. It is run by a powerful clique of individuals from the corporate and financial worlds including publishing and insurance. They are bankrolled by major European and American companies who benefit from the alliance and who can manipulate power without the need for tiresome democracy. There are groups throughout the world who have

246

similar organisations. The Priory of Sion, a French organisation for example, supports the United States of Europe ideal. Many of the Masonic organisations throughout Britain, Europe and America are associated in the same way. You will be aware of course that the outwardly innocent aims of Masonic Societies have long been known as mechanisms for advancement to its members and that there is a distinctly sinister side to them?"

Hal agreed that he was aware that there was probably more to these organisations than met the eye and had always resisted any approaches to him to join. Of course, his reading on the subject had suggested that the majority of Freemasons knew nothing of the more secretive practices and that there was a much more complex purpose known only to the selected few. He had always resisted any organisation that promoted the self interest and advancement through nepotism rather than merit. He recognised the blatant unfairness and yes, undemocratic processes that such organisations espoused.

"So what you're telling me is that all of these undercover organisations, whilst outwardly promoting good work for the security of the citizens they ostensibly serve, actually serve their own members and support them in gaining greater power than the Governments who are democratically elected?"

"That is exactly the case Hal. There is no altruism in these organisations. The notion of democratically elected Governments is a mere chimera; a smokescreen to provide self aggrandisement, power and big bucks to a very few. Governments are mere puppets of these organisations whose influence is huge and unprecedented."

Hal was astonished. He was horrified in fact because he could see the truth in what he was being told. Society was sold an illusion that they had democracy, freedom and truth.

247

What they really had was oligarchs and megalomaniacs wielding power by covert means.

"Everything is manipulated by the process of Freemasonry Hal. All of these groups work together to maintain the World Order as they wish it to be. They underpin and protect the European Monarchy and, now here is the part which you may struggle with, to protect the secrets of the royal bloodlines and the genealogical links to Jesus Christ. Remember, the monarchy as it is today receives the protection from the secret that their bloodline is diluted. These organisations do not wish it to be known that there may be a stronger royal bloodline that may create a counter monarchy outside their control. Our democratically elected Governments are 'sponsored' by the members of these organisations who can manipulate them with their enormous corporate wealth built on the proceeds of war, our various corporations having funded the European war efforts. This has given them tremendous power."

"I guess all of these groups, these Masonic organisations have representatives within the secret services then. Is that what you're telling me."

"Yes," replied Stergios. "The groups are all clandestine and secretive. They network and infiltrate the secret services. They come from Freemasons, the Priory of Sion, the Knights of Malta and other groups. They have been responsible for many political activities; overthrowing and deposing presidents, dictators; the, shall we say, 'removal' of troublesome individuals."

"Assassinations you mean?"

"Yes Hal. Many such operations have raised questions in the past. Think about Kennedy, Monroe. A certain British Princess...? Whilst their deaths have been passed over as explicable, the truth is that there are probably more people who believe they were murdered for political ends than accept the cover stories which were offered."

248

"OK, so you mentioned a Princess. We're talking Diana, right?" Stergios nodded. "At the time she died, there were dozens of conspiracy theories out there and yeah, I know, probably nine out of ten of the British public believe she was killed because she might have been about to marry a Muslim right? And I guess the British Establishment didn't want the situation that the mother of the heirs to the throne might have blood ties with a Muslim family?"

Stergios, clasping his hands on the table in front of him took a moment to consider his response before refilling the wine glasses.

"All of that may be true Hal but it is the tip of the iceberg. In some ways, a convenient reason as to why a princess might have been removed. However, there are far more mundane reasons why it was desirable to have her out of the way; she was at its simplest level a threat to the corporate government and their financial power. First consider her Landmines crusade. To her it was a humanitarian issue to ban the landmines in Angola. There was much of political and financial interest to the industrialists in Angola. There are rich oil and mineral reserves in which Western and Communist agencies all had competing interests. Through the American and European Secret Services landmines were actively donated to the political powers to create civil war allowing the west to buy up oil and minerals at reduced costs. You will find that many civil wars and areas of unrest have been deliberately provoked by the western Corporate World for precisely the reason that they can sell arms and control and manipulate the costs of resources produced by these countries when desperation causes the prices to drop. New weapons can be tested facilitating the arms market to profiteer mercilessly to benefit the western world. Going back to landmines, Angola was just one country using them and buying them. Other countries

249

viewing their success were motivated to buy and fill the pockets of the industrialists in the West."

A chill ran through Hal as he digested the meaning of Stergios' words.

"And Diana of course was a highly popular figure. She wanted to expose all sorts of humanitarian issues and bring them into the spotlight didn't she? I guess if she'd lived, she endangered the secrets of all of these corporate bodies and might have exposed the dirty dealings of the west. It all makes perfect sense that she might have been a very big thorn in the side."

"She threatened the very fortunes of those in the highest echelons. Her influence was becoming greater. People would sit up and listen to her when she became involved in a cause. And the nearer she got to the problem, the closer she got to the sources which she may have eventually revealed."

"Wasn't Diana due to sign a Landmines Treaty shortly after her death?"

It was Kyle who stepped into the discussion now.

"She sure was Hal. She even discussed it with Clinton and his wife who initially supported it. But surprise, surprise, before they got to Oslo, only days before in fact, Diana was dead and the CIA had a word in the president's ear to remind him exactly who was keeping him in office and that if he didn't toe the line, some very dirty linen about to be revealed might be the end of his career. The CIA and other services do like to have people with dirty little secrets in office," he finished scathingly. "So much easier to keep them on message. Without Diana in the way to push for the Treaty, it was a breeze for him to do an about turn on his decision to support the treaty. And that's exactly what happened. A real co-incidence huh?"

Hal couldn't deny that although it sounded farfetched, there was a ring of possibility, even probability to what he was being told. Why would these two agents put their necks on the line to tell him all this if they didn't believe it? Hal gazed at the blue sky now tinged with orange as the sun went down casting a warm glow over the island. Hard to believe that such machinations went on behind the scenes that Joe Public wouldn't even contemplate as possible. Stergios and Kyle paused for a few moments allowing Hal to gather his thoughts and make some notes. It was Stergios who took up the story again.

"At the time, there was talk that Diana had been looking at a number of other humanitarian causes. She'd indicated an interest in campaigning against the nuclear industry on behalf of those suffering from related cancer. There have of course been allegations that others, including a Scottish lawyer and a 78 year old woman were mysteriously killed for showing similar interests and for getting too close to exposing the truth."

"So this, you believe is the real reason that Princess Diana died?" Hal asked. He was astounded by the response.

"That, and an even more compelling reason, Hal." *Good God,* thought Hal, *there's more?* Wasn't that enough to be going on with, he wondered?

"Remember the bloodline, Hal? This is where it becomes highly relevant. Diana was displaying herself as a different kind of royalty. She was flying in the face of the traditional practices of the monarchy and she wanted a New Order in the 'firm'. She wanted a more caring, hands on establishment that would wield its power for good. She wanted active participation as an ambassador. She wanted to heal the ills and change the world. Not something the existing model of royalty would have done in a million years. And, perhaps there was a reason for that." Stergios paused a moment, gathering his thoughts.

"I told you that I had studied the Saunière parchments Hal. They explain the Merovingian ideals. To rule without war

251

and to use negotiation, education and peaceful means to achieve greater aims. To heal the sick and injured, not to harm. Does this raise any questions for you?"

"Well, yes, I guess. Diana's approach seems to have reflected the Merovingian line. But she was only part of the royal family by marriage; a 'commoner' in fact. How does that equate with her position? She didn't have any true connection to the monarchy."

Stergios could barely contain his excitement.

"Hah! That is where you are completely wrong Hal. Diana's family were direct descendants of the Stuart Kings who'd been ousted from the throne by marriage into the House of Hanover in Germany. A politically engineered situation brought us George I through the marriage of James I & VI of Scotland's granddaughter to the Elector of Hanover. Despite efforts to regain the throne for the Stuarts when George ruled mainly from Germany, those trying to restore the Stuarts were unable to depose those in real power; the power of corporate controlled Parliament who actually ruled Britain for the absentee King George. This left the real power of monarchy with the financiers during this period. Now, here is the truly interesting part Hal. Diana's family are direct descendants of the Stuarts but can be traced back to the Celtic Kings of Scotland and then to the Merovingians who were descended from...

"...Jesus and his family from the bloodline of David and Solomon." Hal finished the sentence. "And the Hanovers became the Windsors after the War. So, if I'm understanding this, they carry the bloodline but only in diluted form through marriage in the Stuart line?"

"You have it Hal. The current monarchy is a dilution of the bloodline by the intermingling of the non Judaic Hanoverians with the pure Judaic lineage of the Stuarts. Diana is a direct descendant of the Stuarts and thus, according to the parchments has a stronger claim to the

British throne than those who currently enjoy it. Of course, Diana's marriage was no accident. With her blood mingling in the family, it actively strengthens the monarchy's claim to the throne through her children. Nevertheless, if the secret of the parchments was released, there was a great danger, from individuals such as ourselves who knew the truth, that Diana could have a true claim to the throne and create a new kind of monarchy through her sons; a monarchy that could not be controlled by corporate oligarchs any longer. That was a situation that would never be allowed by those who benefited from keeping the truth undisclosed. Hence, the real reason why Diana had to be removed. The Masonic symbolism and ritual has concealed the truth for centuries." Stergios smiled. "A great deal for you to absorb I think. I have documents and papers I can show you so that you can research the rather simplistic version I have given you Hal. You can do it in your own time once we have created the outline for you. Now, I must leave you good people. I am a little weary now so I shall bid you goodnight. We shall speak again in the next day or two Hal. Kyle and Hal stood up as Stergios rose to leave. For Hal, the information imparted raised more questions than answers. Kyle who was also evidently weary had no real appetite for further discussion and they said their goodnights before heading off to their rooms to be alone with their thoughts.

Chapter 21 – A Thorn in the Side

Kyle tossed and turned alternating between uneasy sleep and jolting into troubled wakefulness covered in perspiration. His dreams took him back eighteen years to the day that he had been called to action on an assignment in which his conscience dictated he could take no part. This was one mission which he and Stergios were secretly avowed to thwart. They knew it was coming; there had been talk about it for months and both men were alerted to the possibility of involvement. On receiving the news they could not afford for their masks to slip. Certain death would follow if there was any suspicion of their dissent. This would be the moment when their professional, emotional and mental acuity would be tested to the full. Their training as double agents had to be used to the optimum or the consequences were dire.

The briefing took place in a dingy dimly lit office deep under the streets of Whitehall. Secret tunnels and secret rooms formed a labyrinth beneath the political hub of power above them. Here, plots were formed, life changing decisions were made and the truly powerful ruled.

It was mid August 1997 and the media was awash with headlines concerning predominantly the love life of the estranged former royal wife. Whilst it all gave great entertainment to the public who lapped it up with undisguised voraciousness, it caused deep agitation to the power hungry leaders of the most secretive organisations in the British Establishment.

Kyle Masters and Stergios Tavoularis sat around the long table joined by a dozen others. All were suited and booted resembling the cleanest cut boardroom members of a multi million pound corporation. Their stiff and sombre demeanour was the only characteristic which might have suggested a more sinister group of professionals was present. At the head of the table was an individual known only to the group as 'A'. He was softly spoken but his voice was nonetheless authoritative and even menacing as he spoke. He was cold, impassive and pragmatic as he announced the reason for their gathering.

"Gentlemen, oh and er, ladies," he added as an afterthought, acknowledging the presence of two women amongst their number, "you will be aware of the unease with which we have all observed the actions of a member of the royal family lately. Without wishing to go into major detail at this stage, it is with regret that I must inform you that you are all required to participate in one of the most covert operations of recent times. Our national security has been laid wide open by the actions of this ahh, certain individual on our world stage and we must now deal with the problem before it causes er, aahm... any more distress and disturbance to our leaders, the family and indeed the safety of the western world. In one week's time we shall be called to action in an operation which will shake the entire globe. We must therefore be slick, quick and calculated in our actions both individually and collectively. In due course, within the next few days, you will each receive your individual instructions. Please ensure that there are no mistakes and that the operation is carried out smoothly. There is no room for error with this one I'm afraid. If we do not succeed at the designated site for the operation, contingency plans have been formulated to ensure that the job is completed efficiently and without margin for questions. This is probably the biggest operation of its kind that any of you will be asked to participate in. It must be clean and it must be final. You may now open the envelopes before you for initial instructions. Please digest the information contained therein and return the papers to the clerk. Await further instructions as to your individual role. That will be all. Thank you."

'A' gathered his papers together, nodded to the clerk and exited the room briskly. Those remaining at the table read their instructions. Some blanched as they saw exactly what their mission involved. It was almost unreal. They were tasked with the removal of the biggest thorn in the side of the British Establishment; a woman whose star shone brightly in every home in the world; a woman who held almost every individual in her thrall; one whose mix of glamour, charisma, compassion, pathos and lately untamed passion for life and humanitarianism had dominated the world's press. Each of those present knew that this was no run of the mill assignment. One slip and disaster awaited them and their organisations.

Kyle and Stergios did not acknowledge each other either within the room or as they left. It was more than their lives were worth for any connection between them to be identified. They had been aware of the gathering storm for the last few weeks and it was their time to climb over the parapet. They would be there at the appointed time; they were already aware of the pre-planning which had gone on before this announcement. They were mutely opposed to everything they were tasked to undertake and they would ensure to the very best of their abilities that this time the agenda of their employers would not be met; indeed that it would be completely subverted. It was time for the corporate oligarchs to be defeated and for the truth to be outed. This was their day.

Chapter 22 – Greeks Bearing Gifts

The emergence of Tasia Artemis as one of their dissident group had been as momentous as it was mysterious. In the secret corridors under Whitehall, she had 'bumped' into Stergios knocking him sideways and causing him to drop the sheaf of paperwork he was carrying to the study. He couldn't help but stare at the tall, elegant and unconventional beauty as she apologised profusely for the 'accident' and knelt down, her Cleopatra bob framing her perfectly symmetrical face, her wide blue eyes carefully and dramatically made up to enhance the stunning natural features of her face.

"Lypámai , eímai tóso adéxia," *I'm sorry, I'm so clumsy,* she spoke in perfect Greek. Stergios was so startled that he fell backwards from his bent position as he hurried to collect the confidential material together. The woman laughed and continued to speak in his native tongue.

"Now, Stergios, I have only a few moments. Listen carefully. I am here to help with your, what shall we call it, humanitarian aims? Very soon, there is to be an assassination of a very famous person who is close to my heart and I think we both know who I am talking about don't we?"

Stergios who had never seen the woman before, said nothing, afraid to acknowledge that he knew anything of the matter of which she spoke. She smiled again.

"It's OK Stergios. I know you are suspicious of me and quite rightly so. I have been sent to thwart those who would kill the Merovingian Queen and to ensure her safe passage. Your life is about to change Stergios and you will be required to guard the Holy Grail until the time is right for her re-emergence. The work you have been doing has been recognised by the higher powers and your diligence will be rewarded."

Beads of perspiration broke out on Stergios' face and he blanched at her reference to 'higher powers.' Had his employers discovered his duplicity? Was this their way of warning him that he was about to face his own demise? Perhaps she was already about to plunge a fatal needle into him. He moved backwards, distancing himself from the woman.

"Don't be afraid Stergios," she said reassuringly as though reading his mind. "The higher powers of whom I speak are not those you fear. I am part of your group and I come to help ensure that you will be successful. Destiny has been set and although you were unaware of it, you have been fulfilling the wishes of the higher order."

Stergios was uncharacteristically rattled by the woman and was wary of responding in any way which might affirm his dissidence. Just then, his phone rang. It was Kyle. The woman nodded to him to answer. Stergios knew that Kyle would give nothing away without their codes being exchanged to signify whether it was safe to speak.

"Please Stergios. Answer your phone. It will affirm the veracity of what I say."

Stergios pressed the button and said, "Hi it's Stergios here, what's new?" Each knew that if the other introduced themselves with this phrase that it meant they weren't alone.

"Stergios," Kyle sounded breathless. "The woman who's with you now. She's cool; she's with us. She's our decoy. She's been working with the target for months as part of our operation. Few people knew about it but I've been briefed by the Doc. Don't say anything if you don't want to. She'll give you instructions and we'll all meet up later."

Stergios, his ingrained suspicion of anything and everyone made no response other than *"OK thanks. Understood."* He couldn't be sure that this wasn't a set up.

"You are a wise man, Stergios," the woman smiled giving her features a strange familiarity. He couldn't quite put his finger on why he thought he recognised her but there was something about her... "You are quite correct to be wary. Now," she continued, "I am glad to make your acquaintance. I shall leave you now so that you can speak with the others in your number who are also aware of me. We shall meet again on Sunday at sunrise next to the standing stones in Avebury. Kyle will accompany you." She inclined her head and her smile was not confined to her lips but radiated to her eyes which were warm and deeply sincere as he lost himself in her presence. She took his hand and he felt a tingling sensation, comforting and reassuring. He was entirely in her thrall as she withdrew her hand and began to walk away from him along the corridor in the opposite direction. She called back to him, "Until we meet again on Sunday, Stergios. *Yassas, andio.* And by the way, you shouldn't be troubled by that shoulder pain anymore," she chuckled.

Stergios turned in amazement to ask how she knew he'd been suffering with an injured shoulder but was shocked to discover he was alone. She couldn't have disappeared so quickly. The corridor was long and only a second had passed. He blinked in the gloomy light, squinting ahead to see if she was standing in the shadows ahead. He walked along the corridor just to check that she wasn't still standing in a blind spot but she was gone. He shook his head in disbelief and continued in the direction he'd begun. He called Kyle and arranged to meet later that day.

"She's something else huh, Stergios?" Kyle was eager to talk about their newest recruit. "I got a call from Stanton to tell me that they'd found the decoy and that she was going to make contact with me." Stanton was the operational head of the dissident few. "Well, when I saw her, I thought, how the hell is she going to be a decoy? She looks nothing like the real thing," he went on excitedly. "But Stergios, next thing I see is she's pulled off that dark wig and hey presto! She's the real deal. Apparently she's had plastic surgery, the works to make her look the part. She's willing to die for this cause Stergios. It's the craziest, wildest, most perfect plan you could imagine!"

Stergios frowned as he listened to Kyle. He was puzzled and intrigued in equal measure.

"She's a strange one, I'll give you that Kyle. She knew something about me that I hadn't told anyone. An old injury that's been playing up lately. I was about to have physio on it. She grabbed my hand and there was this tingling, as though something was passing between us. As she left she told me it was cured. Sure enough, the pain's gone. It's very odd. She just seemed to disappear into the walls under Whitehall after our encounter."

"Yeah, something similar happened to me. She told me my Mom was sick back home but not to worry because although it's serious, she'd be OK. I called home last night and Mom told me she had a cancer scare but hadn't told anyone about it. Turns out she'd had a biopsy this week and she'd just got the results. It was benign. Damndest thing huh?"

"So tell me Kyle, what is the lowdown on this strange creature?"

"I'm told that she's been living alongside the target for months now, learning the mannerisms, living her life with her. She's got a job as an assistant. The target knows who she is. Her name is Tasia Artemis and she's been a special agent working with the CIA and MI5 for about 15 years. Stanton told me he'd never come across her before but she made herself known to him and asked for the gig. She's passionate about creating a new world order and she checked out when he made enquiries. It's kinda odd he didn't know of her though. He knows everyone who's anyone in the service." The target has been fully briefed by our guys about her Merovingian connection and her bloodline. She's also aware that her life is in danger. She's placed her trust in us though and is playing

260

along. That's why she's been taking a higher profile lately in the humanitarian issues. She's laying the foundations for the sea change that we all hope for once the truth is out there. She's been studying her genealogy with Tasia's help and the parchments have been explained to her. She's ready for whatever is coming apparently."

Stergios nodded. He still wasn't convinced that this wasn't a trick. He feared that Tasia may be dangerous. "So, we're up for an early start on Sunday I understand? We have to travel to Avebury standing stones to meet with Tasia she says."

"Yup, Stanton told me that was the arrangement." Kyle finished his Jack Daniels and pulled on his black overcoat. "Best get some sleep then. It's gonna be a long weekend."

Chapter 23– The Devil's Chair

Kyle drove the two hour journey from London to Avebury with Stergios at his side. They arrived in the Saxon village just before sunrise. They parked as near to the standing stones as they could in the National Trust protected area and walked the final short distance towards the stones that loomed over them like eerie lapidified giants. The first glimmer of light was rising over the horizon and within moments the sun rose casting warm shadows over the stones. Kyle and Stergios stood, hands in pockets, looking around the stone circle waiting for contact from Tasia. They didn't have long to wait and their look of utter astonishment amused Tasia as she stepped out from behind the largest stone to greet them. Instead of the dark haired beauty they'd met previously, a tall leggy blond, her hair elegantly short and dressed casually in Capri pants and shirt emerged from the shadows. Her head was bent as though avoiding eye contact until she approached the two men. She raised her eyes, but kept her head lowered in the way characterised by the real thing and smiled in that now famous shy but flirtatious style of the Princess.

"So, what do you think boys?" Tasia asked, her legs parted, hands on her hips, for all the world like a model. Stergios and Kyle were stunned. For a moment, they actually thought they were in the company of royalty. It was only as the light intensified from the warming sun that they realised they were actually in the company of an astonishing look alike.

"It's amazing," Stergios enthused, walking around the woman as though she was a rare museum exhibit. Tasia's eyes followed him as he inspected her from all sides. Kyle was stunned. His heart was beating a little faster as his eyes drank in the beautiful creature who stood before him. He'd never dreamed there could be two of them but he sure wished that if there was a spare he'd be happy to be her consort, so to speak. He was speechless. He couldn't get over the likeness, not only in appearance but mannerism. When she spoke, Tasia used a well mimicked Sloane drawl and sounded identical to the Princess.

"So, handsome," she addressed Kyle, "what do you think? Convincing?"

"I'll say," gasped Kyle. Their eyes met and suddenly he knew that there was a connection between them.

Stergios' interest was far more clinical. He was assessing Tasia in terms of operational suitability. "Astonishing," he said. "It's quite, quite staggering."

"Well I should hope so," smiled Tasia. "It's taken rather a lot of work to become someone else," she laughed. "Transmogrification isn't quite as easy as Harry Potter might lead us to believe. So, gentlemen, to business. We don't have long so we'd better acquaint ourselves since we're going to be such close colleagues soon. She reached into the Hermes handbag looped over her shoulder and pulled out the black Cleopatra wig. As soon as she had put it on her head, the illusion of Diana was gone. It was stunning how much hair could change a person, thought Kyle. However, he thought Tasia was just as alluring as a brunette and quite fancied the idea of having two women in one. It would always be interesting, he thought.

"Come on," Tasia said. "Let's keep moving. We don't want to risk staying in one place for too long, just in case we're followed. The two men had used their training to check out the immediate area on arrival and felt confident they were alone.

"Why did you pick this place?" asked Kyle.

"Oh, I guess because of its pagan history. The Merovingians were mystics and would have appreciated the site for its spiritual properties. And – well, it isn't an obvious city location, I guess."

263

Kyle took in the impressive sight before him, and not just Tasia. The Avebury Stone Circle in which they stood had a distinct mystical quality, even for a sceptic such as he. He could almost feel the centuries of Druids, Wiccans and Heathens who had come to worship and, still did come to worship at the 'living temple' where their ancestors and local spirits were said to roam. As though reading his mind, Tasia picked up on this thoughts.

"It's still frequented by the Druids today," she said matter of factly. "See over there? She pointed to the southern entry to the Avebury henge where there was a cove in the stone. That's called the 'Devil's Chair.' In Druidic rites, the group splits into the God and the Goddess groups. The Goddess sits in the Devil's Chair. She is the guardian spirit of the site. The Druid representative speaks for the Goddess and she is rewarded with flowers and food by the God group. Believe it or not, there are usually ceremonies here on Saturdays and Sundays by different Druidic sects." Wistfully, Tasia moved amongst the stones, caressing each with her hand as she wove through them. She appeared to be lost in her own world and Kyle noticed that there was a strange glow, an aura which surrounded her. He put it down to the early morning light. He was though, entranced. For him, Tasia was indeed a Goddess and he was ready to worship at her feet. He shook himself from his reverie and chastised himself for losing focus. Time enough for such thoughts later. Stergios meanwhile was fascinated in the historical aspects of the ancient site. He too was inspecting the stones with more clinical fascination and had taken himself off to read the various explanatory signs which were placed around the perimeter. Tasia called them both to order and meekly, they followed her command as she told them to gather and walk with her.

"So, Stanton has told you about me?" They both nodded in affirmation. "I think it will only be a matter of weeks

264

before action is taken so we must be prepared. Both my life and hers depends upon it. At the moment, HRH is educating herself in the history and background of what we know from the parchments. She is preparing herself to take on a greater public role and she has begun to make inroads in reconciliation with the family since – well - you know, all the marital troubles. I am shadowing her at every moment of the day; I am living her life with her under cover of being her personal assistant. I know every aspect of what she is thinking, how she is feeling and how she will deal with things. I, in effect am becoming her." Tasia laughed. "I've even taken her place at a couple of functions and meetings with people she's acquainted with and I haven't been rumbled yet." Indeed, Kyle and Stergios couldn't get over the likeness and similarity of mannerism, voice and stature which Tasia had displayed when the wig was removed. It was entirely possible that many people would be fooled.

"When the time comes, your professional training must be slick and precise. There can be no room for error. You have your instructions?"

Both of the men nodded. Indeed, they now had two sets of instructions; the official ones to carry out the planned murderous attack and the other ones, designed to subvert the plan without anyone being any the wiser.

"Good. We shall not meet again until the appointed time. I'm relying on you boys. Please, don't let me down." She smiled, raising her eyes particularly to Kyle who felt the frisson of connection between them again. His heart skipped a beat and he felt the excitement of a teenager on his first date. "Soon, then, gentlemen." Tasia turned and walked slowly away from them towards the car park, her elegant gait drawing Kyle's admiration as her hips sashayed smoothly from side to side with every step. Suddenly, unable to stop himself, and knowing that he could make a terrible fool of himself, he ran after her. Stergios remained in his spot and watched them for a moment before turning his attention back to the monoliths which interested him more.

Approaching her retreating figure, Kyle gently grasped her arm, pulling Tasia back. When she turned to look at him, he didn't know quite what he was doing or what he wanted to say but he tried to articulate a few words.

"Erm, I know this probably isn't the time or place, but could we maybe meet up for a drink? I mean just us? In a social kinda way?" Tasia inclined her head and looked intently at him, a slight play of amusement on her lips.

"All in good time Kyle. I think perhaps we both know that we may have a destiny to fulfil and we must focus on that for now. I can't become embroiled in a situation where I may be seen with you or any of the other members of our group Also the distraction might affect our work. But once we have worked through the first part of our destiny, I would like to think that perhaps we can explore the remainder together. I'm sure we shall." She smiled warmly and, quite unexpectedly and with the spontaneity and charm for which her Doppleganger was known, she leaned over and brushed her soft lips upon his cheek. She giggled impishly and turning from him continued on her way without looking back. Kyle watched her as her figure retreated into the distance where she seemed to melt into the horizon, ethereal as a spirit. He touched his cheek and smiled to himself. For the first time in many years, his tough shell had been cracked and he felt that perhaps there was someone out there with whom he could find happiness. His aloofness had prevented him from forming close attachments, afraid to be hurt again. Something felt different with this woman however and he was determined to discover what it was. Together with the hope he felt, there was a nagging worry that it would not be an easy ride. He knew instinctively that the ethereal beauty who had captivated him was likely also to cause him pain.

266

It was by now fully light and he heard Stergios approaching him over the grassy expanse.

"I think I'm ready to find some breakfast," Stergios said decisively. "Shall we?"

"Yeah, good idea. Let's head for the village."

After a short drive, they entered the chocolate box village with its picturesque Church and quaint cottages. They found a cafe open and they were soon tucking into full English breakfasts with gusto. Kyle was quiet and contemplative. Stergios was buoyed up with excitement and enthralled with the wonders of the historical location. It was he who spoke, cutting into Kyle's thoughts and interrupting his reverie.

"You know, there is something about Miss Artemis. Something quite special."

Kyle nodded appreciatively. "You're right there Stergios. She's quite a broad."

Stergios laughed. "Well I wasn't thinking of her in quite such a common denomination but...," he became more serious. "She's not like us Kyle. I talked with Stanton. She's been involved in top secret experiments involving psychic abilities for use in defence and warfare. She has astounding abilities I'm told. Top of the class in remote viewing, mind reading and telekinesis. She's shown skills in healing, blocking signals and shutting down computers apparently. You know that the intelligence services are hoping to use such skills more regularly?"

Kyle had indeed heard of these practices but he'd always regarded them with some cynicism, discounting them as simply 'cold reading' or mentalism. However, Tasia had surprised him with the information she'd given both he and Stergios although he supposed, being in the secret services, she might have found out the information by quite rational means. Nevertheless, he was intrigued. Something *radiated* from her, there was no mistaking it. And he was determined to discover more, if not now, one of these days.

267

The mismatched odd couple of agents finished their breakfast and drove back to London, each energised by their experiences that day and coiled for the action both knew was coming soon.

Chapter 24 – A Major Gambit

Sometime following Tim's initial contact with the Princess, Tasia had been smoothly installed into the Royal machinery as her personal assistant. Once fully briefed, Tasia's ward, perhaps for the first time ever, had been prepared to do some heavy duty reading to understand the significance of her genealogy and destiny. The idea that she had a greater claim to the throne than her husband both amused her and appealed to her innate desire to make a difference in the world. Tasia managed to keep herself under the radar and was merely seen as an insignificant fixture of royal life in which she ostensibly busied herself with duties which ranged from the mundane ladies' maid to administrator for her employer. She was treated by the entourage with relative disinterest. Her position however allowed her to infiltrate every aspect of the Princess's life and their shared mission resulted in a close but discreet relationship of friendship and trust. 'Advisors' came and went from the dissident security services and together they ensured that the Princess fully understood the importance of the mission they shared. Unfortunately however, her fragile mental state would overcome her resolve and at times like these, she became very afraid and mistrusting of everyone around her. It was natural, of course. A woman in her position could never be sure how far the people in her life could be trusted, particularly as her recent actions made her vulnerable and lonely amidst a powerful institution.

As Tasia settled into her duties, she was soon able to observe and deftly mimic her employer's characteristics. She admired her tactility with people and Tasia emulated the warmth and ability to empathise which the Princess exuded. On various occasions, she witnessed and experienced the devastating effects of her bulimia and depression and the joy she found with her children. Using her empath's skills, Tasia experienced the Princess's range of emotions, the extreme highs and the lows that were equally dreadful. During the deep, dark and uncommunicative periods, when, full of self doubt the Princess's behaviour would be irrational, whisperings amongst her entourage speculated that she was suffering from serious mental illness. Despite the assurances of Tasia and her colleagues, the Princess was often fearful for her safety and had been known unwisely, to voice those fears where she could be overheard. Mutterings of 'paranoia' and 'schizophrenia' could be heard and even the word 'insane' had been uttered.

Tasia was concerned after one such meltdown when tears and histrionics had turned their morning upside down. Everyone knew better than to intervene or reason with the Princess until calm was restored. It was Tasia who tentatively entered her private office where she found her slumped across her desk sobbing, mascara pouring down her cheeks. Tasia approached her with the wariness of a mouse confronting an injured lion.

"Ma'am," she whispered, placing an arm around the other woman's shoulders, "you must be more discreet with your thoughts otherwise we'll all be in danger and our aims will never be achieved," she warned. The Princess though, was in no mood to listen. She was clearly rattled by something that had happened that morning and she pulled herself upright, sniffling and sobbing. Reaching for a tissue from the box on the desk, she blew her nose and wiped away the tramlines from her cheeks that made her look like a French harlequin marionette.

"You just don't understand Tasia," she moaned. "It's OK for you lot. You all know what's going on and you're expecting so much of me. But what if you get it wrong? What if we get found out? Every minute of the day I'm looking over my shoulder wondering if I'm about to get a bullet in my head. I'm afraid to get into my car in case they've tampered with the

270

brakes or put a bomb underneath it. They want rid of me, you know that? Even before we've made the truth known. They all think I'm crazy but I know how they work – and so do you." Tasia knew that it was a world of uncertainty and she sympathised with the terrified woman. It must indeed be like a living hell, never knowing who your enemies might be or what they were capable of.

"Ma'am, please be assured that for all those who might wish you harm, there are equal numbers of us who have a vested interest in protecting you. We are active in all parts of your life and constant checks are being made to ensure your safety. There are unseen officers all around you poised and ready for action. You have friends Ma'am and they are all highly trained and vigilant. Please try to put your mind at rest now. You have to be strong. The destiny you have to fulfil is momentous. Don't arouse suspicion or draw attention to yourself. It's the worst thing you could do at this crucial time." The woman nodded. She understood. However, what she was about to do next would shake the country, probably the world. It was to be her opening gambit to introducing the world at large to her idea of Monarchy. It would gauge her popularity and she would either make the world sit up and listen or be condemned as a lunatic. Her next event had been agreed with Tasia and the allies. They were all holding their breath as they kept their intentions top secret for maximum impact and the avoidance of any preventative action by the Establishment. It was a nervous time for them all and there was a palpable tension in the air to which the Princess now succumbed.

Tasia was an enigma to the Princess. She had emerged from nowhere it seemed. She appeared to know things about her that no-one else could possibly be aware of; innermost secrets and feelings that she had never disclosed or articulated to anyone. When Tasia removed the wig and began to mimic the princess, it was unbelievable – it was like

271

looking at a mirror image. Every so often, when Tasia comforted her, it was as though a mystical experience occurred. The simple laying on of her hands to a shoulder or the warmth of a hug seemed to emanate power and reassurance that entered her body like electricity, comforting and calming her. Tasia's eyes would bore into her own and it was as though they melded into one. At such moments, the Princess was transported to other worlds and times that felt familiar, yet unknown to her. Flowing robes, strange but beautiful lands, walled cities with gardens of paradise and people she recognised but could not name all came to her in pictures under Tasia's gaze. In her heart, she knew she must follow the path that had opened up to her since Tasia and her colleagues had made themselves known. In some mystical and strange way, she knew that she was fulfilling her destiny no matter how difficult the road became. These moments were equally insightful for Tasia, allowing her to use her powers to drink in the very ethos of the Princess, to feel her pain, her joy, her life experiences, her hopes and fears. Tasia absorbed the information into her own being, allowing her to transform herself into the very spirit of the Princess. Unbeknown to her, Tasia had been with her all her life, living each moment vicariously, guiding her to her destiny. Of course, no-one, not even her worldly colleagues would understand the process. Without her, the destiny could never be fulfilled.

Tasia became so adept at impersonating the Princess, she would take on large parts of her life undetected as an impostor. They would giggle like schoolgirls as Tasia fooled even the closest advisors into believing she was the real thing. Her hair appropriately styled, her makeup applied and in a role reversal of immense proportions, the Princess would help Tasia to get ready to undertake public engagements and deal with some of her more difficult moments. It was uncanny how no-one could tell the difference. It was as though Tasia had

272

them all under a spell. For Tasia, it could be difficult as she lived the torment of the Princess. It was unsettling to feel her pain.

Today, Tasia was living the life of her royal counterpart. As an empath, sitting in the royal apartment she felt the emptiness of the limbo that was the Princess's life and felt the frustration of constriction that prevented her from truly embracing a free and stable life. The contradictions of her life weighed heavily; she was neither married nor divorced. When she wanted to go out, she had to be smuggled into a waiting vehicle just to avoid the prying eyes and attention of the paparazzi. Tasia felt the emptiness and futility of loving the dedicated surgeon who consumed the Princess's emotions, knowing in her heart of hearts that she could not anticipate an ordinary stable relationship as other people could. Tasia relived the moments of the Princess's first meeting with her gallant heart surgeon which had left her reeling. Whilst visiting a friend in hospital she had come across the handsome Pakistani surgeon and had quickly set about engineering a meeting with him. She had been full of admiration for his dedication and care and she soon came to understand that he had sacrificed a great deal for his profession. At first, he hadn't known who this flirtatious but caring woman was, a matter which she found refreshing, if a little disconcerting. He was flattered by her attentions though as she sought him out and displayed such interest in his work and deep compassion for the patients he treated. It wasn't long before her obsession led her to immerse herself in the subject of heart surgery and the doctor's Muslim religion, so determined was she that he should fall for her charms and admire her devotion to his life, culture and career. Of course the secret could not be kept for long, such was her profile. Nevertheless, within a short time it seemed that perhaps she had found the love she craved and she even visited his family in Pakistan in the hope that acceptance would lead to the commitment she desired.

273

Perhaps they were both deluded though. Although there was undoubtedly a strong bond between the pair, as an intensely private man, her beloved was unable to see a way forward as she was still married and he shunned the publicity which detracted from his work and even diminished his standing as a serious professional.

If she wanted to step out of the limelight, it would have to be final and uncertain. Tasia knew Diana's reluctance to do that however; the Princess's narcissistic traits telling her that she only existed herself if she existed in the adulation of others. A constant battle waged between her desire for anonymity and her desire for attention. Tasia shivered. Sometimes she wished she too was ordinary and able to exist in the limited world of mortality where she would only have to deal with her own mind and emotions.

It was partly because of the desire to free herself that the Princess had decided to undertake probably the most sensational interview of her life. It was also to be the defining moment in asserting for the first time that she had aspirations of her own for the British throne.

"This is my opportunity to kill two birds with one stone," the Princess confided in Tasia who knew only too well the young woman's highly covert intentions to give a unique interview to the BBC. It was an opportunity to force the hand of the family in granting her the freedom she hungered for and to play the hand of her popularity in guaranteeing a continuing and significant role for herself if the gamble paid off. Of course, it was a gamble, but it was one she was ready to take.

A couple of evenings before the interview in 1995, Tasia met with Kyle to brief him so that all precautions might be put in place. She was uneasy that evening. There were some things even she couldn't control and there was no way of knowing if indeed this was the right time or the right place for the opening gambit of their operation. On the other hand, it would give them some clues as to how they might proceed in the future.

They met in a quiet South London pub on the river and took a seat outside where there were fewer customers and they could see if anyone was in earshot. Tasia looked stunning, Kyle thought as she drew the admiring glances of several male barflies inside the pub.

"It's sure great to see you again Tasia. I've been looking out for you whenever I see the Princess on TV but you never seem to be within range of the camera."

Tasia smiled. "Oh I'm always around Kyle. I just choose to keep my profile low so that no-one bothers me. How are you?"

"I'm good. All the better for seeing you. I was hoping we might have crossed paths again before now. It always seems to be some other lucky bastard who gets to liaise with you though. Guess I'm just the foot soldier."

"Whoa tiger!"" Tasia laughed. "Everything comes to he who waits. There will be a time and a place for us to get properly acquainted. It just isn't now, OK?"

Kyle nodded resignedly and took the bottle of Bud to his lips.

"So, are the plans coming together?"

"Yup," Tasia answered assuredly. "Execution is in place, consequences as yet unpredictable," she sighed.

"You're worried?"

"Aren't you?"

"Yeah, I guess. She's a bit of a maverick so I guess if she doesn't play it as we agreed the whole caboodle could be up. So, what's going down at the palace?"

"She's in control at the moment. The interviewer is so desperate to get this exclusive he hasn't even informed the BBC top brass what's happening. Too many friends of the family in high places there and the whole thing would be scrapped if anyone got wind of it. Anyway, all the staff have

275

been given the day off to make sure no 'moles' can give the game away. We'll need cover arranged to get the crew into the palace. They need to be smuggled in so you'll need to take care of security at the gates. You have enough staff?"

"Of course. Stergios and I will be there and Stanton has timetabled only our guys on duty tomorrow. Everything is organised."

"Good. Here's the anticipated schedule for the day," Tasia handed Kyle a spreadsheet showing the plans for entry and egress of the interviewer, crew and equipment. You'll need to do a sweep before they arrive to make sure everyone is off the premises."

Kyle studied the sheet. "No problem. I'll be there at dawn. Where do I find you?"

"Her nosy butler will be sniffing around trying to get the lowdown on what's going on at that time. I've told him to expect an early change around of protection staff. He's suspicious though. Didn't want to take the day off and tried to insist that he should be around. He thinks the Princess confides everything to him but nothing could be further from the truth. She's put him off the scent and actually arranged some time sensitive errands for him. Now he thinks he's part of some secret liaison with the good doctor. She spun him a line or two and he fell for it. Anyway, just do the usual changeover detail. He'll be despatched around 8 a.m. He probably needs one of our guys on his tail just to make sure he doesn't stick around to snoop."

Kyle finished the beer. "On it!" he said, replacing the empty bottle on the table. "Anything else?"

Tasia shook her head. "Not that I can think of at the moment. It'll be a fluid situation. We just need to stay alert and keep security tight tomorrow." Tasia stood to go. She winked at Kyle as she turned to take her leave. "Til tomorrow, Tiger," she laughed throatily.

276

Kyle, his ardour stymied for the moment simply grinned and said "Grrr... You ain't seen nothin' of this tiger yet, lady!"

"Sounds intriguing," she countered as she sashayed into the car park leaving Kyle just a little hot under the collar with anticipation.

Chapter 25 – The Queen of Hearts

The following morning the air was electric, the tension palpable. The majority of the household had been sent on their way the previous evening and only the Princess's butler remained. As planned, he allowed the protection officers in at the appointed time. Kyle and Stergios were among their number. Irritatingly, the butler refused to be hurried; he had guessed that something was afoot and was determined to wait as long as possible so that his curiosity might be satisfied. Eventually, his procrastination having been anticipated by the Princess and her helpers, he was despatched on an urgent errand that would take him a very long taxi ride away. Instructions had been given to ensure that he could not return until long after the interview was in the can.

Within half an hour of his departure, the crew arrived and were admitted to the Kensington residence with speed and efficiency by all those involved in the project.

Tasia watched as the Princess applied her own make up giving her a particularly dramatic effect. Dark kohl lined her wide eyed innocent expression giving her a melancholy and stunning look. She insisted on doing her own hair to complete the less groomed appearance she was perfecting to add pathos and sincerity to her usual elegant and styled countenance. Finally, she donned a sombre and business like black suit to match the outpouring of emotion which had been carefully rehearsed. It was as though she was marking the death of something. An era, perhaps? Or a presentiment? She was nervous; extremely nervous. She knew more than anyone that her life would undoubtedly become intolerable within the family after this, the ultimate betrayal of her position but she was also excited by the possibilities that may open up to her. A new role, greater autonomy and her heart felt hope that the object of her affections, the noble doctor, would finally accept her as his wife after the inevitable divorce that was bound to follow.

There was much wringing of hands and pacing of rooms at the end of the interview in which it was agreed, the Princess had given the performance of her life. On the day of the screening, the air was thick with a mixture of terror and anticipation as the country settled down tuning in in their millions to watch what everyone agreed would be the most fascinating insight of royal life ever screened. The collective national gasp of astonishment could almost be heard throughout the country as the explosive programme began. Under Tasia's and the others' tutelage, the Princess had pre-empted and addressed matters that she knew would be raised by her enemies and detractors post interview. Her head to one side, her eyes large, frightened and filled with sadness, she acknowledged her bulimia, her attempts at self harm and the deep unhappiness she felt. She disparaged those who would accuse her of madness and squarely blamed her troubles on the Establishment who wanted rid of her and had actively made her daily existence so miserable. It was a clever tactic from her family lawyers who advised her that if she acknowledged these matters, it would make it far more difficult for her husband to rely on them in any later divorce proceedings.

In an atmosphere of pathos, the Princess told of her desire for her marriage to work but the fact that there had been 'three of us in the marriage' had made it crowded. She candidly admitted that after she had discovered her husband's infidelity it had affected her badly but she admitted to one affair herself (fearing that if she did not, her former lover would produce evidence in his possession to the contrary).

Her *coup de grace* however was the one that was important to the group and the most damaging and dangerous to their mission. Sadly, she told her interviewer that she would accept a divorce if that was what her husband and family

279

wanted. She would be content to be 'Queen of Hearts' and would cherish a role as a British ambassador. Few outside the group knew how significant the idea that was being mooted really was. The finale reached its crescendo as she sorrowfully answered the interviewer's question, eyes downcast as she admitted to the world that in her view, her husband was unsuited to the role of King and that her son should succeed the Monarch. The unspoken suggestion hung in the air that he should do so with her firmly in the wings to guide him. The interview concluded and the stunned silence in the room hung over its occupants like a thick curtain. It was everything that they had planned.

The next morning, Kyle, Stergios and Tasia pored over the morning newspapers. Every headline was about the interview which proclaimed the Princess as 'Queen of Hearts' and one party to the 'Three in the Marriage.' Chaos, confusion, horror and terror circled in the Establishment machinery. Disbelief was evident on the faces of all those within the usually well oiled and calm organisation. Public opinion seemed to have gone in the Princess's favour despite best efforts of senior advisors to cast her as a lunatic who should be locked up. Described as a loose cannon, it was clear that action would be imminent. Everyone braced themselves for the storm that was brewing. They didn't have long to wait. After almost immediate advice being taken from the Prime Minister and Archbishop of Canterbury, a divorce was ordered. To Tasia's and the group's great delight, the Princess was also nominated as Humanitarian of the Year. Her profile was already rising and she collected her award in New York. All, so far was going to plan.

Tasia met up with Kyle and Stergios in the secret rooms underneath Whitehall. Stanton was also there for the briefing.

"Ah Tasia, so, how are things progressing?" Stanton asked.

Tasia, dressed elegantly in a blue pin stripe suit, her legs shapely in Louboutin court shoes stretched out beneath the flattering pencil skirt. Kyle could not stop himself from casting an admiring glance but tried to concentrate on the business of the day.

"She's received a letter ordering her to divorce," Tasia smiled, satisfaction clear. "She's definitely working on her terms though. That tape we obtained alleging homosexual practices in the Palace has got them on the run. They certainly don't want that getting out in the public domain. Stroke of genius that one. It's the Princess's greatest bargaining tool at the moment."

"What exactly does the letter say?" Stergios could hardly contain his curiosity.

"Well, basically that she must agree to a divorce. She's making them sweat though. She's had it for a couple of weeks and hasn't responded to Her Majesty. Says she's going to let them wait while she consults lawyers. She also says that she's had a meeting with her husband and he's agreed to a number of her terms."

"Are they terms helpful to the cause?" Stergios asked.

"Mmmm. Definitely. They would certainly keep up her profile if they're agreed. She's insisting it's a no fault divorce, mutual consent, that sort of thing and she wants to keep her home in the Palace, an office at St James and the title, HRH Princess of Wales. Of course, she wants to stay completely hands on with the children with shared custody."

"Good, sounds like everything is going swimmingly so far," nodded Stanton. "Keep up the good work everyone. Keep me informed." Stanton rose, gave a formal little bow to the team and strode from the room clearly satisfied that the operation had been well handled.

"So what now?" Kyle asked.

"We just have to sit and wait to see what happens next," Tasia stated confidently as she too rose from her seat to leave. "Now, gentlemen, I must take my leave. Palace work awaits I'm afraid. I'll be in touch."

Only Kyle and Stergios remained in the room. Kyle felt a little disappointed he hadn't been able to have a few moments alone with Tasia. He despaired that they would ever have the opportunity of getting to know one another better. She was just too damned professional sometimes and he really couldn't gauge what she was thinking. She was a real enigma, but, that's what makes her fascinating, he guessed.

For the next few weeks, the press indulged their readers with every detail of the royal rift they could dissect and analyse from every possible angle. Speculation filled their pages with salacious detail, real and imagined and the promise of a scandal hitherto unknown in the monarchy.

During the following months, Tasia remained at her employer's side, advising her at every turn in order to optimise her position. Eventually, things settled down and the final arrangements for the divorce were reached, largely to the satisfaction of everyone involved in the dissident camp. Life became quiet, the Princess having resigned from much of her charity work and now spending time with her friends and an array of therapists and spiritual advisors. It was exactly what Tasia hoped. She would learn more about the ancient and arcane skills of her Merovingian ancestry and through spiritual growth the Princess would know how to use them when the time came.

Chapter 26 – Emerging from the Chrysalis

Although the media storm abated for a while after that fateful interview, it was a while before matters settled down in the royal circles. Tasia threw herself into her under cover double life, alternating between her role as Personal Assistant and royal double. Both of the women knew it was critical for Tasia to be integrated fully into her role if the plans they harboured were to have any chance of success. At every possible opportunity therefore, Tasia stepped into the Princess's shoes at public engagements where her performances were flawless. With each passing day, Tasia's persona mimicked that of her royal employer and her features and mannerisms became indistinguishable from the woman she impersonated. The Princess could only watch in awe as Tasia deceived the public and cameras into believing she was the real thing.

"My God, Tasia, how on earth do you manage to pull it off every time?" They were flicking through a recording of Tasia's performance at one of the five charities which the Princess continued to support after deciding to retire from public duties.

Tasia paused the screen. "Ma'am, it really is quite simple. People see what and whom they wish to see. Given that as the starting premise it really is very easy to convince them of anything."

"It's almost as though you create a mass hallucination Tasia. Even an Oscar winning actress couldn't do what you've managed to achieve. It's astonishing."

Tasia smiled enigmatically, looking straight into the Princess's gaze as she spoke. For a moment they were truly as one. "Yes, Ma'am, you're right. It is a little like induced hallucination. I learned many techniques in the secret services which are, shall we say, a little unorthodox. You've

283

been studying with some of the best spiritual advisers for a while now. You must understand that occult powers are not just a fantasy but a fact of life. Channelled properly, they are powerful tools which only a few are privileged to comprehend. I have simply been able to perfect the abilities which are part of my heritage, just as they are yours."

"The Merovingian mysticism you mean?"

"Just so, Ma'am. You must realise that you have similar abilities by now surely?"

Indeed, the Princess acknowledged that she had often experienced premonitions and it was true that she seemed to have a strange of gift of bringing comfort to the sick and vulnerable.

"You see Ma'am, it's just a case of learning how to control your gift and use it to best advantage. As long as you always use them for good you will be a very powerful *magus.*"

"A magus, the Princess giggled. "Isn't that some sort of magician? I'm sure I saw a film about it once. John Fowles wasn't it?"

Tasia smiled. "Yes, that sort of thing. It comes from the Greek word 'μάγος' and is also associated with Zoroastrian priests to whom the Roman and Greeks attribute the invention of astrology and magic."

"Oh but it's all so fanciful when you think about it rationally here in the nineties, Tasia. Do you really believe that some of us are endowed with ancient powers?" The Princess sighed and took her head in her hands, struggling with the concepts that Tasia wholeheartedly embraced.

Tasia didn't flinch, but sat back in the armchair and crossed her legs. "Ma'am, time has no meaning in these matters. Ancient powers are reborn through the ages, through the blood. There are things that never die and before science took hold to try and discredit belief, immortality and deity were embraced. For most people, evolution and the constant desire for 'rational explanation' has diluted the primaeval knowledge

284

and instincts which once we all held. Think of the survival instinct. It was paramount when people roamed the wild and dangers of the natural world had to be detected without scientific instruments. Humans had the gift of understanding their environment and relied on premonition and instinct to live. Our modern world has destroyed the greatest gifts of mankind because our reliance on science has made the need for precognition and magic extinct."

It all made a kind of sense to the young woman who longed to believe in something other than the obvious but who struggled despite her voracious questing into the supernatural. She was a woman of the modern age, but something drew her into the arcane and mystical. She just couldn't quite relinquish herself completely to the notion that she was anything special.

"You know Tasia, I feel that I've known you all my life; it's as though you've always been here, like a twin sister or something. You read my every thought, you seem to understand my every emotion."

Tasia smiled. Indeed she had known the young woman all of her life. She had lived her life with her, experienced her pain from childhood to present day. Eventually, the time had come when the synthesis had to be broken and Tasia had to guide her alter ego to her own destiny. Their ancient connection would bring powerful change to a world destroyed by secular pragmatism. A new fusion of the ancient and modern would restore faith in a cynical world of greed.

It was June 1996 and the news was out that the royal divorce was final. It hadn't been without gamesmanship and one upmanship on either side but eventually, the manoeuvring had reached a satisfactory, if not entirely comfortable position for the Princess. She managed to retain many of her royal privileges as well as a healthy financial settlement but, having been burned previously, the family would not permit her to enter into any commercial activities. The family froze the

285

Princess out and Tasia shivered in the chilly loneliness she felt through the woman's senses.

One morning, the two women were working through the daily pile of correspondence when Tasia felt the burst of anger and disappointment build before the Princess stood up, her expression furious as she read a letter from the Prime Minister. On Tasia's advice she had approached him recently to ask if she might take on an ambassadorial role which would allow her to more formally embrace her humanitarian interests.

"Dull, grey, unimaginative little man!" she exclaimed. "He's completely turned me down flat! How bloody dare he? Doesn't he realise I can do more good than all the rest of them put together? He says that the work that I've specifically asked for is, listen to this, 'more suitable for my ex husband!' Well! If it was more suitable for him, why didn't he bloody well think of it then? Why isn't he doing it now? I'll tell you why, Tasia, because he's too bloody busy talking to plants to ever think of doing something useful for people." She sat down heavily and folded her arms, shaking her head in exasperation.

Tasia laughed. "Don't get yourself so wound up. You don't need their permission to do anything. You already have the world eating out of your hands. Use the media for a change instead of letting them use you!"

The Princess's relationship with her beloved doctor had been frustratingly slow to progress and she hoped that now the divorce was complete she could persuade him to marry her. It was becoming ever clearer to both she and Tasia though that he had other priorities and although there was genuine love between them the strain was beginning to show.

"Why don't you do something that might impress him," Tasia suggested. You could possibly kill two birds with one stone if you were perhaps to offer help to Pakistan hospitals for instance? Tasia knew that this would appeal to the young woman but she knew equally well that it would start to create the international platform they now needed for the Princess.

The idea worked magnificently, at least on one level. The work that Tasia and the Princess arranged brought her international acclaim and she was once more in the public focus. Numerous foreign invitations followed and her profile blossomed once more under the rapturous gaze of the world. It was exactly as Tasia and her colleagues intended. The Princess emerged from the claustrophobic chrysalis of royal protocol to become the vibrant epitome of sleek style and elegance much to the disgust of the Establishment who feared that she now put her former family very much in the shadow. Not to be outshone however, the chill winds following the divorce grew warmer and relations were restored with her former husband who now even began to co-operate with his ex-wife in planning joint engagements.

Tasia had to smile. "See?" she had said to the Princess. "They need you more than you need them. They want some of your shine by association again."

The Princess swung her long legs up onto the sofa and grinned, self satisfied with her recent accomplishments and the ability to bask in the glow of having won a very large battle.

"They even want me to do some formal charity work now Tasia! Can you believe it?"

"Oh I believe it alright," Tasia replied, a hint of cynicism in her tone. The plan couldn't have been coming together more perfectly. Of course, it wasn't without a little manipulation from Tasia's 'higher powers'; the ones that most of her more rational colleagues knew so little about.

In the following months, Tasia accompanied and on many occasions substituted herself for the Princess in their enterprise to campaign against anti personnel landmines which were widely used in Bosnia and Angola. Although the family were behind the enterprise, there were those, as Tasia,

287

Stergios and Kyle knew only too well who were muttering dangerously about the damage being done to the British armaments industry.

"God, Tasia, they're never happy unless they're trying to criticise me are they?" the Princess was bemoaning yet another headline from some political worthy who described her as a 'loose cannon' or a 'self publicist' interested only in seeing her name in the papers. Of course the comments hurt them both, Tasia vicariously, but she at least was able to keep matters positive. When eventually the Conservative Government lost to the Labour Government, it was agreed by the incoming Prime Minister that the Princess should have an even greater ambassadorial role. Tasia was thrilled to report the developments to Stanton and her colleagues.

"You're doing a remarkable job Tasia. I don't know how you do it, but please, whatever you're doing, keep it up."

The mood amongst the group became more sombre moments later however when Stanton made his announcement.

"I was called to a meeting last week with various Heads of Intelligence from both the British and American Services," he began. "Whilst we have cause to celebrate our success, it isn't going unnoticed by our mainstream colleagues. Not that we didn't anticipate it of course. Things seem to be progressing rather faster than we'd hoped though."

"Why, what's happening?" Kyle was impatient to know where this might be going. Stanton had an irritating habit of imparting information with dramatic effect so that he didn't get to the point quickly enough for Kyle's liking.

"I'm coming to it Kyle." Stanton admonished him and leaned back in his reclining chair looking for all the world like a Bond character. All he needed was a cat in his lap, thought Kyle wryly. He loves to play the spy to the full.

"There are rumblings amongst the Establishment because obviously, they're not happy about a member of the royal family becoming involved in political issues. Her questioning of the viability of the current House of Windsor in that television interview hit them hard and they're onto the idea that she might be about to try and set up a counter-monarchy with her son at the centre and her as Regent. Obviously her Stuart bloodline, if it becomes public knowledge and arouses interest might lend support and greater credibility to her aims. They're also unhappy that her image has rocketed from 'Queen of Tarts' to 'Queen of Hearts' in the media these days. Respect is growing for her outside the Establishment and they're starting to talk about finding 'a final solution' to the problem. The vested interests of our highest Establishment members are being affected by her campaigns over the landmines. They're afraid it won't stop there." Stanton sat forward again and leaned over his desk. "Anyway, just so you know. I don't think it will be long before we have further instructions. We need to be prepared for anything now. Tasia, what are the plans for the coming weeks?"

Tasia consulted her page to view diary.

"Well we're heading off to Washington where we'll meet the Clintons and there are a couple of other appointments to meet Mother Teresa at a Bronx AIDS hospice and, oh yes," she smiled, "a meeting with American Vogue." The males amongst them raised their eyes at the incongruity of the humanitarian plans being sandwiched between frivolous fashion arrangements but no-one said a word.

"OK," Stanton nodded. "Keep an eye on things and make sure you report in regularly Tasia. I have a feeling it's going to get very hot in the kitchen soon."

Stanton wound up the meeting and the crowd of agents exited the boardroom. Only Tasia, Kyle and Stergios lingered together afterwards.

"Tasia, you need to keep your wits about you. You're in the greatest danger just now. If anyone recognises you from

289

the main service you're going to be a target as much as she is."

A playful smile crossed Tasia's lips and she raised her eyes coquettishly, meeting Kyle's concerned expression.

"Do I detect a note of worry about me Kyle?" she enquired playfully.

"Just a professional interest," he replied unconvincingly.

"Don't you worry about me gentlemen. I am fully equipped to deal with any situation that arises. There's little I can't handle." Noting Kyle's slightly crestfallen look as she dismissed his genuine concern, Tasia softened and gently laid her hand on his. His hand tingled at her touch and at the same time he felt strangely comforted, as though she communicated her own self assuredness to him, skin to skin. She looked earnestly into his deep blue eyes. "Really," she said. "All will be fine. You'll see."

Kyle nodded and managed a smile as Tasia withdrew her hand from his. Stergios meanwhile simply stood aside and observed from a distance the clear burgeoning of affection between his two colleagues. He hoped it wasn't going to complicate matters.

Chapter 27 – Mayhem and Mysterious Murders

Hal's excitement over the story that was unfolding before him grew to obsession. His excitement however was tempered with a dose of scepticism. No matter how plausible his companions' story appeared during the telling, in the quiet solitude of his room it felt less so. Nevertheless, he hurried to his desk at the end of the day ready to chronicle the latest in events in a growing manuscript. Working late into the night, often into the early hours of a new day, he would wearily glance up from the screen to greet the first signs of dawn, surprised to find he'd lost himself yet again in the project that had become his passion. So engrossed was he that he often forgot entirely to eat, missing meals on a regular basis as he immersed himself in the narrative of the lives of those who had summoned him to recount their story. Gone too were the unhealthy snacks that had comforted him when his mind was less occupied. Following Tasia's nutritional advice, the difference was amazing. He felt rejuvenated and a new positivity was taking over his life. Of course, he always kept one eye over his shoulder – there was clearly danger present; but it was exciting to take on this voyage of discovery. He wondered what he would do when it was over. Would it ever be over? What would happen if his book got to market? Where might it take him? Life was less certain now but he embraced it. There were still so many unanswered questions.

Hal caught up with Kyle in the grounds of Villa Artemis where he found him splayed out on his back underneath one of the Mercs.

"Hey Hal!" Kyle greeted him. "Just doing a security check. You can never be too sure." He shuffled out from underneath the car and pulled himself upright before brushing the dry dust from his jeans. "I was just going to have a coffee. Want to join me?"

"Sure," Hal replied as Kyle motioned to the table under the shade of the trees surrounding the grounds where a coffee pot and mugs were already set.

"I was going over my notes last night and I wanted to ask you about some of this parapsychological stuff you were talking about. Tell me more about Tasia's involvement with, what did you call it ... remote viewing; telekinesis? All that stuff," he said to Kyle.

"I don't profess to know a great deal about it myself," Kyle answered vaguely. Until I met Tasia I'd discounted it as just smoke and mirrors stuff designed to spook enemies into thinking there were secret powers being used for surveillance purposes. All I've heard is that there has been a belief within the intelligence services that psychic abilities are accepted and acknowledged as useful in covert activities. Those with the gifts are scrutinised and extensively tested and the results have shown success. Remote viewing is the ability of a sensitive to sit in a room thousands of miles away from a person or activity to identify what's happening in real time. Telekinesis is the ability to move objects without touching them. All the intelligence services are into it. They say Hitler was interested in occult practices and tried to harness these powers in the war. Uri Geller apparently worked for the intelligence services in America and Israel because of his extraordinary skills. It was alleged he might even have used only his mind to knock out all computer systems to help free the hostages of the Entebbe Hijacking"

"It's unbelievable although It would explain a lot of things about Tasia I guess."

"Yeah. It isn't always a gift," Kyle sighed, a hint of - what was it - anger that Hal detected in his voice?" It can be a curse as you've seen. For every time she uses her abilities, a little bit of her is destroyed. It's like an electrical short out and partly why she's so sick now."

Hal nodded thoughtfully. "Another thing I'm struggling with, why were the British and American intelligence services working so closely on the Diana plot?

"OK, so you understand now the idea of Corporate Government? In other words, democracy is dead my friend. It's manipulated by money with decisions being taken at the highest levels to benefit the underwriters whose only interest is to make more money and take more power."

Hal nodded.

"Starting with MI5 then", Kyle continued. "It was first set up to counter German espionage in Britain in 1909. Later, when spies from communist Soviet Union and Fascist Germany infiltrated, MI5 broadened its remit and cracked down hard on anyone on the fringes who might introduce subversive dogma to the country. To this day, MI5 is the British domestic intelligence and counter intelligence agency although it keeps an eye on foreign espionage and terrorism too. Needless to say, MI5 takes a great interest in all high profile individuals who might pose a threat to the Establishment. Think of a certain Princess, for example..."

"I take it they aren't just passive observers though?"

"They sure ain't Hal. They might sound like beneficent protectors of security in British lands but they are ruthless operators. They'll keep subversives under surveillance, brutally discredit them in the media, create smokescreens and kill without compunction if necessary. Think about the leaked tapes from the royal household. Think about a certain protection officer who was mysteriously killed in a road accident when he overstepped the mark with our princess. GCHQ are watching and listening to everything."

Then there's MI6. Formed in 1909 as Military Intelligence Department 6; responsible first to the Monarch, Foreign Secretary and House of Commons Intelligence and Security Committee? OK so far?"

"Yup," Hal confirmed.

"MI6 is full of secret compartments," Kyle continued. "Some really high echelons not even known about by other MI6 members and charged predominantly with ensuring that the British Monarchy is protected personally and as an institution. The Special Operations Executive upholds the corporate and international agenda with the major league players from British and American industry and finance. It's a Masonic structure; highly secretive with connections throughout Europe with various other Masonic organisations. All back the idea of a United States of Europe. It works hand in hand with the CIA which was actually formed by MI6 and, guess what - run by the British and American Godfathers who own the most powerful financial institutions and industries dealing in multinational arms, drugs, fuel and technology who sponsor our respective governments. Mossad and BND are also linked to the CIA."

"So," Hal summarised, "the British and American Establishment, those with major financial interests in political manipulation and the protection of the Monarchy wouldn't have been happy with a high profile peripheral 'royal' messing up their plans I guess?"

"You got it dude; especially one who might have her own legitimate claim to the throne; one that was stronger than the existing monarchy. That could really create some mess-ups huh?"

Hal nodded, frowning. "But the royals and indeed the Clintons were all behind the princess's landmine project weren't they?"

"Oh yeah. At first," Kyle conceded. "The Princess made a speech that was rapturously welcomed in America when she said that she was committed to supporting the Red Cross in their international campaign to outlaw the 'deadly legacy' of fifteen million landmines amidst ten million people in Angola. The Clintons actively and publicly supported her stated ideals, so much so that they intended to endorse a

294

resolution to ban Anti Personnel Landmines at a conference in Oslo which was scheduled to take place 3 weeks after the princess's 'accident' in France. She and Tasia had a highly successful time in America and of course, you know that they went off to Angola to highlight the prevalence and consequences of landmines amongst civilian innocents. They planned trips to Bosnia and the Princess began to take an interest in the nuclear industry. It was all becoming too much for the powers that relied on income from these industries. They couldn't allow the discrediting to continue.

Meanwhile, behind the scenes in the States the CIA became involved in the problem that had arisen within their own Presidency that allowed them to make sure that Clinton could renege on his promise to support the banning of landmines. I'm sure you know that it's in the interests of the intelligence services to have premiers with, shall we say, 'a past'; secrets that might be revealed in the future if they don't co-operate with the Corporate Government. Conveniently, Clinton and his indiscretion with a certain White House intern was hovering over his head. He would need to rely on the help of the CIA when the news came out and he was impeached for perjury and obstruction of justice in the Lewinsky affair. They, of course, knew all about it and were able to give him the support he needed – provided of course he played ball.

"So, how exactly did he manage to renege on his promises?" Hal asked, a little confused.

"Same way they always get around difficult problems. The Princess never arrived in Oslo. The world witnessed her death in a French tunnel three weeks previously. Convenient huh? Clinton was able to withdraw his support for the ban on anti personnel landmines and because Princess Diana wasn't at the conference, the media showed no interest. It all, very conveniently died a death, along with the Princess; or so it appeared."

295

"What do you mean..." Hal asked, "...or so it appeared?"

Kyle smiled wryly. "All in good time Hal. But you get the drift. No deal on the anti personnel landmine issue. Problem solved in the time honoured way. Kennedy, Princess Grace of Monaco, Marilyn Monroe you'll recall, also died in rather mysterious circumstances. They were similarly problems to be removed; Kennedy because he was onto the CIA and wanted to create an alternative defence agency which would work on his behalf. He knew the CIA was running against him and the ideal of democracy. Of course, his desire to end the Vietnam War that was lining the American armaments industrialists' pockets didn't go much in his favour either. Monroe, of course, knew too much about the Kennedys – an arranged 'overdose' for her.

"And Princess Grace of Monaco?" Hal asked.

"Allegations that she was a member of a bizarre religious cult, The Solar Temple. She may have known about Diana's Jacobite connection and the bloodline. She died in a mysterious car accident, co-incidentally driving off a mountain road into the garden of another Solar Temple member. None of these deaths were co-incidence.

"It's unbelievable!" Exclaimed Hal. "Except it's so unbelievable that the very services who supposedly watch over us are actually working for their own ends, it's actually very plausible," he sighed. "So that's why the Princess died in that car crash?"

Kyle shook his head pouring them both more coffee.

"Oh no Hal. It gets far more complex than that. But it was a very big nail in her eventual coffin, so to speak."

Just then the door opened and Stergios joined the two men.

"Hey Stergios. What's new?" Stergios looked tired. More careworn than usual.

"I've just been talking to the hospital. Tasia still hasn't regained consciousness. They're not sure how much longer she can hold on." He looked meaningfully at Kyle. "Or how much longer she wants to hold on." Stergios grasped Kyle's arm and squeezed it in a rare visible display of empathy towards his colleague and friend.

Kyle's sorrow was evident but he took a deep breath. He'd always known that Tasia's time was limited; it was part of the deal. It was her destiny to leave soon and she'd been but a borrowed joy in his life.

Hal remained quiet, respectful of the distress Tasia's illness had brought to the two men but as yet not fully understanding the complex relationships between them or the true nature of their story.

"I've booked the helicopter. It's coming in an hour or so. Why don't we all go over to Chania for a few days? We can be near Tasia and have a change of scenery while we try to complete our work." Hal and Kyle thought it was a good plan and soon they were at the helipad ascending from Gavdos. Hal was relieved to be heading for civilisation. The little island had become quiet as autumn was giving way to the winter months and he found it oppressive to walk along the silent yet still beautiful beaches, never knowing if someone would jump out from the rocks or the trees baying for his life. He had been lucky so far but the more he learned from Kyle and Stergios, the more certain he became that his life was dispensable to those whose interests he might harm. Although he never voiced it, he really didn't know how this book would ever become public. Surely he would be silenced before it ever reached market? Or maybe, if it ever did get published he'd be discounted as just another nutter and conspiracy theorist. He shivered at the prospect. He was an easy target compared to the more high profile individuals who had been so effortlessly picked off for their interference in political affairs but whose demise had been explained away so

297

simply. Hal knew that by his very involvement with Kyle and Stergios his days may be numbered. But now, he had to know the ending. He couldn't walk away. Even Fliss had become involved in some strange ethereal way. If he left now, would he ever have the opportunity of seeing her just one last time? Perhaps that was partly why he stayed. Perhaps Tasia and the two men knew that by invoking her spirit he would be tied in and invested in the outcome. Perhaps Hal was really instrumental in bringing a great truth to the world.

After a short flight the three men alighted from the helicopter in Chania and they were transported by a waiting car to the town. Kyle decided to head off for the hospital immediately to be with Tasia. Stergios, accompanied by Hal headed to the harbour which was still bustling despite the tourist season having ended. Amongst the indigenous Cretans mingled many expats, the majority British, who sat enjoying the late sunshine at the tavernas surrounding the picturesque Venetian harbour. The two men were subdued, each lost in their own thoughts. Stergios looked his usual dapper self in light slacks, white shirt and the customary straw trilby. Hal, never yet having mastered sartorial elegance, still cut a dishevelled figure, more so because his clothes now hung upon his slighter frame. He looked all the more unkempt for the three day growth on his chin.

They had chosen a seafood restaurant this afternoon and the waiter brought them a selection of dishes made from freshly caught produce which they ate contemplatively, Hal's mind returning once more to the heady days of his visit with Fliss. How he longed to see her again. He knew that he would never find anyone who would match her and in truth, he never wanted to. He preferred a life lived with her memory than a life with someone else against whom he would always draw comparison. In an odd way, he was content to exist in this world of intrigue and creative pursuit because Fliss was a part of it. He didn't know what would happen once it was over. He was afraid to think of it.

Eventually Hal broke the pensive silence between them.

"Kyle was explaining the various roles of MI5, MI6 and the CIA earlier. They're scary outfits from what I understand."

"Indeed," Stergios agreed. "They are omnipotent. Once you're in, you can never really get out. If we didn't have Stanton and the others risking life and limb for us to be here, we'd probably be dead by now. The double bluff has paid off for us so far but we never know how long it will last. Already you've seen the evidence that there is suspicion in our ranks. It's being contained for now but every day brings a new threat.

So now you understand the power of the intelligence services and that their existence goes far beyond what is ostensibly security of Britain. MI6 was really set up purely for the protection of the royal bloodline which it does through a highly complex network of Masonic links. It is more powerful than the worldwide web for discovering and concealing world affairs. Because they are all covert organisations, no-one knows about the passage of intelligence between them. We have spies placed in all sorts of organisations, the Knights of Malta, the Priory of Sion; the latter of which was instrumental in the transfer of the Saunière Parchments from France to Britain incidentally. They were first held by an MI6 front company, the International League of Antiquarian Booksellers Museum. France later gave permission for the parchments to be held for a further 25 years when they were transferred in 1956 to an MI6 vault held as 'Classified' in the British Museum. Those documents demand that the Merovingian rights to the monarchy be disclosed and also contain information relating to the Cathar treasures passed down from the Temple of Jerusalem. The information contained in the parchments provide the greatest motive yet for the disposal of our Princess. The political implications for the British

299

Monarchy and the threat to the proposed United States of Europe was great if in fact the parchments disclosed a bloodline traceable to Jesus and his issue which challenges the current monarchical rights to European thrones."

"It's really hard to believe though Stergios," Hal shook his head. "That something so ancient and, well, obscure, mythical almost, could have such an impact on modern day politics and monarchical protocol."

"It's just the link that draws power. People believe in the power of religion and the genetically transferred belief that monarchs are connected to deity. No-one knows how or why the royals are revered but the sources lead us to conclude it is a hereditary belief handed down through religious doctrine through the centuries. Remember, even today the British Monarch is 'Defender of the Faith', head of the Church of England. Therefore the connection is set. In truth, it all comes down to Britain and America's power machinations designed to create a corporate United States of Europe underpinned by the Judaeo-Christian bloodline. The British Monarchy approves because it wants to maintain its illegitimate link with the bloodline. Along with that, organisations prevalent through history have worked with the Churches to maintain the secrets. The Knights of Saint John for instance is a facade for activities in espionage designed to support the concept of corporate Europe. They are concerned with intelligence between the Vatican and the West and have a covert hierarchy that carries out international espionage. The Knights Templar on the other hand defended Jerusalem and became the first financiers setting up early banking systems. Although opposed in their views they each drew their beliefs from the Judaeo-Christian ethos and were allied in the crusades to defeat Islam. They found common ground in their aims and whilst there, the Knights Templar fought to protect the Merovingian claim on Jerusalem, the Knights of St John fought for the supremacy of Rome and the papacy. Whilst the

300

original Judaic bloodline was usurped by political powerhouses, arranging marriages through the Merovingian dynasty it survives today in diluted form through the monarchy supported by the Church of England. This is the Holy Grail for which the Knights Templar fought for political power and which today, Britain and America will fight to the death to protect in the interest of maintaining strong Western power particularly against the Muslims. Hence, the United States of Europe, a powerful American and European alliance. I guess you can see why America is so keen to keep the European Union strong with Britain an instrumental member within it. Against this background, there is a movement, of which we, the 'dissidents' are a part. Our mission is to restore the true bloodline to Britain, perhaps even through an independent Scotland, to prevent the corruption of our world powers which has traditionally only been based on greed and manipulation of democracy. Of course, throughout the centuries, people who have come close to the truth or who may have challenged the current right to the throne have been mysteriously disposed of or discounted as lunatics."

Hal nodded thoughtfully. His understanding was finally beginning to crystallise.

"Hence the questions over who would be the monarch in Scotland if it ever gained independence I guess? And the Princess in our story, through her blood links with France and Britain, which we can trace back to the Merovingians would have been a huge threat because of her Scottish Stuart bloodline as well?"

"Quite so, Hal. With her new ideas of openness and transparency and her desire for typically Merovingian humanitarian ideals, her notions could spell the beginning of the end for the traditional power bases of the various oligarchs within the intelligence services and the Establishment. She began to challenge everything that they held dear. Her popularity could sink the British Establishment, particularly if the suggestion of some kind of counter-monarchy headed up by her as regent to her son could be orchestrated.

Remember, her husband's popularity at the time was sinking to an all time low. The 'People's Princess ' was attracting more credibility and a following worldwide. If this mistreated royal could show that she had a real blood right to the throne, the evidence suggests that her popularity could have toppled the monarchy and her former husband bypassed in his claim. She suggested as much in her television interview if you remember."

It was indeed explosive. Goodness only knew what the implications for him were when it reached the public; if, indeed, it ever got that far. Hal knew already that his life was endangered. How could he ever get this to print, he wondered.

Just then, he looked up and saw Kyle approaching them along the harbour from the direction of the new Chania town. He was waving and he broke into a jog when he saw his two friends sitting outside the rustic fish restaurant, its blue painted shutters and facade matching the sky above them.

"Hey Guys!" Kyle was slightly breathless, more with excitement than the exertion. "Tasia's conscious. She's weak but determined that she should see you as quickly as possible Hal. She's anxious to tell you the final parts of the story. I've filled her in on where we're at so if you can make your way up to the hospital now, she's waiting for you." Kyle having delivered his message slumped into one of the vacant seats and ordered a raki. He downed it in one and ordered another. "Boy I needed that," he said. "You still here Hal? Go on! She may not stay with us for long!" He didn't need telling again. He grabbed his lightweight jacket containing his Dictaphone and notepad and waved a summary farewell to his companions. He hardly had time to think before he arrived at the hospital situated on the outskirts of Chania near the village of Mournies. After a short taxi journey, he alighted at the St

George Chania General Hospital and warily entered the private ward where Tasia, pale and ethereal was propped up with pillows. She smiled wearily when she saw Hal at the door and gestured for him to sit next to her. Stretching out her thin arm she grasped his hand. Her touch was as light as a butterfly's.

"My but you've lost weight!" Tasia smiled. "You've been watching your diet as I advised you?"

Hal smiled and nodded. "Yes, only healthy food and no mixing carbs and protein," he laughed. "Add to that the stress of writing your story and hey presto! A new slim line me!"

Tasia giggled weakly. "As you see, I am a little more slender myself but not on this occasion by design. Now Hal, I think this is the last time you will see me. I have a journey to embark upon very soon. New issues to deal with after a regenerative sleep and a visit to my home and family.

He didn't quite know what she meant so he simply nodded, understanding her to mean that she was slipping away. Deep sadness filled him. She had been a good friend in the short time that he had known her and he would miss their time together.

Sensing his sadness, Tasia reassured him.

"Don't fear for me Hal. This has happened many times before. I am quite prepared for it. It is just the shell that dies; I shall return in another guise at another time when a situation demands it. In the meantime, I am always near my friends, even if they cannot immediately perceive it."

Hal looked confused, a frown creasing his forehead. "You mean reincarnation?" he asked.

"I mean immortality. And yes, I suppose if you mean the transition into another human body in the future, then it is another incarnation for me. Perhaps not reincarnation as you would understand it. I must however return to the clouds above Mount Olympus where I shall watch your progress with interest," she smiled enigmatically so that he wasn't sure if she was teasing him.

Tasia slumped back into the pillows again, the strain of talking to him clearly taking its toll. She was delirious, he assumed. He wondered how much sense he might get from her in this condition. He would have to be careful that her story in completion was not just deathbed ramblings. She appeared to be mouthing words silently now, as though speaking with someone unseen. Suddenly, she opened her eyes and they appeared wider and clearer now as though some hidden strength had been gathered. Tasia managed to pull herself higher in the bed and as she spoke, she no longer had the sleepy slur of moments ago. Her mind appeared active and alert, urgency in her tone.

"Now Hal, we must get on. So, our star was flying high on the crest of the Princess's humanitarian work. You must understand, I use 'our' because I was at one with her, our lives completely interchangeable when appropriate or indeed necessary. It was my job to ensure that she carried out her mission and set the foundations for the future you see. Also, I had to protect her until the moment when her apparent death would occur." Hal sat back and simply listened and allowed the next part of the story to unfold.

The relationship with the heart surgeon was over and Tasia witnessed at first hand the aftermath of the Princess's heartbreak. She didn't just witness it though, she lived it and wondered if she was ever going to be able to get the Princess back on track and focusing again on their work. The young woman was poor with emotional upset and with every rejection, her confidence was knocked badly. However, she was stronger this time and determined that one way or another, she would either get over him or lure him back. Meanwhile, a shock incident shook both women to the core.

It was June 1997 and the Princess was poring over the morning headlines as Tasia entered the office.

304

"Quick Tasia, turn on the television news. Something's happened to the Rottweiler!" 'The Rottweiler' was the term she often used when referring to her former husband's paramour. As the news unfolded, Tasia tried to hide her consternation. It appeared that the other woman responsible for the destruction of the royal marriage had been involved in a car accident when rounding a bend on a country road. It had been a head on collision but she was miraculously uninjured. Mysteriously, the Princess's rival in love, instead of waiting at the roadside where the driver of the other vehicle sat trapped in her car, chose to run from the scene of the accident. It was of course illegal to leave the scene of an accident and it had all caused quite a stir. The Princess was at first blasé about the incident and actually seemed to be quite enjoying the predicament in which her arch enemy now found herself.

"Probably drunk, Tasia. Wouldn't have wanted the police to breathalyse her. Dear, dear! Whatever is the monarchy coming to?" she crowed rather ungraciously. A quick glance at Tasia's face however and her mood suddenly changed.

"What is it Tasia? Why do you look so worried?"

"It – it's nothing Ma'am. Probably nothing, anyway. I'm sure you're right. It'll be a simple explanation."

"Oh my God, Tasia! I know what you're thinking. It wasn't an accident at all was it?"

"Not sure right now Ma'am. Let me make some enquiries." Tasia strongly suspected this was another incident like the bodyguard's motorcycle accident only this time it had failed. The Princess had already connected the two and her jovial schadenfreud had quickly dissipated as she paced the floor, wringing her hands in terror, tears pouring down her cheeks.

"It's a warning Tasia, I'm certain of it. Oh God, it's me next isn't it?"

305

"Yes, but we know that, Ma'am. Don't forget the plans."

"But it could all go horribly wrong. I could end up dead if we carry on with this." Tasia was disconcerted. She had briefed the Princess already that there was a plot afoot to remove her from the world stage. This 'accident' though was a surprise to her. As soon as she was able, she contacted Stanton.

"What's the story on the car accident? We've just seen the papers." Stanton was a little guarded at first, unwilling to commit himself. He realised that Tasia wouldn't have the wool pulled over her eyes however and he gave in. He sighed.

"It seems that the woman has been under MI5 surveillance for a while. Our esteemed superiors feel that we're in such a constitutional mess we need to clean up the act a bit. The talk is that if we got rid of that part of the mess, it might be easier to control things with the Princess. We might even have avoided the need to be rid of her if all talk of marriage to the other woman could be quelled. Everyone acknowledges how blasted difficult it's going to be to orchestrate the 'Death of a Princess' if you'll pardon the expression. If things could have been tidied up nearer to home, there might have been some possibility of uniting the ambitions of the princess and her former husband. It's been bungled though. Target got spooked. Seems to realise that the night of the long knives was arranged for her. There certainly wouldn't have been much protest from the public if the operation had been carried out successfully and it would have served to stop the Princess from rocking the boat too much with her humanitarian work. A warning so to speak."

"But that's not what we want is it? We want to bring out the truth and establish the counter monarchy."

"Yes, but remember, our aims are different from our masters, Tasia. Either way, we could have coped to bring matters to the fore but now it looks as though the original plan to be rid of the Princess is back on. It won't be long now so stand by. Things are about to heat up. There has been talk of a royal marriage to the mistress but the Church is fighting against it and constitutionally, she couldn't become Queen while the Princess is still around. Seems it would be Henry VIII all over again. Church of England would have to be disestablished for that to happen, unless, of course, the Princess were to die."

Tasia was worried. It was all getting very messy. Why hadn't she been informed of this new plan, she wondered?

On her return to the Princess's office, Tasia found her still tearful and nervous.

"I've written my insurance policy you know, Tasia."

"What do you mean, Ma'am, 'insurance policy'?" Tasia asked, a frown of concern creasing her brow.

"A letter. I wrote it at the end of last year. After you told me about my lineage and knowing what they did to Jerry." Tasia was slightly taken aback. She wasn't aware of this and it worried her that anything might have been committed to writing.

Don't worry Tasia. It's sealed and being kept by a trusted source. I've also made a confidential statement to my lawyers. They're keeping it on file should the need for it to be made public ever arise. It isn't much comfort I suppose but I don't want the bastards to get off with my demise scot free!"

Tasia rolled her eyes and let out a gasp of exasperation.

"But Ma'am! What if this gets out before the operation is complete? What's in the letter anyway?"

"Stop worrying Tasia," the Princess replied with irritation. "This is my life, not yours, remember. It isn't exactly easy believing all that your lot are telling me and assuring me that although there is to be an attempt on my life that everything will be fine! Things can go wrong you know! Just look at today's episode. I'm sure that didn't go as it was supposed to. More's the pity," she added venomously.

307

"Anyway, as I said it won't go any further. I wrote a letter on my headed stationery outlining the fact that I knew there was to be an assassination attempt on me. I also stated that I believed my car would most probably be the method of choice. I told my solicitors of my belief that the Queen wanted to abdicate and that both I and that bloody Rottweiler would be disposed of to make way for a more suitable replacement for my ex husband. I told them that if the 'accident' failed they would most probably try to make me look unbalanced after it so that no-one would take me seriously any more anyway. I've known that they wanted rid of me for long enough, Tasia. Look, my brakes were tampered with two years ago – I'm pretty sure now who was behind it. They'll make sure it's a small incident; only me and possibly a few others involved. My home has been bugged for years and I've been told not to 'meddle' in things I know nothing about. It's clear as the nose on my face that there have been plans for me all along. I knew even before you lot came on the scene Tasia. Of course, whenever I became upset about it or voiced my fears, they branded me a complete nutcase. 'Paranoid', 'unbalanced', 'a loose cannon.' It's all so bloody conveniently impossible to prove though isn't it? I've played right into their hands over the years with my bulimia and my emotional outbursts. It's given everyone the excuse to shake their heads when I'm dead and say, 'poor girl, she was completely mad you know. Accused everyone of trying to kill her.' Well, Tasia, they're not going to have the chance. I've put it out there; my prediction. They won't get away with it if anything does happen to me." She fell silent, then, "Not that it'll do me any good at that point but at least my boys will know the truth." The young woman slumped in the sofa, exhausted by her outpouring of terrified indignation. Tasia felt sorry for her and sat down beside her, drawing the young woman close.

"It'll be OK," she said softly. "Trust me. I'm here to take care of you and protect your interests. Don't ever doubt

308

me, Ma'am. We are one and the same, we will live through each other, whatever happens."

The young woman gave a sardonic laugh. "Always talking in riddles, Tasia. I swear I'll never understand what's going on with you."

"Nice cup of tea?" Tasia asked brightly, hoping to keep the mood light. The woman smiled.

"Fixes everything doesn't it? Unless of course you suspect there might be poison in it!" Tasia shook her head.

"I'll make it and taste it for you," she assured the Princess as she went off to the kitchen to busy herself with the mundane.

Chapter 28 – High Days and Holidays

"Things very quickly began to happen after that day in June 1997," Tasia explained to Hal. "A rather unexpected development occurred in the life of the Princess which not only complicated things further but most certainly hastened and sealed her planned demise. I don't know whether other plans might have come into play had our maverick Princess decided not to pursue the course that she did. Certainly our superiors were nervous about the prospect of disposing of her. If they did, they couldn't be sure that the shockwaves in the aftermath wouldn't end the monarchy as it nearly did. However, what happened next sealed the decision for them and we now had to keep our eyes and ears firmly to the ground. We, of course, me, Kyle and Stergios were to be tasked in our formal roles to bring about the finale and ensure that the Princess was silenced for good. As double agents, it was to be our most difficult task; to give the impression that we were working for the Establishment whilst actually subverting their plans. It also turned out to be far more complex than any of us imagined."

Tasia explained that shortly after the 'Rottweiler's' incident, the Princess had decided that it was time for her to consider holiday arrangements for herself and her children. She couldn't compete financially with her husband and she was worried that she might not be able to provide them with anything comparable to their father's holidays. During a visit to the ballet, she had met an old family friend who was also regarded with suspicion and enmity by the Establishment; an Egyptian prestige store owner whose wealth was immense. Knowing of her predicament he no doubt hoped that through his association with the Princess he might be able to manipulate the situation in his favour and garner favour with the British Establishment He had been involved in controversy over his own rather embellished ancestry in the hope of becoming part of the British Establishment and, most particularly of gaining British Citizenship. A colourful character, his own machinations had led him into allegations of political manipulation and shady dealings which had impacted badly on the Tories with accusations that they accepted bribes for services rendered to the old fox.

The Princess accepted his invitation for her and the children to go to St Tropez with him and his family where they could enjoy all the trappings and excitement funded by her benefactor's great wealth. They spent their time on a fabulous powerboat, cruising around the most fashionable locations of southern France, jet ski-ing and diving into the sea. In the evenings they enjoyed luxurious surroundings and mountains of the most exquisite food imaginable.

Still smarting from her break up with her beloved heart surgeon, the Princess was diverted by her benefactor's suave and handsome son who 'happened' to join them aboard the powerboat. She found him generous, eager to please and a hopeless romantic although he was known as a somewhat insubstantial, unreliable playboy whose film career had been largely bankrolled by his father's wealth. It would have been clear to most that the whole situation had been engineered by the young man's father in the hope that his own place in the British Establishment might be assured by the coupling of his son with the Princess who was basking in the light of public adoration and putting the monarchy very much in the shade.

Tasia watched on and experienced the young woman's joy as her new admirer showered attention upon her. As the fireworks began for Bastille Day, they watched in awe. Inadvertently he dropped some fruit and the Princess seized the opportunity for a playful food fight. Suddenly, as though frozen in time, they simply stopped mid throw and stared at each other as though discovering for the first time a deep connection between them. From that moment on, the relationship grew. They flirted and frolicked like children on the boat. All the while, the press followed them, circling the power boat with their own vessels, desperate to get a prized photograph for their newspapers. The Princess decided to rebuke them but at the same time, announced that they were about to be surprised by her next actions. It was a mysterious statement whetting the media appetite for speculation. Was she about to announce her marriage to the playboy millionaire? Could she be pregnant? She treated the press to a display of some very accomplished diving and the press seized upon the slight swell of her belly to suggest that a new life may be growing inside her. Meanwhile, back in England, her husband was trying to launch his own paramour onto the public scene by throwing a lavish 50th birthday party for her. The Princess was deeply satisfied that this was overshadowed by her own presence on the front pages of the daily newspapers and relished the attention deflected to herself.

Tasia spoke with Kyle and Stergios during a trip onshore. She was uneasy about this new relationship. Her two colleagues expressed their own dismay at the latest developments.

"Can't you talk to her Tasia? Tell her that she needs to keep her romantic profile down? Although the public are devouring the stories, it isn't doing much for her credibility as a serious contender for the throne."

Tasia sighed. "There's no talking to her right now. She's fully wrapped up in her own pursuit of romance. It's taking her mind off the surgeon but I actually think she's doing it in the hope he might be jealous and come back to her."

"Is the relationship serious, do you think?" Stergios enquired.

"Hard to say. Although she seems very happy and genuinely delighted by it, she does seem to get rather irritated by him at times. He's too eager to please; like a puppy looking for constant approval. It would get on anyone's nerves after a while. She expressed her liking for a jumper yesterday.

312

Next thing, he arrives with one of every colour for her. She was grateful to his face but discontented when we were alone in her rooms. Said she had enough 'things' and just wanted someone to like her for her. She feels distrustful of him I think." Tasia rang off shortly afterwards but agreed that they would speak later on in the week when they all returned to London.

Tasia took the opportunity one evening of asking the Princess what her intentions were with her suitor.

"Oh, I don't know, Tasia. Sometimes I just get drawn in by the romance of it and sometimes I think it could be something more lasting. We're similar in a way. He's from a broken home and he understands how I feel about my childhood. We both have similar tastes in music and art. Not all the stuffy things my husband was into. I can really identify with him. And let's face it, he's entirely eligible with appropriate resources, shall we say to look after me."

Indeed, the Princess was showered with gifts of clothes and jewellery almost daily. Tasia could see that they satisfied each other's neediness and their mutual enjoyment of the celebrity lifestyle. She in turn loved to receive gifts but her insecurities made her question the young man's motives. She valued even more the companionship and security that he seemed to offer. It was all so different from the undemonstrative and less generous ex husband.

The holiday came to an end and Tasia and the Princess fulfilled a long standing arrangement to go to Bosnia at the request of the Land Mine Survivors' Network. The mission was an enormous success as between them, they shared the limelight and photo opportunities raised by a walk through an area recently swept and cleared of mines, visiting the injured and orphaned and undertaking a generally humanitarian PR exercise on behalf of the charity. It created quite a stir back home with certain Establishment supporters criticising the Princess for political bias and again describing

313

her as a loose cannon. She was stung but undeterred by the criticism which was overshadowed by the praise she received for highlighting what was generally agreed to be a travesty.

Tasia had a little free time after this trip while the Princess jetted off for a cruise holiday in the Greek Islands with one of her female friends. She took the opportunity of meeting up with Kyle and Stergios.

Kyle's eyes shone with pleasure as he took in the bronzed athletic figure Tasia presented as she walked into the Westminster offices. She looked truly beautiful and he wished that the operation was over and they could perhaps get to know each other on a less formal basis. He knew though, that Tasia wasn't prepared to compromise her situation at this stage of the game. It would be dangerous for them both.

Stergios and Kyle were agitated by the latest developments and were eager to know where things were going.

"She's really making waves at the moment Tasia. They're not going to put up with it much longer. Doesn't she realise that probably the worst thing she could do is strike up a relationship with this particular individual? It isn't just the fact of who he is, but what he is. A Muslim for God's sake! There's no way they're going to stand for any kind of formal alliance between the mother of the future King and a Muslim. Especially not with his family connections. If there was any chance of a change of heart in disposing of her, it's fast disappearing with the latest developments." The thought struck Tasia that the Princess's dissident supporters may not be too pleased about the latest developments either. Her romantic choices flew in the face of all sides of this battle and stood to threaten the bloodline historically protected from the Saracens, or Muslims during the time of the crusades. It troubled her, though she tried to brush aside her thoughts.

Tasia sighed. "I'm not sure whether she's serious about him or not. It could just be a typical rebound thing. She

314

doesn't like to be without a consort of some kind. It validates her if someone else is telling her how fabulous she is."

"But what about him? What are his intentions do you think?"

"Ah, now that's a different kettle of fish. I've been eavesdropping on conversations between him and his father. I think he's genuinely keen on her but it's his father who is pulling the strings and he's so eager to please him that I think he'd do anything. It would be a huge coup for his father if he could pull off a marriage between the Princess and the playboy. He'd love to see the Establishment feathers flying over that little achievement. And of course, they'd have to treat him very differently if he was related by marriage to the future King wouldn't they?"

"It's never going to happen Tasia," Kyle said with conviction. "The best we can hope for is that it's just a dalliance that will fizzle out. Otherwise it's definitely over for her. Goodnight and goodbye. Plans are already being hatched as we speak. The fear of this alliance going anywhere is far greater than their fear of orchestrating a high profile accident or the consequences."

"Well, we'll know soon enough, I guess," Tasia sighed. With any luck she might come back persuaded that he's not for her. After all, she's on holiday now with one of her female friends; someone well respected in Establishment circles. She's bound to have a word in her ear."

"More likely trying to pump her for information to carry tales back to the powers that be," Stergios said glumly. "I rather think they'd prefer to be rid of the 'loose cannon' than wait for her to do something else they disapprove of. I very much fear that it's inevitable now."

The story from there was well known to most people. The Princess did not cease the relationship and, almost immediately after her return from the Greek Island holiday, she went off on yet another Mediterranean cruise with her lover. Rumours abounded that she planned to marry him and indeed an extravagant ring was ordered from an exclusive Paris jeweller. The couple were pursued relentlessly by the paparazzi as they returned to Paris from their last cruise which had included a passage around the stunning island of Gavdos where Tasia and the Princess had marvelled at the sight of the old landmark lighthouse destroyed during the war but lovingly reconstructed and located in the midst of vertical cliffs at Aspes. As they sailed around the ragged coastline of Gavdos, they took in the breathtaking beauty of the island.

"It's so peaceful here, Tasia," the Princess had commented wistfully. "Sometimes I think it would be wonderful just to stop the world and get off on an island such as this and live privately and peacefully without the gaze of the world upon me. The Greek Islands just seem so mystical and healing. It's like they have a power all of their own."

"Indeed they do Ma'am," Tasia replied.

"You sound very sure of that Tasia," the Princess, who was leaning on the railings of the powerboat turned to look at her, one eyebrow raised quizzically.

Tasia smiled. "I should do Ma'am. I am Greek and I am intimately acquainted with the mystic properties and the ancient Gods of my homeland. My name means 'resurrection, or rebirth.'

"It's a strange name. Sort of like Anastasia."

"Yes, perhaps a fitting name for those who are reborn. Anna Anderson claimed to be the Russian princess Anastasia. Discredited of course, but aren't these stories always discredited?" Tasia responded enigmatically.

"And your surname, Tasia. It's Artemis isn't it?" Tasia nodded in the affirmative, wondering if the Princess had made the connection.

The Princess giggled. "It's such a strange co-incidence." Tasia waited for the Princess to continue. "Well, my name is Diana, the name the Romans gave to the

Goddess of hunting. Your surname is Artemis, the Greek name for the same Goddess. You are the resurrection of Artemis or the rebirth of Diana." The Princess's eyes widened as she realised the incredible synchronicity. "Why, you're such a strange one Tasia. I sometimes think you've been put here by the Gods just for me."

Tasia said nothing but their eyes met and suddenly the Princess knew. Tasia was no ordinary mortal. Neither spoke, but an air of soothing reassurance descended upon the Princess and she was quite certain now of the spiritual connection which had been made for her protection.

"It is your Merovingian blood Ma'am which has led you to this moment. We Greeks are not so distant from the mystics from whom you descend. They say that Gavdos is imbued with the lifeblood of immortality and that it hides the lost city of Atlantis."

The Princess shivered momentarily as though bringing herself back to reality. "Well Tasia, here's to immortality. I feel as though I could live forever just now. I'm truly the happiest I've ever been. Now, let's go below deck. We need to get packed. We'll be heading back to Paris soon."

Whilst the partying went on late into that night, Tasia took the call they had all been awaiting for so long. It was time to put their plans into action. It was Stergios who contacted her.

"It's set. We've got word to go to Paris tonight. They've decided the Princess is a liability they no longer want to tolerate. We have intelligence that they're headed off to stay at the Ritz and that a proposal of marriage is forthcoming. It's the final straw Tasia. There is also great speculation about the rumour she might be pregnant. The only certainty is her destruction. Keep the lines open for further communications." With that, Stergios hung up. Tasia went up on deck staying away from the celebrations that filled the night with laughter and music. She grasped the metal railings which were cool

317

against her palms and tilted her head to the clear skies and twinkling stars. Closing her eyes, she mouthed words silently, imploring the Gods of old to be with her as the mission she had been sent to complete was about to reach its dramatic conclusion.

Chapter 29 – Putting on the Ritz

From the moment the party arrived in Paris it seemed that they were outrunning the Paparazzi who were eager to capture the first pictures of the couple now rumoured to be planning marriage and possibly anticipating their first child together. The public's insatiable interest had to be satisfied by the newshounds all vying to get that valuable 'exclusive' photograph or quote from the couple or their entourage. The couple themselves were tense as they quickly alighted their aircraft and ran to the waiting Mercedes Benz supplied by their host, the young man's father who was also the owner of the Paris Ritz.

Tasia looked through the rear window of the vehicle in which she was travelling with the couple. Motorcycles and cars were in hot pursuit, cameras flashing behind and beside them. She too was uneasy. One foot wrong on this momentous day and everything would be lost. She had received the code and knew that the planned assassination would be tonight. Kyle and Stergios would be in Paris and even now would be undertaking their own covert plans whilst ostensibly participating in the main event. It was probably the most dangerous time any of them had ever experienced. Any suspicion raised as to their loyalty to the service would mean certain death for them.

It had been decided that the Princess should not be aware of the precise timing or the plans which had been laid for her assassination. She would never have been able to carry it off had she known what was in store for her and undoubtedly the stress would have led to the certain failure of the mission. In truth, it had all happened so suddenly that even Tasia and her colleagues had been taken by surprise. As it stood, the Princess was relaxed and happy aside from the slight tension caused by the chase through Paris to avoid the Paps. If all went to plan Tasia and her colleagues would have the situation under control and she would have nothing to worry about once they had secured her safe passage through the planned incident.

      The day passed quickly after their arrival in Paris. Following a short stop at the Windsor residence in Bois de Boulogne which the couple appeared to be considering as a future home, they headed to the Ritz. Her lover made a detour to the Paris jeweller where intelligence advised he had collected the $205,000 diamond ring rumoured to be an engagement ring. Returning to the Ritz to collect the Princess, they then set off for his home in the Champs Elysees. Tasia and the entourage were advised that the couple would be going to his Paris home and that they would be dining in a local favoured restaurant that evening. Behind the scenes a careful operation was already in progress that would lead to the world's most chilling and shocking news in a matter of hours.

      Outside the Ritz there was a clamour of Paparazzi and journalists waiting for the couple. Try as they might, the hotel staff were unable to remove them from the main entrance. Amongst the crowd, dressed down and mingling with the journalists stood Kyle and Stergios, cameras poised. They were not the only two agents in the mass of journalists, but they were the only two with different objectives that day. Tasia had advised them that nothing would be happening for at least an hour as the Princess's beau had just left the hotel by the back door to carry out his errand with the jewellers. They remained in the hotel where the Princess was just about to freshen up and change. Stergios and Kyle wandered away from the crowd of Paps and walked down the street ostensibly taking a cigarette break and chewing the fat. Stergios had given up cigarettes some time ago but smoking helped him to blend in with the media, many of whom still puffed furiously as an antidote to the alternate boredom and stress which their lifestyle offered.

Kyle was agitated. He had flown in from London only a couple of hours earlier. Just before he left, he'd received a telephone call from one of his contacts at the BBC to say that at that very moment a 'dress rehearsal' was taking place for the announcement of the Princess's death as a result of a car crash. Kyle had blanched at the news. How many people knew of the plans, he wondered? His BBC contact had wanted to know if Kyle knew something which of course, he flatly denied. It was well known that dress rehearsals of this kind happened all the time so that the announcers and programme makers would be able to deal with breaking news of this calibre; but the day before and with such accurate information? It was astounding, he thought. Absurd. Stergios was equally astonished when Kyle updated him on the events.

"Well, what can we expect? The BBC is the Establishment's public voice. The announcers keep their black ties with them just in case you know. However, it is unusually close to home," he mused. "Very dangerous too. Now a number of people in the Corporation will be putting two and two together once the deed is done." A deep frown crossed his brow as he inhaled deeply on the cigarette.

"You look like you're enjoying that smoke," Kyle observed.

"I am ashamed to say that it is a very welcome crutch today Kyle. If I survive this mission, I think I may find it difficult to let them go again. Come on, let's get back to the hotel and look like we're part of the pack. I have to slip away in about an hour to give instructions to our contact in the hotel once Tasia gives us the nod."

Excitement was building as the afternoon passed into early evening. The couple had left for the Paris residence and the Paps had followed closely on their heels and now congregated in the upmarket Champs Elysees where they waited eagerly for them to re-appear.

The Princess was becoming fractious. She was tiring of the attention that had dogged her all day. She was looking forward to a romantic end of holiday meal and the promise of an expensive surprise. She longed to be able to enjoy it without the baying hounds following her every move. She could have no privacy and the strain was beginning to take its toll.

"Oh God Tasia, I just want to get home. I'm so excited to be seeing the boys tomorrow. I wish tonight was over. I'm not sure what's planned for tonight, but I'm a little nervous it could be a marriage proposal." The Princess's beau was getting ready in the bathroom and she whispered to Tasia.

"Wouldn't that be exciting for you?" Tasia asked.

"Oh, yes, I suppose it would be flattering but I'm really not sure about it, Tasia. I have had the most wonderful time and I'm so very fond of him. I would love to see the look on the family's faces if I did announce my engagement. Can you imagine it? Not only would I be marrying a Muslim but this particular Muslim would be the icing on the cake! But I have to be sensible. I think I'm on the rebound and much as I'd love to swipe the self satisfied smiles from their faces, it's no reason to commit myself to marriage. What shall I say if he does ask me?"

Tasia pondered a moment. Even she was finding it difficult to keep up her usual calm and collected front. There were things going on by the minute; coded texts and mobile phone calls passing between her and the main intelligence services with instructions to bring the 'accident' to fruition and between her and the dissidents whose counter instructions had to be juggled whilst still remaining cool not to arouse suspicion.

"Well Ma'am, as I'm sure you know only too well, you must follow your own instincts. I would say though, you must

322

follow your head as well as your heart. Think of the repercussions it could have and how it might impact on your life and relationships with your children."

The Princess looked disconsolate.

"Yes. I can never really have any free will can I? Whatever I do, I will always be trapped into the conventions and propriety of my position, even now when it's diluted and I am apparently a free woman." She sighed. "But you are right of course. It isn't just me I have to think about." She rose from the sofa looking tall and elegant in her blazer and white slacks. "Ah well," she looked at her watch. "Nearly time for us to go to the restaurant." She went over to the window overlooking the exclusive street below, full of chic restaurants and upmarket shops. She paled when she saw how many of the paps had now gathered below. She put her hands to her head and ran her fingers through her neatly coiffed bobbed hair that she was growing into a longer, more modern style.

"Oh God Tasia. Will they never let up? I wish we could just call the police and chase them!" Of course, the Princess no longer had the benefit of official protection since her departure from royal life. She was now dependent on her host's security arrangements which her boyfriend was orchestrating during their Paris visit. It was far more dangerous for her these days and the paps treated her with less respect now that she was more 'celeb' than royal. It seemed that their own intelligence was excellent as well. Probably information was being leaked from those in the know in Paris who might be able to make a decent income by tipping them off from the inside.

It was decided at the last minute that there should be a change of plan. The couple decided they would be better protected if they returned to the Ritz and dined there. At least security there would keep the baying photographers and journalists out whereas a small exclusive restaurant would find it infinitely more difficult to deal with the problem. Tasia sent a

323

text on the 'pay as you go' mobile phone; one of several procured to keep their communications out of the official intelligence services' gaze.

The couple ran the gauntlet through the Paparazzi at the doors of Ritz. Both of them were by now rattled and the Princess was upset. They entered the restaurant where the Princess felt she was under scrutiny by other diners and it was decided the couple would dine in their Imperial Suite away from prying eyes instead. Tasia sighed. It was all becoming very complicated with so many last minute changes in plan. At last she had a few moments to herself and she headed to the hotel lobby where she could see the crowds gathered outside, amongst whom Kyle and Stergios were poised for final instructions.

Tasia felt the phone in her hand vibrate. It was Stergios. He sounded anxious and perplexed.

"Tasia," he gasped. "We don't know exactly what's happening. The official line is that the operation needs to be shelved if they're staying at the Ritz. There's nothing we can do if that's their plan."

"No, it's a really odd decision, but they've decided to return to the Champs Elysees apartment after dinner tonight. I don't know why they just don't stay here to be honest. All they've done is dodge the press all day going backwards and forwards. I think 'he' believes it'll wear them out and they might give up."

"OK. I'll await the official line. No doubt they'll be contacting their man inside as we speak."

Indeed, at that very moment, Henri, the dapper Frenchman was entering the Ritz, called back to duty by his employer's son. He prided himself and basked in his duties as Acting Head of Security for the Ritz. Smartly dressed and cocksure, he strode into the hotel to be greeted with reverence by the desk staff. He took out his mobile and appeared to be taking instructions. Tasia knew that he was the undercover agent for MI6. He had proved to be an extremely useful contact over the years, providing details on the extremely high profile residents of the hotel for the intelligence services. He earned very well, not just from his official role in the hotel, but from the copious cash payments he received from the intelligence services which he distributed amongst several bank accounts.

He might not be strutting quite so confidently, if he knew what the security services had planned for him tonight, Tasia thought ruefully. She shivered. How terrible to know that people were going to die tonight, quite unaware of the dangers they faced as they went about their everyday lives, untroubled. She had to carry out the first part of her official mission now; the first part of the complex jigsaw which would begin the series of events and send shockwaves throughout the globe. She followed the Ritz's Acting Head of Security to the bar where he ordered a drink. A Ricard with water. The two official bodyguards were sitting at a table grabbing a quick snack before their boss gave the signal for them to accompany him and the Princess to the waiting Mercedes. The security man nodded his acknowledgement of the two Englishmen and they exchanged a few cursory words. It was well known that he was not held in particularly high regard by them and it would have been less had they realised that it was alcohol he was consuming, not pineapple juice as they had thought. He strode back to the bar where his drink still sat. Whilst he was occupied with the two men, she had stood at the bar and ordered a mineral water whilst surreptitiously emptying the contents of a phial into the glass of Ricard. She sat down at a table where she could watch. As anticipated, the man lifted the drink to his lips and downed it in a few gulps. He ordered another and drank it more slowly this time. She sent a text confirming that the subject had swallowed the adulterated drink which they knew would slowly take effect over the next hour or so.

325

The call soon came to announce the couple intended to depart and Tasia braced herself. The couple were tense, the Princess tired and eager to get back to London. She'd had enough of the media circus.

Stergios and Kyle received their instructions from those in charge of procuring the death of the Princess and exercised their professionalism to avoid suspicion of their true intentions. It was Stergios who drove a vehicle to the front of Ritz which was intended to be the decoy for the paparazzi who were still clamouring, rumours abounding that the party were about to leave the hotel. Earlier, the Acting Head of Security for the Ritz who would be responsible for driving the target vehicle had stood at the doors, uncharacteristically engaging with the press, promising them that they would have their opportunity of seeing the couple very shortly if they behaved themselves appropriately. He was like a warm-up act, thought Stergios; one moment he seemed to be almost deliberately taunting them, the next appeasing them with assurances that they would have their photo opportunity. It became increasingly frenzied outside the Ritz as impatience and speculation spread through the crowd like a virus. There were many freelancers who tended not to observe the protocol and niceties of those employed by the mainstream news agencies. They were unpredictable and added more danger to an already complex operation. However, the members of MI6 and the CIA who were in Paris that day knew that they would become essential to their cover story once the deed was complete.

As the decoy driven by Stergios arrived at the main entrance of the hotel, Kyle drove the Mercedes intended for the couple to the rear entrance. He had been ordered to collect it from a secret location controlled by his organisation. He knew that the vehicle had been recently 'stolen' from the company who supplied the Ritz with its Mercedes vehicles for transportation of high profile guests. Perspiration ran down his face, the only sign that belied his usual cool, professional exterior. When he'd arrived to collect the vehicle the operative who'd been charged with ensuring its safe hand-over quickly briefed him.

"OK, Kyle, is it?"

Kyle affirmed his identity and flashed his security service badge to the operative who then led him around the vehicle explaining the 'modifications' that had been made to it whilst in their possession.

"So, you may need this information later once this is all over," he began. "The Merc was taken by our boys at gunpoint to make it look like an authentic heist. When we took it into our possession, we changed the engine management microchip over. That means we can now control it remotely. We can take over the operation of the steering and the brakes. The guy who's scheduled to drive tonight, he's one of our boys. An informant. He genuinely thinks he's been drafted in to look after the couple's security on our behalf. Of course, he hasn't been told anything about our plans tonight."

"I guess he must be a dispensable asset to us then," Kyle commented. As the years went by he had become less comfortable with the killing of innocents used as stool pigeons in the service operations.

"Oh absolutely. There's always another one waiting in the wings ready to co-operate with us in providing information. It's a lucrative pastime for these guys who like the idea of being James Bond, kidding themselves they're serving their country and states."

Kyle nodded, an unconcerned smile fixed on his lips.

"Anything I need to be worried about when driving it to the Ritz?"

"No, we won't take control of the car until the right moment. The driver has been briefed to take a different route through Paris. He'll drive through the Alma Tunnel ostensibly to ward off the Paparazzi whom we'll ensure are in pursuit but

327

at a distance. We have a number of our guys both in the tunnel and others posing as paparazzi. They'll have the job of feeding false information to ensure the timings are perfect. When you leave the vehicle, wait for the party and make sure the Princess gets in the back behind the driver. The seatbelt has been modified so she won't be able to fasten it. We have guys poised in the tunnel to assist in 'causing' the accident; SAS, other MI6 agents."

Kyle's heart was beating fast as he drove through the streets of Paris. He knew only too well the techniques being employed here. Known as the 'Boston Brakes' technique to those in the know, a vehicle was reconfigured so that third parties could take over all functions remotely. Technology had been a real gift in these situations. Most prestige cars these days were computerised and they could be infected easily using the on-board blue tooth or mobile phone systems. The technique was named after the small Lincolnshire town and port in England where the SAS who'd perfected it were based. Essential to the success of the operation was the disorientation of the driver. This seemed to be well in hand with Tasia playing the vital role of adulterating his drink which would be followed up by an operative flashing an extremely bright light in his eyes when he drove into the tunnel."

Kyle alighted from the vehicle and only moments later, the Acting Head of Security proudly exited the rear of the hotel and approached the car, taking his place behind the wheel. He seemed relaxed and confident in his mission. He'd been highly trained in high performance evasion and protection techniques designed for only the most elite bodyguard candidates. The man relished the thrill and surge of adrenalin that his job often afforded him.

Close behind him, the couple and their bodyguards came out of the rear doors to the hotel. Kyle quickly and efficiently, in his guise as a regular security services agent ushered the young woman to take her seat behind the driver.

Her lover sat next to her and the two Ritz bodyguards took their places in the vehicle. It was all set. The young woman knew nothing of what awaited her as the car began its fateful journey. Kyle saw that she was relaxed and happy; relieved to be away from the public gaze and heading for what she hoped was to be a quiet romantic end to the evening and her holiday. The last thing he noticed was the woman pulling the seatbelt over her body, her head bowed as she tried in vain to click it into place. She looked up, a slight frown creasing her brow but clearly deciding not to worry about the seatbelt for the short journey to the apartment as she let it go, sliding back into place. He just caught a glimpse of her warm infectious smile as she responded to something said by her lover as the car silently pulled off into the balmy Paris night.

Kyle felt heavy and deeply apprehensive. He had served the official masters and done his duty. This was where he, Stergios and Tasia were about to go 'off script' to carry out what might be the most momentous coup to foil an Establishment plan ever known.

At the main entrance to the hotel, Stergios waited in the decoy vehicle and within moments he was joined by Tasia and Kyle. Tasia was dressed similarly to the Princess and sported her blond wig and dark glasses. As she came out of the hotel accompanied by Kyle, there was an uproar as excitement surged through the waiting paps, closing in and jostling. Puzzlement quickly followed as they realised the 'Princess' was leaving without her lover. Kyle and Tasia pushed their way through the clamour, but one of the waiting paps put out his hand and tugged on her hair. As he suspected it was dislodged and it became clear that Tasia was not their quarry. A surge of angry expletives could be heard from the crowd as they realised they had been duped. They quickly lost interest in the waiting Mercedes allowing the pair to get into the car as the paparazzi dispersed to their motorcycles and vehicles, many of them heading to the rear of the hotel where they now

329

realised the real couple must have been leaving. The mood was black amongst the press who were now determined to pursue the couple. It played perfectly into the hands of those planning to see the end of a very troublesome woman.

Though much was happening at either side of the hotel, in reality it was slick and speedy. A few of the duped paps reached the rear of the hotel just in time to see the real couple's vehicle accelerating away. Those with vehicles close by were soon in hot pursuit behind them and as they gave chase, they were probably only about a minute behind.

Stergios drove off, following the planned route.

"God that was intense," Tasia breathed deeply. "How anyone would want to live like that permanently is beyond me. They'd tear you apart to get what they wanted."

Kyle, who sat beside Tasia in the rear of the vehicle broke from his characteristically cool detachment and reached out to take Tasia's hand and squeezed it. As he did so, he felt the slight electric tingle spread through him which calmed and reassured him. He was thrilled as he felt her hand return his grip. It was the first reciprocal affection he'd ever received from her.

"Not long now Kyle. All being well, we're all going to be better acquainted really soon. We just have to get this right." She smiled. She looked serene and beautiful but still radiated an air of absolute mystery which captivated and troubled Kyle. He looked up to see Stergios gazing into the rear-view mirror.

"Any minute now," he announced as the couple's vehicle came into view just metres in the front of them. It was travelling at around 60-63 mph, Stergios noted. The driver was clearly anxious to keep the paps at a distance. The three agents watched the plan play out. The driver of the couple's vehicle was heading towards a slip road which was a direct route to their destination where they met their first obstacle; a vehicle was parked broadside across it causing the driver to veer quickly away from it towards the Alma Tunnel. The rotary blades of a helicopter could be heard above the tunnel as it hovered, monitoring the procedure from the Paris skies.

The three colleagues were silent, a collective holding of breath as they waited to see whether the rest of the operation would play out successfully. Their very futures teetered uncertainly as Stergios slowed his own vehicle on the approach to the tunnel. None of them wanted to speak, each lost in their own thoughts as the staging of one of the world's most complicated and sensational moments in history played out in front of them. To some of their number it was an extraordinary feat in which they would be proud to have been involved. To the three of them however, it was a shameful abuse by the organisation they had so faithfully represented until they had discovered the shocking truth of the duplicity of the so-called protection agencies.

It all happened in slow motion. Ahead of the limousine in which the couple travelled, blissfully unaware of the plotting and intrigue surrounding them, the white Fiat Uno drove erratically at speed on the approach to the tunnel where it suddenly slowed at the entrance causing the Merc to veer slightly as it braked. Both cars disappeared into the tunnel where another vehicle was ahead. A motorcycle with two black clad riders emerged at the left of the couple's car and then overtook a high speed as the black car in front braked. An intense flash of light, brighter than daylight exploded into the tunnel blinding the driver of the ill fated car. He was already beginning to feel the dulling effects of the potion he had swallowed earlier and his responses were slow. Even then, he tried unsuccessfully to steer the vehicle whose controls, unbeknown to him had been taken over remotely by unseen hands. The occupants of the vehicle barely understood what was happening to them but terror and shock was evident on their faces.

An explosion of sound filled the tunnel. Stergios and his companions had stopped some way behind but within view of the terrible massacre as it unfolded. Their bodies were tensed but their expressions remained professionally impassive and detached lest they betray themselves to their future detriment.

They watched as the limousine veered across the carriageway, completely out of control. Amidst the screeching of brakes which tore through the soul of any person who heard it, the vehicle gave a whooshing sound reminiscent of the final death rattle of a failing patient and signified a clutch pressed down without a change in gear. The electrics in the vehicle extinguished and it hurtled towards its final destination impacting with the thirteenth pillar of the Alma Tunnel.

Within moments, the motorcycle stopped and one of the riders, sinister and menacing in his black leathers and helmet which obscured his features completely got off the cycle and peered into the car. Stergios, Tasia and Kyle held their breaths. They knew that it was the job of the cyclist to verify the success. If there was any doubt that the injuries were less than grave, they would ensure that the job was brought up to standard. What the three colleagues couldn't be sure of was the extent of injury the party may have sustained and what would be deemed acceptable short of death. It would be hoped by the operatives that the injuries would be fatal and matters thus conclude themselves without further intervention which could be dangerous.

It was only moments before they had some indication. The cyclist turned to his colleague and, arms lowered he crossed them. It was the signal that the mission had been accomplished. He clambered back onto the bike and it roared out of the tunnel into the night.

Shadowy figures hovered on the narrow pavement next to the road. It was a dangerous area, not regularly occupied by pedestrians. These were no ordinary onlookers though. They were strategically placed to observe the proceedings, most of them main players, but a select few dissident colleagues.

Within a short time, the accident site was in furore. The press had caught up and some, instead of assisting the injured, callously peered into the vehicle with their cameras looking for the money shot of an injured, possibly dying British icon. They, of course were to become the fall guys in future days and weeks; the most useful decoys the Establishment would use to great effect as blame and recrimination fell upon the world's press. It would not be for many months that details of the incident might truly suggest it was an orchestrated and murderous event.

Chapter 30 – A Fitting Funeral and a Festoon of Flowers

Stergios and his colleagues waited silently in their vehicle as the emergency response team arrived at the scene. All the time they were in contact with those of their number who were close to the accident site, officially tasked with keeping the secret services up to date. At the same time, they relayed information to Stergios and the team who were poised to go into action at the appointed time. At first, good news emerged. An off duty doctor had approached the car in the immediate aftermath and reported that the Princess was conscious and speaking. It was he who had called the emergency services after moving the injured woman's head. He'd reported that her blood pressure was low and that she was sweating, indicative of internal bleeding. He was said to be confident though that the Princess would survive if treated quickly. A fireman on the scene also reported her to be conscious and speaking.

"The bosses won't be pleased to hear this," Stergios commented as he repeated the news to Kyle and Tasia. Tasia nodded. She was relieved. The 'accident' had been more slick than she'd anticipated. She'd hoped that it would prove much more difficult for the Establishment to bring about their objectives.

"Yes, it would have been much simpler for them had she died at the scene. We'll have to make sure we're just as slick."

Kyle was nervous.

"What if she's too seriously injured though? The whole plan could fall apart."

Tasia was impatient with him.

"Then you know what happens next Kyle. Plan 'B' and we all disappear for a while."

The group fell silent again, each lost in their own thoughts and the impact that this momentous day would have on all their lives.

At this point, protocol dictated that anyone of high status involved in such an accident should be taken to the Val-de-Grâce Hospital. This had been the accepted practice in France for anyone of political or royal status to be treated at this military hospital where a highly experienced team of the country's top surgeons and medical staff were on duty to deal with trauma patients. Not on this occasion though. The woman who now laid injured but with survivable injuries was not afforded the privilege of being treated by those who could ensure her safety. Instead, the wheels of the pre-planned operation began and the ambulance which carried its most prestigious patient drove slowly from the tunnel and took a route away from the closest hospital following Government orders to head for La Pitié-Salpêtrière Hospital instead. The ambulance cortege began the four mile journey across Paris assisted by 2 police escorts.

Stergios received the go ahead from Stanton and there was a collective intake of breath from the three agents whose most dangerous mission was about to begin. Even they hadn't realised though, just how difficult their mission would be as they followed the painfully slow cortege on its solemn journey through the city.

"For fuck's sake, why is it going so slowly?" Kyle hissed. Tasia shifted uncomfortably in her seat and, closing her eyes, raised her fingertips to her head which she lowered as though nursing a migraine. In reality, she was using her remote viewing skills. Seconds later, she was mentally inside the ambulance where she saw her friend and alter ego surrounded by medical staff who were trying to keep her stable. The emergency doctor who, unbeknown to the security services had been briefed and was working for 'Operation Merovingian' looked worried and shouted in

335

frustration to the ambulance drivers who obstinately refused to speed the ambulance up. Their orders from their own superiors was to keep the ambulance crawling along, ostensibly because the woman's condition was critical and that the slightest bump could kill her. Insiders knew that it was a decision made to ensure that the greatest delay in her arrival at the hospital was more likely to result in the conclusion they all wanted. Questions would be asked, but they could be dealt with easily by the silver tongued Establishment spokesmen who would ensure the biggest cover up in modern history. In their official capacity, Stergios, Kyle and Tasia were under orders to enter the ambulance at a designated location when it would stop for a few moments near the hospital. At this point, they would complete the termination process. In their 'Operation Merovingian' capacity, their plans were quite the opposite.

As arranged, the ambulance came to its inexplicable halt outside the history museum just two minutes from La Pitié-Salpêtrière Hospital. Seconds later, Stergios parked a short way behind the ambulance. It was dark. The street lights had been turned off to allow the operation to take place unseen as Paris slept in the early hours of the morning.

Quickly and without discussion, the team alighted from the vehicle and they were met by two of their 'Merovingian' colleagues at the door of the ambulance. They nodded wordlessly to each other as they stepped into the ambulance. The doctor was relieved to see them and greeted them warmly.

"You will need to be fast. It's taken far too long to get here. She's fading rapidly."

Seconds later, an identical ambulance drew up behind them and the injured woman was swiftly transferred to the waiting trauma team who took over her care. Tasia, dressed identically to the patient took the place which had been occupied by the injured woman. No-one would have been able to tell them apart as Tasia commenced the most dangerous part of the plan. Accompanied by Kyle and Stergios, she lay on the stretcher and took several deep breaths and began the meditation process which would slow her heartbeat to the extent that it mimicked death. The control, learned from mystics over the centuries would help her to create the greatest deception ever undertaken. Meanwhile the other ambulance, staffed with their own 'Merovingian Operation' agents now sped in the opposite direction to a secret location where the medical staff began tirelessly to keep the injured woman stable and alive.

It was later reported, amidst great criticism of the French medical services that the official ambulance had taken over an hour and a half to make its way over the four mile journey and had inexplicably stopped only two minutes from the hospital. No medical staff had come rushing from La Pitié-Salpêtrière Hospital, which raised further questions, criticism and suspicion over the Princess's treatment. Why, when only moments away from the hospital had no-one rushed down to help the injured woman? Officially, the explanation was provided that her condition had become critical and to move her further might have caused instant death. Unofficially, it was because the real plan was to ensure her death before reaching the hospital.

On their eventual arrival at the hospital, Kyle and Stergios ran ahead of the paramedics who were now removing the stretcher with Tasia's lifeless body from the ambulance. They were met by their own 'Merovingian Operation' medics who solemnly greeted the two agents with a nod. Tasia was rushed into theatre for an 'operation' where it would be reported that 'the Princess' had 'died' of a ruptured pulmonary vein. Tasia played her part to perfection with brief respites when she could bring herself round from her self induced catalepsy as she awaited the inevitable visits and the wheels of state turned to verify her death. The hypnosis

337

techniques she had learned deceived even those closest to the Princess as Tasia's waxen features, rigid posture, controlled breathing and pulse weakened to a state where it was undetectable assured all that she was indeed dead.

Kyle and Stergios meanwhile confirmed the 'Princess's' death to their superiors and oversaw those who came to pay their respects and guarded the 'body' as they had been officially tasked to do. Their instructions were to remain with the body and accompany the coffin when it was flown back to London. The security services were of course deeply anxious that no-one should discover that they had effectively murdered the iconic woman. Kyle and Stergios were however equally anxious that they stayed with Tasia to ensure that at the right moment they could remove her from the coffin and substitute another corpse in time for the funeral and at a point where their double dealing could not be discovered. There were many details to be taken care of. The 'officially' appointed doctor who was supposed to have met the party at the hospital was being held in a secret location having been spirited away by the 'Operation Merovingian' agents and had to be taken care of. With professional detachment, Kyle and Stergios ensured his silence and allegiance to their cause by arranging a warning shot directed at his family should he ever depart from anything but the story he was instructed to tell their superiors; that the excessive delay on the route to the hospital had weakened the patient to such an extent that she could not be saved (and that he had administered an undetectable drug to ensure that she died on arrival at the hospital at any event). He was briefed to say that she had suffered a series of heart attacks and a massive cardiac arrest. She had died, he was to say, during an operation to repair the ruptured pulmonary artery. Their own 'pathologist' conducted the 'post-mortem'. The rest of the staff had been easy to manipulate. It had been an astoundingly smooth and precocious process which neither Kyle nor Stergios could quite believe.

The two double agents were not out of place as serving security agents in accompanying the coffin back to Britain where it was laid to rest in The Chapel Royal, St James' Palace. There, they remained until it was safe to remove Tasia from the coffin and a substitute body placed inside. Tasia was pale but remarkably unharmed from her period of self hypnosis which had helped her to deal with the incarceration with a little help from her friends.

Their duties were over on the day of the funeral and the three of them solemnly dispersed to some well earned leave. Kyle and Tasia agreed to meet the following day. Tasia, ever the master of disguise, sat incognito on a bench reading a magazine. She looked up as Kyle, unusually casual in light coloured Chinos and open necked shirt approached. Although there appeared to be no suspicion amongst their superiors over the operation, they didn't want to draw unnecessary attention to themselves.

Tasia smiled as she stood to kiss Kyle on both cheeks in formal greeting.

"My, don't you look handsome and relaxed," she said.

"So is that the best a handsome and relaxed guy can hope for around here?" he replied in mock disappointment. Tasia shrugged nonchalantly, but then surprised him as she took his face in her hands and kissed him tenderly on the lips. It was the start of a long and loving relationship between two people who would be entwined by so much more than the deep love they shared. Before they were able to consider this though, there was much for Kyle to tell Tasia.

"So tell me, what's the word on the Princess?" Tasia asked eagerly. She had lost so much time during her trance and she wanted to know the details. "Can I see her soon?" Tasia was still holding Kyle's face looking deep into his eyes as she questioned him. She immediately perceived that all

339

was not well as she delved into his psyche through the beloved windows of his soul. She recoiled from him as the answer came to her. "Oh my God! She's dead isn't she? We failed!" Tasia was inconsolable and bent over double as though she'd been punched in the stomach. Kyle grabbed her stooped figure now limp and wounded and he guided her to the bench.

"Yeah, Tasia," he sighed. "She died. We were just too late. They got her at the accident site. Although she was already in a serious condition after the crash she was, with proper treatment, likely to survive. They injected her with a drug to paralyse her organs. The extra delay in the journey towards the hospital didn't help either. Because of that she would most probably have died without their little insurance policy."

Tasia was visibly heartbroken as she wept for the loss of her friend and erstwhile alter ego. They had been like twins sharing every experience and emotion together over the last months. She had assured her friend of a safe passage when the strike finally came. She had failed her, at least in this circle of life.

"But how...? We'd organised everything so that she'd survived – hadn't we...?

"Where is she now?" Tasia asked. "Can I see her body?"

"No Tasia. She's in her rightful place in her coffin about to be honoured by her country."

Tasia nodded. "After all that..." she said disconsolately. Kyle, placing his arm around her shoulders and pulling her head to him, he agreed.

"Yup, after all that." There was nothing else to say as they sat deep in their own thoughts silently comforting each other and wondering where they went from here.

The following day, Stergios, Tasia and Kyle joined the crowds and shared their grief for the woman who had touched all of their lives and who might one day have created a new Monarchy and helped to create a kinder new world. They, like the rest of the world marvelled at the swathes of flowers that carpeted the street outside Kensington Gardens and other royal palaces. A fitting tribute to an extraordinary woman, they agreed.

Chapter 31 – The Sanctity and the Sanctimonious

As Tasia finished relating the end to their 'Operation Merovingian', Hal sat in stunned silence. Drawing his thoughts together he asked, "But how were you ever going to prevent her death when so much had been done to orchestrate the opposite? You weren't even at the scene when the accident happened."

Tasia sighed and shook her head, sorrow, disbelief, even shame evident in her expression.

"Well, here's the terrible thing Hal. Our own dissidents had been involved in the theft of the Merc and the operation to override the computer. Unbeknown to the official agents however, they'd put in their own override system so that our operatives could control the vehicle and lessen the impact. The pillion rider on the motor cycle was one of ours. Ostensibly, he was there to give her a lethal injection to ensure the outcome but in fact, his instruction from our side was to inject a harmless substance."

"So what happened? How did it all go so terribly wrong?" Hal persisted. A tear ran down Tasia's cheek and her face crumpled as she let out an anguished sob. Instinctively, Hal reached over and stroked away her tears. Tasia collected herself and her words stunned Hal into open mouthed shock.

"We were betrayed at the last moment Hal. Stanton gave the order not to override the main operation to kill the Princess and the pillion rider was told to give her the lethal injection. We heard much later that an emergency gathering of the dissident hierarchy confirmed my own fears; that the Princess's attachment to two Muslim lovers could undermine the whole purpose of preserving the purity of the Grail bloodline. Suddenly the two opposing sides found common ground. The Establishment wanted to protect the Monarchy and Corporate Government from a putative humanitarian royal who might undermine their financial and power bases but the dissidents wanted to protect and promote the purity of the Judaeo-Christian bloodline which would be at risk from the very enemy it had fought against through the centuries; the Saracens. Our people feared that if she survived, her headstrong ways and exotic tastes in men could lead to contamination of the precious bloodline they fought so hard to protect. It would have, they said, made a mockery of all they were trying to achieve in restoring the pure bloodline. In the end they decided that it was better to simply allow the now strengthened bloodline to continue through the Princess's children than take the risk it may be jeopardised by her in the future. Of course, they still wanted the truth to be made public which is why Stergios, Kyle and I were sent here. There were two options; either I could pose as the dead Princess and pretend she had survived to be re-introduced years later, or, we simply bide our time and have the truth told at a time when her children were grown up and would understand the importance of their role and heritage. We were not of course tasked with telling the whole truth; the truth that the Princess was killed equally at the hands of those who protected the sanctity of her lineage and promoted the peaceful humanitarian style Monarch she represented. That would hardly engender support from any side now would it?

So you see Hal, you will understand that we have been protected all these years as the time for our role in bringing the truth to the public arrived. However, we have given you the whole truth and whilst this will not be a problem for me much longer, Stergios and Kyle will be in mortal danger from both sides, neither of whom will want the story made public. And so you must also realise that you too are in mortal danger at least until you get the book published. Once it's done no-one will want to draw attention to the fact that the author of a conspiracy has mysteriously died will they?

Hal was numb – shock and the growing fear gnawed at his insides and he thought he might be sick.

"But what were you going to do if the Princess had lived?" he asked.

"We'd always planned to take her over to Gavdos and lay low. We'd nurse her back to health and help her understand her destiny more fully by teaching her about her roots and the mysticism of the Merovingians. She was already very perceptive in that sense and possessed the ability and empathy of healing. I personally would have supervised her more esoteric studies. Once the furore of her death had passed we would have re-introduced her to the world and the full story of what they tried to do would have been exposed, straight from the horse's mouth so to speak. The scandal it would have caused would have raised so many questions and concerns that the cause would be served and in time, she would have to be re-instated into her rightful role."

"Weren't you afraid they'd just try to kill her again? And you..?" Tasia smiled.

"I think it might by that time have been difficult to orchestrate her death a second time, especially with the suspicion already surrounding her the first time. As for us, well, we've always faced danger. When your story comes out Hal, Stergios and Kyle will have to be safely despatched with different identities and new lives."

"What about you?"

"As you see, I'm not going to be around much longer and I'm glad of it. I'm weary now and I've served my purpose; or at least I will have done once the story is complete."

344

Chapter 32 – Bereavement and Farewells

Hal laid his head back against the seat of the taxi and closed his eyes, drained and perplexed after the meeting with Tasia. His mind spun as he tried to make sense of everything he'd been told by the three renegade agents. He had no idea how he would assimilate the tale and create a believable document of all he'd been told. So much of it made sense but who would really believe it? All he had was a tale related to him by three people claiming to have been part of the British Secret Services. He had no proof as to their identities and no way of proving their very existence.

Everything he'd known about the death of the Princess had been called into question and an elaborate tale about switching the bodies with Tasia using superhuman powers to imitate a corpse seemed to be going into the realms of fantasy. And for what? They had failed. The Princess had died in the incident whichever way you looked at it. If Tasia really possessed the powers claimed, surely she could have foreseen that the fate of the Princess had been sealed already? He put the question to Stergios when they met up at their hotel later.

"My friend, I am aware of the difficulties you face here and when your book is published, all we can hope for is that the matters raised are sufficient for the public and those who have a real interest in exposing the truth to question everything that is before them. Indeed, we're living in a world where cover-ups in political life are being exposed daily. This will be another example of the mistrust we must all have. It is our fervent wish that perhaps by showing that there is another role for monarchy, one which will have greater humanitarian impact emulating that of the Merovingian Kings it will be used by those of the true bloodline of Diana; her sons and their offspring. As for Tasia, the days she spent in deep hypnosis removed her consciousness from what was happening in this world. She was in quite another place altogether as our efforts began to disintegrate."

"So exactly what happened after the funeral Stergios? To you and the others I mean?"

"We had to regroup of course. None of us had the heart to continue as agents in the Intelligence Services. It is impossible to fully escape once you are a member but no-one had any great suspicion about us. One by one over the next couple of months, the three of us, beginning with Tasia left the service. She was the first to come over to Gavdos. The island, with its isolation and small population was ideal for us to hide away in the knowledge that if any danger followed us we would be in a position to know about it quickly. The locals would soon warn us if enquiries were made about us. Kyle followed shortly afterwards and I spent my time between the island and Chania which is where I was born. We simply laid low and enjoyed the peaceful life for many years."

"So why now? Why did you want to expose the truth now?"

"The time is coming when the lifetime of one Monarch will be coming to an end. There will inevitably be changes but perhaps not in the way that the Princess had hoped. Her ex husband will undoubtedly succeed his mother and the throne will not pass direct to the next in the Merovingian line as she had wished. However, by placing the story into the public, it is to be hoped that her message will reach her children and when the time comes, they will understand the gift they have been left by their mother. It is all we can do now. Had the Princess lived, we would have waited a few years and re-introduced her to the world. What a shake-up that would have caused when the story of her attempted assassination reached world's ears!" Stergios smiled, clearly enjoying the vision of a future which he had been cruelly denied. Indeed, Hal thought, it would have been an incredible story but were the agents perhaps being naive? Surely if that had happened the Establishment would have taken every opportunity to silence and discredit the woman 'claiming' to be the long dead Princess? She would indeed have presented an enigma similar to that of Anna Anderson, the woman who had claimed to be the murdered Romanov Grand Duchess years after the family had allegedly been shot. Even now there was uncertainty as to the veracity or otherwise of her story which cast her alternately as genuine or mentally ill. Even the existence of accurate DNA testing probably wouldn't satisfactorily prove the Princess to have lived. There were always ways of covering up the 'truth' presented by science. She would never have seen the light of day or been taken seriously as the real Princess. Hal's heart sank as he realised the enormity of exposing any sort of truth in the real world. There were powers out there enormous enough to quell and extinguish the truths which certain people didn't want revealed.

His expression must have revealed how daunted and overwhelmed he was feeling. He felt flat. The task he'd been asked to do seemed impossible. In his own heart was belief in all that he'd learned. To convey that belief to the world would just lead him to ridicule. Stergios' eyes scrutinised him and Hal felt the intensity of the gaze to which he was exposed.

"The other option we considered," continued Stergios, "was to simply continue with the duplicity of using Tasia as a body double of the Princess and re-introduce her to spread the story."

"And you didn't because...?"

"Tasia's superiors decided that such duplicity was no better than the deceit already perpetrated by the political elite. Yes, it would have created a sensation but it wouldn't have been the truth and the truth is what we are fighting for. We are left therefore with the only tools we have; the pen as our sword and the opportunity of raising awareness. The public have always been deeply suspicious about the Princess's death. Perhaps our story will open debate and at least emphasise the doubts harboured by many who question the integrity of our so-called democratic society."

"Tasia's 'superiors'? Hal raised an eyebrow. If she no longer worked for the Intelligence Agencies, who would be her superiors, he wondered.

Stergios smiled sagely.

"We all have a higher accountability Hal. Tasia just happens to be more in touch, shall we say with hers."

Hal was becoming frustrated with the cryptic clues but Stergios could not be persuaded to say more on this subject. He assumed that he was referring to her own religious faith, whatever that might be.

"Now, Hal. Your work here is almost done and it is time for you to return to London and write that book for us. We have people who will help you to get it published. Prepare yourself for the ridicule and criticism that will surely follow. Be sure though, the revelations will rock the Establishment behemoth and suspicion will once more be cast upon political motivations and the future of the monarchy. That's never a bad thing."

The conversation was at an end as Stergios excused himself to return to his room. Hal finished his drink and ordered whisky. He had no idea how he was going to present this story and although he had circumstantial evidence, he lacked anything concrete. The motives he'd been presented for the Princess's death were credible, sure. Enough to make people sit up and wonder, yes ... but to provide any real influence; he doubted that. He was despondent as he made his way unsteadily back to his own room for a much needed sleep.

Hal was awoken by sudden and urgent banging on his door. The sunlight penetrated a crack in the curtains which he hadn't closed properly before throwing himself into bed the night before and he glanced at the clock beside him. It was 10 a.m. and much later than he'd planned to get up this morning. Throwing his trousers on, he opened the door and was confronted by Kyle, clearly stressed and distracted.

"Kyle!" Hal exclaimed, surprised at the unusually dishevelled vision before him.

"Hey buddy," Kyle replied breathlessly. "Listen, I just came to say goodbye. Tasia passed away this morning," the man's voice broke as he relayed the news to Hal. Kyle leant against the door frame and bent over as though he had taken a sucker punch to the stomach. His breathing was laboured as he tried to stifle a sob. Shocked, Hal grabbed the man in support fearing that he was about to pass out.

"It's OK Hal. I'm OK. I'll be fine." Composing himself, Kyle straightened up and Hal could see the pain in his eyes. "I just came to tell you the news. I'm going with Stergios to make the necessary arrangements so you'll be returning to Gavdos alone I'm afraid. The helicopter's organised to leave at noon so you'll need to get yourself to the airport. You'll have time to collect your belongings back at Villa Artemis and the helicopter will take you back to Chania Airport. Your flight back to London is booked for 10 p.m. tonight. Tickets have been e-mailed to you." Kyle spoke breathlessly as though his own life was being sucked from his lungs.

"But Kyle! I should go with you and Stergios. I'd ... I'd like to pay my last respects to Tasia..."

"Not possible I'm afraid buddy. There wouldn't be time and anyway ..." Hal understood. Kyle just wanted to be alone with his beloved Tasia for a while and absorb the enormity of his loss. He remembered the feeling when Fliss had left him. He didn't want anyone else to disturb him as he said his last goodbyes. He recalled how he'd unjustly resented the rest of her family and friends who'd rushed up to see her as she lay peaceful and unmoving, all wanting to spend their own final, quiet moment with her.

349

"Hey, sorry Kyle. Stupid of me. Of course I understand. I'll just go get myself together and be off. Will you be in touch?"

"Sure we will be Hal. We just need to deal with this on our own now. She meant a great deal to me and Stergios. Good luck with everything. Do your best by her huh?"

Hal assured Kyle that he'd do all he could to tell their story and hoped he'd see them both soon. Satisfied, Kyle left, descending the stairs two at a time leaving Hal empty and alone. He was sad too. Not in the way he'd been when Fliss died of course but the finality of death struck him again. It was all too great to contemplate. He could barely comprehend how a person could be there one moment and just gone the next. And of course now, he had reason to question whether it all really ended. At that moment, he felt the light brush of a hand through his hair and he turned suddenly. A faint tingle ran through his body as he realised that Tasia had come to say her own farewell to him.

Chapter 33 – Sangfroid and Saracens

Hal shivered as he stepped from the aircraft into the early morning London air. It was nearly Christmas and a bitter wind cut into him as he walked briskly to the airport terminal building. He'd almost forgotten how cold it could be. The weather exacerbated his feeling of desolation at the loss of another friend and the weight of the burden he'd assumed in retelling their bizarre story. His arrival in London made Gavdos seem so far away and unreal. It had all been like some outlandish dream and now reality was biting. His heart sank as he thought of the task that lay ahead of him. He didn't know if he believed it all himself.

Turning the key in the door of his flat Hal was overwhelmed once more by the feelings of loneliness that had engulfed him until his departure to Gavdos. There, he had felt inexplicably closer to another world and to Fliss whose presence there had been palpable. Now, he was surrounded by the mundane; the emptiness of living his life alone and the stomach sinking feeling that maybe he wasn't up to the job he'd been tasked with. He'd taken their money and hospitality for a few months but was he really able to deliver the goods? Whilst in Gavdos, he'd believed that he could. But now, alone in a cold flat with the isolation of his own thoughts, it all seemed so far- fetched. He was shattered. Maybe things would look different in the morning, he thought forlornly. They didn't...

Hal was greeted with a white-out as he flung the curtains open next day. The snow fell in huge fluffy flakes and the sky was ominously dark. Unshaven, his dressing gown, far too big for him now, was thrown carelessly around him as he put the kettle on and sat down with his coffee at the laptop containing all his notes to date. Prevaricating, he logged into his e-mails and saw that there was one from Stergios. He read it quickly.

'Sorry to have missed you yesterday old friend. As you can imagine, there was a lot to do and as we were Tasia's only 'family' it was our privilege to make the arrangements for her. I know that she was grateful to you for hearing her out and she asked me to tell you that she regarded you as a friend and confidante. Kyle, of course, is deeply saddened but he is strong and he knew this day must come. We have our own work to do in bringing things to a conclusion You will be contacted now that you are back in London by those who can help you in your search for evidence to back up our story. I am sending you something which may help.

In the meantime Hal, good luck with completion of your book. I look forward to reading it.

Yours always,

Stergios

'Good luck!' thought Hal. 'It's going to take a bit more than luck to get this one off the ground, Stergios.'

Hal looked through the list of e-mails, many of them advertising or junk mail and deleted those he didn't want to read. As he made his way through them, there was one from a name he didn't recognise, Albert Godwin. He clicked on it and read the contents.

'Dear Mr Bradbury

I've been asked by Stergios Tavoularis, to contact you to assist you with your understanding of the royal Stuart bloodline which I believe you are researching for a book. I knew Stergios at university when we both studied history and I am now Emeritus Professor of History apparently for my services to ancient times during my career! A trifle pretentious in my view but hey ho! Please feel free to contact me if you feel it will assist you.

Sincerest Regards

Albert Godwin.

352

Hal sighed. He was fatigued and lacking enthusiasm today. The dark, cold day outside merely served to emphasise his despondency as he thought back to the warmth of Greece that made everything so much lighter and easier. He wished he'd been able to stay there to complete the job but he knew he had more information to gather that the internet alone couldn't provide. He gulped down the last of the coffee and made a decision. He'd finish this job then sell up and move to Chania where he would concentrate on building up his writing career. He'd always wanted to write fiction – why not there? The thought instantly cheered him and he felt some motivation to get on with the job and then get the hell away from London. A new life would be just the thing! He clicked the reply button and told Albert he'd be grateful of his help. They arranged to meet in a couple of days' time when the weather forecast promised a let up in the snow. Appropriately, he thought, they met up in the cafe at the British Museum.

Albert Godwin was a white haired, twinkly older gentleman. Older than Stergios, Hal thought. He was dressed in tweed jacket and sported a very dapper pair of tartan trousers.

"Ah, dear fellow, I see you are admiring my leg wear! Thought they'd be just the thing for today. Stuart Hunting Tartan in honour of our shared interest." Hal smiled.

"Very sartorial. You certainly stand out in a crowd," he said admiringly. "Not sure I'd get away with wearing them though." They ordered tea and scones which Albert consumed with relish as they chattered about the dreadful weather and Hal's recent visit to Crete.

"Wonderful history in Crete. Always loved the myths and mysteries of the island," Albert mused. He recalled his visits to Knossos and his fascination with the Minoans who'd been ahead of their times. Hal listened politely as they compared notes about the various places they'd visited on the island. He spoke about the birthplace of the God Zeus with enthusiasm and his visit to the Dikteon Cave in the Lasithi Plateau.

"Couldn't do that journey these days though. It was bad enough negotiating the hairpin bends in the car and the cave itself is for the sure footed. Has a strange air of mystery though. If you concentrate hard enough you can almost feel the Gods around you," he mused. "Which brings me rather aptly to the subject of our meeting today," he continued.

"Sorry?" Hal asked, thinking his companion had veered entirely from the subject of their meeting. Albert chuckled.

"The lady named after the daughter of Zeus, Artemis. Or, Diana, as the Romans referred to her."

"Ah, yes of course," Hal nodded. Albert was not to be deterred from the Gods as yet though.

"Quite a character was the lady Artemis," Albert persisted with the theme which he was obviously warming to. "The Huntress and Moon Goddess, d'you see? By all accounts she could be a bit of a vengeful lass on anyone professing to be more beautiful or indeed better in any way than she. She turned one of her own nymphs, Callisto, into a bear for losing her purity to Zeus who'd duped the poor woman into submission by disguising himself as Artemis. Then she killed Adonis, the God of Love for his rather misguided boasts that he was a better hunter than she," Albert laughed once again as he scrutinised Hal with gimlet eyes making him shift in his seat, a little discomfited.

"It would be easy to draw some parallels with the Diana we're here to discuss," Hal commented uneasily.

Albert nodded. "Indeed, Hal. I was hoping you might see the connection. It seems that our modern day Goddess could, when pushed, also be a lady capable of revenge. The analogy of course doesn't end there. Her own brother rather aptly observed in his eulogy that 'of all the ironies about Diana, perhaps the greatest was this; a girl given the name of the ancient goddess of hunting was, in the end, the most hunted person of the modern age.' And of course, we are here to discuss the real reason why this might have been the case. So Hal, perhaps the poor lady gave away too much of her hand when her father in law said 'If you don't behave we might take your title away my girl,' to which she responded, 'My title is a lot older than yours.' She was of course quite correct but I rather sense that she should have kept a little quieter. Her vengeful nature was evident for all to see when she suggested so publicly that her husband was not a suitable monarch and that she should be 'Queen of Hearts' and Regent to her son as King instead. Unfortunately, her words were too close to home for the Establishment and she sealed her fate," Albert ruminated sadly.

"So it is true then?" Hal asked. "The Princess did have a legitimate claim to the throne?"

"Oh yes indeed. You see the Windsor line is a mix of Germanic or Teuton blood with the Judaic bloodline. It is a dilution of the true Stuart bloodline gained through the marriage of James 1 & VI of Scotland's granddaughter Sophia to Ernst August, the Elector of Hanover. Their union produced George I who succeeded the last of the Stuart Monarchs. Unfortunately, George never really took much of a part in British Royal life, choosing to spend most of his time in his birth country, Germany and never even bothering to learn English. This suited the political Whigs in Britain of course who were made up of the richest oligarchs and financiers of the time. In absence of the monarch in England they enjoyed the 'Whig Supremacy' at this time defeating the Jacobite Uprising led by the Tories. They supported constitutional monarchy, opposing absolute rule and bitterly opposed the Roman Catholic Stuart Kings in Britain. They had successfully deposed James II and James VII from his claim to the throne leaving the way open for the politically manoeuvred Hanoverian rulers. With George I having no interest in Britain, it allowed Parliament, now controlled by financiers to take the lead here. As I think Stergios explained to you, there has been an unseen oligarchy manipulating Parliament and so called democratically elected Prime Ministers ever since. In truth, those leaders with whom we are all so familiar, actually have very little say. They are, even today, merely puppets controlled by the financially powerful oligarch puppet masters. It is always a bonus if those who are elected have things to hide, shall we say. It gives the puppet masters even more control over what happens in power, if you understand."

Hal wasn't strong on history but he began to understand the manoeuvring which had led to the current monarchy.

"In other words," Hal clarified, the Stuarts carried the Judaic bloodline but it was massively diluted after intermarriage from James I and VI of Scotland's children? And the true blood Stuarts were never able to regain the throne after the Whigs became the ruling party in Britain in the reign of an absent George I?"

"Exactly!" Albert confirmed. Since then, various Masonic groups operating within the oligarchy have kept the power base firmly within the Establishment, hiding the truth about the true bloodline of Christ now running only thinly through the veins of the monarchy. There are others who have greater claims to the British throne; a matter kept firmly hidden from public consciousness. Since then of course, the Judaeo Teutons have been the constitutional monarchs in Britain from the Hanoverian Line, through the Saxe-Coburgs and Queen Victoria.

"OK," Hal was desperately trying to remain focused on the complex familial interrelationships which pervaded the British Monarchy. "So, we now have the Windsors. Where do they fit in?"

Albert sipped his tea, his piercing and rheumy eyes bored into Hal, making him feel somewhat stupid and uneducated. History had never really been his thing. Albert returned his cup with a clink on the saucer and smiled.

"Dear dear, what do they teach in schools these days?" his rhetorical question hung in the air as a rather shamefaced Hal returned to his notebook, wishing that Albert would just get on with it. After a few moments, he continued. "Simply put, World War I was fought after the failure to reconcile family grievances throughout the various interrelated European Monarchies culminated in the assassination of Archduke Ferdinand of Austria. Through various allies, war broke out in Europe with Germany eventually declaring war on Britain's ally, France. It resulted in the deaths of over 800,000 British soldiers. The Saxe-Coburgs were embarrassed by their German connections and their German name and to avoid public condemnation and anti German sentiment they changed the royal name to Windsor on 17th July 1917. It was feared, after the forced abdication of Nicolas II, Emperor of Russia that the abolition of all European monarchies may ensue if public confidence could not be restored. The Germanic connections of course remained an embarrassment when Edward VIII, Queen Victoria's great grandson abdicated for love of Mrs Simpson and, rather embarrassingly for the royals, maintained a friendship with a certain Mr Hitler and an interest in the Third Reich. He was an open supporter of facism and Hitler's policies. It was to be hoped that the Windsor name would, over time, cleanse and anglicise the British Monarchy."

"It's all so incestuous when you think about it," Hal remarked. "I didn't really appreciate that all the European monarchs were related, much less that wars would break out between them." He smiled. "Jeremy Kyle didn't exist in those days though, did he?" Albert merely raised an eyebrow in mild disdain. They ordered another pot of tea which Hal wished was a large gin and tonic. They'd been here an hour and

357

hadn't even touched upon the connection between all this and the dead Princess.

"Mmm, yes, quite so," Albert mumbled as he tucked into a large slab of Victoria Sponge Cake he'd ordered with his tea. "Nothing like a traditional afternoon tea with sponge cake is there, Hal?" he said between mouthfuls.

"Very Establishment I'd say Albert," he teased. Albert, choosing to ignore the comment flicked away the crumbs from his lips before taking up the story again.

"Right, so I expect you're wondering where this is leading in terms of the Princess then," he stated, rather than asked. "Well, here it is. Her family can be traced way beyond King James I and VI of Scotland. We can show ancestry to Robert II of Scotland in the 14th century and, now, here's the thing even further to the Scottish Celtic Kings with connections to the Merovingian Dynasty. And who are they connected to?"

"Jesus Christ himself from the bloodline of David and Solomon," Hal concluded.

"Yes! And her bloodline is pure. Not genetically meddled with by intermarrying like the Windsors. The Princess was a direct descendant. Of course, historical documents have been unearthed which provide evidence of all this but the Churches of Rome and England have sought over the centuries to stifle the knowledge. The churches have benefited hugely from dominating religious thought and belief which has served them well in controlling the masses and benefiting financially. The priest, Saunière came perilously close to shattering the religious mythologies perpetuated through the main religious organisations when he found the parchments confirming the bloodline. As you are aware, I think, he was enriched by those documents, now held in secret MI6 archives, when he revealed their contents to the Church."

"Is there any way of being able to see these documents?" asked Hal.

Albert shook his head. "Not a chance I'm afraid. Security over them is impenetrable. However...," Albert hesitated.

Hal looked quizzically as he waited for the old man to reveal his hand. Albert signalled to Hal to come closer across the table as he whispered, "However, I do have photographic evidence of the documents that Stergios managed to obtain. They're in old French but I'm happy to show them to you." Albert produced the pictures which showed yellowing parchments with fading brown writing on them.

"Essentially they confirm the relatives of Christ took up residence in Europe and their connection to the Merovingian Dynasty. We can show the lineage also to the Celts and thus direct to the Princess."

"Can I quote you in the book? And use the photographs?"

"Once, I would have said no. To have these things in one's possession meant certain death. However, I am not so far from death now Hal. I don't fear the truth any more. Yes. Publish and be damned," he conceded.

"It's a strange thing that the very institutions which we all hold in such awe can be so involved in such murderous activities that seem to be putting us all in danger," Hal shook his head in disbelief.

"The Churches are simply other manifestations of man's struggle to control man. We have evidence to suggest that the stories perpetuated in the New Testament about Jesus Christ are really no more than fairy tales. The Church of Rome selectively destroyed or modified the original scriptures. They would probably say that they merely interpreted them. The evidence tends to point to the fact that Jesus was no more the Son of God than you or me. But by transforming Jesus into a superhuman mystic who was responsible for miracles through his links with an omnipotent God, Rome, in becoming the guardian of the legacy became all powerful. Human frailty and the need to believe in something greater than us that transcends death and gives hope of everlasting life allowed the Church of Rome to secure its power base over citizens. The political organisations of the Western World used the myths of Christianity on which to base its democratic control systems and in so doing made the church the agent for political ascendency and the spread of power. Behind our politicians are the oligarchy who manipulate their interests and power through Masonic agencies which wield their influence using ritual and symbolic means cultivated from the Dark Ages and still revered today."

Hal slumped back in his chair. He'd never been naive enough to believe that all was good in democracy but he found it depressing that if what Albert and Stergios had told him, just about everything that he believed in was a facade; a corrupt front serving only very few people in society. Sure, he thought, there will be a knock on benefit to others, but only in the narrowest sense. After all, if the hidden oligarchs were protecting their interests then it must, by default benefit others at least some of the time.   But; and here was the real issue, how much did the system actually work against society? If the Establishment did actually keep people with something to hide in power just so that they could manipulate their own interests, how far did it extend? Corrupt and deviant Westminster figures who could act at will just as long as they did as they were told by the oligarchs behind them and inhibited only by the threat of exposure? It was terrifying to think about and if truth be known, the evidence of just such a world was slowly coming to light.

"You seem weary, dear boy. Am I draining you with all this?"

"No, not at all," replied Hal. "It's just soul destroying to realise that everything that seems to keep our society together is probably no more than a fairy tale based on tenuous links to the past."

360

Albert nodded. "Yes and the greatest fairy tale of all is spun around the monarchy. The mystique of our Royals is kept in place from our subconscious belief that they are somehow special; connected in some way and perhaps second only to God as Defenders of the Faith. And when someone comes to light who can shatter that illusion and threaten to expose the truth, 'accidents' will happen."

"Such as the death of a Princess," Hal concluded.

"Such as the death of a Princess who could upset the comfort of the status quo," Albert agreed.

"What I still don't understand is this though Albert; you say that Jesus wasn't the supernatural being which has always been claimed. If that is the case, then why is it so important that the Stuarts were connected with his bloodline?"

"A good question, Hal. The evidence suggests that whilst not perhaps the 'Son of God' as perpetuated by the Church of Rome, Jesus was the real King of Israel. He is true Royalty. There are records held by the Intelligence Services which suggest that he was a revolutionary usurped by Rome and the investiture of Herod as King of Israel. He stormed Jerusalem with his army on Palm Sunday and for this victory, it is likely that the Romans decided to execute him. The oppressed population were too frightened to oppose or question the Romans. Crucifixion was the penalty for sedition, crimes against Rome, not God, as the majority believe."

"So how did the connection with God arise?" Hal questioned.

"You've heard the term, 'Messiah?'" Albert asked.

"Well yes, of course," Hal replied.

"And your understanding of that word would be...?"

Hal frowned. He didn't really know what it meant. Eventually, shrugging his shoulders, he said, "King, I guess."

"Precisely!" Albert seemed pleased. "But in Israel, d'you see, the rightful heir to the throne is regarded as divine; in other words, God's representative on earth. This is the

361

source of their right and power to rule over others. The word 'Messiah' means the 'anointed one.' In those days of course, there was no 'democracy' but a 'theocracy,' a combination of politics and religion to effect government."

Hal was beginning to see more connections. "And that's why all European monarchs from then to now still have this divine connection and why our monarch is accepted as Head of the Church of England. It derives from the apparent link to the original King of Israel and that is why we revere royalty! Yeah, I get it."

"So you see now why it is so important to our royals that they can claim lineage back to Jesus Christ. They've always been somewhat insecure however because they are not of the pure bloodline who, as we've seen, were usurped with the last of the Stuart line. Unfortunately for them, the Stuart line continued and there are those waiting in the wings today who claim lineage and rights to the throne."

"But what about the stories of Jesus as someone who performed miracles; his reputation as a prophet? Where did they come from?"

"Most will probably be stories Hal, but remember, as the de jure King of Israel, and thus God's representative, who knows? Perhaps Jesus did have mystical powers. There is much to suggest he did and, of course, the Merovingians were well known to have esoteric and psychic powers. When Mary Magdalene and her children fled to Europe, their mystic blood intermingled with the Judaic Teutons who later became the Merovingians. Jesus' family therefore may have been responsible for spreading the arcane powers to the European dynasty. And now ... well, the documents held by the Intelligence Services, brought back from Saunière's village in Rennes-le-Château identify the bloodline as the Holy Grail representing service to the rightful King, true wisdom, the land and the prosperity of its people. This was the Code to which our dead Princess aspired. Her desire to serve her people

362

rather than be served was perceived as her legacy from her ancestors and a great threat to the constitutional monarchy. Her popularity put the monarchy in great peril. Just think, if, as she had wished, the truth had become known about her relationship to the Holy Grail or bloodline, which was conjoined from Jesus' family through the Merovingian Celtic Houses of Dunkeld and Stuart, the public might have demanded her immediate accession to the throne."

"Wow!" Hal exhaled. It was a fascinating whirlwind trip through history but what a story if it was true. The present monarchical line were only pretenders to the throne because they had engineered themselves to conjoin with the blood of true royalty. This could destroy their claim entirely.

Albert smiled. "One other thing Hal. The bloodline is Judaic in origin. It leads back to Israel. Now, tell me, can you see any reason why the Princess's, shall we say ... choice of friends, might have posed another problem to the Establishment and perhaps even those who fought on her behalf...?"

This time Hal understood. "Her choice of friends? You mean her Muslim friends I take it?"

"Indeed. The Princess's last paramour was of Saudi Arab origin and Muslim; his predecessor a Pakistani Muslim. Can you imagine if she had married either, the uproar it would have caused in Establishment circles whose ancestors spent centuries fighting the Saracens and defending a Judaic heritage. They are of course, historically speaking, complete enemies. The bloodline would have thus been tainted irreversibly through any children and placed Islam dangerously close to the British Establishment. Had the Princess managed to establish her right to the throne it may have caused the intermingling of Muslim and Judaic blood into the heart of monarchy. An impossible situation and a compelling reason to destroy her."

363

"There was a belief that the Princess was pregnant at the time of her death wasn't there?" Hal mused.

"Quite so, Hal. And whether it was true or not, it wasn't a situation that the Establishment would allow. Even had the truth of her putative claim to the throne never been recognised, she would have created a half sibling for her children who would carry Judaic/Arab Muslim blood. An untenable situation for the monarchy and its supporters. Potentially it could have destroyed the political foundations held for centuries and allowed destabilisation of everything the Establishment had achieved."

Chapter 34 – Publish and Be Damned

It was dark as the two men said their farewells outside the British Museum. Hal pulled his coat around him and wrapped his scarf more snugly around his neck. The Christmas lights cast a jolly festive glow along the street and he remembered with sadness the days when Fliss would, with child-like wonder exclaim at the festive display each year as they welcomed the season she loved most. There would be no choosing the Christmas tree and no decorations to give his flat the warm glow he'd enjoyed with Fliss. If anything, the festive cheer and the growing discomfort and disillusionment he felt with the UK strengthened his resolve to finish the project and find himself a new life in Crete. It was all that kept him going now.

Hal closed the door on the world and worked like a man obsessed over the entirety of the festive period. It was a welcome distraction from the loneliness that had overtaken him since his return home. His melancholy mood was only deepened by the good cheer and implicit togetherness that Christmas represented. He'd lost Fliss and he'd lost a friend all within two years and misery weighed heavy upon him. He made the concerted decision not to look at a newspaper or switch on the television until Christmas was over. He didn't want to hear about the 'comfort and joy' that everyone else was experiencing, nor did he want to hear about any of the disasters that might be going on elsewhere in the world. His home became a hermitage over the following days as Hal pored over the computer, writing in a frenzied outpouring of prose and reportage. There was much about the Princess's heritage and ancestry that he didn't fully understand so when he wasn't writing, he researched furiously. He stared, wild eyed in a caffeine induced high at the screen as he tried to digest those parts of the story that still evaded him.

He read about the long ago time when the Merovingian dynasty had fused its blood relationship with the Celtic Kings resulting in the continuation of the Judaic bloodline through the Stuarts. Following the crowning of Robert the Bruce in 1306 100,000 Jews had been expelled from France and England, both of which apparently feared the restoration of the Merovingian Kings in Scotland. The Jews were regarded not just as a race and a religion but they took on a far greater political significance.   When political feeling turned against the Knights Templar, Hal found suggestions that they had claimed sanctuary under Robert the Bruce in Scotland, bringing with them the secret documents which proved that the bloodline of Christ, or Holy Grail had survived in Europe. The tremendous strength of this highly trained fighting force had helped Bruce, a direct bloodline descendant, to restore Scottish independence from the English which ultimately reinforced the Merovingian strain. It was said that in return for their help, the Knights Templar demanded the marriage of Bruce's daughter, Marjorie to Walter Stewart, presumably also of Judaic descent, thus embedding the bloodline within their son, Robert Stewart II of Scotland. Princess Diana was his direct descendant.

Scotland was central to the theme and he understood that the English Parliament's desire to unite the Crowns with James VI of Scotland and I of England had been underpinned by the knowledge that the monarch carried the prized bloodline which they desired in their own monarchy for political ends. It was all beginning to come together as Hal ploughed through the ever more complex trail of history.

He discovered that there is a continuing Stuart dynasty and suggestions that there may have been a plan, or at least a strong desire to restore the family as the true monarchy in an independent Scotland and that according to some commentators, Foreign Office documents suggested that the

Princess had been actively encouraged that she was the obvious choice to take up the mantle.

Hal rubbed his eyes, now dry and sore from too long staring at the computer and lack of sleep. He stretched his aching body, pained from the hours of bending over the keyboard. His mind was racing. He thought of the recent Scottish Independence Referendum when Alex Salmond had been keen to assure voters that the current monarch, Queen Elizabeth II would remain Queen of Scotland in an independent country. He wondered why Salmond might not have been anxious to restore the country's own rightful Stuart monarchy given the evidence about which he must have been aware. The answer wasn't far away. Salmond was a keen supporter of the European Union; this was in direct conflict with the ethics of the Stuart line who were actively against the continuation of a corporate and financier led organisation which supported a European Super State.

The jigsaw was starting to show a very detailed and convincing picture of the reasons for a possible assassination of the Princess. Hal thought back to the now infamous interview. Had she really been paving the way for her claim to the throne when he suggested that her husband was unsuitable to be King? Was this what she had meant? That he was a usurper of the true bloodline? She wanted to be 'Queen of Hearts'. Was this her way of planting a subliminal idea in the minds of the public that she could have a greater role? There had also been a suggestion that her son William might 'leapfrog' her ex husband to become King with the Princess as Regent. If this was the case, then she had played a very dangerous hand indeed. Public support might well have created a very compromising situation for the existing monarchy had all the compelling evidence as to the Princess's bloodline become common knowledge.

The documents held by the Intelligence Services, the photographs of which he had in his possession must have

367

been removed from the Knights Templar in Scotland and returned to Rennes-le-Château at some time centuries before the priest Saunière had discovered them. No wonder he became so mysteriously rich. If they truly showed that a distinctive genetic bloodline of apparently mystical qualities existed and that bloodline could be shown to have coursed through the Princess's veins then it would provide an obvious and strong motive for the Establishment to be rid of her. After that interview, her death, which may have been contemplated for a while, could well have become vital for the protection of certain interests. The Princess was quite clear that she supported the idea of a new style monarchy, one chosen by the people. A monarch who would not simply be a figurehead installed by constitution for the interests of the shadowy few but one who would first and foremost look after the rights of the people and justice. There were undoubtedly fears that the Princess's influence over her sons might sway them towards her views.

Hal pieced together the warning signs that might have alerted the Establishment to the Princess's intentions even before the fateful interview. She had without doubt been the greatest thorn in their side for nearly ten years. She had waged war against the 'Firm' tenaciously and with alacrity behind the scenes. She'd been clever though. Relying on the usual distance and reticence of the family, she had used these characteristics to her own advantage. Over the years, her 'Shy Di' image had metamorphosed into the reinvented, elegant and composed woman she latterly became. She engendered fascination, popularity, and respect from the public. It might not have been enough to depose the royal family completely, but, if she was truly aware of her ancestry, coupled with her ex-husband's unpopularity, it might indeed have made it possible for her to engineer the situation where her son, guided by the Princess as Regent, sidelined the future King. The Princess would undoubtedly have enjoyed the prospect of advancing the idea of a counter monarchy, cocking a snook at the Establishment which had made her life such a misery and she had despised with such venom. Hal also appreciated that she had a genuinely altruistic side of her that mirrored the ideals of her ancestry; the Merovingians had passed the genetic blueprint of the Sangraal heritage to her through the Stuarts and she preferred to serve others rather than her position. This troubled the Establishment whose ideals diametrically opposed those of the Princess and thus she loathed them and regarded them as an enemy not unlike the way in which her Judaic forefathers abhorred the Romans and their own politically chosen figurehead, King Herod.

Whilst the claims seemed plausible to Hal as he traced the footprints and the ideology which seemed to underpin the fate of the dead Princess, nonetheless, he feared the incredulity of the public who might find the story a stretch too far. But, maybe not, he thought to himself as he pondered the words on his screen. The public were far more willing to believe that the Princess was assassinated than the official story that she was the victim of a simple accident. Indeed, there were far more obvious reasons why she might have been murdered, but his discoveries brought a more sinister and credible motive to the table which showed that she was probably the greatest threat the monarchy and the Establishment had ever faced. Their days of privilege and self aggrandisement would have been numbered had the truth been revealed.

Hal looked at the word count beneath his typescript. He was amazed to see that he had almost completed ninety thousand words. It was as though he'd been writing in a trance, barely noticing the transition from one day to the next. Wearily, he tore himself away from his desk and pulled back the curtain. Outside, it was a frosty but sunny afternoon. All of a sudden his spirits lifted a little, recalling the pleasure of a bright blue sky and the thought that soon he could spend every day with the sun warming his face and illuminating his darkened spirit. He hadn't even noticed the passing of Christmas and Boxing Day, so engrossed had he been in his work. Glancing in the full length mirror that Fliss had hung on their bedroom door, Hal was shocked at the gaunt and unkempt figure who gazed back at him. He was almost unrecognisable, even to himself.

'Time for some air,' he thought. He needed to get out of the flat for a couple of hours and clear his head that buzzed obsessively with the answers to a mystery he had no way of proving. If only he could get access to the secret parchments, he thought as he showered and shaved in readiness to greet the world again. Finally, dressed in jeans and sweater that engulfed his now skeletal frame, Hal inspected himself and was satisfied that at least he wouldn't scare off small children and animals. He had a haunted, almost crazed look about him. He hoped that fresh air and a good meal would restore a little sanity and normality.

It was bitterly cold as Hal emerged from the flat but it energised him and made him feel alive again as he strolled through the quiet London streets, frost nipping his sallow cheeks. It was Sunday and it appeared that most folks were still nursing their hangovers and culinary excess of the Christmas festivities. He decided to walk in Kensington Gardens and admired the stunning expanse of beautiful parkland, quiet now on this cold winter's day. He imagined the loneliness of the Princess who had wandered these verdant grounds to escape the grand but claustrophobic walls of Kensington Palace and her fears that every move or word she uttered was under surveillance. At least here, she felt she could speak with ease and escape to a world where Peter Pan represented the childlike innocence she adored. Indeed, she would have loved the Memorial play park complete with Pirate Ship that had been erected in her name and drew thousands of children to the Gardens all year round. She would have revelled in the normalcy of children's laughter in those long dark days of isolation, fear and suspicion she must have felt before her death. Hal shivered as he thought of the Princess whispering her terror to a trusted confidante, never quite sure who her friends or enemies were or whether she could ever be truly open. His reverie was disturbed momentarily as a rustling in the trees caught his attention. He squinted into the lowering sunshine and saw a shadow moving swiftly through the leaves. A tall, elegant figure who lithely negotiated the obstacles. He lifted a hand to his forehead to shade his eyes from the blinding light and thought, just for a moment, he saw the familiar figure of the woman he'd known for only such a short time, but who had impacted his life in such a transformative way. She could have been Tasia, Diana, Artemis? Who knew which? To Hal, they had become one and the same. He was unable to distinguish the features of the woman, only the silhouette of someone he was sure he'd once known. Momentarily the figure hesitated and as she did so, he saw her raise a hand in greeting before disappearing into the thick foliage. He raised his own hand in hesitant response as another feint rustling sound preceded the appearance of a young deer gambolling through the trees seemingly in pursuit of the woman. He knew at that moment that Artemis had returned and Hal smiled to himself, comforted as always by her mystical presence.

Presently, refreshed by the walk and the mists in his head clearing, Hal made his way back to the Borough of Chelsea streets where life appeared to be resuming. More people had obviously decided that it was time for a stroll and he felt as though he was back in the living world, released from his self imposed Hadean prison. He didn't notice that another figure was surreptitiously tracking his movements, disappearing into alleys and doorways behind him as he paused for a moment, first to buy a copy of the London Herald before settling into a nearby cafe where he planned to eat his first proper meal in four days. Where had the time gone, he wondered? Hal could barely recall sleeping or even moving from his desk since he closed the doors following his meeting with Albert. He scanned the menu and plumped for the all day breakfast. It was only as he felt his mouth watering at the aroma of fresh bacon, eggs and sausage sizzling on the grill behind the counter that he even realised he was famished. He was also beyond exhaustion. No wonder he'd looked like a crazed madman when he saw his reflection in the mirror this morning. As he devoured the plateful of food in front of him, Hal gazed out of the window, watching the post Christmas sales get into full swing as shoppers now came out in droves ready to spend their gift vouchers or return unwanted gifts for something more desired. He'd forgotten the last time he'd actually wanted to buy anything. Money and things had ceased to have any interest for him since Fliss had gone. There was no nest to build; no plans to re-decorate or even furnish a new home any more. All he knew was emptiness and indifference. He thought again of the possibility of a new life in Crete when the book was finished. He would get himself a little apartment overlooking the sea. It would have a balcony and he'd buy a blue table and chairs which, set against the brilliantly whitewashed walls, would provide inspiration for his own Greek Odyssey. He felt an unfamiliar flutter of excitement. Perhaps he could find life again, he thought. He would be a frequent visitor to Gavdos to pay tribute to Tasia Artemis, the woman who had led him there.

Hal ordered a coffee and remembered the newspaper he'd bought. He unfolded it and immediately blanched as the headline screamed out at him.

"UCL Emeritus Professor Found Dead in Possible Ritual Killing"

372

Hal didn't need to read on to know to whom the article referred. He almost didn't read on at all as a wave of nausea hit him and beads of perspiration broke out on his top lip. He thought he was going to faint and lowered his head attempting to steady himself as his head spun. At that moment the waitress returned.

"Sir? Are you OK?" Hal took a deep breath and raised his head.

"Yes, thank you. I think so. Sorry, I just felt a bit dizzy for a moment.

"Here's your coffee." The waitress placed it down in front of him. "Can I get you some water or something? The coffee's still a bit hot."

Hal nodded gratefully. "Yes, that would be very kind. Thanks."

"No worries," she replied and went off to fetch the water. Finally, after a couple of glasses of water and a few sips of coffee, Hal steeled himself to read the article.

'UCL *Emeritus Professor of French Mediaeval History, Albert Godwin was found dead in his Marylebone flat yesterday afternoon. Police are investigating the death which they say is being treated as murder. Professor Godwin was found by his Housekeeper returning after her Christmas Day break. She immediately alerted the Police. No specific details have been released as yet, however, neighbours who heard the Housekeeper, Mrs Emily Armitage's screams have reported that it was a 'scene of carnage' as they found Mr Godwin 'butchered' and 'disembowelled.' Police have refused to confirm or deny the details of the Professor's death but witnesses were reported to have described it as a seemingly ritual killing reminding them of tales of Jack the Ripper.*

UCL President, David Thomson said that news of Professor Godwin's death was a terrible shock to everyone and that he would be sadly missed. Since his retirement,

Professor Godwin continued to give regular lectures and seminars, imparting his specialised knowledge of the Merovingian Dynasty, an ancient French Monarchy, to students of the University. 'His expertise and knowledge will be irreplaceable,' Mr Thomson said.

Investigations are continuing into the death. As yet no suspects have been discovered and there is no known motive for the killing.'

In a daze, Hal folded the paper and paid the bill.

"Are you feeling better now?" the waitress enquired with concern.

Hal shook his head. "Just heard some bad news," he said vaguely.

"Oh, sorry to hear that," the waitress replied. "Such a bad time of year for sad news isn't it?"

"It is, isn't it?" Hal agreed as he bade her farewell.

As he walked back to his flat, a voice nagged insistently in his head. *'It's you next, it's, you next,'* it said. *'Let this be a warning to you. You don't meddle in things like this.'* Over and over the voice goaded him. Fear chilled his veins. He walked quickly, hands flung deep in the pockets of his thick overcoat. He knew that this was no co-incidence. It was a direct warning. If they'd caught up with Albert, they'd be after him again soon. What was it Albert had said to him? *'To have these things in one's possession meant certain death. However, I am not so far from death now Hal. I don't fear the truth any more. Publish and be damned.'*

Well, it had been a prophetic comment. Albert might have feared death if he'd known how he'd meet his end. He had certainly been damned.

Hal was reluctant to go home. He knew that if they'd caught up with Albert, they weren't far behind in coming for him. What to do? As if in answer, his mobile rang. He looked at the screen and Stergios' name came up. Before he

374

pressed the answer button, Hal looked behind and each side of him. The street was quiet apart from a couple of shoppers returning home.

'Hello?"

"Hal! Thank God! I've just heard about Albert. Have you seen the news?"

"Yes, I've just read a report in the London Herald. I'm scared Stergios."

"As you should be."

"Thanks for that Stergios, you're such a comfort," he replied with heavy irony.

"Sorry – didn't mean to make things worse. Now listen Hal, I don't have long. We're almost there now. I have you under surveillance but you are in danger. Here's what I want you to do..."

Hal followed Stergios' instructions. He returned to his flat and immediately e-mailed his as yet unedited manuscript to him. He e-mailed it to himself as well and then cleared the hard disc of his computer completely. He removed all history and cookies cached on the system and hastily changed his passwords. He flung as many of his clothes as he could into a large suitcase and packed his laptop into its case. He took a final look around his flat and then shut the door behind him for the very last time. He clambered into the taxi he'd called earlier and soon, he was heading to Heathrow where he'd be catching a flight to Paris. He had a couple of people to see there under Stergios' instructions and he would complete the manuscript and deliver it to a publisher who was waiting for him in the city. Stergios had arranged a safe house for him. He just hoped he could get there before they caught up with him.

For Hal, it was a stressful few hours. Arriving at Charles de Gaulle Airport, he retrieved his luggage and hailed a taxi to the Montmartre address Stergios had provided for him. On arrival, Stergios had assured him, Madame

Sauveterre would be awaiting him. Montmartre was the artistic district of the city famed also for the Moulin Rouge. Now, in the early hours of the morning, the lights still glowed and the famous Windmill of the Moulin Rouge gave the district an air of bohemian vibrancy. Had it been any other time, Hal would have been thrilled to be there. Tonight though, he was apprehensive; unsure as to the contact he'd been provided by Stergios and fearful of any followers who might yet be in pursuit of him. Knowing the characters he was up against, he must be an easy target.

His destination appeared a little less salubrious than he might have expected. It was a side street in the northern Paris '18th arrondissement.' Nervously, Hal thanked the taxi driver and paid the fare. He also asked him to wait a moment until he ascertained he was indeed in the right place.

"Umm, attendez un instant, s'il vous plait?" He asked the driver in faltering and scarcely remembered school day French. The driver appeared to understand him and remained with the engine running as Hal rapped the ornate door knocker. It echoed ominously in the quiet street. After a few moments, he heard footsteps behind the door which was thrown open revealing a dimly lit hallway with stairs apparently leading to various landings and apartments. He was confronted by a woman, perhaps in her late 50s or early 60s who, he thought rather unkindly, looked like a throwback to a Dickensian madhouse. Her wild grey hair was loose and unkempt; she wore a long skirt and bohemian frilled top, a patterned shawl thrown carelessly over her shoulders. She looked Hal up and down, somewhat warily, he thought, before stepping outside to look up and down the street as though checking to see whether he had been followed. Seemingly satisfied, she smiled.

'Bonsoir Monsieur. You are Hal, yes?'

376

Hal confirmed his identity and as she hurriedly ushered him inside with a '*come in, come in,*' he turned and waved the taxi off before the door was closed behind him.

"*This way,*'" the woman motioned for him to follow her up the stairs to the second landing where they entered her apartment. Hal scanned the small room which doubled as a sitting room and kitchen. She invited him to sit at the table and bustled off into the partitioned kitchen where she poured him coffee from a filter machine. He accepted it gratefully.

"So," she began. "I am Madame Sauveterre. At least," she smiled enigmatically, "that is how you will know me for now. In your language, Mrs Safe Haven, I believe." She chuckled throatily as she lifted a cup of the filter coffee in her gnarled hands and drank some of the black strong liquid inside. *'Of course, thought Hal. Stergios and his appetite for appropriate names.'*

"Thank you for taking me in at such short notice. It must have come as a bit of surprise to find you have a house guest from England."

She stared at him with piercing eyes which were not unfriendly, but slightly unnerving in their intensity. They scrutinised every inch of him as though studying a specimen in a Petri dish.

"Not at all," she replied calmly. "I've known you were coming for quite some time."

Hal's expression must have revealed his surprise at her comment. How could she possibly have known he would be coming here?

"Really? I had no idea I'd be visiting France. It was something of an impromptu arrangement for me," Hal replied quizzically.

The woman emitted her throaty chuckle again as she pulled out a packet of Gauloise from a pocket in her skirt and offered him one.

"No thanks. I gave it up years ago."

377

"Very wise," she conceded, nevertheless proceeding to light the cigarette from which she drew deeply.

"You must be very tired Hal. Don't worry. You will be safe here. There are friends around us and, shall we say, a very early warning system which is generally accurate. If there is to be trouble, I will be the first to alert you," the woman assured him. "Now, I also need some sleep, so I will show you to your room and we can talk in the morning." Hal concurred with some relief. He was indeed overtired by now. So much so, he wasn't sure he would be able to sleep. With all that had happened in the last 24 hours, he wondered if he could ever sleep again. However, something in the woman's manner and tone gave him reassurance. There were three doors off the main sitting room and kitchen and Madame Sauveterre threw open the first.

"I hope you will be comfortable Hal." The room was a little dreary, but clean and comfortable enough. The wooden floorboards were *au naturel* and contained a single metal bedstead, the mattress covered with blankets and ornate bedspread, a rug, a small wooden wardrobe and, as the woman had indicated, a small desk and chair adequate for him to continue working. The French windows opened out onto a balcony overlooking the street. Green Louvre shutters were at either side and the woman scuttled over to close them for the night.

"Don't feel you have to get up early in the morning Hal. I shall be here whatever time you awaken. We can talk then. For now though, it is, I think, time for all good people to be in bed."

Hal smiled as she backed out of the room and bade her goodnight. He really didn't want to think any more so he undressed down to his shorts and tee shirt and threw himself gratefully into the bed. He switched off the dim bedside light and fell into a deep dreamless sleep.

Chapter 35 – The Theosophist's Theory

Hal was awakened the following morning by the sound of voices in the next room. It took him a few moments to orientate himself as he rubbed his eyes and wondered briefly where he was until recollection of the previous night's mercy dash to Paris returned. It was like a movie, he thought incredulously. He felt a stab of nervous apprehension as he contemplated the day ahead. It was cold in the room and he shivered a little before reaching for his clothes and grabbing a thick sweater and socks from his suitcase. Once dressed, he threw open the shutters to reveal a narrow street below. He stepped onto the balcony. It was indeed very cold out there. He surveyed his surroundings for a few moments, taking in the other apartments and balconies in various states of repair and disrepair. It certainly had a character of its own. I really am an artist in my Paris garret here, he thought. Absolutely the place for the stereotypical struggling writer. Not quite to his taste though. Stepping back inside the room, he secured the French windows and stepped out into the kitchen/sitting room. There, at the kitchen table sat Madame Sauveterre. She reached over to turn off the radio, the source of the voices that had awakened him.

'*Bonjour*, Hal. Did you sleep well?'

"Indeed, I did Madame, thank you. I was exhausted. Mentally exhausted, I think. A great deal happened in the last few days."

"Yes, Stergios has briefed me. You must be very afraid Hal. I am sorry for you."

Slightly discomfited by her matter of fact acceptance of his clearly endangered life, Hal merely said that yes, it wasn't a position he enjoyed. Madame Sauveterre stood up and headed for the kitchen.

"Croissants and coffee OK for you? It's all I have in for breakfast I'm afraid."

"Perfect!" Hal replied more cheerily than he felt.

While the woman busied herself in the kitchen Hal gazed around the room. It was filled with some strange artwork, some of it quite creepy, he thought. There was a great deal of what looked like traditional religious icons mixed with figures that looked like Gods and Goddesses of various cultures, both modern and ancient. Included in the artworks was a picture of a beautiful fair haired woman in Grecian dress aiming into the distance with a bow and arrow, a deer by her side. Hal didn't hear Madame Sauveterre as she appeared by his side and placed warm croissants and coffee on the table in front of him.

"I see you are admiring my gallery," she said, bustling back into the kitchen.

"Indeed I am. You have a very mixed collection here. All religious depictions I take it?"

The woman inclined her head. "Yes, in a way. It's slightly more complex than that. I saw you looking at Artemis." She smiled. "She is the one responsible for you being here *hein?*"

"In a manner of speaking..." Hal frowned, slightly puzzled. He was disturbed by the drawing on which his eye alighted next. It was a symbol of some sort; it looked a little Masonic, but different. As he studied it, he saw that a snake created an outer circle, its head meeting its tail and encasing a Star of David which itself contained another symbol which he recognised as the Egyptian Ankh. More disturbing, he noted a circle containing a swastika between the snake's head and tail and above that, some writing which he took to be Sanskrit or Arabic in origin. Around the outside of the large circle created by the snake were the words, *'There is no religion higher than truth.'* Well ain't that a fact, Hal thought.

Curious, he asked the woman what the symbol meant.

"I'm very glad you asked that Hal," she replied in her thick accented but fluent English. "I am what they call a *theosophist.* This is the symbol of the Theosophical Society. A theosophist is, I suppose a philosopher of the divine. Translated from the Greek θεός (*theos*), God and σοφία (*sophia*), wisdom. It means literally, the wisdom of God. We are interested not just in traditional religious study, but more the esoteric philosophies. We seek knowledge of the mysteries of being and nature and hidden knowledge about the divine. It is a highly spiritual study of philosophies and esoteric groups which include anything from Gnosticism, Freemasonry, Astrology, Spiritualism, Rosicrucianism and many, many more. We seek enlightenment through understanding of the relationship between humanity, the universe and the divine to discover ultimate salvation."

Hal listened, fascinated. "The symbol – I guess it represents many religious facets then. The serpent of the Bible, the Jewish Star of David, the Ankh. But what on earth does the swastika have to do with it?"

Madame Sauveterre laughed. "Most people see the swastika in its stigmatised context rather than its religious context. Long before the Nazis got their hands on it, it was a sacred and auspicious symbol in Indian religions. It represents a lucky or auspicious object. Unfortunately, its meaning has been subverted, *perverted*, even by its use by Nazi Germany. The Ankh represents *breath of life* and the symbol above is Sanskrit for the chant *Om* representing an all encompassing mystical entity and the very first vibration of consciousness. You probably know that the *Om* is used in meditation."

The woman hesitated a moment to allow Hal time to digest the new information.

"So," he considered the emblem again, "it represents in a way, all religion as being one? Is that it?"

381

"I think you could say that. The aims of Theosophists are to create an Universal Brotherhood of Humanity without distinction of race, creed, sex, caste or colour; to encourage study of philosophy, science and religion and investigate the unexplained laws of nature and the latent powers in man." She poured Hal more coffee as she warmed to her subject.

"I won't bore you with details but it is a form of mysticism and is embodied in the New Age Movement and occultism in the west. It originally came from Judeo-Christian religions but now it is more universally regarded."

"Ahh," it dawned on Hal. "So the Merovingians would have been regarded as a Theosophical sect I guess."

"As you say, Hal. The Kabbalah emerged in 12th century Southern France. This was the theosophical basis of Jewish mystical development and is embedded in Western esotericism. It is our belief that back in those times, the earth was ruled by ancient occult adepts forced into exile."

"We're talking about the descendants of Christ? The ancient Bloodline carried by the Merovingian Dynasty."

"You're much more educated on these matters than I thought Hal." Madame Sauveterre was clearly pleased. "Stergios has taught you well."

"And I guess this is all linked to the dead Princess?"

"Indeed. The ancient Theosophists believed that there would be a restoration of the bloodline during the New Age, which of course Hal, is now. We are no longer governed by the dogma of any one Church. However, there are those who are suspicious of the old beliefs. Again, the hatred of the Jews some would say is deeply embedded in the restoration of the bloodline which many would say is a Zionist takeover plan. However, the more enlightened of us would say that the restoration is secular in nature, combining the beliefs of many for a political solution to be reached."

"Enter the re-emergence of the Stuart family and the nominated person to represent the bloodline – Diana?"

"Exactement!" replied the old woman. "The birth of the New Age is upon us Hal. We have nation warring against nation, earthquakes and famine. All predicted by Christ as the dawning of a time when the bloodline must re-emerge and strive for political and social justice. Diana was the obvious choice with her popularity and humanitarian presence. The populace would have supported her as the counter monarch had the truth been revealed before her death. That is why we are all now endangered. Even now, the bloodline continues to course through the veins of her family and particularly her children. If they seize the Merovingian ethics it could spell disaster for the oligarchy."

Hal couldn't help but see the connections within connections which always led back to the same common denominator, Diana.

"And of course," he mused, "the Princess was a champion of the New Age wasn't she? Presumably because it ran through her genetic makeup. Her interests in spiritualists, clairvoyance and all the rest of it stems from the Merovingians."

"Indeed, Hal, the connection is clear. The Stuart Kings themselves were also reputed to have knowledge and wisdom of a higher power. The Princess was thought to bring peace and healing to the sick, just as Christ's bloodline was said to have done."

The pair sat in silence for a few moments allowing the discussion to rest between them. For Hal, the synchronicity was evident. Planned co-incidences set in motion centuries ago having an impact on the modern day. It was irresistibly obvious in many ways.

"Now, go and put your coat on Hal, I want to show you something."

A short while later he sat in the passenger seat next to Madame Sauveterre as she negotiated the Paris roads competently and decisively in her little Renault pointing out

383

various places of interest as they went. It was still comparatively quiet on the roads, a matter for which Hal was grateful. He was a nervous passenger at the best of times and didn't relish the thought of rush hour Paris. Within twenty minutes, they arrived at their destination and Hal shivered. They were at the *Flamme de la Liberté* overlooking the now infamous Alma Tunnel where the Princess had met her end.

"People tend to treat the Flamme as the unofficial memorial to the Princess," Madame Sauveterre explained. Indeed, there were notes and flowers laid there; messages of condolence and allegations of murder were written on the notes and on the bridge in graffiti. Looking down over the bridge, Madame Sauveterre motioned Hal to join her. "See Hal, this is the exit to the Alma Tunnel." He leaned over and watched for a few moments at the constant stream of traffic passing out of the tunnel. He felt sad and found it disturbing that a woman of such vitality and elegance had met her death in such a soulless and grey place.

"Can we go inside the tunnel?" he suddenly found himself asking, the urge to be close to the point of the Princess's death compelling.

Madame Sauveterre chuckled. "I think it would be unwise Hal. There is a narrow walkway for people servicing the tunnel to use as access but you take your life in your hands in there. French drivers are not so slow, as you see. I think you are feeling a, how shall I say it ... strong connection, yes?" He nodded contemplatively.

"That is not so surprising. The Alma Tunnel has magical and spiritual properties."

"What do you mean?" Hal asked. He had the feeling that this wasn't just a sightseeing trip. As throughout his journey with the dead Princess, there was more than met the eye to this excursion.

384

"You've probably noticed Stergios' fascination with names, their meanings and connections," Madame Sauveterre smiled.

"Yeah, he always likes to find significance in everything," Hal agreed.

"Diana, or Artemis, whichever you prefer, was the Huntress and also the Moon Goddess of ancient times. The Merovingians were originally exiled in Arcadian Greece but moved later to France. She was otherwise associated with the pagan Goddess, Gaia, or Mother Goddess who was worshipped by the Merovingians."

Villa Artemis and *Villa Gaia,* Hal thought. OK, so more connections. He sensed that he was about to hear something of new significance. He thrust his hands deep in his pockets. It was getting colder.

"Paris was named by the Merovingians Hal. They had a close connection with the City. She extended her hand over the bridge. *Pont de L'Alma* itself had great significance for the Princess's ancestors. Madame Sauveterre reached into her own pocket and pulled out her Gauloise and lighter. She took a deep draw from the cigarette, its strong aroma filling the air between them. "Yes," she continued. "It is a pagan sacrificial site Hal. A place where people gathered to invoke the Moon Goddess Diana and petition her for help."

"Wow! That's a bit of a strange co-incidence isn't it?"

Madame Sauveterre merely looked at Hal as though he were a little backward. Her expression said, *co-incidence Hal? No co-incidences here. It is all as it should be; as it was planned.* It didn't take him long to realise that his rather under developed sense of the spiritual was hampering his understanding and empathy with his companion.

"Sorry." He said. "No co-incidence, right?"

"Hear me out Hal and then make up your own mind about that. Now, not only was this a place of worship and supplication to the Moon Goddess; it was also a place where people would come to settle their disputes, usually in a fight to the death." Madame Sauveterre took one last draw from the cigarette she was holding before continuing. "Legend has it that the person who won the fight in terms of strength and survival was actually deemed to be the loser in reality. The winner was the person who died, because in disputes settled at L'Alma, the victor goes immediately to Heaven where they remain with the Gods until they avenge their own death. The story goes that using the moonlight and the power bestowed by the Gods, they are empowered to manipulate events on earth to their own advantage."

Fascinated, Hal listened to Madame Sauveterre's story. His mind was beginning to make connections again.

"I guess we could say that there was a dispute settled between the Princess and the Establishment on 31st August 1997 then?" Hal mused.

Madame Sauveterre was pleased. "As you say Hal. Not only that, but the very night she was killed is regarded as highly auspicious in the pagan calendar. That night is known as 'The Dark of the Moon.' It was the night before the new moon and the only night where there is no moon visible in the sky. It is said that on subsequent new moons, the dead will have the opportunity of finding vengeance and justice channelled through Diana the Moon Goddess."

Hal nodded in understanding. "So you're suggesting that the dead Princess as the 'winner' in her dispute has the power to find retribution for her killers at the time of the full moon."

"I shall leave you to ponder the possibilities. You have now lived through some strange times. You must weigh up the evidence for yourself."

"One thing I don't quite understand," Hal began. "You're telling me about what we would describe today as paganism. If the Merovingians were essentially Judaic and

386

believed in Christ as the true Messiah, how does that all fit together?"

"Quite simply, the so-called pagan religions became absorbed into our mainstream religions. Today they are regarded as an 'Earth Religion.' Many pre-Christians worshipped polytheistic deities as did pre-Islamists. As the main religions developed, many of their festivals, including for example the Roman *Saturnalia* was absorbed and became what we would call Christmas today. Remember, the Merovingians did not regard Christ as the Son of God. They believed in the Godhead but Christ was essentially the true and original Judaic blood King endowed, most probably with occult powers passed into the Merovingian line through his family. Hence the belief in the power of the Holy Grail. All of these Gods have merged into the single God of today's mainstream Judaic/Christian religion. Taking things a step further, the Saracens or Moors are the Arab Muslims descended from Herod, the usurper of the throne of David. Although he was a practising Jew, he was an Arab on both sides of his family. Thus the Saracens are the enemies of the Judaic Christians and hence the reason for the crusades and the perpetuation of this enmity throughout the Middle East today."

"And," Hal concluded, "just another reason for the death of the Princess. Her love for an Arab Muslim."

"Correct, *mon cher.* For the Judaic Christian Establishment of the Western World, the Princess brought danger in many guises; true claimant to the throne who threatened the cultivated Monarchy of choice for the Establishment Oligarchs and the time honoured power and control of the Churches; potentially also the wife of a man whose own religion has been long held the greatest adversary of the West. Put it all together and ... well ... we know the result. The potentates of the oil rich Arab countries would love to have their share of the political kudos in the Holy Grail. Had she married her lover, she would have conjoined the blood of the Saudi Royal Family had she produced more children. An untenable situation for the West, wouldn't you say."

Indeed, Hal could see what an incendiary mix all of this could have been. He could also see that the Establishment would stop at nothing to prevent such an unpalatable situation occurring; nor seemingly the apparent supporters of the Princess's lineage.

"Thank you, Madame Sauveterre. This has been a revelation. It's helped me understand so much more. Now, I would like to show my appreciation by taking you to a nice warm restaurant and buying you dinner. Would you do me the honour?"

Madame Sauveterre's face lit up. It had been a very long time since she had dined out with a gentleman.

"In that case," she said coquettishly, "how can I refuse?"

The pair headed for a restaurant recommended by Madame Sauveterre which lay between the *Sacre Coeur* and the *Moulin Rouge*. She told Hal that the 17th century building which housed it was a favourite of Renoir and Picasso. He could see why as they approached the picturesque restaurant dominated by one of the two remaining *moulins* or windmills remaining in the city. There, they enjoyed the cuisine of the bistro before heading back to Madame Sauveterre's apartment where Hal settled down to work on the closing chapters of his book.

He spent the following ten days feverishly working in the little room provided for him by Madame Sauveterre. He felt strangely safe in the apartment with her. There was something so reassuring and knowing about her that when she told him she knew he'd nothing to fear from the outside world just now, he believed her. Like Tasia Artemis, she had an *other worldly* understanding and knowledge that he felt he could rely upon. She had assured him in any case that there

388

were members of Stergios' and Kyle's group keeping an eye out for anything untoward. Still, Hal barely left the flat. He just wanted to finish the book and get on with his own life. Once it was out there, it would be pointless killing him except for revenge. The damage would be done by then though and the enemies would be less inclined to dispose of him than discredit his story and work on damage limitation. Killing him once the book was published would merely serve to support the conspiracy theory he espoused.

It occurred to him that there must be some footage of the Princess's engagements still located on YouTube. Curious, he scoured much of the available material. Tasia had said that she was always at the Princess's side during engagements, when not actively impersonating her. Hal scrutinised the videos carefully. Tasia had said that she merely observed and attended the earlier appointments with her boss but try as he might, he could find nothing that showed the presence of Tasia with the Princess, much less anyone who closely resembled her. He also closely inspected the Princess to see if he could spot Tasia during one of her alleged impersonations. Still, he could find nothing that might suggest that anyone else was masquerading as the Princess. This might of course have been difficult bearing in mind the shocking likeness of Tasia and the Princess. The videos weren't always close enough for him to distinguish anything, even had it been possible to see a difference. Indeed, thinking back on Tasia without the Cleopatra bob, he really couldn't have said that he wasn't looking at a slightly older Princess. This was the true mystery of the situation he'd been embroiled in for so long. He could see that everything about the story Hal had heard from Stergios, Kyle and Tasia had the hallmarks of truth, or at least some kind of truth. It was entirely plausible that a centuries old secret might have led to a challenge for the throne and that shadows behind the scenes would have their own reasons for wanting to keep that

389

information quiet. The story about Tasia's involvement with the Princess however was slightly less credible and Hal wasn't entirely sure that he'd ever find the truth as far as this element of his book was concerned. It troubled him because his lack of answers diminished the substance of the Princess's claim to the throne and how he'd come by the information. He hoped that one day he'd discover the truth of it all. For now, he had to content himself with the facts as told to him and the research he'd carried out to substantiate them and hope that the world would accept that there was evidence that at least highly questionable deaths had occurred in the Alma Tunnel on that fateful night.

Hal read all he could on the so called 'enquiries' that had occurred after the accident which still left many questions that even the final inquest had failed to satisfactorily answer.

Allegations that the driver had been drunk and had been driving too fast because the paparazzi were in hot pursuit were highly questionable. The press cars were some way behind the Princess' vehicle having been fooled with the decoy at the Ritz thus delaying them. In fact, it was known they only caught up after the crash. The driver had received expert training and both bodyguards who survived the accident testified that he had not been drunk. Claims of an alleged mix of Prozac and alcohol in his blood were debunked as the effects of such a cocktail would have caused distinctly odd behaviour. The driver of the mysterious Fiat shown by forensics to have collided with the ill fated Mercedes was latterly discovered dead. The man, a reporter, had been following the Princess during the last week of her life and was reported to have been an MI6 informant. Whilst officially his death was recorded as suicide, his body was found inside his burnt out car which had been locked from the **outside.** A fireman had latterly come forward to say that he believed the body also to have had two bullet holes in his head. The reporter's office had been broken into at the same time as his apparent 'suicide.'

There were so many questionable factors relating to the death of the Princess. She was a staunch believer in the use of a seatbelt but on the night of the accident she had been unable to fasten it as it was faulty. The vehicle being used had been mysteriously 'stolen' yet returned before being used on that night. It was known that the security services were able to modify cars such as that one so that they could control it externally. Was that the reason it had been 'stolen?' Indisputably it all accorded with the facts relayed to him by Kyle and Stergios. Why, Hal wondered, had the authorities refused to allow the car to be examined by Mercedes, the very people who would be able to testify as to its condition? He knew the answer of course – they would have discovered the tampering that had gone on during its disappearance. And of course, there was the flash of light and the motorcycle, the method known as the 'Boston Brakes' commonly used by the SAS, evidence from whom in recent weeks had emerged indicating their likely involvement at the scene of the incident. Sitting back after reviewing the evidence, Hal's unease grew. What chance did he have in light of all this murder, mayhem and intrigue? He almost wished he was still chomping sausage rolls at his desk in London dealing with the vapidity of celebrities.

Finally, just after 1 a.m. ten days after his arrival in Paris, Hal dotted the last 'i' and crossed the last 't' in his manuscript. It was finished. He was dissatisfied with the conclusion having been unable to verify Tasia's, Stergios' or Kyle's identities or their position as secret agents. They would have to remain a mystery until the next journalist perhaps was able to delve deeper or papers came to light 30 years hence which might shed light on those mysteries. He had done his job though. He had told the Princess's story as he'd been asked to do and though he could reach no conclusion, the circumstantial evidence was enough to raise some very serious questions, he thought. He was satisfied with the work and for the first time in days, he went to bed and slept a deep, dreamless sleep, a burden having lifted from his shoulders.

Although it was January, it was unseasonably mild in Paris as Hal made his way to the final appointment arranged for him by Stergios. He was off to deliver the manuscript to a literary agent who was willing to read it and hopefully find a publisher. Hal knew how difficult it was to get agents these days so he was grateful for the help from Stergios and the strings he had obviously pulled to get him to this point. The agent had agreed to come to Paris on a trip paid for by Stergios. It was envisaged that he would remain in Paris to work with Hal on any amendments and editing needed before returning to London to seek a publisher. They had decided not to work anymore by e-mail fearing the possibility of interception so Hal had carefully tucked the manuscript into a plastic envelope and sealed it before heading out into the cold winter sunshine of Paris. It lightened his heart that soon he would be free of the manuscript and he could properly start to make plans for his new life. His next book, he resolved, would be a work of complete fiction. Something to provide him with the escapism he now so longed for. Hal headed for the Abesses Metro in Montmartre having bade Madame Sauveterre a cheery '*à bientôt* and he now found himself speeding under the city towards Champs-Élysées where he was to meet the agent at Hôtel Plaza Athénée on the Avenue Montaigne. Hal smiled to himself. *Trust Stergios,* he thought. *Athene's Hotel.* Always the Graeco connection.

It was a Monday morning and as Hal alighted the Metro, he was caught up in the early commute. Gripping the plastic parcel under his arm, he came out onto the crowded Avenue and tried to find his bearings. According to the map, the hotel was on the other side of the road and a bit further ahead. He looked at his watch. He was fine for time, he still had 15 minutes before the appointment. Walking up the Avenue, he admired the opulence of the famous shopping area, not unlike the upmarket Knightsbridge in London.

Hal stopped at the pedestrian crossing and pressed the button to cross the road. Moments later, the signal turned green for him to cross and he stepped off the kerb, the hotel just in sight on the other side. Half way across, he became aware of the roaring of an engine and his heart leaped into his mouth. He only had seconds of awareness before the motorcycle, with black clad rider and pillion passenger rushed straight towards him and without any apparent attempt to avoid him slammed into Hal's body which had been shocked into momentary paralysis. Hal was vaguely alert to the excruciating pain that shot through his frame as he was thrown several feet into the air with the impact and his body, like a rag doll came crashing down in front of a moving vehicle which was unable to avoid him. Simultaneously, the package containing his papers was thrown aloft and, unnoticed by other shocked pedestrians and traffic was swiftly located by the motorcyclist who sped off into the distance through the busy avenue.

It must have been some minutes before Hal came to. He felt strangely numb and it took him a few moments to realise what had happened. There was a crowd of people gathered around him and two women bent over him. Even had he felt less disorientated and increasingly sore, he doubted he could have followed much of what they were saying to him. With an increasing sense of urgency however, Hal simply wanted to flee. He sat up despite the crowd's protestations for him to remain still and looked around to see if the manuscript was nearby. It was however nowhere to be seen. Hal's first thought was that the emergency services would no doubt be on their way. He was also certain that this had been no more 'accident' than that of the Princess. Therefore, he concluded, the emergency services may have

393

been arranged prior to his accident and their mission may, just as it had been with the Princess to ensure his demise rather than his survival. Stiffly, he rose to his feet and he was surprised to find that he could move more easily than anticipated. He indicated to the crowd that he was fine and he pushed his way quickly through the gathering to the pavement amidst protestation and excitement. He headed back to the Metro and somehow negotiated his way back to the Montmartre flat. Entering, he found it empty. Madame Sauveterre had probably gone to pick up her groceries from the various stores she favoured. Hastily, he penned a note thanking her and without specifics told her that he must leave immediately. He gathered his few belongings together, including the laptop and made his way to the airport. He was heading for Chania. The time had come when he could think of nowhere else to go where he might be safe. Even there it was touch and go, he knew. He just hoped he could disappear into anonymity and now that the manuscript was in enemy hands, perhaps they would have no further interest in him. A long shot though. They weren't daft enough to believe he'd have deleted all records of the book.

Although he appeared to be simply walking wounded, Hal knew that the accident had been serious enough to cause him traumatic injury. He was amazed and thankful that so far, apart from a strange haziness, he didn't seem to have much in the way of pain. In fact, he thought, he felt rather well. He must have slept through the flight (or perhaps lost consciousness) because when he awoke after what felt like only a short nap, the plane had landed and he had no recollection of his journey through the airport at Chania. He resolved however that he wouldn't stop here yet. Stergios and Kyle were still on Gavdos. He would go there first and seek their help. He hadn't dared stop long enough to telephone or e-mail and he didn't want to risk being traced through telecommunications which he was certain now must be under surveillance. To prevent being tracked through the GPS system on his phone, he had thrown it away before heading to the airport.

Hal retraced the steps of his first journey to Gavdos, finally alighting from the ferry the following day onto the familiar beach at Karave. As usual, there were cars waiting for the ferry to arrive with provisions and for the odd passenger to head back to Crete. This time, he had no means of transport but managed to clamber onto a truck and hide under a canvas awning. He kept his fingers crossed it would be returning to one of the villages where he might know someone who could contact Stergios and let him know to pick him up. It was a bumpy and uncomfortable ride and he couldn't see where he was going. Still though, Hal remained calm and focused on his destination and plans. Eventually, the truck fortuitously came to a halt in the small town familiar to him, Sarakinikos. This was a relief. He'd go to the taverna that he'd frequented so often with Stergios and ask them to call Costas who operated an occasional taxi service during the tourist season. Stergios and Hal had often left the cars in Sarakinikos when the red wine had flowed a little too copiously and relied upon Costas to return them to Villa Artemis. A little frisson of excitement fluttered through Hal's stomach as he thought of returning to Villa Artemis where he'd rekindle his friendships and mourn the loss of their mutual companion Tasia. It had been difficult for Hal during the last weeks; he'd felt cast adrift back in London and France and he'd hankered after the peace of the Greek islands and the comfort of familiar faces who'd experienced shared adversity.

Hal was feeling very weary now. He suspected that he needed medical attention but somehow his determination to return to Gavdos had given him the superhuman strength to overcome whatever injury and pain he'd sustained. It was a miracle really – to be thrown bodily into the air by the force of that motorcycle and then run over by another vehicle and then

395

actually *survive.* He recalled the sickening blow of the bike but couldn't recall what had hit him afterwards. It must have just been a glancing blow, he thought gratefully as he approached the taverna. It was quiet and neither of the familiar owners appeared to be around. A moment later a middle aged man appeared from the kitchen area and began to lay the tables for dinner. No doubt a few locals would pop by later for an evening meal, thought Hal, remembering the regulars he'd often seen at the taverna. Hal approached the man, whom he didn't recognise and asked for a beer. He thought it prudent to at least buy something before asking him to call Costas. The man frowned, barely acknowledging him then disappeared in the back returning empty handed some while later.. Something about the man's demeanour made him uneasy. He sat a while longer somewhat awkwardly enjoying the evening sun and realising the man intended to ignore him, he decided to move on. He resolved to make his own way to Villa Artemis concluding that the unfamiliar waiter perhaps spoke no English and certainly didn't appear welcoming. It was possible to walk, he guessed. It would take him perhaps an hour under normal circumstances but his limbs were groaning with aches and pains which was unsurprising given the trauma they'd sustained less than 24 hours earlier. Hal rose unsteadily and quickly scanned the tiny village which, although familiar, appeared different from his recollection. There were subtle changes; a lick of paint here and there; the supermarket had been modernised; the road was less dirt track than tarmac now. Hal supposed that the island must have decided to spend some money during the quiet season so that it might become a more attractive destination for the tourists later on. He didn't relish the thought of being there when the influx of naturists, sun seekers and walkers descended on the island to disturb the spirituality and equilibrium he'd been so fortunate to enjoy.

396

He set off on the fairly lengthy walk to Villa Artemis. He couldn't believe his luck, or indeed his own temerity, however when a few yards later he came upon a car; co-incidentally a small black Mercedes parked at the kerb. The window was open and, characteristically on an island like Gavdos, Hal thought, the keys had been left in the ignition. Hal only considered the situation for a moment. He cursorily glanced around and finding no-one anywhere near, he opened the door of the Merc and sat behind the wheel. He felt terrible of course, but hell, after all he'd been through, he was sure that he could, with Stergios and Kyle's help, explain to the owner that he'd simply borrowed the car and intended to return it immediately afterwards. There was a very small police presence here but he thought he'd probably be able to get the car back even before it was noticed missing. It was only as he pulled away in the direction of Villa Artemis that he realised this was actually the car which had been placed at his disposal when he'd first arrived. He breathed a sigh of relief. It belonged to Villa Artemis anyway. He wondered who'd been driving it into Sarakinikos. It wasn't usually driven by either Stergios or Kyle. Maybe one of the Villa staff, he thought. Oh well, they'd find their way back he guessed. He'd have a bit of explaining to do but the thought no longer fazed him. Once a gentle and law abiding citizen, he was now a hardened fugitive in fear for his very life. Hal smiled to himself. Who'd have believed that the pastry loving slob of yesteryear would have become embroiled with MI5, MI6 and the cover up of probably the most famous assassination in British history. Intrigue and conspiracy was now his life.

Hal turned off the main road onto the track leading to Villa Gaia and drove slowly along the familiar uneven road, a flutter of nervous anticipation filling his chest as he thought of the reunion with old friends and the story he now had to tell them. After only a few moments though, he became confused and disoriented. To his right, he saw the old shack he'd

397

passed on an almost daily basis when travelling into town. Although nothing new, the shack had been a couple of hundred yards further on than Villa Gaia. Hal used the passing point near the shack and turned to retrace the way he had come. How could he have missed Villa Gaia? It stood just off the road for goodness sake. It wasn't as imposing as Villa Artemis but really, driving up this road, you couldn't fail to see it. This time Hal drove too far in the other direction but still, there was no sign of the Villa. He abandoned the car and decided to walk in between the only two points at which the Villa could have been situated. He ascertained the location at which he was certain the Villa should be between the shack and the point at which he'd left the Mercedes. All he saw was a clearing, large enough for the house to occupy, but – no Villa Gaia! He recognised the landscape well enough as he walked down the slight incline towards the area where the villa ought now to be. He also recognised the area in front of him where the garage should have been located. The rhododendron bushes that had flanked the villa were there but nothing else. Perplexed, he knelt down, hoping to find some foundations; anything that might prove that he hadn't gone completely mad. There was nothing though. Absolutely nothing to suggest that the clearing was anything but that. An area maybe reserved for development but not yet started. Hal frowned, perspiration dripping down his temple as a mix of fear and panic began to overtake him. How was this possible? Even if the building had been torn down in recent weeks, there'd be something, surely to indicate its former existence? Hal struggled to lift himself back up from his knees which were groaning in pain from the accident. *'Accident,'* he thought. *'Attempted murder,'* more like. He tried to think rationally. These intelligence agencies were capable of just about anything. They could make anything happen and cover their tracks just like conjurors. Maybe, for some reason, Kyle and Stergios had decided to make the Villa 'disappear' after

Tasia's death? Perhaps it was a very carefully staged cover up so that their own traces were extinguished? Wearily, Hal dragged himself back to the Mercedes and turned it around again, determined to face the next enigma. Putting the car in gear, he drove slowly up the hill towards Villa Artermis, his heart pounding and dread filling his chest as he wondered what, if indeed anything or anyone would greet him as he drove over the brow of the hill.

Hal's worst fears were confirmed as he drove up to the familiar location that had once housed him and enchanted him with its breathtaking views over the sea. He pulled up in the vacant space that had once been occupied by the gated courtyard, his breath coming in short gasps. Steadying himself, he opened the car door and stood in the vast emptiness where Villa Artemis had once stood. This time though, it wasn't completely clear. Hal half walked, half staggered across the old 'courtyard' and came upon the remains of a building, its foundations still evident but the walls torn down to a few stones and rubble. Moreover, although it had been a building of some size and substance, it certainly wasn't the modern build of Villa Artemis. These stones were decades, possibly even centuries old. Walking around the foundations, Hal could determine the layout of various old rooms and even the remains of a fireplace but there was nothing reminiscent of the sumptuous villa he'd lived in until so recently. The old building occupied exactly the site of Villa Artemis and would have to have been completely removed in order to erect the new structure. Hal became more and more perplexed. The intelligence services might have been extremely clever but to re-create this scene in such a short space of time? No, it was impossible!

Exhausted and fraught, Hal shaded his eyes with his hand and scanned the entire area. Apart from the familiar surroundings he'd enjoyed during his stay here, there was nothing. No sign of the sumptuous and opulent villa with its

399

colonnades and marbled entrance he remembered. Hal jumped, disturbed by the sound of a car engine. Looking quickly around, he searched for a place to hide fearing that he may have been followed after all and that out here, he was a very easy target. Terrified, he realised that there was nowhere he could conceal himself. It was just a large open space with a pile of rubble which wasn't high enough to hide a child. The bushes were too far away for him to reach even if he'd had the strength to run.

Hal almost laughed in relief when he saw the familiar truck belonging to Manolis, a neighbouring farmer and occasional Villa Artemis gardener with whom he'd been on nodding acquaintance. He waved the truck down and was thrilled to see Manolis's sun dried wrinkled face looking back at him.

'Manolis,' Hal shouted as he shambled painfully towards the open window of the truck. "I can't tell you how good it is to see your face here! What on earth has happened to Villa Artemis? Where is everyone? I've been down to Villa Gaia as well and it's gone too!"

A deafening silence lay between the two men. Manolis gave no indication that he'd even recognised Hal and far from his usual habit of exchanging pleasantries, a frown shadowed his hostile expression. He merely shook his head.

"Villa Artemis?" Manolis queried, alighting from the truck. "Villa Artemis has been gone for over 100 years when the lady Tasia departed this island. Look – you can see what remains of it. And Villa Gaia, you say? The last remains of that house were removed ready to build on about 10 years ago. The developer they say went bankrupt before work started and it has remained empty ever since."

"But Manolis, you must recognise me! Hal? I stayed here barely a couple of months ago. I was Miss Artemis' guest. You were doing the gardens..." Hal's voice trailed off in

400

horror as he caught the dismayed expression of the old farmer who was shaking his head.

"I don't know what you're talking about, I'm sorry." The older man shrugged and scrutinised Hal as though he were a lunatic. "Tasia Artemis is long gone from here and remains only a distant legend. Few will venture here after dark though. They do say that she returns to her favourite island when the moon is full to dance in the garden. The legend says that she was the true Goddess Artemis descended from Mount Olympus and that she comes to spend time back amongst the mortal world when she is needed. It's been a long time since I heard of anyone seeing her though. Most people as I said, stay well away from here."

"No, no, no, Manolis, you must be mistaken," Hal heard himself exclaim in desperation. "What about Kyle, the American? Stergios the historian? They used to give you instructions for maintenance of the gardens when Tasia, Miss Artemis was too sick to speak with you herself. Manolis..." Hal wanted to shake the man into admitting his recollection but he simply frowned, seemingly bewildered by Hal's ranting.

"I'm sorry *Kyrie*, I have no idea what you are talking about. I am not even Manolis. My name is Nikolaos. Now, I must be on my way. I would suggest that you leave here before darkness falls too. Can I give you a lift?" Manolis or *Nikolaos*, as Hal was now expected to think of him was already clambering back into his truck, eager, it seemed to be away from this madman.

Suddenly Hal felt as though all energy had been sapped from his body. There was nowhere to turn, no answers to be found it seemed. He thanked '*Nikolaos*' for his time, realising that even if the man was lying, there was no way of getting any more information from him. He told him that he could drive himself back to town, indicating the Mercedes parked haphazardly in the old 'courtyard' of his memory. Hal watched as the truck's wheels spun in the dirt

401

and coughed as it threw up dust in its wake. He listened until he could no longer hear the retreat of the engine in the distance. It seemed unnaturally silent once the man and his truck had gone. No wind blew the trees and bushes, no birds sang and the cicadas were hushed. The air felt thick and cloying. Hal fell to his knees and collapsed onto the rough, barren ground and thankfully lost all consciousness from a mind in turmoil and a body broken and bruised.

A sweet sound of strings and tinkling of delicate bells drew Hal back into awareness. He was lying on a lush green lawn where the birds were singing once more and the cicadas called playfully to each other. He felt warm and comfortable. Reluctant to open his eyes fully just yet, he simply lay where he was listening to the mellifluous and haunting melody that seemed to emanate from the air around him. He smiled to himself contentedly. He just wanted to stay here basking in the relaxed and peaceful space cocooned in a womb of safety and yes, joy.

It was the gentle nudging of something against his face that finally convinced him to peel open his eyes. When he did, he laughed and stretched out his arm to cradle the smooth, friendly head of the baby deer which was gently pushing him from his slumber, its warm nose stroking his face and its deep brown eyes gazing into his. Seconds later, he felt a light hand grasping his arm and elbow, tenderly lifting him into an upright position. A tingle filled his body, like electricity; energising and flowing through him, healing and soothing. As he rose into a sitting position, he could feel soft flowing fabric and a familiar scent in the air, delicate and evocative. He lifted his face to the person who cradled him in her arms and saw that it was Tasia, warm and vibrant, smiling down at him.

"Welcome back Hal. We've been waiting for you," she smiled. Her hair was in the familiar short blonde bob and Hal couldn't decide if he was looking at Tasia or the Princess. One simply merged into the other, he thought.

402

"Tasia! But – you're dead. Aren't you...? Hal rubbed his temple as though this would sort out his confusion.

Tasia smiled at him indulgently and when she spoke her voice was serenity itself. "What is death Hal? I have never experienced it. We simply move from one life to another until our work is done and it is time for pastures new."

Hal looked around. They were in the gardens at Villa Artemis. There was the house in all its glory, just as he remembered it.

"I don't understand Tasia. Before I collapsed – it was just *rubble*. The Villa wasn't here. According to Manolis or *Nikolaos* as he called himself earlier, the Villa hadn't stood for hundreds of years. Tasia smiled as she stroke Hal's hair.

"Don't perturb yourself Hal. You're safe now and you shall have your reward."

"Reward? What for? I've been paid already and I was planning to move here; to Chania."

"And so you shall. You are here to stay now. Your work is complete and you have served us well."

"I don't understand. Why are you here? You died. In the hospital. Tasia, you have to tell me who you really are."

"Of course. It's why I'm here now." Hal pulled himself from her grasp and his gaze met hers, piercing and knowing. Her smile melted his impatience. "Hal, we are all many people. In fact, we are all 'spirit.' We can be whomsoever we choose to be and we can either do good or bad. Who am I you ask? I am Artemis, daughter of Zeus, Goddess of Hunting and the Moon. I am family of the bloodline of David and Solomon; I am a Merovingian Queen and I am also Diana, whose broken body could not be fixed and who won the battle against her enemies in the sacred Pont L'Alma tunnel in Paris. I am Tasia, Hal, *'Resurrection'*. Throughout the centuries, I have been many people and taken on many guises to ensure that eventually the world will be brought to heel and stop the endless destruction by its people. I cannot guarantee the

403

result because we are legion and in each lifetime I work with good spirit and bad spirit but I try to bring truth in the hope that each incarnation will create greater understanding to guide all returning spirits toward protecting their earth and promoting goodness and justice."

"Tasia, you're talking in riddles again," Hal groaned. From what you've said am I to take it that you and Diana were one and the same; not different people living separate lives." Tasia smiled and nodded.

"It's hard to understand Hal, but yes, that's what I'm saying. My spirit co-exists with the human host and I work through that person to try and influence the future. It isn't always easy. Even the Gods can be swayed by human failings and circumstances with other returning spirits' involvement can defeat our purposes. It is why I could not save the Princess to continue her humanitarian efforts and the bloodline. I did all I could of course but there are powerful and evil spirits who can outmanoeuvre our best efforts."

"And your mission with Diana – what exactly was it?"

"The Greeks, with guidance from their Gods were the fathers of democracy Hal. Those Gods created the bloodline to promote the purest of motive throughout world monarchy. But there are many who wish to pervert purity of motive; those who prefer their own selfish interests and comforts than work for the greater good. We saw how democracy was being subverted and how it is manipulated by money and subjugation of people to gain power. The Gods of old decided that the truth must be exposed. The Princess was the perfect vehicle for this. We could show the world by telling her story how the bloodline was diluted for the interests of power and that the adulation of government and monarchy as it stands was misplaced. The fact that Diana died in the Alma Tunnel of itself had people questioning. How many actually believe that she died in an accident? Year on year, evil is exposed in Government and now, thanks to you, the truth about the

404

European Monarchs will also be told. It may not have an instant result but the story is out there and gradually there will be more and more questions. The weak really *shall* inherit the earth Hal because the bloodline, one way or another will be restored and it is our hope that it will be in the telling of your story and the realisation of the Princess's blood family that they do have the power and influence to change things and make a truer more honest world. The oligarchy will be exposed and the choice of monarch will become possible once the story is known. No longer will Government have the power to install its puppet kings. It is the legacy of their Merovingian blood. Diana could have had a major influence but we were defeated this time. We will not be defeated next time."

Instinctively, Hal understood Tasia's words. He now understood that she was no ordinary mortal. Suddenly, the bizarre events of his recent life now made perfect sense. But almost as soon as he came to this realisation, another thought abruptly disturbed him.

"Tasia! You don't understand though. I had an accident in Paris. I was on my way with the manuscript to the literary agent Stergios had arranged for me. I was crossing the road and ..."

"You were run over, throwing the manuscript aside in the ensuing chaos. Yes, I know Hal. Of course I know. But don't worry. We managed to, shall we say, recover it shortly afterwards. It is in good hands. In fact, it is being published as we speak."

Hal's expression belied the shock and amazement he felt at being told his book was being published.

"But how...? Tasia it was only 24 hours ago that I had the accident. How can that possibly be true? I need to get back to London and sort out the publishing deal if that's the case."

405

"You still don't understand do you Hal?" Tasia smiled at him. "Hal, your accident happened in mortal terms, years ago. It's just that it seems it was only 24 hours ago to you. It's much easier than remembering what happened in between times; the *aftermath* of the accident which can be so very traumatising. The spirit needs time to heal, ready for its next journey. But it's done now. You're here and you're healed and you're going to have contentment for a long time before your next mission. You've earned it – questions are already being asked back amongst the mortals and changes are already afoot. Questions are being asked as we speak; not just about the death of the Princess and the old world order, but questions over your own death. You've become a national enigma Hal, a celebrity in your own right. Posthumously, of course." Tasia's serene smile lit up her beatific face as Hal's eyes widened in final comprehension of all that she'd said.

"You're telling me that I'm dead too, aren't you?"

Tasia said nothing but her eyes said it all.

"Don't be sad about that Hal. The rewards are great. In fact, here is yours coming now.

Hal followed the direction of Tasia's gaze and there, coming towards them was Fliss, as beautiful as the day he'd met her. His heart rose in joyful anticipation as Tasia stood and took his hand. As she did so, he rose from his seated position to stand in the Elysian Field that he had known as Villa Artemis's gardens and courtyard. Fliss smiled and broke into a run towards Hal. As she reached him, they flew into each other's arms and the true meaning of bliss became knowledge to both of them. They had been promised eternity together and it started now.

Bibliography

Belzer Richard & Wayne David – *"Dead Wrong 2, Diana Princess of Wales"* Vigliano Associates 2013

Botham Noel – *"The Murder of Princess Diana"*, Metro Books (2006)

Campbell Lady Colin *"The Real Diana"* Arcadia Books (2005)

de Sède Gérard *"The Accursed Treasure of Rennes-le-Château"* Les Editions de L'Oeil du Sphinx (2013)

Gregory Martin *"Diana The Last Days"*, Random House (1999)
Hutchins Chris and Thompson P, *"Diana's Nightmare – The Family"*, Christopher Hutchins Ltd (1993)

Junor Penny – *"Charles Victim of Villain?"* Harper Collins (1998)

King Jon – *"The Cut Out"* – Create Space Independent Publishing Platform (2014)

King Jon & Beveridge John *"Princess Diana, The Hidden Evidence"* SPI Books (2002)

Made in the USA
Charleston, SC
03 November 2015